For Ganesh,
Remover of Obstacles

For Ganesh,
Remover of Obstacles

✦

a novel

Sujoya Roy

iUniverse, Inc.

New York Lincoln Shanghai

For Ganesh, Remover of Obstacles
a novel

iUniverse books may be ordered through booksellers or by contacting:

iUniverse
2021 Pine Lake Road, Suite 100
Lincoln, NE 68512
www.iuniverse.com
1-800-Authors (1-800-288-4677)

ISBN-13: 978-0-595-34556-4 (pbk)
ISBN-13: 978-0-595-79303-7 (ebk)
ISBN-10: 0-595-34556-5 (pbk)
ISBN-10: 0-595-79303-7 (ebk)

Printed in the United States of America

This book is for Ganesh,
Remover of Obstacles,
and for those generous souls amongst us
who silently remove obstacles
without expectation of
praise or gain.

Alarippu is the first number in a typical *Bharatanatyam Arangetram*. It is a simple invocation, offering obeisance to the gods and the audience. Performed solely to the sound of syllables set to the beat of a drum, no story is told. Beginning with a standing, decorative posture, the dancer gradually incorporates all body parts. By building slowly, the *Alarippu* introduces the audience to the potential of the dancer, which should be fully expressed by the end of the performance. The pure "*nritta*" movements of *Alarippu* relax the dancer's mind, loosen and coordinate her limbs and prepare her for the dance. Rhythm has a rare capacity to invoke concentration. *Alarippu* is most valuable in freeing the dancer from distraction and making her single-minded.[1]

#

1. The summaries of each section of the Bharatanatyam repertoire are synthesized from a number of sources:
    The Dance in India. Publications Division, Ministry of Information and Broadcasting, Government of India, 1964.
    Bharata Natyam, Sunil Kotari. Marg Publications, Mumbai 1997.
    "Bharatanatyam Dance" at www.geocities.com/Tokyo/Shrine/3155/bnatyam.html/ Annapoorna Annand.

1

"Toss anything published before 1980," mom commands, "and box anything published after that." Krishna gets on with it, undivided by sentimentality. The twenty years in this office are over; she'll salvage the remains and move on. I lean against the flimsy metal bookshelves, lingering on the crackling, yellowed pages of the leather-bound hard-covers, reluctant to bin books I'm sure will one day be valuable. "Come on, get going!" mom urges, "Let's get this over with."

I watch my mom's diminutive figure hunched behind the enormous, faded steel desk of post-war density as she struggles to pull a clanking file drawer out all the way. I wonder at how somebody in her position put up with such a cruddy office all these years. She was always traveling, barely there, she'd tell me. Still, the tinny, aluminum-framed "moveable" mint walls (which never once budged since installation), the whining fluorescent lighting, the teetering aluminum guest chair with its worn, tweed covering, the slanting, mismatched bookcases jammed in between filing cabinets of varying heights. No man at the U.N. would have tolerated that environment—in fact, none at her level did. Even when offered a bigger, better office in the Secretariat building, it was easier not to move she claimed; plus, why not just stay where her colleagues knew she could be found? At least she had a spectacular view of the East River—though what point was it when the office was arranged so that her back was to it and even with her chair raised to the highest setting, her eyes barely cleared the window ledge.

Backlit, mom's outline seems even tinier. I notice she's lost weight, gotten gaunt in the six months since my father died. I seem to have found what she lost. So many endings, I'm thinking to myself as I pluck another Econ book full of formulas and tables from the shelf, flipping to find the publication date. Yet, there's nothing but single-minded efficiency in mom's demeanor as she examines dog-eared manila folders and stacks them expediently into neat piles for "toss," "forward" and "keep." I, by contrast, have been dawdling over every award, photograph and memento displayed, suggesting every so often "this one seems important, mom, wouldn't you want to keep this one?" "Nope," she responds resolute, "Where am I meant to store all this stuff in a one-bedroom apartment, and what good is it to stare at when I may not even be working anymore?" She's got a point. Best, I suppose, to just let it go. It's impossible to know whether she'll really get the consulting work she's been angling for once she retires. Plus, she'll be working from home, and she can download anything she needs off the Internet.

Moving to D.C. will be good for her, I'm sure, even if it's a small condo. What's the point of a huge house in the NY suburbs with dad gone and no more office? Plus, she'll be closer to Suhasini and the children—the only two people on the planet capable of delighting my mom into insouciance. In fact, had we pulled, at their age, the kind of stuff my sister's kids get away with nowadays, we'd have been walloped across the continent. In the case of Aarti or Mulund, they could set the carpet aflame and my mom would celebrate as though they'd invented fire. Still, they're good for each other. And without dad to over-indulge, the kids are ready and willing victims.

"Sushila!" my mom shakes me out of my reverie, "How is it at the bank? I read about the layoffs. You feel safe there?" Mom issues these casual inquiries on occasion, thinly veiled anxiety over my security because I'm "thirty-something," as she might say, and unmarried. "It's fine, mom." I mollify. "The layoffs won't affect the New York office. Don't worry. I feel safe…Too safe, in fact." Oops. Shouldn't have said that. Here it comes. "What? What too safe? Lucky, you should be considering yourself!" she barks back impatiently. I find it uproarious that her accent and sentence structure revert to South Indian when she's irritated. She swaps her v's and w's and lapses into sing-song. "For your own good I bring it up! So many people losing jobs, and you always dreaming of leaving the bank…writing, if you please…throwing away your M.B.A. One of these days you won't have that option! What if they just let you go? Then what? Who to fall back on then? I hope you're doing your share there, not loafing off like some common American." "Moooooooom!!!!!" I wail, "It's all just fine. I'm not loafing off. My job's fine. I'm fine. They love me there. I'm not going anywhere. And Americans work plenty hard." She starts a comeback, sighs loudly for my benefit, then drops it. We revert to our duties in chilly silence. She knows I've been wanting to leave, go back to the writing I'd always intended to pursue as a career but didn't, caving to standard Indian parental pressure to study something that would "guaranty my financial stability." But I know it's not the right time with dad gone now and all. I can hang in for a while longer, I suppose. No harm. It'll make mom feel safer, which is well worth it.

Perched on a step-stool up against the bookcase, I can see my own reflection on the window panes. Ugh. No make-up, hair piled into a scraggly heap, an oversized tee-shirt, scruffy jeans, and is it the glass or are those really all the extra pounds I'd rather not quantify? From mom's perspective, I imagine, I am certainly not the pretty, proper, petite and pliable Indian daughter of whom to be proud. I can't carry off a sari (I thought I'd unravel on my way up the aisle at my sister's wedding and wind up in nothing but a slip at the altar, the red and gold silk unfurled in a trail behind me.) I can't speak a single word of my parents' languages (well, to be fair, they spoke no Indian languages in common either, so we grew up speaking English at home, or Spanish or French or the language of whatever country the U.N. had us sent to that year). And, much to mom's disappointment, I patently refuse to date Indian men. They're entitled, acquisitive, ambitious, white-wannabes, with an embarrassing mama's-boy twist. They expect to be catered to and I just won't do it. They would never dare treat a white woman the way they behave with Indian women, all presumptuous and superior—in my generation, anyway. It's appalling. Worse, they have no capacity for introspection; and, they don't even recognize it. The boars.

In the long run, mom's probably right. Maybe there's something in staying with what's safe. I've dabbled with writing on the side, but I haven't done anything meaningful since college (an article here and there, but nothing substantial.) It was a juicy dream long ago, but now maybe it's just a fantasy. I could never make a career of it. Too late. Near impossible to get published these days in any case. Plus, I'm good at the bank. And truth is, I've come to rely on the income and the lifestyle it affords. Why upset the apple cart? Stay with what I know I can do for sure. Fact is, I like feeling productive every day; I like crossing stuff off my to-do list at day's end and setting up plans for the next. I like bullshitting with the mail-guy who's somehow decided I'm Hawaiian. Maybe punny, witty e-mails and travel logs to friends and colleagues I consider clever enough to get it are enough of a creative outlet. There's a certain satisfaction in the stellar yearly review (despite which the bank can't justify a corresponding bonus—but glibly supplies the expected "cost of living" increase and compensatory meaningless title change for me while the executive management gets multi-million dollar rewards.) Maybe contributing my energy and imagination to an exploitative, rigidly hierarchical, fundamentally inhumane organization that never questions the righteousness of purely materialistic goals or the way they justify socially irresponsible (if not offensive) means is just fine in the long run thankyouverymuch.

But no. For mom it's a much more practical matter. If you start questioning the context of everything you'll never do anything at all. Anyhow, from her perspective, doing your duty (which in my case is following through on a career based on the Ivy League education for which my parents paid dearly) has more value than indulging your heart's desire. That's exactly what's wrong with this country, she'd charge. Nobody does what he's supposed to. They just do whatever they want. God, mom probably grizzles at the result she's produced in the children department. I must seem so brutish and stubborn compared to Suhasini. My tiny mom…My own mom who's sacrificed every security, every luxury, every penny to ensure that my sister and I could live educated, comfortable, safe, reliable lives. And, unlike Sunny, I won't comply. I constantly threaten to disrupt my safe job (I've moved to three banks since starting my career 15 years ago, and mom can't imagine this disloyalty), I'm not inclined to reproduce (there's so much world to see!), I won't even date the right men for her benefit. Imagine what satisfaction it would give her: two down, none to go.

Still, I wonder if mom knows how desperately lonely it feels to be the defiant one—even if by American standards I'm still a goddam saint. I'm sure she imagines I sit around gleefully victorious in my insubordination, thinking up clever ways I can displease her next. There's no winning. I try hard to be dutiful, respectful, willing, acquiescent to her will. In fact, I set off on a whole career path based on my parents' choosing! Yet it must come through that I do things begrudgingly, threatening always to rock the boat, though I barely make a wave. Instead, I'm living my real life hiding in the lifeboat hanging off the side, making occasional but prominent appearances on the main deck to look like a vital part of the crew.

"Hey mom, this one's from 1975, but it's signed by the author. Maybe it's worth keeping." I wave the crimson cloth hard-cover in the air from the step-ladder. "Oh right," she replies curtly, "that one we keep. Just put it in the box." It's a medical text; not economics or statistics like the rest. I'm puzzled. I flip through it some more. The dedication reads *'To Krishna whose courage enabled a life I could never have otherwise dreamed of.'* Underneath the dedication, in hand-writing before the signature *"You remain an inspiration. KN."* "Hey Ma, is this dedicated to you? Do you know this doctor guy?" Mom looks up at me exasperated. "Stop wasting time and just put it in the box, will you? We're never going to get through this." I know my mom enough not to pursue this further. She's never liked discussing herself or her past and gets grumpy when I push it. She dismisses all inquiries into her childhood with phrases like, "Oh what does it matter now? That's ancient history!" She really does move on, this 65-year old demographer, with steely determination and remarkable courage. She's crabby already today, so despite nagging curiosity, I deem it best to drop the subject, stuff the book in with the "keepers," and eventually, we get through the packing.

All cartons are stacked and labeled. A small, yellow "Post-It" jammed with excruciating detail in mom's painstaking block-print tops each of the boxes and the files to be forwarded in the outbox. I hoist the one carton of keepsakes she's reluctantly agreed to hang onto (mostly my urging.) There's only one thing that she really took care to keep: an ancient looking ink pen that sat prominently in its well on her desk all these years, with its dried up, hexagonal Indian Ink bottle, stopped with a disintegrating cork. Mom looks over the dingy room once to see if anything's forgotten. She unhooks her sensible, multi-pocketed purse from its familiar resting place behind the door, slings it over her shoulder, flips off the light-switch, and heads straight for the elevators without turning back.

2

The family astrologer assured them that today would be auspicious for Krishna's *arangetram*, so she tried not to worry. Still, alone and just thirteen on a makeshift stage before the whole temple *sangha*, her entire extended family and the Nadghars, (who had traveled all the way from Bangalore just to see her dance) she couldn't help but be nervous. If she performed precisely she would deserve the ankle bells she wore for the first time today—inducting her into the rare society of *Devadasis*. More important, she would please the gods, who would then certainly look upon her family with favor.

Awaiting the first beats of the *tabla* from the musicians seated on floor-mats nearby, Krishna fixed her gaze down the center aisle on her composed *nattuvanar*, determined to draw courage from her beloved Jyotsna's placid demeanor. The smartly-dressed audience chatted in hushed tones, and Krishna dreaded their whispering about her. They were probably commenting on her age, her outfit, her posture, her audaciousness; doubting her, even as she stood frozen, doubting herself. Worse, the kohl made her eyes itch. She wanted to squeeze them shut with every blink and feared the whole audience could see them twitch. She certainly couldn't meet the gaze of her expectant parents, cross-legged on mats in the front row. But she noticed that they had sandwiched the Nadghars between them—probably to better gauge their reactions. This made her even more nervous. Little Sindhya was bouncing on her haunches and waving enthusiastically beside Amma, trying desperately to get Krishna's attention, unaware that her sister was not free to acknowledge her from stage. Krishna yearned to scoop her youngest sister up in her arms and whirl her around the stage as they had done this morning to Sindhya's infinite delight. Instead, she severed that impulse, reminded herself that distraction was insolence to the deities, and concentrated on calming down, remaining still and maintaining the statuesque perfection of her initial pose. The heady scent of jasmine from the garlands she wore in her hair comforted her somehow. She traced with her mind the painstaking path of a single bead of sweat trickling down the small of her back, fighting with every stiffening muscle the impulse to wipe it away.

At the first slow thuds of the *tabla*, Krishna was relieved at being unleashed. As the singer joined in, chanting her initial syllables, Krishna found that just as Jyotsna had promised, her body couldn't help but follow the practiced routine. After seven years of rigorous training it was natural and inevitable. Her tension dissolved instantly into the focus required for her moves. Her eyes danced first, bouncing left, up, right; then her neck jerked instinctively to the singer's "taiya-tai-taiya," and as more syllables commanded the introduction of more body parts, her shoulders, then her arms, then her torso joined in. Not even her eyeballs were to veer from the prescribed movements. *Bharatanatyam*, it had been drilled into Krishna, was no forum for personal expression. The devotional dance form existed for almost 3000 years before her, and it was not for her to interpret, improve or augment but only to execute as faithfully as the *Devadasis* she followed.

For her debut, Krishna had mastered the ten key features of her physique so that each could be controlled in isolation, any combination could be commanded together and all could be directed in concert. Her feet, her legs, her hips, her torso, her shoulders, her arms, her hands, her neck, her corneas and even her eyebrows were scrupulously given over to the defined ancient motions and the poses, like those on temple friezes, known to gratify the gods. The few connoisseurs in the wide-eyed audience would certainly notice if her dance strayed even minutely from the established, but it was the gods to whom her family would ultimately answer.

Krishna's *Alarippu* to Ganesh was not only traditional with respect to Hindu initiations but particularly meaningful for the Nayampallis, as years ago, after having birthed three girls in succession, Amma had promised Ganesh her devotion if he removed the obstacles to her producing a son. Since Kishore, Krishna's elder brother, had emerged, Amma fasted faithfully and the family properly made grateful offerings of sweets to Ganesh on the fourth day after each new moon, though *Ganpatti* would normally be celebrated only once per year. Krishna knew that Arna would scrutinize her precision of form in offering garlands in the four cardinal directions and coconuts to the portly elephant god, as her father wished to remove any obstacles to Krishna's betrothal—which he expected to bring about this evening, after his daughter's performance. All these weighty things flashed through Krishna's nimble mind as she started her routine. Still, within the space of just the *Alarippu*, Krishna's jittery self-consciousness vanished into concentration as she gave over to the demands of the dance.

During the rhythmic *Jatisvaram* that followed, speedy and exacting on the feet, Jyotsna closed her eyes. Rather than watching her disciples' movements, something in which she had confidence, she listened for stray jingling from the new bells at Krishna's ankles—any rattling that didn't conform to the tabla's beat. Krishna's precision at this age was perhaps her greatest strength. Jyotsna, usually unflappable, was slightly on edge tonight. There were only a couple of gurus in the audience, but they would evaluate not only the dancer, but the skill of her *nattuvanar* in teaching the dance as well as her judgment in determining Krishna's readiness for a debut. There was no denying that Krishna was young for an *arangetram*, potentially opening her to harsher criticism. But then again, these days in the backwaters of Mangalore, not many had sufficient exposure to *Bharatanatyam* to make much of a fuss. Her teacher had been impressed by Krishna's determination and her diligence as a student; the way she would end a class still fumbling with a particular move and come back two days later having perfected it. A naïve and curious spirit, Jyotsna evaluated of Krishna, cloaked with unlikely self-discipline. So Jyotsna was relieved when the *jatiswaram* was well received. Still, Krishna was only twenty minutes into a two hour performance where she would have no rest. Her stamina was good, (an advantage of youth), but the *varnam* could be her undoing. Luckily, adding expression to rhythm in her *shabdam*, Krishna proved that her competence in adhering to a demanding beat was enhanced by a capacity to introduce expressive gesture. As Jyotsna looked over the audience she was gratified at their pleased expressions. For the moment, they were satisfied, and Jyotsna was relieved.

Arna had behaved cool as coconut water all day long, in the hopes that his air of confidence would be infectious. He stared straight ahead at his daughter, feigning unwavering confidence in Krishna's talent (of which he wasn't at all certain till this moment) so that the Nadghar's wouldn't doubt his conviction and thereby question the prospective alliance. Amma reveled in Arna's seeming self-satisfaction and, unable to help herself despite Arna's cautioning against this, constantly stole glances at the Nadghars. A god-fearing man, Arna couldn't understand how his wife could show such little faith after having been assured by the astrologer that all would work out if it were undertaken today. Amma had unwavering faith in her daughter's gifts, but little in the Nadghar's capacity to recognize them. She was a compassionate, attentive young mother, given to indulging her children and worrying about them in a way that Arna never would.

Deepa, Sandhya, Shakuntala and Kishore were simply stunned: when had their little sister developed such poise, confidence and skill? Shaku was certain that with this display of talent, far more impressive than the *vina* recital which had not long ago won her own betrothal, Krishna's engagement would be sealed—and her parents would then have only Sindhya to worry about. Kishore was comforted that his insistence on rendering the younger girls more marriageable by teaching them the classical arts would be vindicated. He was sure that his idea of inviting the Nadghars had been a good one, and expected that based on this showing, Krishna's dowry would not be too onerous to his parents. Deepa thought her little sister was too painted and over-adorned, and that such ostentation was unbecoming to a *Chitrapur Saraswat Brahmin*, even if it was traditional to a *Bharatanatyam* dancer. She was not at all certain that a spectacle like this, followed by a reception, was appropriate to the community, even if the Swami had given his blessings. Where in this, she wondered, is our commitment to not living beyond our needs? She pondered whether the Nadghars were nationalists or colonist-sympathizers and whether this flagrant show of nationalism would rouse concern in them. And what if they deemed such showiness insufficiently humble in a daughter-in-law? Sandhya worried over whether the cooks who had been hired to assist *M'am* for the reception would be meticulous in matters of cleanliness, and whether the bearers would have properly set up the food for the reception (she heard no noise from the tents outside, and this troubled her), and why on earth hadn't Sindhya been left at home? She was shifting and fidgeting so much she was probably distracting the struggling Krishna on stage!

An hour into the performance, after delighting in the way the light glinted off the fancy jewels adorning her big sister's neck, hair and ears, waiting for the moments she knew Krishna would kneel so the pleats on the front of her costume would fan out between her knees (she loved that motion) and wondering whether the pointy brass links on her belt hurt every time Krishna bent over, Sindhya was bored and restless. She heaved exaggerated sighs of exhaustion and alternately flopped on either her mother's or her sister's knee, waiting for this thing to end because she'd forgotten to check today on how the eggs were doing in the nest. She ogled the fancy outfits of the guests, thinking to herself how very dapper and proper her father appeared, kitted out in a full length *kurta-kameez* for the special occasion. She reveled in the scent of cloves that came off Amma's simple silken sari. She gazed adoringly up at her mother, noticing how attentive, anxious and eager she seemed, then fanned herself in random spurts with one of the dried banyan leaves *M'am* had cleverly fashioned into fans to combat the mugginess.

For her *varnam*, Krishna had selected a crowd pleaser: the popular tales of love between Lord Krishna and the married commoner, Radha. Jyotsna thought back to how she had warned Krishna against this choice. "You will turn the audience away if you don't dance it just so child. Krishna and Radha are, after all, the most popular couple in Indian mythology." Krishna had been stubborn about the selection, however, ignoring her *nattuvanar's* warning. She knew it was a popular saga of love and would gain her much audience favor if well performed. Krishna pleaded with Jyotsna to get her approval, "But it's my favorite. And so very sad how Lord Krishna adores Radha but he could never marry her. It moves everybody so that he must be dutiful and marry into royalty instead. I know that I can make the story come to life since I love it so!" Jyotsna satisfied herself that the stories of the couples' dalliances and Radha's infamous jealousies and longings, would give the dancer plenty of opportunity to express the nine classical emotions. Its capaciousness made it a wonderful selection, although still an ambitious one for a debut dancer. Surveying the crowd, Jyotsna now concealed her concern that a dancer so young may be unable to convincingly express love or compassion. As she looked around she realized that even adults had trouble conveying these sentiments with words at their ready disposal. Jyotsna plunged back into doubt: had Krishna's displayed unusual abilities or had Jyotsna been won over by simple fondness for her own disciple? But Krishna had been so enamored of the love stories and so bull-headed over staying with this theme. She practiced diligently to prove her skill to her guru and at some point Jyotsna had decided to trust that with enough guidance, Krishna's capacity for *abhinaya* would defy her age.

By the time her *varnam* came around, Krishna, though tired, had relinquished her insecurities and found herself well in her stride. Jyotsna tried bucking up her own confidence. It was too late to worry now anyway. Jyotsna was encouraged that despite the cloying humidity of the late morning, Krishna had barely broken a sweat and moved confidently into the "acting" that made the *padam* portion of her *varnam* such a challenge. The singer would repeat one lyric several times to test the number of ways the dancer could express a single sentiment, then move onto another. It was the sole improvisational segment of the repertoire, and an experienced audience would have been persuaded only by subtlety. Krishna felt her body riding on the music, and from the corner of her eyes she noticed friends and relations tapping hands on folded knees and swaying with the melody, which encouraged her and boosted her flagging energy. As she danced the well-known verses about Radha and Krishna's legendary romance, Krishna remembered that by evoking personal memories, her face could magnify the proper emotions—emotions she'd been warned by Jyotsna were perhaps too complicated for a girl so young.

The elegant Jyotsna could see that the crowd was pleased. Krishna had hit squarely on expressing anger borne of jealousy. She so convincingly conveyed disgust that some in the audience even grimaced along with her. Fear was not so difficult for a child to display, nor wonder, nor joy. Jyotsna, like any *nattuvanar* with pupils so young, had been creative in inducing the more evolved sentiments. She had taught Krishna to think of events that might make her feel a certain way on stage. "What makes you feel tender-hearted and sympathetic?" Jyotsna had inquired of Krishna at practice. Krishna recalled the affection with which Sindhya would bring home a stray, scraggly kitten and plead with *M'am* for it to be fed. This immediately filled her with the warmth she was meant to communicate as compassion. For peace, Krishna had confessed to Jyotsna, "I feel so safe when Amma sometimes comes into bed with Sindhya and me and hugs us to sleep in the middle of the night. It makes me feel like the whole world is perfect." For valorn, Krishna recalled her pride when her father joined the local independence marches and the dignity there could be in a defiance so resolute. For love, Jyotsna had worked with Krishna to come up with a combination of rapture (the way she reveled in the smell of roses), adoration (the way she marveled at watching a *Devadasi* like Jyotsna dance); and desire (the way she relished the sweets Amma would make to celebrate *Diwali*.) The mingling of the three came as close, Jyotsna determined, to what a girl so young could convey as love. It appeared, in Jyotsna's assessment, to be a near enough facsimile, and it seemed to pass muster with today's audience—many of whom appeared glazed over after two hours of performance and unabated heat. The stifling schoolroom which had been converted for the purposes of this recital was not built for this capacity, and little breeze was coming through. By this time, weary guests were fanning themselves lazily and shifting impatiently on their mats.

Krishna was relieved when her *tillana* was over. She performed her final *mangalam* in obeisance to the gods and then to the audience. As she backed slowly off the stage with the music fading, she quashed her need to pant. The nerves that concentration had abated for the dance began once again to surge. They eclipsed her exhaustion. The music trailed off into silence as she waited expectantly, suppressing her trembling, in the corner of the room. Sweat now poured down Krishna's back bleeding dark patches into the iridescent folds of her green and gold-brocaded costume. She was flush with anxiety awaiting the audience response. Unwelcome tears welled up in Krishna's eyes. What, she thought, if nobody applauded? The five seconds when the room fell silent felt to Krishna like they might never end. She glared beseechingly across the room at Jyotsna who was powerless to initiate the applause—it would not have been her place. Kishore, deciding that he was in as authoritative a position as anyone, began to clap. The sheepish crowd, which had only been awaiting the lead of an expert, eagerly followed suit now, clapping and cheering the performance. Deepa scrambled to her feet, tip-toed up to Krishna hunched and in a hurry (as though the whole audience couldn't see her) and pressed into Krishna's hands the colorful cluster of roses she was meant to present to Jyotsna. Sindhya was tickled that the roses she'd helped snip this morning were finally going somewhere special. As Krishna made her way to her *nattuvanar*, quivering with nerves, eyes planted on her own feet so as not to seem to acknowledge the applause which she secretly delighted in, Jyotsna smiled widely and scanned the charmed crowd.

Jyotsna noticed that only two in the audience did not express their satisfaction: Arna (who would not have wanted to seem big-headed, though pride was bursting through his lofty demeanor) and Jyotsna's own guru, Bala, who had instead made her way to the Nayampallis in the front row and appeared to be bowing to them a *namaste* implying her departure. Jyotsna graciously accepted the roses from Krishna, then watched her affectionately as Krishna knelt in *vandana*, touching the feet of her guru with both hands, and rising while motioning a circle with her palms to bring them together, covering her hands with her eyes and then clasping her hands together with a bow. In turn, Jyotsna pulled a single, pink rose from the plump and fragrant bunch and returned it to Krishna with a warm embrace. Krishna collapsed, drained and breathless, into Jyotsna's arms, as the audience clapped in acknowledgment of Jyotsna's tutelage and Krishna's exhausting performance.

The applause died down and the crowd began to rise tittering their uneducated criticisms and admirations. They made their way toward the tents that had been arranged outside the doors, where the *prasad* would be served. Krishna did not expect congratulations; those would be reserved for her parents and her teacher. Deepa and Sandhya hustled Krishna to the outhouses where they would help her clean up and change into a new sari for the reception. Then Krishna was expected to personally thank each of her guests for honoring her with their presence. As her sisters tossed well-water over her sweltering, not-quite-yet womanly body, Sandhya urged Krishna to scrub her face as much as possible to take off all that awful painting. Krishna reveled in the cool water and took every occasion to cup it into her hands and gulp down as much as she could. Her sisters scolded her for not waiting for boiled water. The restless Sindhya had been made to feel useful by staying well away from the washroom, and "safeguarding" Krishna's fresh sari from the splashing water. Krishna welcomed the lavishing attention of her sisters, efficient as it may have been.

Meanwhile, Jyotsna jostled her way through the appreciative crowd, catching Bala just as she was about to slip out the doors. "Aunty? You are feeling alright?" Jyotsna inquired. "Oh yes, my girl, only I have a long trip home and should start making a move now" Bala replied unconvincingly. "Aunty, I must ask. You were not pleased with the performance? You did not applaud it. You think she is too young? I have introduced her too early?" Jyotsna's giant eyes implored Bala's reassurance. "Jyotsna," the wizened Bala replied thoughtfully, "the girl has great potential. She has strong technique, and much poise. She will surely develop her *abhinaya* with maturity, although it is very good even now. She has promise." Jyotsna thought all of this very complimentary. "Then what is it, Aunty?" Bala paused while some of those milling around passed by and someone congratulated Jyotsna on having identified a prodigy. Then, drawing closer, looking somewhat apologetic, Bala whispered "There is too much pride yet in her, Jyotsna. She dances for the audience, not the gods. It is only her upbringing and her youth. It is not her fault. She has been taught to perform properly. You have done an admirable job. When she surrenders fully, she will be able to inspire." Jyotsna felt ashamed for being unable to discern this weakness. A worthy teacher should be able to make out this essential attribute in a dancer. "She wasn't ready." Jyotsna acknowledged, visibly disappointed. Bala was quick to reply: "*Hare*, things are different now, *baba*! Gandhiji says it's a matter national honor to bring back our heritage. We must revive *Bharatanatyam*. The colonists have suppressed this dance for long enough! Just because they don't like us to take pride in our history, doesn't mean it is right for us to comply. If her dance lacks some spirit now, it cannot do so for long. You are doing the right thing by unveiling young talent. Just think of how many will learn our stories through this performer! Let her dance! She will mature, and then we will see her give more. So, we display good looking mangos that are not yet ripe to eat! Doesn't matter. At least the people know how a good mango should look!" Jyotsna thought over her guru's words. "But Aunty, good looking mangos don't always taste so sweet and the sweetest mangos don't always look so good!" Bala smiled, "Yes, my girl, but all the sweetest mangos take time to ripen. See that the youngster dances publicly as much as she can bear. When she has tired of the audience, she will relinquish herself. Then maybe we can have some nectar worthy of the gods, eh?" Jyotsna took the point and escorted her mentor to the bullock-cart, its exhausted buffalos dozing alongside their driver, under the blazing Mangalore sun.

At the *prasad*, where she now appeared in a creamy, silk sari bordered with gold and tightly plaited hair, Krishna made sure to thank each guest for coming. Krishna was the fairest of her sisters. Her Father was exceedingly satisfied with her appearance, as amongst Brahmins, to be pale-skinned was tantamount to being beautiful, and the two "*gori and gomti*" would often be uttered of women in the same breath. She was still girlish, but growing shapelier despite the rigor of her dance practice. Krishna's thick, black hair was a stunning contrast to her pallid skin, and her dark, enormous, deep-set eyes were pleasantly balanced against the pout of plump lips. Yet, it was Krishna's self-imposed reserve that made her most attractive. Unlike Sindhya, she no longer had the luxury of exposing her natural vivaciousness. Krishna worked hard at suppressing her intrinsic sparkle in favor of the composure expected of a girl her age. This dutifulness imparted a kind of glow to her. An obligatory propriety betrayed the tumult of a restless spirit.

Some in the audience told Krishna she was a born dramatist. Others said she was very beautiful or graceful. Her school-teachers were highly laudatory, and said they now knew why she ran off after classes instead of staying to play like the other children. Kishore-dada, usually parsimonious in his praise, said she was turning into a presentable young lady and that she should keep up the good work. Krishna, though bursting with pride, deflected all praise exactly as she was meant to. "All credit goes to my guru," she replied, her head bowed in humility, her hands clasped behind her back. "Thank you but your kind words should be addressed to Jyotsna-Aunty," was another ready response. She noticed that Arna and Amma were staying close to the Nadghars. That the Nadghars had stayed on, rather than begging off for their journey home, was a good sign. She imagined they were negotiating a dowry and wondered what her parents would have to give over to "win her a first-rate Bhanap husband," as Kishoredada liked to say. She was nervous about approaching and was keeping the scariest for last. After making thorough rounds, however, there was nobody left to thank and Krishna had to make her way toward her parents and the Nadghars. For reassurance she sought out Sindhya, who had set out a tea party beneath the skirts of the tables where the sweets were laid out. She grasped Sindhya by the hand and edged up beside their father with all the confidence she could muster.

Arna and Mr. Nadghar were deep in discussion about the progress Ghandiji was making and how small things like going back to locally spun cotton were much more than symbolic gestures. The compact Mr. Nadghar was pontificating as Amma and Mrs. Nadghar looked on with interest and nodded in agreement. Krishna and Sindhya stood in silence waiting to be acknowledged. Sindhya, who had grown impatient and wanted to get back under the table, tugged at the tails of her father's *kameez* exclaiming "Krishna-akka wants to talk!" Arna, who held a general notion that children should be seen and not heard, exempted his youngest from this dictum. He collected her amiably into his arms, "This is our youngest, Sindhya" he introduced, "and you can see that we will have much work to do in keeping her hushed before we'll be able to find her a suitable match!" Amma nodded her ascent with pursed lips, and Mr. Nadghar smiled appreciatively, "Yes, it must be burdensome to have so many girls," he sympathized. Then addressing Krishna he remarked, "Your father assures me that in spite of your talents, you

have an acquiescent disposition, and I should be very pleased when you are wedded to my son." Krishna wasn't sure how to deflect this compliment. She wasn't
even sure she had heard one. All she heard was "wedded," and smiled dumbly,
fixing her eyes on her henna-painted feet as she thought up a response. Soon she
answered meekly, "I am grateful that you came, sir. If you were pleased with the
performance, Jyotsna-Aunty deserves all credit. If you were not, then it is my own
fault." The dour Mrs. Nadghar, having evaluated Krishna's statement, knelt
down to address Krishna more closely; "It is the gods who must be pleased child,
not we! And we shall learn of their judgment in time, won't we?" "Yes maddum,"
was all Krishna could reply, not daring to look into her future mother-in-laws
eyes. Krishna scolded herself for not thinking of this on her own, her eyes downcast, tears burgeoning. She bowed a hasty *vandana* to each of the Nadghars, and
not waiting to be dismissed, scurried from the tent toward the outhouse behind
which she hid to burst into floods of tears. The day's pressures and the unexpected terror of impending marriage to a stranger overcame Krishna all at once,
casting her into mighty, heaving sobs.

"You must excuse our daughter," the ever apologetic Amma broke in, as she
tried to make out where Krishna had disappeared in such a hurry, "she will have
had a difficult day, you can understand, and must be quite weary." "No apologies
necessary," replied Mr. Nadghar good-naturedly, as his wife's face grew decidedly
skeptical, "you should be commended that she has learned to do her duty despite
being so taxed. I will be pleased to report to our son that upon his finishing the
medical college, he will have a well raised young lady to call his own." "He will
indeed be surprised that we have found a fitting *Bhanap* girl with a proper boys'
name!" Mrs. Nadghar injected somewhat derisively. Arna jumped quickly to
explain: "Krishna's *namakarana* landed on the feast of *Janmasthami* so we were
moved to name her after the mighty river which is the namesake of Lord
Krishna," then, he added genially, tweaking Sindhya's chin, "and our river flowed
into an ocean!" The group chuckled at the well-timed pun. Sindhya liked being
named after something so big as the ocean. She flashed a wide smile, then
remembering that humility was expected of a proper lady, quickly buried her face
in her father's shoulder to hide her shameful pride.

Jyotsna remained to help tidy up after the last guests trailed off that afternoon.
Krishna had been coaxed out of her misery by Sandhya who had explained that
Krishna wouldn't be leaving home until after she finished her high schooling.
Didn't Krishna know that they are, after all, *Chitrapur Saraswat Brahmins* and
Saraswati is the goddess of learning? Krishna was expected to finish high school
before getting married, or else how would she be able to entertain an educated

husband? Krishna smiled because she knew her clan was named after the river down which they had migrated from the North Western planes almost 5000 years before, not after the goddess. Still, she was encouraged to hear that this marriage was still four years off and she wouldn't have to leave home until then. She was even more pleased when, upon departing, Arna hugged and commended her for behaving so properly, and even added that it was a rare day when a daughter helped to lighten a man's burden—which she had taken to mean that her dowry must have been manageable. After Arna and Kishore had left for home, only *M'am* and the women were left to transport the soiled dishes, move the wooden tables back into the classrooms, take down the tents, and restore the two-room schoolhouse for Monday's classes. They labored together in the oppressive heat and gummy humidity of the pre-monsoon season, coordinated by Deepa's wordless yet officious commands.

In the midst of her cleaning Amma glanced down to find that the intricate *rangoli,* so painstakingly poured this morning by Deepa, had been gashed and muddled. She was pained to find that the fine yellow powder surrounding the concentric red pattern was now streaked across the delicately laid paisley figures, the elaborate geometry now smudged beyond recognition. Careless passers-by swishing saris or dragging their feet must have wrecked the gorgeous design. Amma resented the enormous footprint of a man's sandal imprinted smack over the central motif. It looked almost deliberate to Amma, who immediately thought herself silly for imagining such intentional defacement. No, she corrected herself, the ornate *rangoli* is poured from fine dusts precisely to remind us how easily anything, including a carefully composed life, can vanish with the slightest disturbance.

As Jyotsna struggled with the diminutive Amma to take down the festive and fragrant garlands they had so arduously strung up the night before, she queried in Kannada, "Ratna-bai, Bala-bai believes Krishna should dance as much as possible. She thinks it is proper to contribute to the movement and that Krishna will be teaching many people their lost culture. She says Gandhiji would support it." Amma processed the implications of Jyotsna's suggestion. "She is promised now, Jyotsna-bai, thanks to you! There is no more need to make show of her. Now she must concentrate on her studies." Jyotsna attempted another approach, "but her studies would not suffer now that she is fully trained! And what a waste of so many years of practice for only one performance! I myself studied and performed together at a time when *Bharatanatyam* was much more prohibited than it is now; and I managed even to contribute some little bit to the family purse!" Amma considered the proposition again. "Arna would not like this idea, Jyotsna.

You must put it out of your head. How is Krishna to attend high school if she must travel to perform? And what will the *sangha* think of this showiness?" Jyotsna, a *vaishya*, had always been stumped by these orthodox Brahmins: on the one hand they idealized education and culture, on the other, they fiercely guarded their community from any outside influence. She made another attempt, "Ratnabai, Krishna will have to go to Bombay in any case to take her yearly exams. If only then she could offer some performances as I have, just think of the service she will be doing! There are so few of us keeping the dance alive, and so few willing to learn under these circumstances! And I will always be with her to chaperone. We might even dance together! You have been courageous and taken the chance to educate her like this. There is much promise in her, even Bala-bai says so! I must respectfully ask, how can you waste all this training?" Amma responded in her gentle, patient style, "Jyotsna-bai, you have been a part of our family all these many years. You have been an important influence on Krishna's development and because of your labors we have won her a good husband. That was our purpose, and it is now accomplished. Arna is not likely to agree to this. It is not my decision anyhow; I can only support what Arna decides." Jyotsna, ever diplomatic, conceded some flattery, "You are a devoted wife, Ratna-bai. It is not right for me to ask this of you. I will speak to him directly. He is a reasonable and educated man. I am sure that he will see how the gods are better served by making a temporary sacrifice. Thank you for your advice." Amma was left baffled by the conversation. She did not think she had imparted any advice.

That night, Krishna, spent and relieved that this day was over, stroked Sindhya's forehead as they lay side-by-side in the small cot that dominated the humble room they shared. "What did they really think of me?" she wondered to herself, going over in her mind the events of the day. "They said so many nice things…but were they only being polite?" Just as she herself had been trained to restrain her dissatisfactions, Krishna imagined that others spared her due criticism. She suddenly recalled that her marriage had been arranged today. She was relieved that Lord Ganesh had made that possible, but a vague fear overcame her as well. She shuddered, but stifled her natural revolt in favor of responsible resolve. "When I am married," she imagined, "I will be just like Amma; devoted to my husband and unfailingly dedicated to my family. It will be a pleasure to give up my wants to satisfy theirs. It is proper." Her body stiffened against the prospect, but it would have been wrong not to think it…after all, her father had worked so hard to ensure her proper betrothal. Yet she couldn't deny her antipathy for the stern Mrs. Nadghar. "I will come to love her, I am sure, when I know her better" Krishna assured herself, doubting the likelihood. Then thoughts of having to leave home crept slowly in. "I don't want to go away the way Deepa, Sandhya and Shaku did. It was so sad for Amma and so terrible for the rest of us. And what must they be doing, so lonely in their new homes far away?" Krishna strained back her tears so as not to alarm her young companion. Anyway, she thought, she had no choice about it. What point was there in blubbering? She calmed herself with the knowledge that it would be a long time before she'd have to go. Still, she wished it could be longer.

Meanwhile, Sindhya remained wide-eyed and sleepless. "*Akka*," she whispered. "I didn't check the eggs today and now I can't sleep." "Oh Sindhya," Krishna replied exasperated, her voice crackling from tears suppressed, "the eggs are fine, I'm sure. They will be there in the morning and we can check them then. Close your eyes now." "No *Akka*," Sindhya retorted steadfast, "tomorrow you will go to school before I wake up and then *M'am* will say he's too busy to lift me and Amma will say she's too short! We must go now! What if they popped?" Sindhya liked the sounds of certain words in English better than in Konkani: the ones that sounded funny to her or sounded just like what they were supposed to mean were her favorite. "Pop" and "bumbershoot" came up frequently of late. Krishna stifled a giggle. "Hatched, baby, eggs don't 'pop'." Sindhya slid into a whine, "What if they hatched, then? Can't we see, please, *Akka*, please?????"

Born premature, with precarious beginnings, Sindhya had always remained petite. Her miniature hands and tiny feet, the button nose on her minute face, even the smallness of her voice, infused Sindhya with a defenselessness that easily tugged at the stalest of heartstrings. So Krishna, though exhausted, motioned silence to Sindhya and climbed off the low bed. She lit the small oil lamp at their bedside and the two girls in thin petticoats tiptoed barefoot through the meager, single-story house, out the back door, past the well and across the courtyard to the huts that served as a depot for their fathers' grain brokerage business. Along the ledge of the corrugated tin roof that Arna and *M'am* had curled at the edges to fashion a gutter for the monsoon seasons, a purple sunbird had tucked a sac-like nest which now cupped its delicate eggs. Krishna lifted Sindhya to balance standing on her shoulders and then handed the frail Sindhya the gas-light. Sindhya held it far out in front of her to find the nest along the gutter. "Is the mother there?" Krishna asked. The truth was, she was just as interested in the progress of the nest as Sindhya. "No," came Sindhya's little voice, "no Mummy. More that way." Sindhya motioned left with the gas-lamp, holding on to the gutter with her free hand. Krishna shuffled over, commanding in a whisper "Be careful not to touch them!" Moving the gas-light closer to the sac, Sindhya counted off, "One, two, three, four, five." Sindhya pointed at each egg as she counted, her littlest finger tip grazed the last one. She didn't understand why it shouldn't. "They're all still here! They've gotten bigger! They're alright!" she confirmed, relieved. "I told you they would be; now let's get back to bed." Krishna whispered. The girls dismantled their balancing act and scurried back to the house hand in hand.

The next day, while Krishna was at school and Sindhya was helping Amma hang the washing, Sindhya glanced across the dusty courtyard and thought she saw something leap off the edge of the grain shed. "Amma!" cried Sindhya racing toward the shed, "The eggs hatched! They're flying!!!!" Sindhya arrived at the broken egg-shell on the ground, a single fragment had chipped off the surface and she could make out a yellowish beast squirming, its beak and clouded eye clearly distinguishable through the membrane still engulfing it. Amma came after Sindhya and both bent over the wriggling critter. "It hasn't hatched yet, baby, it looks like it's trying." Amma evaluated. She squinted up at the gutter where she could see the dazzling sunbird protecting her nest. "I don't know why it fell. Maybe it's been thrown from the nest," explained Amma to her quizzical daughter. "There might have been something wrong with it. Unless it only fell out on its own."

Sindhya considered the situation as she squatted over the egg in her hand-me-down school frock, inspecting it closely, afraid to pick it up. "Why won't mummy come to fetch it? Because it's so ugly?" Amma worried that she had said too much, then giggled "No baby, it's not ugly. It's just isn't ready to come out yet. It wasn't fully cooked. Maybe mummy doesn't know how to count and hasn't noticed that it fell out!" Amma thought she'd made a good recovery. "Then we can give it back to her!" Sindhya exclaimed excited, "She'll be so happy!" Amma reached out to collect the egg and the piece of shell beside it. She carefully pressed the fragment into place to cover its matching hole, attentive not to pierce the sheer membrane still protecting the fetus. "No, *ammu*, once something foreign has touched it, mummy won't take it back." Amma said the word "foreign" in English. "We'll have to see if we can keep it warm and maybe it will hatch when it's ready. It doesn't seem too damaged from the fall." Amma now worried that she'd given her little daughter too much hope. Perhaps she should have let nature take its course. Sindhya looked very upset, inquired "What's forn?" "Foreign is something from outside, something that isn't its family. Sometimes when something foreign touches an egg, mummy-daddy think it smells wrong so they won't take it back. It's better if we take care of it now. Yes *ammu*? We must find some cotton wool to keep it warm." Amma solicited Sindhya's cooperation. Sindhya remembered touching an egg last night. She wondered if she was "forn." She liked the idea of helping the egg and being able to watch it closely every day till it got better. Sindhya followed as Amma carried the egg gingerly across the courtyard and into the house to solicit *M'am's* insight.

After school that day Krishna headed automatically for the squat bungalow across the river where Jyotsna taught dance and music lessons. She skipped along the path thriving with bowing coconut palms and dense with bamboo thickets. She marveled at the way the brilliant bougainvillea could cascade down just about any structure, wind itself around any wayward stump. The walk to Jyotsna-Aunty's was lush and shaded and took Krishna past the sluggish, green river, where she often stopped to gaze out at the longboats, with their reedy fishermen pulling in the last catches of the day. More than that, Krishna looked forward to the delicious *lassi* Jyotsna offered her after school and before dance-class—even though Sandhya had once said it was wrong to accept food from a *vaishya*. Krishna didn't care. She didn't understand how if the same cow made the milk that was turned into the *lassi* it should be any different if a non-Brahmin served it. After all, Jyotsna could drink the *lassi* Amma gave her, so why shouldn't she do the same?

On her way to Jyotsna's, Krishna was supposed to be memorizing her Shakespeare verses to recite tomorrow but her mind kept wandering. She remembered years ago overhearing Arna and Kishore-dada arguing over whether she should be allowed to take dance classes and how nervous she had been the first time she went to Jyotsna's bungalow. Arna had called Jyotsna a "dirty *Devadasi*" when Kishore had tried to convince him that if Krishna were to learn *Bharatanatyam* she could also improve her Sanskrit. Kishore pled a strident case: "Teaching the classical arts to the younger girls will make it easier to marry them off, Arna. Now with so many *Bhanap* boys leaving the hometowns and making love-marriages with non-Brahmins, it's our duty to make sure that the girls marry into the community. What makes you think the girls will have any chance at decency if we don't make them stand out? And the cost of the dance classes will be minimal compared to the embarrassment of an unmarried girl, no?" Krishna had been surprised to hear her brother assert himself so strongly before their father—especially over her. Arna had only agreed to an initial three months of classes to see if Krishna "took to dancing" and said that Amma would have to meet this "supposed" teacher and see if she was fit to influence a Brahmin.

Amma had taken Krishna to Jyotsna's bungalow after much trepidation about what she believed was a ridiculous plan to earn interest in her girls—although her opinion would not have been welcome. "We will only be observing the class to see if it is decent, yes?" Amma explained to Krishna on the way so as not to engender any expectations, "And don't you touch anything nor accept any offerings. These women have all sorts of schemes to draw you in." They had been greeted at the door by a bubbly Jyotsna dressed in garish colors, who after introductions had to Amma's surprised dismay, immediately taken to calling Amma by the over-familiar "Ratna-bai." Before Krishna could get her mother's approval, Jyotsna had whisked them both over to the straw mat where four other young girls sat waiting for class to start. Jyotsna announced that before any dancing, they would listen to an old story. The girls seemed pleased with this notion. Jyotsna, who Amma estimated to be in her early thirties, folded herself gracefully into a seated position on the floor mat before the eager cluster and motioned for the girls to make a circle around her. She had an easy manner with the girls, and this, despite her general skepticism, Amma appreciated.

Krishna found she'd never seen anybody tell a story the way Jyotsna did. She made big gestures and funny faces the way a boy would. She looked up proudly rather than down humbly. Jyotsna laughed without covering her mouth and shrieked loudly in mock fear or delight, all of which Krishna at first thought quite unbecoming of a lady. Jyotsna would purposely leave out words in her stories so the girls could fill in the blanks. Jyotsna would say certain words in Sanskrit as well, and have the girls repeat them until each of them had pronounced correctly. She let them interrupt her with questions (which was never allowed in school) and didn't scold them for making mistakes (which always happened in school.) When Jyotsna made a motion to enhance the story, she would encourage the girls to make it as well, helping them place their arms or fingers in the special, proper positions. "The thumb," Jyotsna explained, "always signifies Brahma, the god of gods; the index finger," she noted pointing at each of the girls', "signifies the human self or 'ego.' When you make a circle touching the thumb to the index" (Jyotsna showed the girls, curling her fingers into position), "you are joining your spirit with the spirit of god!" Krishna had learned the meaning of her first *mudra*.

Jyotsna was unlike any of Krishna's aunties or sisters or teachers. Even though she was slender and petite, somehow she seemed bigger and brighter. Krishna thought she had never met so lovable a lady. Even Amma had forgotten herself and gotten wrapped up in the story-telling that first day, her eyes widening with delight as Jyotsna brought to life the well known tales Amma so cherished. And though Krishna had been clumsy in the dance portion of the class, Jyotsna had told Amma that Krishna had promise. "I can tell," said Jyotsna, "by the way your little girl pays attention. She will pick up the background with ease." Amma liked her girls to be complimented, and though she was wary of this unmarried *vaishya* who had made her own living by dancing and who knows what else, she sensed that Jyotsna was kind-hearted and harmless to children and probably a good teacher (as long as only the stories and dancing were conveyed.) She reported to Arna precisely this. That evening Amma watched Krishna repeat the story to Sindhya with the same animation and inflection that Jyotsna had used. "And when you touch the thumb to the index," Krishna motioned dramatically, "you are joining your spirit with the spirit of god!" From the next day on, Krishna went to Jyotsna's bungalow every day after school for classes, except for the days when Jyotsna was performing or teaching out of town.

Over the last seven years, Jyotsna had grown on the Nayampallis—particularly as it appeared that Krishna's dance lessons were contributing to her general education in Hindu mythology. The Nayampallis appreciated that Jyotsna would frequently walk Krishna home when her private classes went past dark, and that she made sure Krishna did her homework while she waited for her class to start. It was obvious to Amma and Arna that as Krishna's dancing had improved, Jyotsna had become just as dedicated to Krishna as Krishna had become to the dance. They valued Jyotsna's commitment, and little by little accepted her into the fold despite her being of a suspect caste. Still, Amma thought it was scandalous that Jyotsna had no qualms about talking back to men—particularly in defense of the classical arts. Jyotsna had once put Kishore squarely in his place when she had implied it quite uneducated of him to assume that all *Devadasis* were prostitutes. (Krishna had later asked Amma what that word meant and Amma had simply said she shouldn't repeat such dirty things.) Jyotsna had admonished Kishore with skill and subtlety. "Any learned historian would know," she said, implying that Kishore was neither of the two, "that the *Devadasis* only inherited a bad reputation when certain *rajas* began to forcibly take the sacred temple dancers as courtesans. You who are so well versed in the *Vedas* would know that by doing this they not only defiled the girls but also offended the gods!" Jyotsna went on, as though this were common knowledge amongst the educated. "As you know, the *Devadasis* never had opportunity to restore their dignity. Those *rajas* were co-opted by the English invaders, who promptly suppressed the classical arts so that our own people wouldn't learn and spread their proud history in this manner. Had my own grandmother not taught me the dance in secret, this important means of devotion would now be forgotten. And isn't *Bharatanatyam* now contributing to the cause of self-rule? Doesn't Ghandiji agree that the classical arts are integral to self rule?" Kishore conceded, leaving room to regain the upper hand, "I will have to research this further, but if your claims are true, you have elevated my understanding." Amma felt shame to be so pleased that her prized son, Kishore, had taken a lesson from a *vaishya*—and a mere woman at that.

Krishna had paid close attention to the discussion, but at age nine had not understood it one bit. As she skipped toward the bungalow this evening, she understood it all much better. She knew that *Bharatanatyam* had to go underground, as the colonists were threatened by its propagation of Indian mythological stories that might vent more nationalism. She liked the intrigue surrounding what felt like the mischief of dancing *Bharatanatyam* when it was informally forbidden.

Jyotsna was surprised to find Krishna at her door, since technically she was no longer a student. Krishna strode inside as usual, slung her satchel into the corner of the room as she always did and awaited her *lassi*, apparently unaware that there was no more need for classes. Unsure how to respond, Jyotsna relied on the comfort of habit and headed to the kitchen to fill a glassful. Instead of bringing it out to the salon as usual, she called Krishna into the kitchen and motioned her to take a stool at the small center-table. "Krishna," Jyotsna said, placing the frothy yogurt in front of her, "I didn't have the chance to tell you yesterday that you made me very proud. Your performance was excellent. Even Bala-Aunty said so." At this, Krishna's eyes lit up. She knew well the regard in which Jyotsna held Bala, and she could think of no higher praise. "Bala-Aunty thinks that you should start performing publicly with me. Do you know what that means?" Krishna sipped at her *lassi*, imagining the implications, then suggested, "Then I will not be going to high school?" Jyotsna smiled down at Krishna, "Oh no, I'm afraid you won't be able to escape high school my girl! But I have spoken with Arna and he has agreed that sometimes when I go to perform in Bombay or other places, you can dance with me. What do you think of that?"

With pounding heart, Krishna recalled the one time she had seen Jyotsna perform. Rahul-dada had just married Shakuntala-akka and had arranged for Arna, Amma, Sindhya and Krishna to travel to the Bombay suburbs to see Shaku in her new home. As a surprise, he had taken the whole family on an outing to see Jyotsna perform at the Opera House. Krishna remembered how exciting it had been to see her very own teacher all dressed up and on the high stage under so many lights, with so many spectators. Rahul had arranged with Jyotsna for the family to have special seats right up front, so Krishna's eyes were almost level with the bells around Jyotsna's ankles. Bala-Aunty had welcomed the audience and made an introduction, saying that Jyotsna was one of the "brightest stars in the *Bharatanatyam* sky because she personified the devotional aspect of the dance." (Krishna had to ask Arna what that meant.) Jyotsna danced six numbers during which Krishna sat mesmerized. She had never seen anything so radiant in her life. She noticed that when Jyotsna danced, she didn't seem at all like her usual self. Something about her disappeared and something about her magnified. To

Krishna, it didn't look like Jyotsna was dancing *Bharatanatyam*; it looked like *Bharatanatyam* was moving Jyotsna to dance. The audience cheered and clapped loudly after the fifth number and then everybody stood up and called for one more. It was after this spectacle that Krishna redoubled her efforts at dance class—she wanted to look just like Jyotsna on stage one day. From that moment on, she wanted to be applauded and cheered. She wanted the glamour of the stage, the thrill of the praise and the ability to so move a crowd. She knew it was wrong in her tradition to call such shameless attention to herself, but Krishna was awe-struck and irresistibly compelled. So at the suggestion of real performance, Krishna couldn't conceal her eagerness: "I would dance with you on a big stage?" she inquired excited. "Not always a big stage." Jyotsna explained, "Sometimes only a small stage. Sometimes at the houses of important people. Sometimes at schools or colleges. But Arna says you must keep up your good marks in school. Do you think you can do that? We will have to practice only before performances. Henceforth, you will not have to come here every day after school. We will fix up days to practice before performing. Sometimes if we must go far away, we will travel together and we will stay in the houses of nice people who want to help us show others about *Bharatanatyam*. Most important, we will be contributing to a very worthy cause." Krishna couldn't believe her ears. She would be doing something virtuous for nationalism, yes, but she was going to be sensational like Jyotsna! She wouldn't be so nervous about going away from home as long as Jyotsna was with her. As for Jyotsna, she could barely believe that Arna had conceded. He had agreed that spreading the myths and stories through *Bharatanatyam* could help the Gandhian cause, and a devoted nationalist at heart, he was willing to let his daughter contribute.

3

I've been dreading the whole move thing but it turns out that unpacking's quite easy. Mom, I should have figured, travels light. Besides the furniture, there are only about 20 other boxes—not even big ones. Sunny rolls her eyes as she heaves one onto the kitchen counter. "Mom, it must have taken longer for you to label this thing than to pack it!" She's right, the contents, right down to "strawberry print pot-holders" are listed neatly in black magic marker, on not one, but two sides of the box. As we unwrap and unravel, I am awed by mom's capacity to have redacted the paraphernalia of a sprawling, suburban, four-bedroom life down to the essentials needed for a "junior-one," urban retirement. She seemed almost relieved about the process of paring down, somehow unburdened. After every garage sale or visit by the Salvation Army, she'd go about her business self-satisfied and resolute, like she'd just come back from a teeth-cleaning, smarting from the lingering sting but confident it was the right thing to do. She already seems comfortable here in her new D.C. apartment, with everything compact, within reach, so much easier to control.

I'm assigned to hooking up the computer and assembling the desk and book shelf in the corner that we now call "the office." Mom glowers at me signaling that she's displeased with my wire management skills. "What? I'm just making sure everything works before I wind up the cords!" I whine defensively. "Good idea..." She retorts, somewhat suspicious. "I should think you wouldn't expect me to live with that jungle of wires." Done with the untangling, I set myself to shelving books. We agree they should go up by subject, not author. "At this age, I can barely remember what I'm looking up, less who the heck might have written it!" mom quips, irritated at what she perceives as her declining faculties. She's exaggerating or being humble. Her memory's still better than Sunny's and mine put together: last week she rattled off the prescription number for her blood pressure medicine by heart. "For heaven's sake," she hazarded when the pharmacist and I eyed her with equal astonishment, "I've been calling in for the damned thing once a month for five years. I probably recite it more often than my own name!"

I run into that medical text again as I'm unpacking. I've thought about that dedication several times since I spotted it, and figuring mom's in a peppier mood,

I venture another inquiry. "Hey ma, here's that medical book by your friend. Sunny, did you know some secret admirer dedicated a book to mom?" Sunny reaches for the book as I offer it. "Don't be silly, Sushi," mom promptly reverts, intercepting the hand-over and piling the book on the shelf without looking at it, "nobody dedicated anything. Now get back to unpacking you two." Sunny, undeterred, plucks the book from the shelf and starts flipping through it. "Sunny, now put that back and get to it. You two will do anything to avoid working." mom adds, trying to distract us with guilt. "Hey ma," Sunny insists, "is this really dedicated to you? It's so nice! What on earth did you do to change this guy's life?" "Don't be ridiculous, Sunny, put that thing down now. I didn't change anybody's anything. Now will you girls get back to work?" mom retorts, unconvincingly. I tease, "Mommy has a fan-club, mommy has a fan-club..." Miffed now, mom elaborates on her faux irritation, "If you girls will stop fooling around we might get done with unpacking before I turn 70!" Sunny winks at me and smiles as she re-shelves the book. It's obvious mom's keeping a secret. Being modest by nature, she'd never let us in on it, even if it were something impressive or perhaps especially if it was. She's never been the type of mom to regale us with stories of her glory days, the way dad was apt to do. On the contrary, she enforces her reserve with consistency. On returning recently from a PTA meeting where she accompanied Sunny she commented, "I hope you're not chumming up to Aarti and Mulund the way these American parents do. It's no wonder kids lose all respect when they're glibly told all about their mother's old smoking habit or how 'cool' their dad was in college. Kids don't need to know all that, they need to learn by upstanding example." Sunny tried to defend a more open approach but ended up frustrated and complaining to me in the end. I reminded her that mom hasn't even undressed in our company since either of us was in kindergarten.

Later that night, I'm on the fold-out couch in mom's new living room. I can't sleep. I survey my surroundings in the silvery moonlight that seeps through the curtains, spotting some framed photographs on the side table beside me. There's one of the four of us not long before dad died. We are standing in front of the Washington monument smiling compliantly for the camera. Dad has one arm wrapped around mom beside him, and mom, despite being the shortest, has arranged Sunny and me in front of her and is clutching each of us by one shoulder, hiding as usual. I put the silver frame down and pick up another, a sweet black-and-white of Sunny and me, she at seven, me about two or three, both of us in frilly sun-dresses. We are barefoot in some sort of garden, a sliver of rose-bush visible behind us. We are both squatting and looking up. She's arrived, swaddling me in a hug from behind while I was intently scratching something into the dirt with a stick. Sunny's beaming into the camera, glad for the attention. I seem startled, worried, but on the brink of putting on the right face for the camera. Truth is, I looked troubled, even back then. As I examine the photo, I start wondering whether mom's just going along with all these changes in her life, not letting on how hard it really is. Is she putting on the right face just for us? On the other hand, she seems like she's doing just fine. She seems less lonely than she was back at the house. Bumping around up there really was no good for anyone. And maybe all this change is a good way to keep herself occupied, body and mind. It makes me think I should be looking into some changes of my own—a good way to keep myself occupied, body and mind.

It suddenly occurs to me that I haven't checked my e-mails all weekend and there might be something from the office. I log on, lowering the volume on the modem so as not to disturb mom in the bedroom. Despite all my worrying about her, I can hear her snoring faintly through the door. The sleep of the just. After checking my e-mails, I start messing around on the Internet. It occurs to me to run a Google on that doctor's book. I quietly take it down off the shelf and flip around to find the right info. I tap out the author's name off the title and stare at the screen as a list of results appears. Four medical texts show up on the Amazon site; 1969, 1975 (that's the one!), 1979, 1986. An article indicates that he's a professor and researcher in the University of California system. But the synopses talk more about the books than their author. Then I find a cluster of studies on technical medical subjects; a couple in full text. I skim through them and find an e-mail address for him at the end of one. Divining a hint of scandal in the air and feeling strangely curious and bratty, I decide that if mom won't give, I'll figure it out myself:

From: sushilarao@youhoo.com
To: knadghar@calberk.edu
Subject: The Control of Highly Infectious Diseases
Date: Fri, 8 Mar 2000 00:28:48—0800 (EDT)

Dear Sir:

I wondered if you'd kindly indulge my curiosity on a quick inquiry. I was recently interested to find your 1975 publication "The Control of Highly Infectious Diseases," on a bookshelf in my mother's office. The dedication in it was an appreciation of Krishna. The book was autographed personally by you. I'm just wondering whether the book was dedicated to Krishna the deity; or per chance Krishna Rao—nee Nayampalli (my mother)—or whether it was another Krishna (after all, it is a common name.)

I would welcome hearing from you. I hope you do not find my question improper. I would understand if your dedication is private and you consider my inquiry inappropriate or personal.

Sincerely,

Sushila Rao

In the *Jattiswaram*, the element of melody is introduced, making the dance richer. This pure dance number increases the complexity of the steps but also requires a dancer's stamina and self control in maintaining astonishingly sculptural poses while the rhythmic music calls for movement. The purpose of this dance is to show the technical skill and accuracy of the dancer in meeting a demanding beat, as well as mental strength in resisting the urge to follow the tempo, by holding challenging postures.

#

4

The sunbird's chicks hatched a full week before Sindhya's egg, and she became anxious that it wouldn't learn to fly before the monsoons came. *M'am* had managed to keep the egg swaddled so it grew at pace with the nested ones while Amma made frequent suggestions conveying pessimism over its prospects. She reminded Sindhya that even human babies weren't named for a few months after their birth, since the chances of survival were so low. Still, every morning after washing up Sindhya visited the small shrine in the house to pray. Since bringing back the egg, in addition to all the usual thanks and praises to various gods and forebears, Sindhya asked for a blessing on the sunbird and all her chicks (including the "forn" one under her own care). So, frankly, did Amma. After daily prayers, Sindhya sped directly to the kitchen for a status check.

One afternoon, *M'am* heard peeping from the shelf where the egg rested. He hastened to fetch Amma and Sindhya. The squawking chick had hatched and broken through the very spot where it had been damaged. The creature chirped and squealed and seemed never to be satisfied no matter what the ever-solicitous *M'am* fed it. When Arna was consulted, he questioned whether it was proper for the group to interfere quite so aggressively in gods plans for the expelled chick. Still, he dictated that if it were to remain under the care of the household, "all gym-cracks" related to its feeding would have to be performed outside. There was some controversy over whether *M'am* (also a Brahmin, as he handled the food) should get one of the gardeners to collect worms for the chick, as a vegetarian diet seemed unsuitable to its needs. It was agreed there would be no harm in feeding worms to the needy chick as that was the pattern of life. Arna, somewhat incredulous over being involved in this ridiculous matter for the benefit of his youngest, decided that *M'am* could take on the fairly distasteful job of delivering the worms with pincers into the chicks' squawking beak. Sindhya said she didn't mind collecting worms, as they were readily available in the humid pre-monsoon season, but she was strictly forbidden to do so. For now, Arna had barely enough time to distribute the stocks in the granaries before they became impossible to store or transport during the monsoons. He didn't want to be further bothered with such frivolous domestic concerns.

M'am had some reservations in the context of a Brahmin, and strictly vegetarian, household over whether this feeding of worms would be appropriate. He was not delighted over the prospect, but carried out his work with a keen devotion. His family had serviced the *Nayampallis* for generations, and he was grateful to be in the service of upstanding Brahmins. The skeletal, bald and bow-legged cook, a toothy smile ever stretching from ear to ear, carried out his duties cheerfully and wobbled his head agreeably to what he assessed as even the most repugnant of requests. He could, he reasoned, have ended up working for a family beneath him, as his brother did, and was content just to be gainfully employed. When Sindhya would ask him what his real name was, and why he could address her as Sindhya while she was allowed only to address him by the title of "uncle-cook," he merrily reminded her that he had seen all the children grow up even since they were "sitting in the mango tree," and was thereby justified in calling them by first name. A generous soul by nature and a Brahmin-by-the-book, *M'am* deposited extra coins in the jar by the outhouses for the *nightsoil* collectors after Arna had already paid the due amounts. Arna knew that when *M'am* made a bargain at the market, he kept the difference for the *harijans,* who it was understood also had their place in society and subsisted on such kindness. From *M'am,* Arna never asked for receipts.

Sindhya was delighted with her new-found rearing functions and closely observed *M'am's* ministering to the ever-hungry chick. She inspected closely as the worms were delivered into the chick's beak. She watched mournfully as the worms wriggled, then disappeared down the tiny gullet. Sindhya eventually wore *M'am* down so that she could help to feed the frail chick (never in Arna's presence), careful always to use her right hand, just as all Hindus should. In a short time the chick grew sturdier, finding its feet, and shedding its fuzz in favor of feathers. Sindhya gave it plenty of attention, on occasion telling it stories from the ones that Krishna would tell her at bed time. She doled out advice on how it would eventually have to find its own worms and learn to fly. *M'am* enjoyed listening to Sindhya's colorful retellings of Indian mythology modified for relevance to a bird. Amma learned that when Sindhya was nowhere to be found she was likely in the vicinity of the kitchen porch worrying the sunbird. The chick came to know Sindhya and *M'am* well, and stopped squawking immediately upon seeing either of them approach.

As for Krishna there was no question that, just as all her siblings, she would excel in her high school entrance exams. To study, she had Sindhya drill her with random questions on everything from ancient history to English vocabulary. The exams required mostly rote memorization and in helping Krishna study, Sindhya ended up absorbing much more than she realized. The easiest questions for Krishna were always in math. She learned her times tables so well, that she could make surprisingly long calculations in her head. She loved the way math was so reliable and efficient. It wasn't messy like English class, with all sorts of exceptions and irregularities. If you did it methodically and precisely, like *Bharatanatyam*, math always worked out. So it was no surprise to her parents, nor cause for much celebration, when three weeks after her visit to Bombay, Krishna's examination results arrived in the mail. Amma had not only prayed to Ganesh but fasted for an extra day during the week of Krishna's exams, to which she attributed the fact that Krishna had qualified for high school entrance "with mathematics honors." The batch of qualifying students from the Mangalore area would be expected to report to the girls' high school on the first weekend in June. Arna promptly arranged for Krishna to ride daily by bullock-cart with the other two qualifying neighborhood *Bhanaps*, as the closest high school was 30 kilometers off. It was common for *Chitrapur Saraswat* Brahmins to pool resources, or cooperate in any endeavor that would ensure perpetuation of their clan. Sindhya thought it very exciting that Krishna shouldn't have to walk to school any more. She herself would be starting at the lower school this year and was certain to have to walk, even in the rains.

After finishing her entrance exam, Krishna practiced daily and diligently with Jyotsna for their first performance together. Though the neighboring state of Madras was rendered autonomous since 1937, it was still governed by a colonist as far as Arna was concerned. Arna reasoned that increasing numbers of Indian troops were getting deployed and used as "cannon fodder" to fight the Allied War just as Gandhi's "Quit India" campaign was taking root. As a result, it seemed to him that more numerous English envoys were visiting Madras and other southern strongholds. In what Arna assessed was amongst British measures to placate the population growing more interested in self-rule, over the past months, restrictions on cultural events had been lifted or permissions to hold them no longer required by the colonists in charge. The Baroness Rankeillour, wife of the Governor of Madras, had, as a result of this increased freedom, come upon an *Odissi* dance recital. She found it charming and convinced the Governor that a performance of folkloric dances might be interesting to visiting dignitaries. Jyotsna had been contacted to represent the *Bharatanatyam* tradition at the next Governor's ball, and had promptly recruited Krishna for the show, which would also include *Kathakali, Kuchipudi* and *Odissi* dances. Transportation, lodging, a substantial per diem payment and all meals for a week were to be provided to all performers by the Office of the Governor, but the instinctively cautious and conservative

Arna took some convincing. In the end, he insisted that if they must go, the two would stay at the home of his trusted *Bhanap* cousin, not far from the Governor's mansion at Fort St. George. If they had to practice with the musicians, the Governor would surely extend the courtesy of transporting the performers to and from what he was certain would be a safer and more sanitary environment than a hotel which would accept "all kinds." Beyond that, Arna didn't require much persuading, as he was too occupied with ridding the granary of its stores before the rains. Jyotsna made arrangements to comply with Arna's requirements. The Office of the Governor advanced RS300 for pre-performance expenses. Jyotsna immediately delivered RS200 to the Nayampallis so they would be predisposed in favor of permitting Krishna to dance, and spent some of her portion hiring a tailor for new, matching, costumes for Krishna and herself.

This would be a different kind of performance for Jyotsna. The audience may include Indians, but she understood that the show would have to interest the foreigners who may not know the mythology nor understand the devotional aspect of the dance. Given only fifteen minutes to perform, she felt compelled to choose a fast-paced, dazzling and demanding number that relinquished *abhinaya* in favor of stringent *nritta*—it was precisely the kind of piece at which a technically accomplished novice would excel, and a more experienced dancer might eschew. Krishna would be sure to delight, as she was growing more striking daily and as Bala had confirmed, was naturally oriented toward pleasing the audience. But dancing with a partner would be new for Krishna, and would require a great deal of practice for both. Rehearsing before the rains was trying enough. The unyielding humidity, the thickness of the air, made the dancing cumbersome and both dancers were quicker to frustrate and fumble. Krishna also underestimated how tricky it would be to coordinate with another dancer. She was used to ensuring that her bells jingled to the rhythm of the musicians, and now they had to jingle in sync with Jyotsna's as well. To appear symmetrical on stage, Jyotsna ensured that even the arcs of their arms and the angles of their bows were precisely aligned. Perfectionists by nature, the two took great pains to match up even the width of their smiles.

Sindhya flew shouting through the house when the driver arrived to collect Krishna for the journey to Madras. Amma was helping Krishna to pack the valise reserved for Arna's long trips, which he agreed to relinquish for this special occasion, when the unmistakable roar of a motor vehicle drew the whole neighborhood to glare at the door of the Nayampalli household. "It's come! It's come! Jyotsna-Aunty's here with a driver and a big white motor-car just like the *rajas* have!!!" Sindhya cried, hurrying toward the girls' bedroom. Amma, her own long hair disheveled, rushed to help Krishna close the suitcase as *M'am* delivered to the driver a hot tiffin-carrier filled with *idlis, sambar, parathas,* and *dal* for the trip. He also supplied plentiful mangos, including Krishna's favorite Alfonsos—juicy, ample, ripe and in ideal season. The driver emerged to help with the luggage and, being used to the excesses of dignitaries, was happily surprised to find only one small bag to load. Even Arna surfaced from the granary office to see what all the fuss was about. He took the driver aside and, for the benefit of the attentive neighbors, loudly interrogated him as to his years of experience and safety record. He admonished the driver to make sure there would be no unscheduled stops and insisted on learning the precise route to be taken although in earnest, it made little difference as Arna knew few of the roads in the direction of Madras. He nodded in approval in any event, then slipped the driver RS20 to "ensure the safety of his cargo." He knelt to hold Krishna by the shoulders and impressed upon her the importance of behaving herself like a proper Brahmin and making her country proud. Then he pressed a letter into her hands to be delivered to cousin Prakash. Krishna knew that it probably contained some if not all of the money that Jyotsna had delivered earlier that month. No Nayampalli daughter would ever subsist on favors.

Amma, her heart swollen as though she was losing another girl to marriage, embraced Krishna tearfully, "I will pray for your safe-keeping every day. I will ask for blessings on your journey and many happy returns for your dance." Amma got so emotional, she had to remove her nose ring and accept a hanky from Arna in order to blow her nose. Wondering what could have moved his wife to appear outdoors with loosened hair and irritated by the blubbering, Arna scolded Amma's whimpering, "She's not going to fight in the war for heaven's sake, she's going to Madras for a mere week and will be safely in Prakash-Uncle's hands. Now let the party make a move else they will lose the precious daylight needed for the drive." Sindhya was crying for no reason other than that she had rarely seen her mother do so. Krishna hugged and kissed Sindhya and promised to bring her something special from her trip; she told her not to cry because that meant something bad was happening, but something good was happening so she should be happy instead. She climbed into the back seat elegantly, keeping her sari tucked under her just as she saw Jyotsna do. She noticed for the first time how many neighbors had appeared at their doors or windows to witness the spectacle. She felt special and liked the feeling. The car pulled away with Krishna waving wildly out the open window, and *M'am,* Amma and Sindhya waving back from behind as Arna headed back to the granary. That night, Amma dotingly ladled an extra bit of *dal, rice* and *sambar* onto each plate, as much to Sindhya's glee as Arna's consternation. *M'am* would have to readjust his portions, he commented. Krishna's gallavantings shouldn't justify overindulgence at home.

Uncle Prakash's home in Madras was not so different from Krishna's own; and the "twinkle toes," as Leena Aunty had dubbed them upon arrival, were each given their own bedroom as Prakash and Leena's daughters had grown up and married some years ago. Krishna had never had her own room, as before Sindhya came along, she shared the room with Shakuntala. She worried about whether she would be able to sleep without Sindhya to embrace, but was consoled by the giant batik of Ganesh that hung opposite the bed—where she could see it clearly on laying down. The journey had been tiring once the glamour of a car-and-driver had worn off. There were lots of rocks, stones and pot holes which made her bounce and jiggle more than on a bullock cart, and it seemed that things went past so fast in a motor-car, Krishna barely got a chance to look at them before something else of potential interest came whizzing at her. In the car, Jyotsna tried to prepare Krishna for the ostentation of Fort St. George. She queried the driver to learn more about Madras and the Governor's ball. The driver, George, was a Christian and it was obvious to the passengers, from his coloration, limited vocabulary and servile demeanor that he had been a "*bhangi*" converted for the purpose of economic mobility. When Krishna asked a question about a town or monument, George would answer "Please, *Mem Sahib,* this is the postal office." Or "Please *Mem Sahib,* that is the statue of Nandi only." George was the first person ever to call Krishna "*Mem Sahib*" and Krishna giggled to herself upon being addressed as a grown-up. From then on, for the next week, she became used to being addressed as "Miss, Madam, Ma'am, Mem Sahib, Lady, and even Krishna-bai."

No matter how much Jyotsna tried to explain, Krishna was not prepared the next morning for the splendor of Fort St. George. She had never been inside the walls of a proper Fort nor crossed a moat or been waved through the daunting entrance gates to anything. It never occurred to her that all the activities of a normal city would be enclosed in the walls of the garrison. The red brick buildings with ornate towers were imposing in size and improbable in quantity. The buildings looked different from the squat ones she was used to, and reminded her of the drawings she had seen in English picture books. The Fort even had its own post office and a giant Anglican church! The Governors' residence was also inside the fort walls; and the gardens here were so well tended that not a single withering petal could be spotted amongst the plentiful rows of rose-bushes lining the walks to the buildings. She had been at some spectacular Hindu temples where each wall was avidly sculpted and each spire was painted in vivid colors, but those seemed somehow vulgar, riotous and in woeful disarray compared to what she now beheld. Here, by contrast, everything was square, even, prim and neat. It looked like every inch of the whole fort had been polished. Even the roads were perfectly paved and spotlessly clean. No animals roamed the streets, and not a single orchid seemed to grow wild or randomly or out of place. There were no fallen trees nor even nuts on the ground! Krishna noticed that there were hardly any women about, except the haggard sweepers in faded cotton saris, bent over their short straw brushes, endlessly pushing dust off the walkways and entryways, careful not to look into anybody's eyes. She never understood why they couldn't attach a long stick to the end of the brush so they wouldn't have to stoop; Arna had concocted such an implement for Amma when her back-trouble started, and it, in combination with properly timed oil massages, had been a great relief. As the driver headed through the wide boulevards to the gymnasium where the dancers would be meeting the musicians for their first practice, Jyotsna noticed the many dapper Indian men in uniform stealing glances at the ladies in the back seat of the white sedan.

Their first practice day was only with the musicians; and once they had coordinated their numbers, the rehearsals went quite well. The next days Jyotsna and Krishna met the *Odissi, Kuchipudi* and *Kathakali* dancers and also got to watch them perform. Krishna didn't like the *Kathakali* one bit. She thought the big masks were silly and that without the ability to show facial expression, there was no reason to repeat the musical lines so frequently. The men who danced the parts, however, were jolly and good natured. One of them had a big paunch that reminded Krishna of the one Kishore-dada was developing. She was amazed that he could excel as a dancer nevertheless and resolved to tease Kishore-dada that it wasn't too late for him. The *Kuchipudi* seemed to Krishna only like an interpretive form of *Bharatanatyam* with fewer rules. The four dancers told a contemporary love story instead of drawing from mythology. Krishna liked the idea of it, but didn't understand how this dance would work to please the gods or educate the people. The *Odissi* dancers made Krishna's heart pound. Their dance was slower and more fluid than *Bharatanatyam*. The dancers' bodies curved and bent more; a stark contrast to the way her own movements were so angular and clipped. They told a familiar story from Hindu mythology as well, but in a different way than she had learned. Jyotsna explained that *Odissi* dancers also used to be *Devadasis* in the state of Orissa and that only recently had they too experienced a revival. She was very pleased to see this art form grow. That evening at the dinner table, much to Prakash-Uncles' surprise, Jyotsna and Krishna were chattier than he imagined possible, and had a great deal to report. When Leena-

Aunty asked Krishna why she had so enjoyed the Odissi, Krishna felt shy to explain. Jyotsna remarked that perhaps it was because in general, the dance was more graceful, and less clipped than *Bharatanatyam*. What Krishna couldn't grasp, was that the Odissi dancers' movements were highly alluring and sexually charged. They emphasized the feminine form in all its curvilinear glory, and when the Odissi dancers performed, they made Krishna feel something like naughty inside. In the next days of practice, Krishna worked hard to stress the s-shape of her poses more like the Odissi dancers did. Jyotsna reprimanded Krishna for the delay this caused in meeting the beat, and wondered aloud if Krishna was tired or had some injury to her hip. "Aunty," Krishna replied in justification, "I'm only trying to make the gestures bigger for a bigger stage, just like you said!"

On the day of the performance, the practice was moved to a raised wooden platform on the lawns under the vast balconies of the Governor's mansion. Gathering at the stage, the dancers were met by an imposing Indian Lieutenant, tall and smartly dressed, who spoke officiously as though addressing a troop of new recruits. "I am the organizer and the master of ceremonies for the festivities. You should think of me as your commanding officer during your stay." He paced back and forth in front of the awed dancers and clicked his heals after each sentence, no matter what its importance. "You understand that you are only performers here and not invited guests." (click.) "You will not at any time consort with the guests," (click) "chat with the guests," (click) or approach the guests" (click) "and if you can avoid it, you will refrain from even looking at the guests." (click click.) He went nose to nose with the portly Kathak dancer and screwed up his eyes accusingly, "You understand, sir?" The dancer nodded guiltily and shrunk back. The officer added that the audience would enjoy the performance during the dinner which would be served at the multi-tiered balconies of the house and at the tables arranged on the gardens. As he spoke Krishna noticed that the tables were being set with fine, gold-bordered china, gleaming silverware and more varieties of glasses than Krishna had ever seen. The Lieutenant pointed out stage locations where the musicians would sit and the pathways for the dancers' entries and exits. He motioned at where the Governor and his wife would be seated and sternly reminded the dancers "You will remain entirely and strictly in the areas outside of the dining premises and you will not stray for any reason." "Mixing with the guests will not be tolerated." "And to ensure your proper composure, you will be under the constant supervision of an officer who will also tend to any other of your needs." He motioned to a lanky officer standing by, indistinguishable from any of the others, except that he was now assigned to follow the dancers around. Krishna followed Jyotsna's lead in smiling and nodding graciously as the self-important Lieutenant barked his rules on and on.

So astonished was Krishna by the opulence surrounding her, Krishna barely caught the Lieutenants dictums. From the lawns of the garden she could see clear through the windows of the mansion. Krishna admired from afar the intricate woodwork on the walls inside the house, giant shimmering chandeliers, and enormous paintings of fancy white ladies in billowing pastel-colored gowns arranged around them like birds squatting in their own nests. A stern officer in monocles seemed always to be standing behind each seated lady, bands of gold embroidery at his sleeve, medals and badges emphasizing his lapels. She knew these people were important, probably former Governors, but they all looked pretty much the same to her. Krishna was pleased to recognize the familiar portrait of Queen Victoria, although she had never seen one quite so huge. She appreciated Queen Victoria but worried a little for the Princess Elizabeth and imagined that if she were just a tad prettier she might have fewer troubles than her mum.

Krishna thought she best use a washroom before practice began and after inquiring with Jyotsna, the Lieutenant called for a young officer to escort Krishna through the back entrance and the mansion kitchens. The officer led her past the busy catering halls, where she was horrified to encounter a table supporting three giant and bloody legs of some sort of beast (she knew not what poor creature had suffered this fate.) The smell and sight of this barbarism made Krishna nauseous and almost faint, and she scurried faster to keep up with him, relieved to be heading to the facilities. At the end of a hallway the young officer stopped abruptly and wordlessly opened a door which he motioned her to enter, then closed it efficiently behind her indicating that he would wait. Krishna found herself in an alien setting. The room was tiled and white like most washrooms and the wash basin seemed familiar enough, but there was no hole in the tiled floor, nor any stoppers to place ones' feet, and no buckets with which to wash. Instead, an oddly shaped, somewhat oval seat with a glazed ceramic base seemed to dominate the room. A long chain-cord with a wooden handle hung over-head, which she imagined was connected to the fancy electric light above. Krishna was flummoxed. A roll of paper had been cleverly attached to its own pocket in the wall in a way she'd never seen before. Krishna gazed at herself in the large mirror over the sink. She was not used to seeing so much of herself at the same time. She mostly used hand-mirrors and on occasion could see her bent reflection against a motor car or blurred against the glass of a city shop. The figure looking back at her didn't seem like the Krishna she was used to. Her chest seemed bigger, and she thought that made it look like her waist went in, when before it used to just go straight down. Her frock concealed wider hips than she used to know. It had not occurred to Krishna that in addition to growing taller and stronger, she was evolving a new shape. She closed her eyes; adopted a classical *Bharatanatyam* pose, then opened them again. She stuck her hip out further to the right and straightened her back. This, she thought, was what the *Odissi* dancers looked like, and she was pleased. Then she remembered that the officer was waiting for her outside. She considered climbing onto the sink and relieving herself there, using the faucets and her hand to wash herself and drying with the roll of paper. Then she reconsidered, knowing that something about that would be wrong.

Krishna sheepishly knocked on the door from the inside. The officer opened it and started to walk away expecting Krishna to follow. "Mister," she heard herself plead, meekly at first. When he didn't respond, she cried "Sir!" The officer turned, concerned and headed back toward her: "Something, Mem Sahib? No paper? Sorry Madam, I'll fetch and come," he started to go. "Mister, no!" Krishna cried somewhat desperately this time, embarrassed. "There is paper. Only, there seems to be…" Krishna was unsure how to complete the sentence. The officer looked at her quizzically. Suddenly something dawned on him and he suppressed a snicker. "One moment, Mem Sahib. I come." He proposed, smiling. The officer shuffled off in a hurry and left Krishna standing embarrassed at the door. Cooks with long aprons in silly, lopsided, white hats swished past her looking determined and concerned; she took in the smells wafting from the kitchens, none of them familiar, although all of them rich and heavy for the season. There was no cumin or coconut in the cooking going on. A young man in white garb came hurtling toward her behind a trolley balancing a giant cake shaped and decorated just like the Governor's mansion. It was a magnificent replica decorated with fine filaments of silver and gold leaf. Krishna could not imagine that it would be eaten and destroyed. Presently, the officer returned with a troubled looking Anglo-Indian lady in tow.

The lady must have been forty years old but she wore a school frock just like Krishna's, except that it was longer and black and white, not grey and white like hers. She was tall and wore thick black stockings and flat shoes. A small and useless white cap was pinned to her hair, which was pulled back into a bun. Krishna thought her awfully comical, like an overgrown schoolgirl who had outsized even her cap. She looked down at Krishna, narrowing her eyes, "I'm told you are one of the dancers?" "Yes, Madam" replied Krishna promptly, sure she was somehow about to be humiliated. "I am the Baroness Reinkellour's mistress. And you are from?" continued the maid. "Mangalore, Madam." Krishna responded. "And in

Mangalore, you have no Westerns?" the lady elongated the "lore" so to Krishna it sounded like a whole other place. "Yes Madam, we have one movie house nearby and I have seen the talkies of Mr. Gene Autry, Madam." At this, both the officer and the maid doubled over in laughter. Krishna did not know what was so funny. She also didn't understand why the picture show was so important when all she wanted to do was relieve herself. The maid composed herself and continued mockingly, "And in all these talkies you see, young lady, you have never seen a Western toilet facility?" Krishna was upset. She had only been to three or four of the picture shows in her whole life and the lady made it sound like she went every day. And nobody ever saw the toilet in any picture, did they? Krishna shook her head no. The maid huddled Krishna into the washroom and closed the door behind them. She raised the toilet lid, and pointed at the resultant orifice. Krishna peered down at the hole, feeling stupid. She had only to raise the lid, which she did not realize was there, and things would have been fairly self-explanatory. The maid detailed the proper technique and pulled the cord to show Krishna how it flushed. Krishna covered her ears at the alarming sound of the flushing and peered continually down the drain, amazed at the swirling water. It was still unclear to Krishna how she was meant to clean herself if there was no vessel to transport water from the basin to the toilet bowl. She thought she'd better not ask, and when finally left to herself, simply wet as much toilet paper as she could with which to clean. After washing her hands in the basin, she fixed herself in the mirror, pulled the cord mightily and walked confidently out the door to be led back out to the stage by the still smirking officer. Krishna had used so much toilet paper that entirely unbeknownst to her the bowl flooded right out into the kitchen hallway, upsetting the cooks and caterers who slipped and skidded as they rushed busily by.

The afternoon was passed in organizing stage directions for musicians and performers and setting the order of programming. The dancers were told that the Governor would be making a small speech and toast prior to dinner and that the Lieutenant would present each dance with a description. Most important for Krishna, they learned that the *Bharatanatyam* dancers would be first. Contrary to being nervous about this, Krishna liked the idea of getting it over with. She had learned at school recitations that if you lead, you don't have to compare yourself to everybody who preceded you and build up your nerves; instead, you get to finish up and everybody compares themselves to you. Plus, at school, it seemed that anybody who volunteered to be first got some credit for bravery. One of the army barracks quarters nearby had been allotted to the dancers to change into their costumes. They would be fed there, then change, and be driven back to the ball at performance time. At the barracks, Krishna told Jyotsna about the toilet incident and Jyotsna laughed heartily, remarking, "You never know what sorts of things you can learn when you're away from home, do you?" Krishna was pleased that Jyotsna didn't shame her for not knowing about Western toilets. They agreed that the use of only toilet paper, or rather, the failure to use water to wash oneself, was clearly unsanitary. Arna would later comment that it was typical of British short-cut methodology.

When Krishna was in full costume, her eyes lined with kohl, her lips, finger tips and toes painted brightly red and her sparkling gold jewelry affixed, she felt transformed into a more substantial version of herself, and she positively glowed. When they gathered to depart, the jovial *Kathakali* dancer, winking at Krishna, jokingly asked Jyotsna "But what have you done with your partner? You have sent her away and brought a very beautiful and grown-up one instead? This one hasn't practiced! How will she know what to do?" Krishna felt shy to receive this kind of attention from a male stranger, but she also liked it. It was not her custom to accept compliments quite so directly, and she didn't know how to respond. She remained quiet and kept her distance from the men for the rest of the evening. Instead, she followed closely with her eyes the graceful movements and demeanor of the *Odissi* dancers, all of whom seemed to be in their later teens and twenties, and whose transformation from saris to costumes seemed to her much more glamorous and dramatic than her own. Their jewelry was of silver instead of gold, and they wore fan-like head-dresses that she imagined required some balancing. As the youngest in the group, however, Krishna still appeared to draw the most attention, even from the *Odissi* dancers who treated her like a younger sister and insisted on being called by the more familiar "*didi*" instead of by name.

When the group returned to the mansion, they were led to the garden entrance and directed to wait behind the hedges enclosing the lawns. The officer who had escorted Krishna to the toilet that morning guarded the dancers from crossing into the garden until summoned. From between the bushes, Krishna scanned the brilliant scene, noticing how magnificent the mansion now appeared, all a-twinkle with lit candelabras, shimmering glass-ware and glimmering china. There must have been two hundred guests milling about. The elegant ladies wore simple, close-fitting gowns of satin with bared shoulders, healed shoes and sparkling, opulent jewelry. Unlike the bright and brocaded saris that she was used to seeing at Indian functions, English fancy-dress seemed gentle and subdued. Most of the men were in military uniform but others wore stark, black suits with white shirts and little bows around their necks; maybe, she imagined, they were meant to look like gifts. At some of the tables in the garden, be-turbaned fanning-wallas waved giant peacock-feather fans for the comfort of those seated, and worked hard not to make eye contact with the pampered guests.

Krishna fixed her gaze on a fine-featured, English rose seated, cross-legged at a table nearby. She wore a sparkling tiara around the bun into which her golden hair was stacked, ringlets tumbling sloppily away from the crown. Her ease in this setting gave her the confidence of a woman older than her youthful looks betrayed. The charmeuse silk of her soft yellow gown slid languidly about her elongated legs when she shifted or turned in her seat, revealing creamy seamed stockings and strappy sandals clinging to delicate feet. She inhaled slowly, leisurely from a cigarette attached to a slender stick, and beaming, daintily clinked her tall glass against that of the several gentlemen who seemed to come out of their way to greet her. There was a dazzle about her enhanced by the smile in her eyes and an elegance that Krishna found alluring. Krishna noticed how she seemed to speak so boldly with the men and sometimes tossed her head back in gales of exaggerated laughter, something she'd never seen an Indian woman do. She wondered what it would be like to be so free of self-consciousness. Krishna spotted only five or six Indian ladies in the whole party, two of them in colorful and elaborate nine-yard saris heavily embroidered in gold thread. She imagined they were *Ranis* or possibly even consorts, but even they remained humble and inhibited. Indian servants, dressed in white *kurta-kameez* and stiff white turbans, wove between the few guests seated at tables with silver platters of tid-bits or replete with glasses; some empty, some full. Krishna didn't understand why only Sikhs were hired as waiters. Jyotsna explained that this was like a costume, that probably none of the servants were actually Sikh. Krishna thought the party was truly brought alive by the small orchestra that played on one of the balconies. She liked the music of Beethoven and Mozart that on occasion came over the radio prior to the war reports that Arna tuned into, but she had never seen anybody dance waltzes in real life—only in the picture shows. She thought it scandalous how the English ladies danced tightly up against the men in public, then changed partners and danced tightly up against the new ones!

Krishna was shaken out of her reverie when bells were rung to direct guests to be seated for dinner. As had been warned, the Governor made a speech thanking his honored guests and hailing the allied forces for their continuing, valiant struggles. He had everybody raise their glasses to the British Empire and then remain standing for a solemn singing of "God Save the Queen." He said that tonight's entertainment would be unusual and that he hoped the guests would find the local folklore as charming as his wife recently had. He said he believed that it was important for the empire to learn more about the native traditions if it was expected to improve on them and to maintain stable relations. He said he thought this was one small step in that direction, then exited the stage to much applause. When the Lieutenant took the stage, he made only a brief introduction, explaining that four classical forms of Indian dance would be presented by highly trained artistes from neighboring states. He said that some of these had sacred and others had secular value. Then he mispronounced *Bharatanatyam*, which Krishna thought was ridiculous for an Indian, and in his curt and efficient fashion simply said "without further ado…" as he backed off the stage.

Krishna and Jyotsna were allowed to pass into the garden just as the musicians began. Krishna had not expected blinding lights directed at the stage and barely made it up its steps. When she got to her starting pose she realized she could not make out the audience for the brightness of the lights. She was somewhat relieved at this, as she worried about their reactions, never having danced in front of so large, so male, or so white an audience before. As she began the dance, she concentrated on delivering it to the gods, but knew her mind was more concerned about what these fancy foreigners would think. Nevertheless, her feet moved swiftly to the practiced routine, and every time her eyes could meet Jyotsna's, whose rapture on stage remained captivating, Krishna was reinspired to concentrate on the dance. Krishna could hear chatting and clinking of glasses in the background, but insulated by the barrier of lights and still focused on exaggerating her movements, she quickly became comfortable being unable to see the audience and soon felt like her dancing was truly for the gods. The footwork was demanding and the hot lights made Krishna feel like she was dancing on the sizzling surface of a *dekchi* oiled with ghee. The performance was over faster than she had expected. As the dancers backed off the stage (never turning their backs to the audience) gales of loud applause seemed to waft up from over the lights. Krishna felt like she was walking on air. She loved the attention, never having had the appreciation of strangers quite like this. She understood that her family or friends might admire her dancing out of courtesy, but this feeling of being liked by an unfamiliar audience was new and intoxicating. Even the dancers who greeted them behind the stage were cheering and clapping with delight. The funny *Kathakali* dancer scooped Krishna up by the waist and twirled her around with glee, exclaiming in a thick accent, "*batcha*, you have gotten us off to a wonderful start!"

Krishna, tired, but stimulated by all the excitement, caught her breath behind the raised platform which she peered over to catch the next performance. To improve her vantage point, she edged around to the side of the platform away from where the other dancers were, but still remained hidden from the audience.

From this position she could see both the dancers on stage and the audience and was pleased to notice their smiling faces and the way they seemed to point at certain movements or make comments while the *Kuchipudi* dancers gestured and twirled. The young officer scheduled to watch them did not call Krishna back out beyond the hedge, and in fact was nowhere to be found. The audience seemed genuinely to be interested in the dancing, their necks straining to see over the heads of those up front. As Krishna tapped to the music, following the dancers' feet, transfixed, her hands perched on the edge of the stage, she felt a hand cover her mouth and another grasp her around the waist from behind. The Lieutenant pressed against her as he commanded in her ear, "Do not scream or kick. Do not make a spectacle of yourself or I shall make sure your parents learn what a dirty, undignified girl you are." Krishna froze. She did not know what the man meant nor why he would say such things; she could feel only the jabbing buttons of his jacket, the steely cold of his belt buckle against her back, his hot and sour breath in her ear and his insistent hand pressing against her waist and sliding slowly downward. She instinctively thrust her elbows against him, but now he dropped the hand from her mouth, turned her roughly to face him and gripped his arms tight around hers as he forced his whole weight against her, so her face was now jammed against his chest and her arms were pinned beside her. The Lieutenant pushed soggy lips against Krishna's neck in a way that made her feel disgusted and tried to press his mouth against hers, though she turned her face, squeezing her eyes and lips tight to avoid the onslaught and struggling to get away. He drove rough kisses into Krishna's ears, squeezing with his hand the flesh of her back and buttocks, whispering "No need to act so coy. You've made no secret of how well you can perform. You must be getting much practice offstage to be so seductive when you're on it!" Had Krishna screamed, her voice would not have been heard over the music. Between the stage and the hedges on this side, in the dark, nobody was likely to spot them. In any event, Krishna had been raised as too polite to act on her own behalf. She knew something terrible was happening but did not know how to stop it; she only heard that she would be shamed before her parents if she were to resist. Her throat clenched, she felt her knees buckle, and in an instant everything went black.

When Krishna awoke she was laying in a cot at the barracks where the performers had changed clothing earlier that evening. Jyotsna and an elderly, alarmingly pink, bearded old man with a moustache and round spectacles hovered over her. She opened her eyes slowly, disoriented, and started to raise herself on her elbows. "She's awake!" noticed Jyotsna "thank heavens! Are you alright, *ammu*?" Krishna nodded groggily as her eyes came into focus. The bearded man in his crisp black suit and bow tie immediately bent over her, reaching to feel her forehead with his hand. Krishna recoiled instantly. "Her responses are quick!" announced the doctor sounding glad, in his snappy English accent. "It was only a little exhaustion, I would imagine, combined with the heat from the lights. Fluids and rest and she should be back on her pretty little toes by the morning." He smiled mildly at her and helped her up to sip a glass of water, which she drank thirstily. He added as she drank, "such an energetic performance in this weather had to have its consequences, didn't it?" The Lieutenant, who Krishna hadn't noticed was seated on the cot beside hers, jumped in promptly with mock admonition, "You gave us quite a scare, young lady, fainting like that! Had I not been passing by and noticed you faltering, you might have broken your bones in that collapse! And what luck that the good doctor was in the audience to make sure you were alright! What a big commotion you might have caused!" The Lieutenant seemed genuinely concerned and relieved. Krishna was petrified to see the Lieutenant, and then suddenly ashamed. She knew not where to look or what to say. She thought for an instant that perhaps it had all been a dream. Had she simply fainted from exhaustion and dreamed the Lieutenant's attack? Still, something in her was disquieted. She felt repulsion toward the Lieutenant and could not bear to look up at him. His mere presence made her anxious. She began to tremble and sob. "There, there, darling," Jyotsna consoled, embracing her. "You only had a little scare. We worked you too hard didn't we? First your exams, then all the practice, and the travel and the excitement of the show? Nothing to be worried about, now. You're just fine. And you did very well! How many times I've collapsed from exhaustion after dancing! It's part and parcel of the effort. We'll take you back to Prakash Uncles' and you'll rest and you'll be just fine." Krishna wanted to say something but no words would emerge. She just sobbed and leaned into Jyotsna, glad for her company and the protection it imparted.

The doctor took his leave announcing that he should return to the party and inviting the Lieutenant to return with him. "Well," said the Lieutenant, "now that we know the young lady's alright, I can resume my duties back at the ball." Addressing Jyotsna he assured "The driver awaits to return you to your housing whenever you wish." Then he added reassuringly, "And don't you worry, Madams, I understand that if we shared this incident with anybody, the girls' parents may worry about her constitution and prevent her from dancing in future, so I can assure you that it will not be reported. No harm was done in any event. I am just pleased that it was nothing more serious than a little fatigue." With that, he strode out of the barracks with the doctor. Krishna now hugged Jyotsna even tighter and whispered through her sobs, "You won't tell anybody, will you

Aunty? I did nothing wrong, did I?" Jyotsna was ever amused by the propensity of devout Hindus to feel blameworthy over matters far beyond their control. "What in heaven is wrong with falling ill after so much strain? We know you're a strong girl after all! You proved so at your *arangetram*. We all have the right to rest, and your body decided it was time! Now don't you worry; we need not tell anybody about this and everything will fall into place like normal. In fact, I believe you must be blessed! How lucky you are that the Lieutenant broke your fall and brought you immediately to my attention!"

Later, laying in bed at Prakash Uncle's house, Krishna fell sullen and deep in thought. She went over in her mind the consequences of disclosing what had really happened. "If Arna finds out I was harmed, he surely will not let me travel again. He will say he was right in his reluctance to let me dance and I will never be allowed to dance away from home." Her arms felt sore and she found only a slight bruise on her forearm, where the Lieutenant must have pressed her so roughly. Her knee was mildly scraped, though she knew not from what. She did not feel sore elsewhere, just sore at the Lieutenant. "Why would he pick on me for his meanness like that?" she wondered, quickly realizing that she might have brought his manhandling on herself by working so hard make her moves more coquette. She was overcome with shame. She soon apprehended that she could not share this incident with anyone, as she herself was surely responsible for it. Even the Lieutenant had said so. Krishna felt the sting of loneliness, the isolation stirred by a secret to be kept. She stifled her tears. Self-pity wasn't warranted if she herself was to blame.

On the way home in the car, Krishna resolved that despite the painful incident, she had enjoyed her first dance trip. She chirped optimistically at Jyotsna. "When can we have another performance away?" Jyotsna now knew that Krishna had loved the glamour of travel, the unusual sights and the people so different from what she was accustomed. Krishna had felt special and appreciated, and had seen things she could never have imagined. She understood instinctively that this was something of which she wanted more, and determined that it was worthwhile to simply put the attack out of her mind. And with the same discipline she showed in her *Bharatanatyam* practice or in her studies, in that instant, she simply did. Krishna decided she would never mention being wronged. Immediately, a sense of loneliness set in.

Still, returning home after her "adventures in Madras" as Arna soon came to refer to them, was an immense relief for Krishna. She raced into the house, found her way to her mother and wrapped herself around Amma with all her might, bursting into tears as though this were a parting rather than a homecoming. Arna commented that it was obvious that distance truly did make the heart grow fonder. To Sindhya's great delight, Krishna indulged her with heavy detail on all aspects of her trip, making sure not to mention even the existence of the Lieutenant. She reported on it for days on end, answering questions, even from *M'am*, about how the "Western" worked, and for Amma about the fancy English dresses and the horrifying food in the kitchens and the spotlessly clean campus. She understated everything to do with the performance simply claiming "It was just like at my *arangetram*, except I couldn't see the audience because of so many bright lights." She was happy to hear from Arna that the letter Prakash Uncle had conveyed home reported that she and Jyotsna had been the best and most undemanding of guests. Krishna had never quite so much appreciated the comforts of the familiar. After her first trip away from home without family, and particularly after her awful experience, she looked differently at the way Kishore-dada and Arna were so protective and strict with the girls in the family, something she had always accepted unquestioningly but now could better understand. She squeezed Sindhya more tightly when they went to bed every night, somehow wishing to shield her from the burdens of growing up.

The beginning of high school opened Krishna's eyes even wider. She was one of only a handful of Brahmins, with only two others from her own *gotra*; and though the other school girls also had excellent academic qualifications, she had never been amongst such variety. While the preponderance was Hindu and Muslim, some girls were Christian, and others were Zoroastrian. The Muslim girls would stop whatever they were doing at certain times of day, pull out small prayer mats, and bend down in prayer. Krishna was intrigued at their head-dress and the way they all prayed in the strange and guttural sounds of Arabic even though their everyday language was Kannada. She concluded that the main Muslim god must speak only Arabic. The Christian girls seemed the most outspoken and fearless to her, and Krishna admired their audacity. She knew that many of them were converts and understood from Arna that it was likely that they had converted in order to escape the confines of caste, but unlike Arna, she didn't hold that decision against them. She thought it quite amusing that one could choose a religion the way one could choose which color hair ribbon to wear that day. It had never occurred to Krishna that she might opt out of being a *Chitrapur Saraswat Brahmin*. "Wouldn't the gods be insulted and angry" she asked her companions on the way to school one day, "if we all just picked another god to praise?" Her schoolmates were equally baffled by the notion. They confessed to each other that they admired the courage of the Christian girls in persisting in the colonists' religion despite the threat of the wrath of their known gods. One of them commented, "They must be very willful to go on praising that Jesus in plain sight of the angry Shiva!" Not for one instant did it occur to any of them that conversion implied a rejection of the Hindu pantheon altogether. Krishna somehow thought of converts to other religions as having an additional set of gods and rules to obey on top of the Hindu prerequisites.

While at school she still excelled in mathematics, Krishna's most intriguing class was "human health." It was the only class for which Krishna's parents had to give a special written permission for her to attend. Krishna did not understand why. Mainly, the teacher spent unreasonable amounts of time describing in detail the functions of each most minute part of the body, both male and female, convinced that thorough explication of the elements would impart appreciation for the whole. Large drawings of human figures were posted beside the chalkboards. All the muscles and bones and veins of the body were shown on them in lurid colors, and their Latin names identified. Here, she learned about the *lingam* and the menses, and soon also became accustomed to losing her Muslim schoolmates for four or five days monthly as a result of this catastrophic event. She also learned in detail how human babies developed after the spermatozoa left the *lingam*, entered the *yoni* and traveled to the ovaries from which fertilized eggs dropped and grew in the womb.

Growing up, Krishna had frequently seen the naughty *mithuna* carvings on temple friezes: the bulbous bosoms of small-waisted ladies getting pinched by mischievous gods, ample-bottomed women clinging with wrapped legs around the waists of men with pained expressions on their faces. She had considered the carvings silly, the way they seemed always to be climbing all over each other naked—a ridiculous thing that no clean person would do, certainly not a Brahmin. She had been taught at the temple that those sculptures were a reminder and warning that *kama* would impede spiritual liberation and was therefore to be avoided. She also once heard that the maligned Devadasis were defiled by overindulging in desire. However, not until now did she learn that this same *kama* resulted in the production of babies! This perplexed Krishna a great deal. "How could *kama*," she asked Jyotsna one day, "something so improper, be the only way to have children, something we celebrate with such joy?" Unlike Amma might have, Jyotsna did not become embarrassed at Krishna's questions or glibly assure her that they would be resolved upon her marriage, but rather calmly described things in ways that Krishna could understand. "*Kama*," Jyotsna patiently explained, "can be very pleasurable to both men and women. But it is over-attachment to *kama* that impedes spiritual growth. Understand?" Krishna nodded that she got the gist. Jyotsna went on, "You see, the gods wish for married couples to express their love for each other with the passion of their bodies, but when they overindulge, just like with anything else, the gods are displeased. It becomes inappropriate, you see? You can never be liberated if you give yourself to excess." Krishna thought she understood. Jyotsna assured Krishna further, "One day soon, you will understand this sense of *kama* better, and once you do even your dancing will improve. Your *abhinaya* will show the tension between having so much desire and knowing that you must restrict it." Krishna imagined it like her craving for too many of M'am's delicious *phuranpolis* and the queasiness she felt after having overeaten when she knew she shouldn't. When she thought upon it further, she was highly gratified by the notion that the wicked Lieutenant would never attain liberation because of his obvious inability to restrain his rampant *kama*.

5

Once Krishna got accustomed to the volume of school work and the yearly examination schedule, she was happy to attend the distant high school and adjusted easily to the variety of students from different backgrounds—something her parents, who had been home-schooled, had never done and were wary of on behalf of their children. One never knew what unwholesome influences lurked outside the known. Harder for Krishna were her increased responsibilities at home. In an effort to prepare her for marriage, Arna commanded Amma to involve Krishna in all aspects of homemaking, just as Deepa, Sandhya and Shaku had done prior to their weddings. Whereas before, Krishna was expected to remain out of the kitchen when *M'am* was cooking (as Sindhya still was), now Krishna was to assist and learn. When the milk was delivered just after dawn, *M'am* coached Krishna in the making of curds based on cultures from yesterday's batch. Without his ministering however, Krishna's yogurt often emerged too runny or too firm, resulting in waste that Arna frowned heavily upon. It was only after much experimentation, including gauging the likely heat and humidity of the day, that Krishna came upon a somewhat reliable formula. She was bored by having to sift lentils and grains meticulously to cull the impurities, fragments of husk and critters that made their way into their containers before cooking. She keenly observed how coarsely or finely *M'am* ground the aromatic spices to concoct marinades for his variety of dishes. The first time Krishna ran to fetch paper and pencil to take down a recipe, Amma and *M'am* poked good-natured fun. "Proper Indian cooks don't use measures like in a chemistry experiment!" scolded Amma, "good cooks know the quality of their dishes by sight and scent!" In fact, it was preposterous to assume that one batch of cardamom seeds or fennel would be equally fragrant as the next. How could one "measure" such unreliable elements? Krishna learned to cook based on what each dish should look, feel and smell like, and depending on the varying strength and weakness of each seasonal ingredient.

The new homemaking program meant Krishna was sometimes allowed to accompany *M'am* on market days. He taught her how to choose produce in season and how to sniff through their skins to identify the ripe fruits and vegetables and select the legumes and grains that best combine to maximize protein in the vegetarian diet. Krishna loved the chaos of the market. Monkeys staged coordi-

50

nated raids on the booths to make off with whatever they could; creative vendors juggled hairy coconuts or hard, green mangos high in the air just to draw attention to their stalls; dark, diminutive women with immense silver nose rings squatted on their haunches behind massive, toppling sacks of grain, pouring measures of them from three feet in the air onto the gleaming brass plate that counterbalanced a giant lead weighted scale before each of their booths. Though Krishna enjoyed the trips to the market, she had learned her lesson well at the Governors' Ball and never veered far from the protection of *M'am*. *M'am* was loyal to some of the vendors, the ones the family relied upon for proper products. Krishna liked the familiar ones as well. They wouldn't make her uncomfortable by trying to flirt the way others sometimes did. Occasionally Krishna was sent to fetch some kohl *kajal* or incense to burn at the shrine. The cosmetics stalls featured over-painted ladies who waved heady perfumes of sandalwood and tea rose under Krishna's delighted nose. Krishna would follow *M'am's* lead in bargaining for a bottle of coconut oil (a popular cure-all) or powdered henna (for *mehndi*), as she was never allowed the extravagance of scent nor cosmetics off-stage. It was vulgar and improper for a *Saraswat* Brahmin to draw attention to herself in such a manner—particularly if she was betrothed.

Krishna never saw *M'am* more animated than when caught up in the bargaining joust. The ritual rarely varied. The vendor would confidently pitch his highest offer. *M'am* would scoff and exaggerate scanning the market to find a comparable stall. The vendor would revise slightly, as though accommodating, and *M'am* would promptly counter with half the figure. The vendor would turn away as though deeply offended, then flick his hand at *M'am* in a motion of dismissal. *M'am* would begin to move away, shaking his head in mock disappointment. The vendor would shout out a more reasonable compromise, which *M'am* would round sharply down. Then, muttering to himself, the vendor would reluctantly crumple the goods into sheets of newspaper and jab them in M'am's direction. As there never seemed to be any change behind the counter when any coinage over the agreed price was relinquished, *M'am* readily produced exact change. The same ritual played out hundreds of times per day at the market, and Krishna could identify it without hearing words or reading lips. Through *M'am's* banter, Krishna absorbed the acting skills essential to economizing on purchases.

One time, *M'am* encouraged Krishna to try it for herself. She would be bargaining for butter to make the *ghee*. *M'am* would stand out of view of the salesman while pretending to look over the goods at the next booth. Krishna strode confidently up to the rotund vendor. "How much per pound today?" she queried like a pro. The frowning vendor looked her over, arms crossed in front of him, his price contingent on his assessment of the wealth of the buyer. "Aren't you Shiva-ji's little girl?" he inquired in response. "Should the price of the butter depend on my father's name?" Krishna barked back with moxy. A smile spread across the pot-bellied vendor's lips, "With that sort of come back, you must be Sanat-ji's daughter then." Krishna wouldn't give, "Have you run out of butter that you have to make small talk, sir?" Krishna had flubbed. By addressing him as her superior, she'd given way. "Just one rupee for you." The man barked back. "Hmph," Krishna retorted, crossing her arms, "What, I look like a *rani* to you? Fifty, and not a paisa more." "What?" plead the vendor, "you want me to tell my wife I was giving away the butter today?" He appealed to what he imagined was Krishna's sense of family honor. "Hah! Your wife will be pleased with the profits, I'm sure!" The man tutted and shook his head in disappointment, "Look, 80 paisa or I'll be thrown out of the house." Krishna took a lesson from *M'am* and pretended to scan the market for other vendors, muttering so she could be over-heard, "There must be somebody who wants to make a sale of butter today." The vendor took the bait, "No self-respecting goat-man will give you any decent but-ter for less than 70, child." Krishna kept taunting, "I think I see Babu over there, he won't insult my intelligence." She started to move away. "Fine," said the ven-dor, "You can have it for sixty-five. Final offer." "Sixty, and you have a deal." Krishna barked back promptly, urging the change at him. The vendor shook his head lamenting his fate, took the money, and turned to dole out a pound on the scale. Krishna, cross-armed and mum, inspected the scale closely as the butter dropped in. "Eh!" she voiced when the butter measured just a hair under a full pound, "Cheating the buyer won't get you any repeat business." Krishna was sur-prised to hear herself pipe up like that. "Vulture!" the vendor charged back, smil-ing mischievously and shaking another dollop off his spatula onto the scale. He handed Krishna the wrapped butter with a nod, "Pleasure." He announced, all arguments forgotten. Krishna, satisfied at her accomplishment, struggled her way past the crowd to *M'am* and dropped the purchase in his sack. "Only sixty!" she beamed at *M'am*, proud of her first bargain. "Golly, a charmed girl." *M'am* pro-nounced, raising his eyebrows "We must have you talk the river out of flooding its banks next rainy season."

During weekends, summers and school breaks, Krishna performed frequently with Jyotsna. The Nayampallis came to appreciate the small sums that these recit-als brought in, particularly when performances were at government or private functions—many of which were hosted by guests from the Governors' Ball. Additionally, due to revived interest and more liberal policies, the dancers were called upon to perform more widely in neighboring states. They danced devotionally at temples, and at schools and colleges for the benefit of public education and the furthering of the nationalist agenda. Small articles appeared in local newspapers praising their work, which Sindhya collected painstakingly and showed off proudly at school although her father would have been aghast at this display of conceit. Arna received letters from Governors and *rajas* thanking him for permitting the talents of his daughter to benefit the public (over which he was privately highly satisfied.) Kishore worried that all this attention might compromise Krishna's wedding should the Nadghars come to learn of it. How could one respect a girl who was constantly on such display? Arna was consoled in that Mr. Nadghar had proven himself a committed nationalist and would surely understand how performance of *Bharatanatyam* contributed to the cause, although it might expose his future daughter-in-law more than the usual *Bhanap* wife.

The Nayampallis only attended performances when they were conveniently nearby. But Krishna relished her contact with the fascinating world outside of Mangalore. At home, she filled Sindhya with details about the colorful way Maharashtrian ladies dressed unafraid to draw attention to themselves, the incredible number of spires at the Meenakshi Temple in Madhurai, the strange shapes of the Portuguese buildings in Goa and the miraculous way the Shore Temple at Mahaballipuram seemed to float on the Indian Ocean when the tide came rushing in.

As Jyotsna had expected, on entering womanhood, Krishna's *abhinaya* indeed improved and she was better able to manifest love and longing. Krishna could tell that the audience response was different from the past—more emotional and effusive. Bala soon commented to Jyotsna that she had never seen a dancer so technically accomplished who was still unable to give over to the pure joy of dancing. "It's as if Krishna will not allow herself this pleasure," Bala commented. Jyotsna intuited it as adolescent self-consciousness or chalked it up to her ascetic Brahmin upbringing. When Krishna watched Jyotsna dance, it was precisely this quality of surrender that Krishna knew she lacked. Jyotsna could see that though Krishna's body knew what to do she still over-thought her motions. Abandon was squarely in opposition to the rigorous technical training of all other aspects of *Bharatanatyam*, and it was difficult to give over. No matter how much bolder she had grown at the market or through her dance, Jyotsna estimated that for Krishna, having to be so submissive, dutiful, asexual and silent at home made it all the harder for to be free on stage. Bala's studied eye observed further, "when Krishna's spirit comes through in a performance it is only momentary and accidental. Just when she should give over to it, the girl seems to remember herself and retreat into mechanical movement." Otherwise, the taut geometry of her form was unparalleled and the precision of her footwork unmatched. Jyotsna conceded, "Yes, even if she lacks passion, her beats are formidable, and nowadays I often struggled to keep up."

As the months passed, Krishna undertook her homemaking lessons with dedication and skill although still not with the least enthusiasm, except on the welcome outings of market day. She felt she was posing as a homemaker rather than learning to be one. When *M'am* had the day off, Krishna took responsibility for the main evening meal, and quietly endured the families' abundant criticisms and hard-won praises. Nowadays Arna also had Krishna pay closer attention to passages of the *Vedas* that she hadn't focused upon before. A *dharshan* or sacred festival day at the temple often included readings of the scriptures, which the younger children without Sanskrit training would usually fidget or sleep through. On the long walk home, Arna took pains to stay close to Krishna and found convoluted ways to emphasize by example the lessons about the consequences of defiance, of transgressions against tradition, and of straying from the Brahmin way. "It is not only a privilege but a responsibility to be born a Brahmin. As the *Vedas* tell us," Arna instructed, "your duty to your community, your family, your husband and your children should precede your own will for the good of all." Krishna listened intently, hoping desperately she would be a good Brahmin and make her family proud by subverting her will. She inquired "But how is it that we got so lucky to be Brahmins anyway?" Arna explained, "We have collected virtues in our past lives. Just like when you study for a test at school you can be sure to get good marks. Your high birth in the next life is assured if you behave properly and do your duty. And if you are very virtuous, perhaps you can surmount the cycle altogether and attain *moksha* as do the saints." Krishna knew, even from her dancing, that only by submitting the self and the selfish could such liberation be possible.

Krishna recognized that all this preparation would ultimately be in service of another home, and the idea of leaving hers still filled her with dread. High school would end in just over a year, and she would be taken from all that was familiar. Krishna could not imagine herself married the way so many of her classmates dreamt, nor even acting like a wife. She found herself paying closer attention to the interactions between Arna and Amma, her siblings and their spouses. She noticed, without question or challenge but simply as a matter of observation, that the women seemed to exchange their wishes for the protection that the men bestowed. After her experience with the Lieutenant, this did not seem to Krishna like so bad a proposition. Still, it appeared to her that even though Arna was supposed to be in charge of the religious education of the family, Amma fasted far more often than he ever did. Yet Arna had gained status as a pillar of the *Chitra-*

pur Saraswat sangha in Mangalore. It was well known in the community that he tithed a full fifteen percent of the family income to the temple, participated on several of the National Committees, including the one which had determined whether *Bhanaps* should be allowed to go abroad for education. They had resolved that travel would be permitted on a case-by-case basis, depending on what sorts of skills the boy might be able to bring home; otherwise, he may choose to marry and settle abroad, a waste to the community which would contribute only to its diminution. Recently, when a *Bhanap* girl from the neighboring town had threatened to stray into a love marriage with a *kshatrya*, it was Arna who had been called upon by the girls' parents to intercede and talk some sense into her before she made such a disastrous mistake. (Krishna couldn't imagine how anybody would be so foolish as to enter the insecurities of a love marriage. The community would not support or assist in the upbringing of such children; and the gods would be enraged, never bringing anything but hardship to such a household.) Yet, despite all Arna did in public, it seemed to Krishna that as a wife, mother and homemaker, Amma had the harder and more thankless job, rarely getting to assert her own will. Krishna imagined she'd never be up to that sort of effort.

Arna was gratified that Krishna's travels enabled her to appreciate the way she was invariably welcome in any other (even a strangers') *Bhanap* home. Jyotsna too had benefited from this community, and gleaned some of the value of its stringent ways. *Chitrapur Saraswat* Brahmin homes were all alike in their customs, habits and values. Unlike the Christian, Muslim or non-Brahmin homes Krishna had seen (although these usually belonged to wealthy dignitaries), *Bhanap* homes were simple and sparsely furnished, without evidence of waste or shows of excess. Even if they belonged to affluent members of the community, there were few trinkets and decorations about the house, and not much in the way of luxury. Krishna learned young that living beyond one's needs was improper, as anything that she had or consumed beyond her need assured that somebody on earth lived without. This was another responsibility of being a Brahmin of which Arna constantly reminded her: "recognizing that while past lives may have elevated one to this standing, living sparingly enables others to live comfortably." The community took this precept seriously, and no matter how wealthy or educated a family might be, it would honor its heritage by remaining austere; conserving, recycling and reusing. Though Ghandiji wished to advance the untouchables, a notion that made orthodox Bhanaps grizzle, his commitment to asceticism conformed closely to Brahmin philosophy. Krishna sometimes heard his moving speeches on the radio now, and felt gratified to uphold this standard.

Sindhya attended her new school with much enthusiasm and withstood the constant comparisons to Krishna with congenial grace, since she admired her sister as much as Krishna's former teachers had. One day, the purple sunbird which had made itself a fixture in the kitchen for years, flew off and didn't return. Sindhya was inconsolable. Amma had taken pains to warn Sindhya repeatedly that once the bird was strong enough to fend for itself it may take wing. But awareness doesn't prevent sentiment, and Sindhya's tears would not abate. Even Arna comforted Sindhya, "Why without your tending, the sunbird may never even have hatched." Krishna added, "Just think, because you helped it grow, maybe it will find its own friends and grow a family of its own." Still, Sindhya moped for days. Unfazed by the experience in the long term, throughout her elementary schooling, Sindhya continued her habit of adopting strays. Arna growled about foolish sentimentality when a recently arrived cat birthed six fumbling kittens by a haystack in the granary. Within a month, between the seven of them, they consumed almost the entire day's milk supply. Arna resolved that as soon as the kittens were strong enough, he would transport the whole feline family far away in a bullock-cart on his next visit to one of his farmers. While Sindhya was at school one day, he did just that. Much to his frustration, the cats found their way home before Arna himself returned that evening. Sindhya was none the wiser. Arna resolved that he'd forever have to take care of one brood or another, and Sindhya announced at school one day that she was going to become a veterinarian or a doctor when she grew up. Her teacher smiled patronizingly, knowing that the chances that Sindhya's future husband would permit her education at this level would be low.

At the high school, Krishna consistently led her class in mathematics. Arna teased her one eveing upon her return home: "You must have been a very good boy at school." He had opened a letter addressed to Krishna from the Office of Academic Excellence of the Maharajah of Mysore. It was addressed to Mr. Krishna Nayampalli, as usual assuming that Krishna was a boy. He read aloud "You are cordially invited to compete in the principality's mathematics contest, the winner of which will be awarded a full scholarship for study at the Central College in Bangalore on condition that he pursue an engineering or mathematics curriculum." Arna speculated the invitation must have come about because the several high schools in the principality now had to maintain British standards, requiring reporting on student performance to the Office of Academic Excellence. Krishna's mathematics examination results were amongst the highest in the state, and one hundred accomplished students had been invited to compete for the scholarship. Arna presented the letter as a matter of information, with the intention of praising Krishna indirectly for her efforts, and encouraging Krishna to tutor Sindhya, who seemed to be struggling in this area. He pretended to continue reading, "But if the winner is promised in marriage, it will be ridiculous as she will be too busy to become an engineer." He smiled as he handed Krishna the letter. Krishna made a face at her father, understanding that there was no point in competing. She was not disappointed by this assumption until the next day, at school, when one of her peers boasted about how her brother was invited to the contest and would surely take the prize. Suddenly, Krishna was spellbound. She knew she was better at math than the boys and wanted to prove it. "I know I could outdo any of those boys, including your brother!" She announced, uncharacteristically boastful. Her schoolmates giggled and covered their mouths in embarrassed admiration. At the first class break, Krishna marched over to the school-mistress' office to learn what would be required. Two day-long examinations would be administered in Bangalore after which non-qualifying students would be eliminated. All finalists would have to solve two problems as fast as they could, being timed by observers. Whoever solved the problems correctly in the least amount of time would win the scholarship. Krishna was not focused on the idea of obtaining the scholarship or going on to higher education. She was gripped by the notion of proving that she could beat the boys she'd likely be up against. She also knew that Arna would never grant her permission for such a vain endeavor, and couldn't imagine either defying him, or managing the logistics of getting to Bangalore three times for the required exams.

On her way home from school that day, Krishna was lost in thought as the bullock-cart bumped over the pot-holed lanes. She was daydreaming about the thrill of winning the math competition when one of her schoolmates shook her out of her reverie: "Krishna, I thought I saw your father at the astrologer's last weekend. Do you know if your chart matched with your fiancé?" As he had done with Krishna's sisters, Arna would have determined if the couple was compatible prior to arranging the marriage so as not to have to back out of a deal. "Hmmm," Krishna responded non-plussed, knowing graduation was only eight months away, "Maybe he was only consulting for the proper date for the wedding. That is not yet fixed." Her friends became excited. Neither of them had been promised yet, and both were eager for the honor. They deluged her with questions, "Have you chosen your saris yet? Have you drawn up the guest list? Have you read your compatibility charts?" Krishna was listless and uninterested in the discussion. "Nah," Krishna replied nonchalant, "What have I to do with any of it? Even if I have my own wishes, I must do as my parents please." She reassured herself as much as she did her friends, "Arna would not have arranged the wedding if the charts were not well matched, and he thinks it a bad idea to share them with us anyway; he worries about self-fulfilling prophecies." Respecting Arna, the girls agreed this was a very wise approach. "Are you pleased at least with the looks of your fiancé?" One of the girls ventured sheepishly. "I have not yet met him," Krishna stated plainly, "and most likely will not until just before the wedding. He studies far off in Bombay. Anyhow, I have school to finish off and don't want the distraction." Krishna tried to change the subject. The truth was, she hated the idea of marrying and moving away and thinking about it made her worried and nervous. But her mates persisted in their excitement, reminding her that soon the wedding preparations would start in earnest. They teased that they had never seen so blasé a bride. Krishna's mind, unmoved by her friends' enthusiasm, kept straying to what great fun it would be if she could take that test. As the bullock-cart drove past Jyotsna's cottage, Krishna bolted up in her seat. She had devised a plan. She would tell Arna that there were performances in Bangalore on the exam dates, enabling her to travel there unquestioned. She had taken the train to Bangalore with Jyotsna a number of times by now and knew how to go about it. The pocket money she had saved over the years would surely suffice for the train tickets, and she could get to and from Bangalore on the same day—as long as there were no breakdowns on the train.

Krishna carried out her plans with the stealth of a scorpion without breathing a word, not even to Jyotsna, her most reliable confidante. She wrote promptly to the State Office of Education confirming her participation in the examinations. She mentioned to Arna nonchalantly one dinnertime that she had been asked to perform a week from Saturday in Bangalore, but that she and Jyotsna would be gone only for the day. Her heart jumped when Arna wondered aloud "Perhaps even the Nadghars can attend your performance, after all, they live right there in Bangalore." Krishna had to come up with a good excuse, "No Arna," she exaggerated a sigh to make it seem burdensome, "It's a private benefit, not a school or temple function. In fact, there won't even be a stipend this time." Krishna felt sickly at lying to her father. Still, Arna considered whether it would be appropriate for Krishna to be in Bangalore without calling on her future in-laws, and whether they might be offended if they were to learn of her visit. Krishna quickly reminded Arna that she had been to Bangalore with Jyotsna at least five other times over the last years and had not had to burden the Nadghars with a visit on those occasions. Arna reconsidered, "Hmm. Now that I think about it, it might be inappropriate for you to visit unaccompanied by Amma and me. And listen, you make sure that you and Jyotsna return home directly after the performance, eh?" Protectively, Arna didn't let on why. He had begun to read about ugly events between Muslims and Hindus on the streets of Northern cities. Tensions in the country were running high. He didn't want the ladies caught in any ugly incident. Krishna was relieved by Arna's decision, and cleverly talked *M'am* into accompanying her to the train station on market day to purchase her trains tickets in advance of the travel date—which she explained Jyotsna was unable to do due to her teaching schedule.

On the Saturday of the first exam, Krishna awoke early and packed her *Bharatanatyam* costume exactly as though she were off to a performance. She was nervous about all the deception, knowing there was defiance in her heart, but she could not stop herself from going through with it. She parted with her parents tensely, pretending to take the familiar walk to Jyotsna's from where the two would head to the station. Amma, noticing that Krishna seemed more anxious than usual, queried "Haven't you practiced enough for this show? You seem to have more than the usual jitters, my girl." Krishna explained that it had been some time since the two had practiced the dances they would present today, and perhaps she was only apprehensive about the numbers. Then she felt guilty for lying to her mother. The Nayampallis went about their normal day as Krishna ran to the station just in time for the Bangalore train. She was relieved that at this early hour, not many passengers from her small town were waiting on the platform, and none were known to her. Krishna had booked her seat in the ladies' compartment, which had only two other passengers: one pregnant, and asleep; and the other a sizeable merchant of some sort, surrounded by bundles, with whom she couldn't communicate for lack of a common language. Over this, Krishna was quite thankful, as she would not have wanted to be questioned about her adventures.

Four hours later, Krishna arrived at the Bangalore terminal, where she had to ask directions to the Central College. She looked for elderly, well-dressed couples, who she knew she could trust for accurate information, and spoke in English when she enquired. Luckily, it was only a short walk away. Krishna had never in her life walked alone on the streets of any town but her own. She did not like the way she was ogled by strangers; nor the comments that were directed at her by male passersby. In a city like Bangalore, it seemed most people walked on the streets rather than the footpaths, as the sidewalks were lined with beggars and merchants, and the dusty streets were only occasioned by motorcars or bullock-carts and bicycles. Krishna followed the same procedure, and upon arriving at the registration desk was confronted with some confusion since she was mis-categorized amongst the boys. As she had remembered to bring her high-school identification and class-marking papers, there was no question as to her identity and after some shuffling of papers and stamping of documents, Krishna was informed that she was one of only six girls participating in the examination. The girls would be given the same examination, but in a separate room, for the comfort of all. Krishna felt lucky to have appeared early for the exam, as it gave her some time to eat the *phuranpolis* that *M'am* had packed for her, while inspecting the other contestants as they registered. The exam went easily for Krishna, and as she sat on the train headed home, relieved that it had gone without incident, she felt a new and sneaky kind of joy. There was a deep satisfaction in covert defiance when overt rebellion was unacceptable. Back at the house, everything was just as though she had returned from another performance. Only Amma noticed that Krishna's costume didn't seem to need the usual cleaning, but chalked it up to it having been a short show on a cool day.

The weeks at school proceeded normally until Krishna returned home one afternoon to find Amma in tears at the front stoop of their little house. Krishna jumped off the bullock-cart aghast and ran toward Amma trailing her heavy satchel behind her. She imagined something horrible had happened—probably to Sindhya. "Amma, what is it? Where's Sindhya?" Amma looked mournfully at Krishna, then directed betweens sobs, "Go to the granary office to see your father. Go now. And take care." She hustled Krishna through the house, weeping. Amma was a young mother, having produced her first child at sixteen. Soft by nature and trained into acquiescence, she could not bear to discipline the children herself, and left that task up to Arna, who, fifteen years her senior, believed discipline to be his paternal duty. Amma was mourning Krishna's fate in advance. She had some idea what Arna might say and that punishment would be harsh and intuited that Arna's stubbornness would make for tensions in the house long after this episode would pass. As she hurried toward the granary, Krishna couldn't imagine why she would have to seek out Arna there—something she'd never been asked to do before. Rushing past the well, apprehensive over bad news about some family member, Krishna was relieved to spot Sindhya bothering *M'am*, who was filling copper pots to boil for baths.

When Krishna arrived breathless at the granary office, she found Arna seated behind his immense wooden desk, deeply engrossed in the large account book spread out before him. He looked up irritated, pushed his spectacles up on his nose, motioned for Krishna to enter, then hunched back over his accounting, ticking and crossing for a good couple of minutes while Krishna remained standing (she would never take a seat without being asked), catching her breath, and wondering what tragedy had befallen the family. Arna's demeanor did not betray anything in particular and as Krishna waited for her father to attend to her, she imagined the possibilities. Perhaps Shakuntala had lost the baby, or Kishore had been recruited to the war effort, or maybe this had something to do with her own wedding—perhaps she would be lucky and it was off! Arna snapped the account book closed abruptly. Krishna shuddered. He glared at his daughter, clearly angry, but also pained. "What," he started softly "have I done as your father to deserve your defiance and disrespect?" Krishna was baffled, she answered honestly, "nothing, sir." Arna grew louder now, scolding through gritted teeth: "Nothing! How dare you imagine that I have done nothing for you! Who has ensured that you were brought up in a respectable Brahmin household? Who has kept you well fed, clothed, well educated, and well looked after? Who on this earth has encouraged your dancing and assured your wedding into an upstanding family? Who, I ask you, who has done all these things?" Krishna cowered now. She did not understand where this line of questioning was going. "You have, Arna; you've done all of these things with Amma. And I am grateful for them." "Grateful? Grateful!?" questioned Arna indignant, "Do you show how grateful you are by defying your parents? By behaving as though you are not subject to rules? Is this how you show us how grateful you are?" Tears burgeoned in Krishna's eyes. Arna had never been so cross with her, and she began to suspect he had learned of the exam, but could not imagine how. "No, Arna, please." Krishna pleaded, "Why do you chastise me this way?" Arna mourned, "I do not know what I did in a past life to deserve so insolent a daughter! I can only imagine that this Jyotsna of yours has had this menacing influence on you! I knew there would be something wicked with this *Bharatanatyam* mischief. In fact it has done nothing for your character! No child of mine has ever defied me in so embarrassing a fashion! And a girl, at that! We might expect this from a lad, but from a girl? Or is she just a common strumpet?" Arna leaned across the table and narrowed his eyes at Krishna now, "How can you know no other Bhanaps saw you waltzing through the streets of Bangalore alone like some common girl? Or did that Jyotsna devil take you there?" Krishna let out the breath she didn't realize she'd been holding. Somehow her Father knew about the exam. It did not occur to Krishna to explain herself, she flew immediately to Jyotsna's defense: "Please, Arna, don't blame Jyotsna-aunty for my failure. She didn't even know." Arna was incredulous: "Then you admit to your trickery and deviousness? Do you think that just because you have become a dancer you are special in this family? That you are exempt from the guidance of your parents? You admit to shaming and disgracing your family like this for no good reason? What did you think you would gain by it? What were you doing other than risking your own safety, compromising your decency and the respectability of the family? What would have happened if the Nadghars had come across you there?" Krishna bowed her head in shame, tears flowing freely down her face, she responded between sobs, "No, sir, I am not special. Yes sir, I have disgraced us all and I am very sorry for it. I shall never offend you like this again." Arna knew from experience that it was important to break the tendencies of teenage rebellion at once, before a danger-ous pattern developed. He was immediately pleased that unlike Kishore, who would never admit to an offense, at least Krishna was honest and seemed promptly remorseful. This somewhat restored his usual calm, officious tone. He pronounced: "I am not interested in why you would do such a thing, but I have decided that you will perform only once more before your wedding. I am only permitting this because Amma tells me that Bombay University has scheduled it and already paid expenses in advance. But you can consider your gym-cracks with this *Bharatanatyam* finished. It has obviously had a dreadful influence on you. Anyway, it will serve you no purpose in your husband's house. You make sure to ask your Mother's forgiveness before you step back into my household. And you are dismissed!" Arna flipped his account log open, and slumped down noisily in a huff.

Krishna backed out of the office in tears, but couldn't bear to face Amma and ran to her own room, throwing herself on her creaky cot to weep. She was angry and sorry and felt despicable and confused. She knew she was suffering for assert-ing her own will. Sindhya trailed in not long afterward, wondering what drama had caused Krishna to run twice past her without even the slightest greeting. "Have you hurt yourself?" asked Sindhya innocently. "Leave me alone!" Krishna sobbed loudly, "I have hurt myself; and I have hurt Amma and Arna and the whole family. I am too willful and indecent, and now everything's ruined!" Sindhya didn't understand. She did not feel like leaving Krishna alone. Instead, she hopped up on the cot and stroked her sisters' hair just the way Krishna did when Sindhya skinned her knee or lost an erstwhile pet. Krishna lay strewn on the bed, sobbing, embarrassed at being caught in a lie and ashamed of her behav-ior. Sindhya, puzzled by her sister's grief, petted Krishna gently and absentmind-edly while twirling her tongue around a loosened tooth, unhindered by the tangy taste of blood and propelled by the satisfaction of yanking its from its root. Moments later, as she felt Sindhya's hand stroking her hair, her little sisters' pity did not feel right to Krishna. She was convinced that her actions did not deserve such compassion. She resolved to compose herself and go to Amma for forgive-ness. Krishna willed herself to stop sniveling as though turning off a tap. She steeled herself, wiped her eyes, and explained to Sindhya somberly that she was unhappy because she was no longer allowed to dance because of something improper that she had done. Sindhya too became disappointed. "But you love to dance! And you are so good! Even the newspapers say so!" she offered, as though the decision had been Krishna's alone. Now Krishna resented her marriage even more. It was certain to keep her from the dancing she so loved.

Krishna washed her face and went in search of Amma, who, unable to keep from fretting, had holed herself up in the shrine-room to pray for mercy on Krishna's behalf. She jumped when Krishna opened the door. Krishna fell immediately at her mother's feet in a bow of *vandana*. Amma began to bawl and hugged Krishna tightly, rocking her as she hadn't done since Krishna had last fallen ill. Before Krishna could utter a word in remorse toward her mother, Amma consoled her: "We will ask the gods forgiveness together. Now come and sit beside me. I know you didn't mean harm, *ammu*, you were only being impulsive. Everything will be alright soon." Coaxing her daughter from her almost fetal position into crossing her legs, seated before the altar crowded with statuettes of Ganesh, Krishna, Vishnu and Durga, all garlanded with fresh jasmines and fogged in with the heady smoke of incense, Amma began to chant in a whisper to Gayatri, the mother of the *Vedas*, the purifier, the destroyer of sins…"O beloved Mother, at the present moment I have taken my body as the self owing to ignorance, through my impure intellect. Give me a pure intellect which will enable me to know my real nature. Give me light and knowledge." Soon, Krishna joined in beside her mother, closing her eyes in prayer and feeling graced at the way Amma didn't even demand an apology, but instead granted Krishna immediate reprieve.

Amma felt this daughter to be too hard on herself. She did not know how to convey to Krishna that even the gods sometimes allow for folly. She knew only how to teach by example, so she forgave Krishna promptly and wordlessly: a simple shift of heart that Krishna would never permit herself. As Krishna chanted along with Amma, she basked in waves of relief. When their song was over, Amma wiped the tears from Krishna's eyes with the corner of her worn sari. Cupping Krishna's face in her warm, used hands she reassured her tenderly, "We will have so much to prepare for the wedding, *ammu*; you will not miss the dancing at all. We will bring beautiful saris for you; and everybody will wonder how we managed to keep so fair and beautiful a girl unmarried for so long!" Krishna burst into sobs again.

For the remaining school year, Krishna avoided Arna as much as she could, often claiming to have to study in preparation for her final exams. She never boasted to her classmates again. As expected, she and Amma traveled frequently to and from Bangalore to gather fixings for the trousseau. Mrs. Nadghar sometimes joined the expeditions, usually inviting the travelers over for tea after the shopping. Since the talents of her future daughter-in-law had brought her some status amongst her friends in which she was only delighted to revel, Mrs. Nadghar seemed much more indulgent and pleased with Krishna these days than she was at their first meeting. "You have turned into quite a lady," she remarked, uncharacteristically, and welcomed Krishna into what she called "your soon-to-be home" with unexpected hospitality, insisting that Krishna now refer to her as "Aunty" if not as "Sangeeta-bai." Krishna found the Nadghar home very similar to hers, but recognized she would always feel like a guest here. She still hated the idea of having to go. It would never feel like her own.

Nowadays Amma intermediated between Krishna and Arna, ensuring that she relayed Krishna's preferences on matters regarding the wedding on the rare occasions when these were relevant. Krishna kept from thinking in too much detail about what would happen after the marriage; she determined that it was inevitable and fretting about it would not make it better. High school would end in March, her certificate exams would be held immediately, her last performance would be in mid-April, and the wedding was set for mid-June—prior to the monsoons, and at an auspicious time according to the astrologer. Because it was improper to gossip and there was no reason to, much to Krishna's relief, Arna didn't share her transgressions with anybody in the family. Even Sindhya remained unclear about what had happened. Kishore, Deepa, Sandhya, Shaku and the others simply understood that once she were married, Krishna would no longer dedicate any of her time to dancing. This seemed natural to them and appropriate to a *Bhanap* wife. Krishna gleaned from Amma that Arna had learned of her adventure by opening a letter from the Mysore Office of Academic Excellence informing Krishna that she had passed the first examination, and inviting her to the next round. Arna never shared that letter with Krishna, having been warned by the astrologer long ago that this daughter was already too proud, independent and headstrong, and would need less praise and more disciplining than the others to be properly contained.

Perhaps because she knew it would be her last performance, but also as a further excuse to avoid Arna's company, Krishna put more effort into her practices with Jyotsna nowadays. One day Krishna ventured to share with Jyotsna all the gory details of the exam cataclysm. She confessed, "And now I am so ashamed. It was prideful and stupidly inconsiderate. I don't even know why I did it. I just wanted to show that I could!" Jyotsna tried to contain her pride over Krishna's defiance by behaving disappointed both in Krishna and in Arna's response. Yet, she was privately delighted that Krishna had asserted herself for a change, even in her own little way. She was tired of seeing girls constantly quashed into submission. The predominant attitude that a woman's sole role should be as wife and mother didn't sit well with Jyotsna. She understood its value, recognized the benefits such an attitude produced for the community, but noted in her own experience that some people, even women, often had a different calling. Jyotsna resented on Krishna's behalf that her considerable talent should be stifled just because it issued from a girl who should be married instead. She could see that there was a fire in Krishna that her tradition kept from burning. She could also see that no matter how much sand were thrown on them, these flames may never burn out. They might smolder quietly and explode some day if Krishna didn't let the embers glow just a little.

Still, Jyotsna knew that once she was married, the chances of Krishna's continued dancing would be low unless by fate or chance her husband were remarkably liberal or failed to immediately impregnate her. She thought it best not to hold out any hope when there was an impressive incidence of honeymoon babies amongst *Bhanap* couples as far as Jyotsna was concerned, and the likelihood of Krishna's continuing to dance was almost eliminated by that trend. Jyotsna reasoned that perhaps she had garnered the most she could over the years from this excellent prospect, and was glad for having tutored Krishna and danced with her as long as she did. She could only hope that some day Krishna would ensure that her own daughters learned the dance, and thus perpetuate an important tradition. Though Jyotsna did not speak these things, (why plague the girl, when she already felt so burdened?) when the two practiced together now, it seemed to both them like each step was weightier, each move suffused with unprecedented import. As it would be her last performance, Jyotsna chose demanding pieces that would showcase Krishna's skills. This program, for a mostly Indian audience, was entirely dedicated to *Bharatanatyam* and would include only Jyotsna, Krishna and a couple of Bombay-based dancers with whom Jyotsna had enjoyed dancing in the past.

On the evening of the performance at the University, which none of her own family attended, Krishna was unaware that her intended was in the audience. He learned from the University newspaper that Krishna Nayampalli would be dancing at the Chancellor's Invitational Cultural Programme. Intrigued, Krishna's fiancé, who had never before set eyes on his bride-to-be, was delighted to have such an opportunity. He informed none of his friends at Grant Medical College, nor his parents, of his intention to attend. Although his father had assured him that the girl was fair and lovely by any standard, and more importantly, *"Amichi gele"* (one of us), the boy was intent on seeing for himself what he would be getting in this bargain. The handsome, jaunty, boy arrived at the theatre early to secure a good seat and prepared himself mentally to be thoroughly disappointed. He had resigned himself long ago to his arranged marriage and had consoled himself that as long as she was truly a trained dancer, she might at least have physiological advantages.

Backstage, Krishna fiddled with her jewelry, folded and refolded the pleats of her costume and paced so much that Jyotsna had to hold her still so the jingle bells around her ankles wouldn't distract the dancers on stage. The local dancers performed first today, giving Krishna the chance to grow even edgier. They were both talented and experienced and although one was quite young, it was obvious she had the swiftness and precision necessary to accomplish more demanding footwork as she matured. It was odd to Krishna to evaluate another dancer like this. Just shy of seventeen, she was no longer the youngest at these events and was relieved of that pressure, though she realized she missed the attention it bestowed. Krishna had convinced herself that this performance held her last opportunity for redemption from her misdeeds. She buzzed with fidgety energy, fearing she'd be unable to control it in time for her entrance. Jyotsna noticed Krishna's uncharacteristic jumpiness but chose not to mention it for fear of making it worse. When, finally, she and Jyotsna took the stage, the normally demure Krishna felt herself trembling like a petrified novice. Remembering the Hindu dictum about soft intention being more effective than rigid will, at the opening invocation, she simply set her intent on gratifying the gods. And from the first beat of the *tabla*, Krishna was, for the first time in her dancing, transported as though a vast, knowing, force eclipsed her mind and unleashed her body into the dance. She put no concerted thought into her movements, yet somehow they came easily, almost playfully, as though dancing were happening to her. So overwhelming was this sensation that Krishna instinctively resisted it at first, forcing herself to concentrate on the grounding sound of her jingle-bells. This focus somehow intensified the feeling, as though now the tinkling of the bells propelled Krishna in the direction of her next natural move. Krishna felt lighter than a plume of smoke, freed from burdensome mindfulness, diffused into euphoria. When it came time for the footwork of the *jattiswaram*, Krishna and Jyotsna had to face each other momentarily. Their eyes locked. In Jyotsna's blissful countenance Krishna glimpsed the freedom of surrender. Drawn in, she succumbed. Krishna at last gave into *Bharatanatyam*, and it gave back through her. For the next thirty minutes, the captivated spectators reveled with the tireless performers in the pure ecstasy of devotional dance.

When the music slowed and it was time to back off stage, Krishna had not yet come back into herself. It took a few seconds of panting before she recognized where she was and what she was meant to do. When she came to, for the first time in her many years of dancing, Krishna made an unplanned move: she turned to face Jyotsna who was standing on one leg, frozen in the pose that Krishna should have been mirroring. Krishna dropped her required stance, strode over to her *nattuvanar* with hands clasped as if in prayer to the beat of the flustered musicians' *tabla*, and spontaneously bowed deeply to Jyotsna in *vandana*, tears streaming down her face. The roar that came up from the audience, which Krishna had entirely forgotten was there, nearly knocked both dancers off their feet. As usual, Krishna could not see through the blazing lights, but she needn't see the elation that she could feel. Although they should have been backing off the stage by now, Jyotsna remained still, calmly balanced on one leg, the very embodiment of *Nataraja*, Lord of the Dance. And Krishna remained crouched and quivering at her guru's feet. The music could no longer be heard over the cheering of the audience. It occurred to the flustered stage manager that poor Jyotsna would have to remain in that impossible pose forever (indeed, he was sure she could have), unless he closed the curtains, which he promptly did.

Now the audience screamed and clapped even louder demanding that the dancers return. Jyotsna dropped her stance behind the closed curtain, knelt to collect Krishna who seemed to her suddenly like the seven-year old she had first met; wondrous, nervous, unguarded, and embraced her with all her might. The stage manager pushed the opening dancers out on stage to take a bow with Jyotsna and Krishna, also something unrehearsed. It was not in the tradition of *Bharatanatyam* dancers to take bows. The last piece was always a show of appreciation to the audience and the gods. Just before the curtain opened, Jyotsna astutely commanded "*Mangalam!*" All four dancers, following Jyotsna's practiced lead, conjured a rotating bow in the four cardinal directions, and one to the audience, which continued to stomp and cheer. The Chancellor of the University was compelled to take the stage to commend the dancers and thank the audience for their attendance at "the most moving and splendid example of what Indian culture has to offer that this humble stage had ever witnessed." Ambling home that evening, Krishna's pie-eyed fiancé didn't notice, for a change, the wretched beggars or the unrelenting horns or the stench of standing water in the pot-holes of Bombay. He was intensely, irreversibly, inconceivably, in love.

A Chancellor's reception for the board, faculty and performers followed the show. Krishna and Jyotsna rushed to clean up and change into saris as a bicycle rickshaw awaited to take them to the Faculty Club. The chandeliers sparkled and the mahogany railings were polished to equivalent gleam. The guests milled about the opulent galleries, lounging on the velvet sofas and admiring the antique wall-hangings. The generally inert faculty greeted the arriving dancers with enchantment and appreciative applause. No less than five lofty professors of this, that or the other approached the intimidated Krishna to commend her. They used words like "radiant" and "exquisite," "moving" and "inspired." Unlike at her *arangetram* where Krishna had practiced words of humility, at this event, she was mightily stumped. She tried to recall what she'd said at her debut, but couldn't utter what now seemed so hollow and insincere. Instead, she just smiled with eyes downcast, grateful for the praise, but somehow letting it pass through her and to the gods and Jyotsna—who really deserved it. Krishna sensed she had been carried through this performance. She did not feel gifted or proud, she felt lucky and blessed.

Krishna was not used to "mingling" the way Jyotsna could, so she stayed close to her *nattuvanar's* side, occasionally nibbling on a passing *pakora* (which she knew she shouldn't), or gulping thirstily from a series of what seemed like unreasonably tiny glasses of chilly water lined up neatly on a somewhat baffled waiter's tray. She knew this behavior was unbecoming of a lady, but at the moment was irrelevant to a thirsty dancer. It was just when she got up the courage to ask the waiter for "please, a very, very large glass of water" that the nattily outfitted Chancellor of the university marched up to Krishna and Jyotsna with a twinkle in his eye and a smile wider than she thought should fit on his oblong face. He dismissed Jyotsna's *namaste* and instead clapped bony hands around hers, exclaiming in an exaggerated accent, "In ten years of knowing you, dear girl, I have not seen you dance as you did tonight! I did not think it was possible for a professional with your mastery to improve, but I say, you have astounded me this time and I fear you must share the credit with the talented artiste at your side." Krishna liked the way the Chancellor's words spilled out breathily from him unhampered by pause, and the way his British accent seemed so absurd emerging from so typically Indian a face. The Chancellor was a friend of Bala's family, and Bala had introduced him to her student when Jyotsna was a young dancer and he a young professor, hoping their families might agree to a wedding. The Chancellor's mother, on learning Jyotsna was a dancer, had flatly forbidden such a union, and so things floundered before they had even begun. Jyotsna had heard from Bala that his mother had recently passed and she took a moment to acknowledge it. "First, let me express most sincere condolences," Jyotsna looked up at the Chancellor grievously, "it is not easy to lose the one who gave you life." The Chancellor took a deep breath and gazed at Jyotsna in somber thought. "You know," he uttered, considering, "tonight's performance made me forget this heartache for just a short while." He quickly snapped himself out of his reverie and abruptly addressing Krishna, added, "Young lady, it is my understanding that in addition to your considerable stage talents, you stand first in your class in mathematics and have ranked amongst the top twenty students in Mysore on your high school certification examinations?" Krishna didn't know how the man would have learned these facts, but conceded their veracity by smiling and nodding, her hands clasped timidly behind her back. He continued officiously, "It was the infamous Balasaraswati, who recommended your talents to my offices who informed me of your outstanding achievements." Jyotsna was surprised to hear that Bala would have talked Krishna up in such a manner. "My dear Miss Nayampalli," added the Chancellor curtly, without pomp or prologue, "I have had the opportunity to consult the governing board and some of the faculty members. The university is in a position to offer you a full scholarship, including room and board here in Bombay, if you would agree to showcase your considerable talents at the scholarship benefits, fundraisers and other cultural events as may arise." The Chancellor spoke quickly, as though if he let the offer sink in, Krishna might not take it. "I would imagine this would be a very attractive offer if you have not yet decided upon a university placement. We recognize this is an unusual solicitation, but I did not want to undertake the formalities without ensuring that the response would be affirmative, as it would simply waste our precious few resources, if you grasp my meaning. You do understand and forgive the approach, do you, considering?" That was all the Chancellor had to say. After his rushed monologue he stood silent, smiling his face into a triangle, anticipating unqualified enthusiasm from his addressees.

Krishna was stunned; Jyotsna, agog. Krishna blinked and smiled appreciatively, trying to grasp the implications of the offer. Jyotsna stammered on Krishna's behalf, "Mr. Chancellor, sir; this is indeed an opportunity of a lifetime, but you should be made aware that Krishna is expected to..." Krishna interrupted, surprising even herself "raise such a gracious offer to the attention of my parents, sir. I am a *Chitrapur Saraswat* Brahmin by upbringing, you see, and it would be improper..." Krishna had said enough. "I see," replied the Chancellor, deflated, "It was our belief that your talents would add considerably to our offerings here at the university in view of the growing clamor for more Indian culture and the..." He stopped himself, realizing that his cause was hopeless, improvising solutions as rapidly as his mind could process. "Would it?" he inquired pensively, "Would it be helpful if I were to write to your father, and perhaps also to the National Council? After all, wouldn't it further both the reputation and contribution of the community to have such a worthy representative at the university? We have had so many lads of yours here—such a work ethic! Much to be proud of, what with the cooperative housing systems, and the funding mechanisms, and the industriousness...Yes, this explains everything, of course. You are certainly a product of the values of your community, young lady. Indeed..." Krishna thought the Chancellor would never hush up. She persuaded him that there was no need for him to raise the matter with her parents as she would do so herself. Jyotsna stood by Krishna, aghast at what had come over the girl, but allowing Krishna to represent herself, as she may never again. Jyotsna was simultaneously amused and disappointed. Had it been any other one of her students, there would have been little question. After the Chancellor took his leave, thanking the dancers and urging Krishna to let his office know directly should she be able to start courses in July, Jyotsna gazed in wonderment at the discomfited Krishna. Krishna realized that she'd been forgetting herself all day. She had danced boldly and outside of herself, she had defied thousands of years of tradition by throwing herself down before her *nattuvanar* on stage, and now she had misled the Chancellor of the University of Bombay about her certain (married) future.

A rickshaw transported the dancers on the long haul through Bombay to Shaku and Rahuls' home in the suburbs for the night. The ride felt endless, and the tired dancers rode side by side in dazed silence. Jyotsna did not want to raise the matter of the scholarship, although she wondered why Krishna didn't admit that her marriage would prevent her from accepting. Jyotsna reasoned that perhaps Krishna thought it impolite to turn down such a generous offer. Deferring the response to a politely written refusal may have been easier for Krishna than a rejecting the offer in person. Meanwhile, Krishna's mind burbled with optimistic scenarios of approaching Arna with the news, postponing the wedding, or at worst, obtaining the Nadghars consent so that she could attend the university. She pictured herself engrossed in the pages of a thick, leather-bound tome, stacks of books piled up on either side of her at some solemn library table. She saw herself sitting in a large lecture hall, a pencil tucked behind her ear, listening intently to a bespectacled, befrocked professor bellowing the titillating knowledge of the ages purely for her erudition. She imagined herself on the platform of today's auditorium, proud with cap and gown, waving a sheepskin at the audience, her parents beaming at the very front. The distraction was futile, but Krishna indulged it nonetheless on that dreamy ride home. Meanwhile, Jyotsna sat at

Krishna's side, mightily satisfied with her student. Krishna's final performance had been her most passionate. Perhaps, Jyotsna considered, it was most compassionate left unsaid.

Krishna did not return to Mangalore with Jyotsna as she was meant to the next day. Shaku was happy to have Krishna stay over a few days and sent word home with Jyotsna that she would be safely seen onto the regular train next week. It would give the sisters a chance to spend some time together and do some more pre-wedding shopping in Bombay to lessen the burden on Amma. Shaku imagined it would be helpful to give Krishna some exposure to her own household, which was more urban and comparable to the one she would occupy in Bangalore. Rahul was happy to write to Arna on this matter, as he imagined that Krishna would be good company for Shakuntala during this uncomfortable third month of her pregnancy. A week later, when the couple delivered Krishna to the train station nearest their home, she said her fond and tearful goodbyes, uncharacteristically clinging to Shaku's embrace in public and waving dolefully from the window of the lady's compartment. She was meant to change to the interstate line at Victoria Station, but didn't. Instead, she searched the whole platform for a familiar face (there was sure to be somebody she knew going home to Mangalore) and was relieved to come across a neighboring family (not *Bhanaps*, but still reliable) headed that way. She entrusted them anxiously and gratefully with a letter to deliver to her house. She explained fretfully that she was expected to return home, but would be delayed due to her sister's difficult pregnancy and was headed back to the suburbs instead. She had come all the way to the Victoria Terminal in the hopes of finding somebody to inform her parents of this development.

After handing over the letter, Krishna walked briskly toward the ticket counters but hesitated at the end of the platform. Red-caps jostled past her, their wagons piled high with toppling luggage; she watched the chai-walla on the platform dispense a cup of milky tea, tilting long pours back and forth between two cups, improbably distant from each other, so it would cool and thoroughly enjoying his own high-jinx while his bemused client looked on. She took a slow turn to absorb the cacophony of the train station—the bedlam for which she would be opting over the safety of home. A distinguished, overdressed foreigner brushed by her, then stopped, turned and looked her over with lascivious intent. She was reminded of the disgusting Lieutenant and shuddered. She had a momentary change of heart and started toward the train, but it hissed and hooted twice and she halted again further along the platform and watched it chug away in huffs and grumbles. When the train was entirely out of sight, Krishna, now resolute again, traded in her ticket and pocketed the few rupees which in addition to her satchel containing some saris and her dance costume, now constituted all her worldly possessions. Next, she turned up at the doorstep of the Chancellor of the University of Bombay.

May 7, 1940

My Dearest Amma and Arna:

My heart aches to imagine the pain that this message will bring you. It is my most sincere wish to cause no further trouble or hardship for the family for which you have worked so hard. I am most grateful for, and most undeserving of, all the care and blessings you have ever bestowed upon me. Please be consoled and assured that it is not your wardship, but my own willfulness that brings this decision about. I expect neither forgiveness nor support. I understand every consequence, including the shame I bring upon you in the *sangha*, for this decision. Even Jyotsna-Aunty does not know of it, so please do not blame her.

I shall remain in Bombay in order to attend the university. I have been offered a scholarship that allows me to continue to dance. I have felt the power of Bharatanatyam now, and I feel it to be my passion and my calling. I know that I can dance with all my heart, but I am too willful to be so exemplary a wife and mother as Amma. I am consoled in knowing that dancing is a way for me to contribute personally to Ghandiji's worthy efforts. There are so many well-bred ladies who work in Bombay for a living. I will dance, and in this way I expect to be able to compensate you someday for the dowry which I know you will honor your word by conferring.

I am burdened and ashamed to think of your disappointment with me. I have not met your expectations nor honored you as you deserve. Please consider that I might have dishonored you more as a reluctant wife. I can only hope to please the gods by dancing and so be absolved for my transgressions against you and against the *sangha*. Please do not think that I take pride in them.

I do not deserve or expect any reply. I will write to you weekly, wanting nothing in response. I will pray for you every day of my life. I will pray that someday you can forgive me. I will pray for you to be lucky and blessed with health and abundance. I will pray that the gods do not bring vengeance on your household for my misdeeds. I will pray that, unlike me, Sindhya grows up to be the excellent kind of daughter you deserve. When you explain to her that I have not been a good sister, a good example or a good influence, I beg of you please to let her understand that I have loved her anyway, and do love her still, with all my heart, as I do you. I hope that you know how much I miss you already.

A loving daughter would not be so bold, but even then, I offer this letter with all respect and humility.

Your ever-loving,

Krishna

6

Technically, the smell of curry caused the fire. Everyone had complained that I hadn't cooked Indian in ages, so I'd spent the prior evening grinding spices and marinating and the next day chopping and frying and setting up for the dinner party. I'd whined my way through it, not because of the labor (repetitive work can be somewhat meditational,) but because no matter how you ventilate, all that simmering somehow makes the whole apartment absorb the smell of curry. It settles into the carpets, hugs the walls, even seeps into the bedding—and worse, it wafts out into the hallways broadcasting "Desi in da house!" Because I detest that propensity of an Indian household to assault the senses with the clinging remnants of curries long past, (self-loathing therein noted, thanks) just before my guests arrived I'd put out a few aromatherapy votives—the ones that come nested in those thick, squat, fogged glasses—in an effort to mask the smell.

The dinner earned honest praise despite the spiciness of the main dish which caused lots of tongue-fanning and refilling of water glasses. Nobody mentioned Sofian, which was really decent of them. That's why I love my friends. Since it was the first time I'd entertained alone since he moved out (it's been three months now) I'd expected it all to be harder. I realized in the middle of serving that he'd never done a damn thing to help anyway. He was entirely unsupportive of my additional family burdens after dad died, and had, if anything, become more distant just when I needed the most bolstering. He was, to be fair, fed up with all the lying and had said from the beginning he wouldn't marry a non-Muslim.

As far as my family was concerned, he was just a roommate, a sub-letter of the second room and bath. Moroccan by birth, though raised in France, his religion meant he'd never have passed muster with mom or dad. I kept him a secret. We actually started out as flat-mates, evolved into friends, then lovers. One thing led to another. We found ourselves cooking dinners at home together, catching a movie on occasion, eventually starting to check in with calls or e-mails to find out if the other would be home that evening. Looking back on it I realize he probably just wanted a caretaker, a mom (he was five years younger than I, new to and alone in New York,) and I was probably acting out covertly the defiance against my parents no Indian child dares undertake overtly. Also, after dad's death, any comfort would have done, so even as the feeling grew that Sofian was the wrong guy (none of my closest friends ever trusted him—too slick they warned, used to riding on his looks,) I ignored the signs, overemphasized the slightest of his attentions, made excuses for our intellectual and emotional incompatibilities (what with me traveling so much for work.)

Three months ago I came home a day early from a business trip, heard the shower going, noticed the bed in disarray, and wondered what Sofian was doing home on a Wednesday at noon. Must be sick, I figured. I don't know who was more stunned, the petite, pigeon-toed Asian girl (Japanese? Korean?) who stepped out the bathroom door expecting Sofian, or me. "Oh my god," she gasped with valley-girl drama, "We didn't think you'd be back till tomorrow! I'm so sorry...I'm so, so...I'll just get my stuff..." She scurried to collect her clothes, clutching my bathsheet around her; a meaningless bra, jeans, a tiny pink cashmere sweater and thong I hadn't noticed tossed across the easy chair. They were all there when I'd come in. I stared in stunned silence at nothing in particular. What was happening didn't fit in my head. She retreated nervously into the bathroom. I surveyed the bed: my bed, my sheets, my pillows dented with another woman's imprints. I dove at it, tearing off the linens, savage, enraged, flinging them in a heap across the room. The girl slipped out the door in the midst of my rage. My instinct was to chase after her as I heard the front door click shut. I ran toward it in a frenzy, not quite sure what I intended to do, and lunged for the door, slamming a finger against the hard metal handle and bending it back so hard it sent pain searing up my arm to my elbow. Then I stopped. I gripped the hurt finger with my free hand, leaning against the door, nothing but anguish coursing through me. A purposeful calm came over me as I stood there. I headed for the phone, picked it up, and dialed Sofian at work. "Come home now," is all I said when he answered, all businesslike and composed, "pack up your shit and get the hell out."

By the time he got home I was a cowering mess of tortured tears, huddled, clutching my knees at the foot of the stripped bed. He didn't even try to console. He said nothing, in fact. He just found a suitcase and started opening drawers noisily and throwing stuff in as I sat on the floor whimpering, tears scudding down my cheeks. "Can I leave some stuff till I find a place?" He asked eventually, gruff. I nodded without looking at him, just wanted him out. Then he added as he was leaving, as if to excuse himself, "It's just, you know, you've been a real drag lately. We stopped having any fun." The rage surged back up in me but I didn't lash out. I somehow didn't feel the right to complain. In fact, by the time he came back a week later to collect his things, I'd convinced myself that indeed something I had done had caused his infidelity. I'd dissected all the whys and wherefores, wailed my head off, swallowed my anger and somehow become willing to settle. I asked him not to leave, and even apologized that perhaps I'd been in mourning too long. I actually thought maybe we could work things out. He left anyway. Selfish bastard. I never told anyone why we split up, how humiliating it had all been. I just let my friends believe it simply hadn't worked out.

In what now seems to me an improbable stroke of foreshadowing of the fire, I'd used some unfamiliar chilies in the marinade, making for more piquancy than I'd expected. Other than adding sugar, which might ruin the rest of the flavors, I'd taught my guests that proper Indians know that water doesn't do much to quell the fieriness on the tongue: you need to damp it out with rice. So there were barely any leftovers and the *basmati* was polished off entirely. We'd gone through eight bottles of wine and were well past dessert and into our second cups of tea when someone smelled smoke and just then the fire alarm went off in the hallway. The firemen guessed that the candle in the bathroom had burst its glass container, caught fire to the towels stacked beside it, setting the hairdryer aflame, which lit up a hanging towel, and by the time we got to it half the bathroom was a blazing, smoky, toxic rage.

I don't know what combination of courage and foolishness caused two of my guests to venture in there, but had they not had the presence of mind to throw the bathmat into the tub, turn on the faucets and slap out the flames with the wet mat while somehow turning the shower hose on the burning heap, it could have all been much worse. By the time the firemen tromped up five flights of stairs (they arrived grouchy and exhausted), the place was a right mess but the fire was out. The greatest damage was actually caused by the firefighters themselves, whose heavy equipment left deep slashes on my walls and whose boots, after sloshing about in the soup of water, ash and molten plastic on the formerly white marble floor of my bathroom, tracked that mélange through my antique Isfahan carpets and into the hallways as they checked the walls for electrical damage and any lingering flames. The Super, unhappy to be roused from the comfort of his sofa, arrived to inspect and said it looks worse than it probably is. He guessed the bathroom would cost about five hundred dollars to fix and, to my relief, it could get done this week.

Nothing puts a damper on a dinner party quite like a massive fire. After a flurry of window-openings and hearty hackings, a round of recountings, reassurances, congratulations, and cleverly strategized picture taking for insurance purposes, there were tight hugs all around combining relief with disbelief, and then everybody filed out, with sincere offers to help clean up—which I politely refused—it's a Sunday after all and everybody has work in the morning. So here I am, with a sink-full of mucky dishes and a flooded, scorched bathroom; licks of flame-print running up the walls, soot glommed onto the shower curtain and (inexplicably) on the ceiling, and ashes speckling undecipherable patterns on the mirrors. I'm too jazzed to go to bed and the chances of sleep, under the circumstances, aren't promising, so I've set myself to cleaning up. I've conquered the dishes and the kitchen, figuring it was something I could accomplish and knew how to do. Despite the wide open windows on a below-zero night, the smoke still hangs in the air and burns my throat (and I'd been worried about the smell of curry!) So with a scarf tied round my face to filter my breathing, I've valiantly taken on the bathroom, working from the top down, so that the bits of debris end up on the floor and I can sop it all up, perhaps into the plugged tub and then fill up garbage bags from there.

I am thinking about recent events as I collect the remains of my former bathroom. I'll tell Suhasini about it all in the morning, but recognize there's no point worrying mom about the fire. It's over, and it'll be cleaned up. Anyhow, she'll just freak out about my safety and my capacity to manage on my own. Particularly now that she's still grieving, I will continue to protect mom from my pains and struggles as I always have. Though I may not know the details, I sense she's had enough of her own. So I've shared with her nothing about Sofian—just cheerfully reported that he'd gotten his own place and I was looking for a new roommate. That's the way it is between us. Mom and I keep a safe and cordial distance. She doesn't ask questions to which she'd rather not know the answers, and I don't go looking for advice I know I'm not likely to take. It tends to work out.

It's 3 a.m. I'm kneeling beside the bathtub, verily impressed with my own efficiency, wringing out a formerly favorite towel (now scorched and tattered), when a single, viscous tear rolls down my cheek and I fall into the familiar abyss of the "mean lonelies." The loneliness isn't something that comes over me and then vanishes the way a grumpy mood or a wave of joy or gratefulness might. Instead, it lurks; a context ever ready to consume me. It has no particular affinity for day or night, and no identifiable triggers. It can snatch me, almost vengefully, out of the most cheerful of moments, reminding me that happiness isn't legitimate if not shared; and of course, in difficult times it can suck me into its vacuum with a most self-satisfied glee. Even though I am by nature optimistic, enthusiastic, gregarious, it receives me into the certainty of hopelessness and isolation, reminding me that nothing connects me to anything or anybody and threatening that nothing ever will. I cannot reason my way out of its void (it does not respond to logic) and there's no "reaching out" from its mercilessness. Consoling, well-meaning reminders that I am "so lovely, so smart, so cultured, so healthy, so wealthy, so lucky," that I have "such a rich social life, such a loving family, so much to be look forward to and be grateful for," have no effect on its persistence. A shrink once suggested that it's probably just rage, stuffed down and unexpressed. I may integrate these things intellectually, but in the throes of this emotion, all I am is deserted. I am unutterably deficient, excluded. What I sense is this: the loneliness is not about who I am or what I have now. It has been there for me as long as I can remember, it was there long before me, and it will not be extinguished by my efforts alone. Avoidance of its relentless threat corrals me into my worst decisions (Sofian), my most pathetic responses ("don't leave me!"), my most desperate measures (always staying safely below mom's radar.) It breathes life into my nightmares; it sucks life out of my dreams. So, on the cold, wet marble floor of a luxury apartment on the Upper East side, a "lucky," self-reliant woman with nothing to complain about kneels trembling and whimpering softly into a soaked, ashen towel, feeling insufficient and alone.

From:	knadghar@calberk.edu
To:	sushilarao@yoohoo.com
Subject:	The Control of Highly Infectious Diseases
Date:	Oct 03 2000 00:28:48—0800 (EDT)

Dear Ms. Rao:

Kindly forgive the long delay in my reply. I was called away on an emergency to Kenya in March and have only returned last week. I am still catching up on backed up e-mail.

In response to your inquiry, the book you referenced was written by my father, whose name I share. After partition he left India for Kenya where he founded a rural hospital to treat infectious diseases. He authored several books and articles on the subject. As we are both doctors, or I should say, he was (I went to Kenya because he passed away) I am frequently mistaken for him. Except I work for a teaching hospital in California and infectious disease is not my field.

I had never paid attention to the dedication, and can only imagine it was to Lord Krishna, but regret that I cannot enlighten you further. If you do learn anything more, I would be interested, as the dedication has now begun to intrigue me too!

Best wishes,

Kamath Nadghar, M.D. PhD

The movements of the *Shabdam*, which follows the *Jattiswaram*, tend to be more leisurely and meditative. For now, the dancer need no longer prove technical skills so mechanically to the beat of the musicians. Rather, the music slows to enable the dancer to demonstrate a capacity to convey feeling.

#

7

The monsoon winds raged outside, pelting angry rain against the brittle glass of her clattering dormitory window. Krishna gazed dolefully at the limp stack of letters bundled on the night table of the narrow, ill-lit room which now served as home. Jyotsna was heartbroken at delivering them, sadder in fact than Krishna was now. Ten thin, damp envelopes returned to Krishna unopened, conveying to her the rancor that now dwelt in Arna's heart. Amma might never have she had written. Sindhya, Krishna imagined, felt confused, abandoned, maybe even betrayed. And the rains seemed endless this year, punishing, self-righteous.

Upon receiving Krishna's letter, Arna, impervious to the downpours, had stormed over to Jyotsna's bungalow incensed. Jyotsna was singing a handful of small girls through their steps, when the door flew open, slamming and setting the whole flimsy structure abuzz. The girls, terrified by the soaked, ranting, lunatic at the door, ran squealing to a corner of the bamboo-floored room and huddled, hugging each other and cowering as though fending off the gales. Arna, dripping pools of water into the makeshift studio, flew at Jyotsna pointing and bellowing, "You dirty whore! You have turned my precious daughter into a useless outcast! What right have you to interfere in my family this way?" Amma skidded in behind, beseeching in a placating tone, "This is unnecessary, Arna; lower your voice. You are embarrassing us with unfounded accusations." Arna shot back at her, "Enough from you! What has this to do with you?" Jyotsna, who had backed slowly away from Arna trembled mildly but maintained composure. More than anything she had been startled and was concerned for her students. "Arnaji," she proposed firm and calm, "losing your temper with me will not help whatever is the situation." Jyotsna, having established herself as the cool-headed observer, now assumed an attitude of haughtiness that rudeness cannot penetrate. Arna didn't apologize, but adjusted the madness out of his voice and turned the encounter into a terse interrogation on the events that had led to this catastrophe, all played out before a tiny, tremulous audience and Amma who had been relegated to her own silent place. After getting his fill of whatever scant information Jyotsna would supply, with the decorum and detachment of a tolerant prosecutor, Arna stomped off to the temple to see if he could obtain Swamiji's counsel, leaving the disconsolate Amma to clean up his abusive mess.

Amma's helplessness irritated Jyotsna, though she understood its source. Amma was trained to be dependent, conciliatory, apologetic and Jyotsna knew she had stayed behind to make amends. Jyotsna coaxed the girls out of the corner and urged them to sit in a circle in the middle of the room. "The mats are all wet!" one cried, "because uncle didn't even take off his sandals!" Amma, realizing that neither had she removed her shoes, now slipped them off discretely as she waited for Jyotsna to deal with the alarmed girls. "Yes," said Jyotsna, irritated but self possessed, "Did you see how angry uncle was? So angry, he must have forgotten his manners!" Jyotsna raised her arms to her hips, tutting and making use of the conflagration. "We are lucky, you see, just in time the gods sent us uncle so you girls could learn! Can you make an angry face like uncle's?" Small faces twisted into scowls with knitted eyebrows and fierce eyes. Amma couldn't help but giggle to herself at the apt depictions of Arna. "Very, very good!" Jyotsna encouraged. "Now when we must dance anger, you can remember uncle and make the proper face, no?" The girls nodded, brightening. "But what have you done to make uncle so angry?" one student inquired with legitimate concern. Jyotsna considered her response, "When you yourself are cross at something sometimes you kick a pebble hard to get out of your way, isn't it?" The girls remained interested. "Well are you mad at the pebble?" The girls shook their heads. "That would be silly, wouldn't it?" Jyotsna continued, "I think uncle isn't really angry with me. I think he is only angry, but I am like the pebble in his way." Amma was impressed by Jyotsna's skillful approach. Jyotsna had continued her lesson and calmed the students as well. She was pleased that when the girls were collected, they left with smiling faces.

Now Jyotsna knew that Amma would have to apologize on her bullheaded husband's behalf, something he had neither the courage nor gallantry to do himself. Amma corralled Jyotsna around her small kitchen table as Jyotsna poured Amma a lassi, which Amma gently and tearfully refused. "Jyotsna-bai," she offered meekly, "you have even told the students that Arna is not angry with you. So you know this. Still, I am very sorry for his behavior and his vicious words to you." She looked down at her own hands like a guilty child as she continued, "These you must see as the result of his embarrassment. You know that he would only be so bold with kin." Jyotsna, seeing Amma's noble intent and sympathizing with the humility involved in having to make amends for her husband's flubs, sprang to reassure Amma, "I know that I am not at any fault in this matter, Ratna-bai, I did nothing to influence Krishna's decisions. She has taken her own path." Amma composed herself now, scrunching a corner of her sari to wipe tears from her eyes. "I know that Krishna has always had defiance in her, even the astrologer told us this when she was born." She tried to give Jyotsna her due, "Yet with your tutoring, she had gained such discipline. Now this happens. She pridefully forsakes her fate!" Jyotsna reframed Amma's assumption. "Perhaps, Ratnabai, this is her real fate and what had been planned for her was not." Now Jyotsna felt sorry for Amma's lot. Both women knew that Arna's anger was borne of fear for Krishna's safety and the embarrassment her behavior portended in the community. The shame of breaking an engagement, and the implication that Arna was unable to raise his daughter to contribute to the *sangha* were burdensome for a man in Arna's position. How could he, of all *Bhanaps*, fail to raise a dutiful daughter? Amma, forming a wan smile through downcast eyes, admitted sheepishly, "Arna would never recognize where Krishna's determination and stubbornness came from." Then with a defenseless glance at Jyotsna, Amma's resigned eyes finally spilled the plump floods of tears she'd been holding back since morning. She heaved sobs so deep and desperate they moved Jyotsna to add her own. On a wobbly kitchen bench, the two women sat side-by-side in an embrace, rocking each other and weeping over the pitter patter of rain on the roof. They wept for the inevitability of loss and the anger of men. They wept for their own powerlessness and their own guilt. They wept for the damage done and the damage yet to come, and for Krishna and Arna and Sindhya and each other. They wept until they were good and dry, and with a penetrating look, Amma expressed to Jyotsna all the words she could not utter—words she knew Arna would not allow—forgiving, encouraging words she knew Jyotsna would somehow convey some day to Krishna. Then awkwardly, begging Jyotsna's forgiveness, Amma took her leave.

"It is ghastly," complained Krishna "that I should have put you through this." Krishna couldn't express enough remorse for putting Jyotsna, the least blameworthy, through that painful ordeal. She imagined the scene that Jyotsna had described and plunged into grief. She was much comforted that Jyotsna showed no bitterness toward her and also proffered no judgments or opinions about her decision. Jyotsna looked around at Krishna's sparse quarters bemused. Never would she have imagined that this proper, obedient girl, this model daughter, this meticulous purist could have undertaken so bold and defiant a venture. Jyotsna wondered whether Krishna was really strong enough for all this. Had she truly considered the consequences? Had her upbringing ever exposed her to the indignities, the humiliations she was likely to bear as a single woman in a world fashioned by and for men? Jyotsna gently suggested, "Krishna, have you had the misimpression that the life I have been given has been comfortable or easy?" Krishna, cross legged on the floor, was taken aback by the question and looked up at Jyotsna puzzled. "I do hope," Jyotsna added, "that you hadn't modeled your path after me in any way. You know that our circumstances have been meaning-fully different. My parents perished when I was so young, and without brothers and sisters and only my grandmother to raise me, I had to contribute early to the family purse. Since she was a dancer, I learned her craft. Even if I had been arranged to marry, I would have had to work for my dowry, so I had no incen-tive. And I wanted to take care of my grandmother more than some demanding husband. You understand?" Krishna took the story as a mild warning, of what, she did not know. "I have had the luckiest of circumstances, Jyotsna, this I am grateful for. Only I have always feared that something in me could not live up to the expectations of my upbringing. This dancing I know I can and must do." Krishna said no more by way of explanation. Jyotsna felt some relief of exculpa-tion. Krishna inquired meekly, "Will you be terribly put upon if I ask you to keep bringing news of my family?" "It is no inconvenience," Jyotsna replied with empathy, "but I fear I will have little to offer. When Arna came last week to bring me your letters to return, I tried to convince him to make amends, but he was firm." Arna had showed up again at Jyotsna's unannounced, but had at least waited for her class to be over this time. Jyotsna thought she would hear an apol-ogy, but none came. She had not closed the door on Arna for Krishna's sake and had suffered being treated like a mere messenger when she tried to reason with him. Jyotsna continued, "Arna believes the only way to teach you a lesson is piti-less excommunication. No family member is to contact you and he said nobody in the community will be recruited to recover you." Jyotsna was sorrowful at delivering the tidings. Krishna, knowing this would be the pattern, was unmoved. Jyotsna remembered to add, "He said he would consider forgiveness only if you apologized personally and retracted your wayward path by quitting this university and coming home. He would, he said, still have to evaluate the sincerity of your repentance. But he assured me, just so you know, that he would entreat the Swami not to issue a formal excommunication." At least, Jyotsna was relieved, that would leave the door open to Krishna's contrition.

Krishna knew that through continued contact with Jyotsna she would at least be able to gather precious news of her parents' wellbeing. Jyotsna's class was larger this year than usual—a sign that Indians were paying attention to the need to restore their own heritage. So Jyotsna was much in demand in Bombay as else-where, and was pulling new students along. It was likely that the two would be able to meet up frequently. Krishna asked Jyotsna only one favor: that she deliver a letter to Sindhya at school so that Krishna could explain herself. Jyotsna agreed wholeheartedly. She saw no reason that so tender a heart as Sindhya's should be broken. Ten days later, as Sindhya was skidding home along the mucky road from school, struggling against the obstinacy of an inside-out bumbershoot, Jyotsna came running after her uncovered, barefoot and beaming, spattering broad and joyful bursts of mud with every footfall. It had been a long time since Sindhya had seen Jyotsna-aunty, and in the messy downpour of that windswept, muddy lane, urgent rivulets of water carving ever deeper lesions into the rich earth, it lit their hearts to behold each other. Jyotsna emphasized that Sindhya should keep this encounter and letter to herself, and promised to find Sindhya again when next she could.

September 12, 1940

My very dear Sindhya—

You must be very cross with me for staying away so long. If you feel hurt, you are right to be cross. A good sister would never want you to feel bad. A good sister would not leave you without saying goodbye. It is very important that you know that just because I have had to leave home, it does not mean that I do not love you. I love you very much. I think of you every day. I miss you very much. I wish only for good things for you. I pray for you. I wish that I could be with you. I remember your sweet face and it makes me gay, even when I am most sad.

You must wonder why, if I care about you so much, I am not home with you. I do not know what Amma and Arna have told you about why I have gone away. Whatever they have said, you must believe them. They must have told you that I have spoiled many plans and injured the people, like you, whom I love the most. I did not want you to get hurt, but I know that you must be. You might be very confused, because you have not done anything to me that should cause me to hurt you. Even I am hurt! It is very hard to be away from everybody who is so dear to me. I am often lonely. I miss home and I miss you.

It is difficult to explain why I cannot come home even though I miss it so much. I have disobeyed Amma and Arna, but I am not willing to change my decision. I have not done as they would wish for me and I have insulted the sangha by putting my will before theirs. You already know that this is not a good way to behave. The Vedas tell us that the gods do not favor those who do not do their duty. We must all fulfill our part in the community so that the world can continue to thrive. Even though I know this, I feel like I have another more important duty: a duty to dance. For me, it feels like dancing is the reason why I was given the blessing of life. Even if it takes me away from the people that I love. Even if it makes Arna very disappointed, I believe this is my part in the community.

When you are bigger perhaps you will understand, or Amma will be able to tell you more. For now, please do not behave like I have. Obey Amma and Arna. Be pleasing and respectful at home, in school, in temple and with everybody you meet. The Vedas say: make all that you do a sacrifice and you will have the grace of the gods. I know that Arna forbids you to write to me, so do not disobey him. I will send messages to you with Jyotsna-aunty, but I do not wish for you to be punished, so you must be careful with them. You must also know that even if you do not have word from me, you always remain my favorite and most pleasing thought.

Your ever loving akka.

October 20, 1940

My dear Krishna-akka:

I am not cross with you. I miss you all the time. Arna says I must forget you but I will not. So do not worry.

I have good marks at school. There is a new teacher. She is an old maid but she is not strict and she is Banap.

We have also a new bullock baby. Bunty. Bunty cannot pull the cart yet. I wished you had been here for when Bunty came out. He was funny.

I know Arna will not let you home but I think I will come to Bombay because M'am says I am almost big. He is sad too.

I said to Amma about your letter. She said it is our secret. She said I can write to you but she cannot. She says you understand. She says you know that she loves you even if she cannot write. Amma told me one more secret. She said one time Lord Krishna said Arjuna must make war with his own family because nobody really ever dies. It is more important to do our duty. Maybe you are like Arjuna. But it is not like a real war with killing people.

I have your pencil box now. Do not worry. I am keeping it for you.

With love from Sindhya

The Nadghars were surprised at how heartbroken their son was over the news. It had taken them such efforts to convince him to finally make a match, that they had gathered he was not entirely disposed to marriage. Now they found themselves having to console him that so unruly and strong-willed a wife would be a lifelong aggravation. "I never liked her in the first place!" Mrs. Nadghar recalled. Mr. Nadghar added, "And just think how the children would suffer with such a willful mother. Better to learn of her impropriety now than to uncover it once inexorably bound." The lad remained disconsolate for some days, dejected as much as humiliated, as such a unilateral withdrawal from the engagement cast suspicion on the character of the abandoned fiancé. What would the sangha say of him? His mother assured him "You are a worthy doctor now, and a prize to anybody. You are a credit to the community as well. You should have the pick of any girl you wish and not have to settle for a strumpet." His father chimed in, "Yes, you are old enough now, why don't we select your bride together?" This notion cheered him immensely. Something to look forward to.

The novelties of college life were Krishna's main distraction from the constant burden of guilt. She had never before sat in classes beside boys, and did not like the way they glared at her, scanning her shamelessly from head to toe, lascivious, brazen. She felt contaminated and shriveled under their unrelenting gaze, squirming like a salted leech. She resented that in their boisterous company, the academic confidence she used to know retreated into self consciousness and doubt. In the lecture hall, the boys' arms would bolt up, eager to answer a professor's query. Rarely did the girls raise their hands, and seldom were they called upon if they did. Erroneous answers from girls stirred cackling and snickering from the boys, behavior the jaded professors did nothing to control. There was some respite in the classes of lady professors, where the boys were compelled to show a modicum of restraint. Krishna learned to contain her cleverness in class, startling her lecturers at exam time. They might have reviewed her written work more skeptically had her name betrayed her gender—had they even known who she was. To spare her parents' good name, she shortened it to "Nayam" for the purposes of all non-legal documents. It was, she resolved, the least she could do.

There were six other *Bhanaps* in Krishna's entering class, all boys, and (thankfully) none from her *gotra*. She learned this only by recognizing their surnames at roll calls. She imagined that they would have recognized her name as well, wondering what must have befallen her when by now she should be married. Perhaps they would have surmised she was barren. Krishna kept away from them as much as all others of their species. She took care to choose seats next to girls in class. Preferably plain, studious ones in simple saris or unembroidered *salwar kameez;*

ones that looked familiar from the women's dormitory, or ones that reminded her of somebody from home. Only a handful were Brahmin, and at first she gravitated toward them, though Krishna no longer knew if she deserved the designation. Over time she found that dark or fair, slim or hefty, Muslim or Hindu, the other girls in the hostel were consistently bright and determined, and despite the competitive environment, forged a cautious camaraderie, a muted alliance founded on what they did not realize was their common alienation. Krishna soon determined to shy away from companionships. It eventually led to her having to tell her shameful tale, so in time she opted for anonymity and relative solitude. Still, she could not help but be fascinated by the other women. Those Krishna liked best came from farthest away and spoke nothing in common with her (neither Konkani, Maharathi nor Kanadda) but an English accented heavily by their own language. She queried the Northerners ceaselessly on the subject of snow: how to protect from it, whether it hurt one as it fell, how to walk through it in a sari, and what to wear on ones' feet. She was incredulous at the number of girls who claimed their families supported them entirely in their quest for education even at the expense of marriage. Some of them were studying to be physicists or even medical doctors, believing sincerely that it was just as much their right and responsibility to pursue a higher education as it was that of a man. Krishna inclined her ear on occasion to listen through the thin walls of her room to the small band of Gujarati girls who would gather, giggling next door, trading gossip and singing heartful songs in unison, their voices quivering with nostalgia. Incomprehensible words carried to Krishna over unfamiliar tunes the sweet solace of shared wistfulness, a borrowed consolation. Krishna sang no Konkani songs to herself. They rendered her unproductive, distracted her from her schoolwork, and took her to times and places she deemed best not to revisit.

Krishna's dance appearances grew increasingly demanding over her years at college. Her initial university-sponsored performances at several Bombay venues drew considerable attention and substantial crowds. The fundraisers and benefits at which Krishna was showcased earned the university both income and unexpected kudos for, as the student paper put it, "it was high time that educational institutions began fostering the lost culture by sponsoring the education of such talented propagators of the classical arts while enabling the artists to share their talents." Indian nationalist fervor spurred by Mahatma Gandhi's increased influence in all matters social and political converged in a timely fashion with Krishna's personal ambitions. In the center of Bombay, in a university setting where so many resources were available, she read the nationalist papers avidly and stood, half concealed by her draping *dupatta*, timidly at the back of the student-sponsored lectures and teach-ins on the Quit India movement. Something about the passion of the speakers made Krishna nervous. They professed commitment to unimaginable changes: integration of the untouchable caste into the main-stream; redistricting of the States to fit cultural and linguistic norms, not for the convenience of British economic aims; free and universal education to the univer-sity level—even for women. Krishna's veins throbbed with fury at hearing how the British empire had robbed India and other colonies of their god-given resources and misused their native populations, even exploiting the caste system for its own material gains. Her heart thumped with joy at the promise of an India free from English control. Her throat clenched to learn of the imprisonment and detainment of Gandhiji at the Aga Khan's palace and his sacrificial episodes of fasting to protest British rule. In a show of solidarity, Krishna added another day of fast to her week; one for the gods, her ancestors, her family, and the teachings passed down, and one dedicated entirely to the movement. She persisted in fast-ing even on performance days (a weak body, it was emphasized, was borne mainly of a weak will.) The small shelf that served as her dorm-room shrine, crowded with statues of Vishnu, Shiva, and Ganesh, and a small, garlanded photograph of Shrimat Anandashrama Swamiji now, like several other shrines throughout the country, included a picture of Gandhiji as well. As there was no *Bhanap* temple she felt comfortable attending, she fashioned her own rituals at home, reading the *Vedas* daily for reassurance and inspiration.

Jyotsna never failed to marvel at how much Krishna changed from one visit to the next. Her confidence had surely grown along with her education. She no longer restrained her opinions, though she delivered them in the apologetic tone of somebody overstepping her boundaries. And Krishna's dancing had trans-formed so there was defiance in it. She never worried any longer about remem-bering a step. They fell in place unbidden, unsolicited, unencumbered. She began each performance now with a silent meditation, dedicating her dance to her par-ents and beseeching Ganesh to remove obstacles to the cause. The resulting moves were grander, stronger, nearly acrobatic. In the growing circle of connois-seurs, Krishna became known for movements so brisk yet so expansive, they defied the probabilities of metered time and limited space. She would catapult dramatically across the stage in perfect form, just short of bursting through the confines of *Bharatanatyam* tradition, her bells snapping promptly to an unforgiv-ing beat. Some in the audience marveled, others tutted disapproval. Jyotsna lav-ished in Krishna's glory. Bala frowned with disappointment, "Her pride has grown, not diminished. What good is that for whom?" Still, it was undeniable, her *abhinaya* was moving, fulsome and sincere. No longer girlish but sumptuously womanly in form, Krishna was breathtaking on stage. A dazzling, powerful beauty came streaming through her, no longer compromised or tentative. Though she rarely rode on rapture in performance the way she sometimes had, now Krishna felt incorruptible when she danced. She felt whole on stage, pure, unblemished, intact.

Messages from Sindhya were still passed through Jyotsna, who remained ever obliging in filling Krishna with any news she could gather about the family. For Shaku and Rahul's son, Amma had, much to Arna's consternation, chosen the name "Aniruddha"—the manifestation of Lord Krishna as the One Who Cannot be Obstructed. Krishna's eyes twinkled at learning this. She took it as a small act of subversion and support on the part of her mother. Even if it was unintended, she liked to think that naming her nephew after such a powerful form of Lord Krishna was a small allusion to her. Sindhya had risen to the top of her class at school, and was already promised to a medical student, though not from nearby. Arna, thinking far ahead as a responsible father should, had purposely written to *Bhanap sanghas* far away soliciting correspondence from interested parties. This reduced the likelihood of the parents hearing of Krishna's vagaries from any source but himself, who could portray the situation in a more palatable fashion, without casting doubt on the manner of his children's upbringing. Krishna understood Arna's reasoning. If he were to seek a groom from a nearby village, Sindhya was likely only to be accepted, under the circumstances, to a widower or someone meaningfully older than she. Arna would sacrifice the proximity of his daughter in favor of her contentment. Sindhya's fiancé, of the Nayel family, lived in Calcutta, 1500 kilometers from Mangalore. Once she was married, Sindhya would likely move away and rarely see her family. Krishna recognized that her insubordination brought consequences far beyond what she had foreseen.

Krishna increased her course-load. Her inclination toward precision became a compunction to perfectionism. She read all assignments twice, and redrafted her papers in so meticulous a handwriting, it was hardly distinguishable from print. She began a routine of awaking at 4 a.m. to pray, meditate and study before classes, spent all day at lectures or the library, and didn't allow herself sleep until midnight. She ate infrequently, sparingly, punishing herself by remaining always slightly hungry. She agreed to every invitation to dance, irrespective of her work-load, another form of penance. She minimized interaction with all others at the hostel, opting for a solitary confinement. The girls began to view her as snobbish and unfriendly, putting on airs now that her dancing was so well known on campus. Her professors in the math department began calling on her for unembellished, clear responses after disappointing replies from the boys. She was infallible. "But can she cook?" a fellow would shout from the back of the room, rousing rounds of muffled laughter. Instead of averting her eyes in shame anymore, she learned to stare down the boys in class or in the hallways, wordlessly attacking their lewd advances with glares so venomous, the boys cowed, turning on their heels and scampering off in the most expedient direction.

One September morning Krishna noticed it was light out by the time she awoke. A weariness lay heavy on her shoulders. She must have overdone it at last night's performance. She looked at herself in her small hand mirror, noting that her face seemed gaunt, almost green. She relegated it to the quality of light and remembered that there would be another performance tonight—at the Alumni club. She was running late already and the day had not yet begun. She scurried to her duties, ignoring a vague nausea and unshakeable fatigue. Dressing at the Alumni Club, for all she tried, Krishna could not manage to fasten the backing to her earring. Her frustration intensified as she twirled the trinket in vain, twisting it at every possible angle, this way and that, repositioning it repeatedly between uncooperative fingers trying to meet the grooves it was meant to catch. Her hands were shaking now, tensed and desperate, she nicked her ear with the shorn rim of the golden backing, sprouting a single drop of blood which skipped down her finger, settling against a glimmering bangle. Krishna stopped her struggle. She blinked down at her wrist, still holding the earring back between her fingers. A tear met the spot of red blood at her bangle, then another. Krishna breathed in deeply. An obstinate earring was not going to reduce her to tears right before a performance. She sopped the blood and tears with the edge of her costume, wiped a hand carefully across a cheek so as not to rub off the kohl around her eyes, and closed them, choking back whatever else might try to escape. "Pray," she insisted. Krishna prayed for strength and forgiveness. She asked blessings on her family and on Gandhiji. She offered her dance to the gods. She calmly affixed her earrings.

Minutes later, in the wood-paneled Common Room of the Alumni Club, before a crowd of 150 distinguished gentlemen and the Chancellor who always introduced Krishna as "our own treasure and my personal discovery," the jingle bells around Krishna's right ankle came unlatched as she was dancing. The leather strap studded with bells dropped off her foot and in her next motion her right heel landed hard upon it, stinging sharp through her tendons. She skidded on her own bells, twisting her ankle and etching a jagged gash into the waxed teak floor of the social pavilion. She landed with a thud on her side, her head at the knees of a stunned musician cross-legged on the floor. The music stopped. The crowd waited for her to rise. Krishna remained on the floor, clutching her ankle, heaving great sobs and wailing louder, she knew, than the pain in her foot justified. "Is there a doctor in the house?" cried the Chancellor, taking command. There were twelve.

"No Miss, it is not the ankle that has kept her here so long," explained the tidy, diminutive nurse to the fidgeting Jyotsna, who stood distressed at the foot of Krishna's bed, "the healing is complicated by the malaria. Her fever hasn't broken. We continue to dispense quinine, but her temperature remains too high." Jyotsna repeated her original question more pressingly; "But the ankle, is it broken? Can she walk on it? Can she dance?" Unfazed by Jyotsna's pleading tone, the nurse flipped efficiently through the papers on her clipboard, scanned the scribblings over her half-glasses, then pronounced, "Miss, it is not possible to tell. The x-ray indicates fractures to both the calcaneus and talus. For now, the foot is immobilized and the pain is almost certainly quite grave, but because the patient is so non-responsive, we cannot determine the extent of it. It is feared that the foot will not bear weight for some time." Jyotsna absorbed the implications of the news. She had no idea what a calcaneus or a talus were, but she needed only hear "fracture" and "no bearing weight" to understand that Krishna was not likely to get up and dance. And what of her scholarship? What of her studies? She would surely miss the remaining semester. What of her exams? A small group of students followed a doctor into the infirmary, pausing at the bed beside Krishna's. "You may remain here another half hour, Miss," the nurse reminded Jyotsna, "it is not likely, however, that the patient will awake. She has episodes of delirium—entirely normal under the circumstances—when she shifts and speaks, but her language is garbled and nonsensical, even in her native tongue. Good day." Jyotsna watched quietly as the nurse hung Krishna's chart at the foot of her metal cot and moved stealthily around the rolling trays and carts to the bed of the girl next door, also sound asleep.

A cluster of lab-coated medical students approached and the doctor leading them politely inquired of Jyotsna in a whisper "You are a family member, Miss?" "No," replied Jyotsna absent-mindedly, then correcting herself, "well yes, an auntie. But not a blood relative, no." "Would you mind, Miss, if the students and I discuss the patient?" he continued, posing the question that really concerned him, more affable than the nurse who preceded him. "Not at all," Jyotsna offered, "please, as you wish." She moved around the bed, closer to Krishna, who lay limp with shallow breath and sweat on her brow. Somebody had taken care to plait her hair into two neat braids which rested beside her ears, long to her elbows, limp at her sides. The braids made her look younger, like the girl Jyotsna had known at nine or ten years of age. But her face was gaunt now, not fair but pale, her cheeks and eyes hollowed. Though still so young and vibrant she now seemed to Jyotsna a portrait of deflated youth. Jyotsna kicked herself for not requiring Krishna to take better care of herself when they had last met. Jyotsna had noticed how Krishna's blouses were hanging off her and had only commented that she had become so devoted to her studies she must not have made time to eat. It had not occurred to Jyotsna that Krishna may have already been ill. Standing there, Jyotsna made out what she could understand from the doctor's explanation to the students, observed as he sought a pulse and as he questioned students on likely treatments.

The Chancellor had been obligated to inform the family of the accident. Jyotsna wondered, as she stood observing her little ward, how it was possible that Arna and Amma could keep away under the circumstances. This was more of Arna's stubbornness, she was sure, still trying to teach Krishna a lesson by leaving her alone in her illness and surely ignoring Amma's pleas on Krishna's behalf. Jyotsna had learned of the telegram from Sindhya, but only a week after it arrived. "KRISHNA NAYAM ADMITTED COLLEGE INFIRMARY. ADVANCED MALARIAL & FOOT FRACTURE. PAYMENT REQUIRED FOR TREATMENT. PLS REPLY OFC OF CHANCELLOR." Sindhya had sent a letter along with Jyotsna, who caught the next train to Bombay upon learning the news. Jyotsna remembered the letter now, rifled through her purse to find it and slipped it under Krishna's flat, insufficient pillow. "It's from her sister," she informed the onlookers, "for when she wakes up." The doctor jumped to boost Jyotsna, "The patients' strength is coming back slowly. It is only a matter of time. Her fever reduces only slightly every day, but one notes a steady improvement. No fears, Madam. One is able to treat malaria quite well." Jyotsna appreciated the encouragement. She stroked Krishna's forehead tenderly, cautiously, felt the clammy, glistening skin and wondered "What of her now?" Resolving to do something, anything, Jyotsna collected her belongings, bowed a quick *namaste* at the small band of white-coats, and headed for the Office of the Chancellor.

For twelve days and nights Krishna lived in her dreams. She was a twittering, purple sunbird being fed and tended by *M'am* and Sindhya till she got her chirping fill. She flapped madly in the cramped nest, striving to take wing, then sprang one day and fluttered, ecstatic into the courtyard, skittering to the edge of the well. She floated higher on a current, circled like a bride around the fire three times over the main house; then soared over the granary, past the cashew plantations and the canals of Mangalore, crossing the swollen banks of the Gurupur river and out to the shimmering, turquoise ocean. She landed on the wooden rim of a Chinese fishing net rising out of the water heavy with doomed, flopping fish, their slick silverblue scales already relinquishing iridescence, their gills puffing in desperation. She mourned there as the net ascended, then sprang from it to soar back to the land where on a flimsy papaya tree she pecked at the tender fruit, hopped curiously from branch to lush, green branch, then fled again, this time higher, past orange desserts and crystalline lakes and golden fields shimmering from the heat. She felt the sun on her wings and squinted into it, relishing the freedom of her flight. In her feathery form she didn't have to try, she didn't have to struggle, she had no duties, no worries, no rituals to perform. She was carried on the wind and land wherever she may, the bounteous earth sustained her. She flew even further, to mountain tops cascading with snow and alighted, shivering, on their glimmering peaks, enjoying a softer landing than ever she expected. Even from that distance, something called Krishna home. When ready to return, she knew she'd find her way.

In the richness of her dreams, the Bhagavad Gita came alive. Krishna sat on the chariot of Arjuna pulled by four bucking horses, laden with the golden crown of royalty, equipped with quiver and crossbow and a breastplate of gleaming brass. She was Arjuna the troubled, the blue Lord Krishna on the chariot at her side. Arjuna was torn between duty to his calling and love of his kinsmen, who opposed him in battle. In her dreams, as Arjuna, Krishna saw her own family across the battlefield and grieved. She did not wish to harm them: not for sovereignty over the three worlds nor for victory in battle. Helpless, heart and mind divided, she heard the words of Lord Krishna reverberate through her in response. Fixing her mind only on her duty, executing her responsibilities with pure devotion to God, she would be absolved from her transgressions. After all, Lord Krishna explained, death is *maya*—a mere illusion in the material world. Trusting this, Arjuna should not fear to do his duty in fighting, as none of his kinsmen could really be rubbed out. To do one's duty in service and devotion to god, setting aside pride and worry in favor of shear surrender would absolve Arjuna of all sins. There should be no need to grieve, Lord Krishna comforted Arjuna, as nothing would truly ever be lost.

The intervals lengthened between bouts of fever. A blush of color returned to Krishna's face. She did not remember her dreams or visions. At first light one morning, as the portly nurse on duty took her temperature, Krishna stirred and squinted her eyes at the crisp brightness of the white ward. Through the filmy curtain across the room she could see out the window the verdant branches of a magnolia tree fluttering in the breeze, rapping against the pane. It was not raining anymore. She knew not where she was nor could she remember getting there. Her belly gnawed at her. She blinked softly at the nurse, recognized the setting as a hospital, thought it must be a day or two since she slipped and suddenly became flushed with embarrassment. The nurse greeted her pleasantly, "How is our sleeping beauty? Tired? Hungry? Any pain?" Krishna attempted a reply, a reedy voice piped out, "Hungry please." Then added, "My foot…aches." The nurse smiled down at Krishna, concentrated on taking a pulse, "You've managed a broken foot. It's immobilized in a cast. See?" She lifted the gauzy sheet below to expose the trapped ankle, colorless toes poking out behind the jagged edge of a glossy cast. "I'll fetch the doctor and something for you to eat. Veg?" Krishna nodded, tried to lift herself on her elbows and too feeble to rise, crumpled back onto her pillow. Then, alarmed, she noticed the tubes and needles latched to her arm, and winced. "Not too much movement, yet, *atcha*?" warned the nurse in a whisper, "You've only just woken. Rest. When I bring the food, I will help you up." Pressing Krishna's arm with a look of reassurance, the nurse jostled past the equipment obstructing her, and waddled laboriously through the double-doors that swung, creaking behind her.

Parched, lightheaded, and listless, Krishna couldn't muster the strength to do more than scan her cavernous quarters. Girls lay sleeping on cots to either side. Unable to count her companions, she listened for the sounds of their breathing identifying two fulsome another two labored, and wondered what ailed them. Her foot throbbed. Burbling plastic tubes, steely clamps, whirring gauges and starchy linens seemed to stretch from one end of the elongated ward clear to the faraway other. Too weak to shift her uncomfortable position, she stared up at the stark, white ceiling, knowing now that the gods had rendered their judgment and punished her for her defiance. A broken foot would obviate her scholarship and her earning potential, leaving her without option but to return home. Such punishment would not have been meted had she identified her yearnings as pride and surrendered to the duty of marriage. Amma would surely be merciful. If Arna forgave her, the penance would be severe. There would be no possibility of marriage now, a shame she could not imagine bringing upon her family's good name, nor one she imagined that she herself could endure. A loneliness overcame her unlike anything she had felt before. It was a stark and desperate isolation. A knowledge that she was connected to nothing and nobody with no possibility of relief. It mingled with the searing sting of shame. Krishna began to shiver. The dark hollow in her belly expanded over her, eclipsing any spark of hope. Too terrified to weep her sorrow, too frail to moan her frustration, she sobbed hard and trembled fitfully like a papery leaf quivers on its branch at the whim of the monsoon winds.

The brisk clop of the stocky doctors' feet did not lift Krishna from this abyss. He noticed instantly the horror in her eyes and rushed to reassure her with a compassion she never expected from men. "Nothing to fear," he comforted, in sing-song English, his kind eyes melting at the helplessness before him, "worst is done, child. Fever is fully broken!" he assured, widening his eyes as if to a toddler, wobbling his head in enthusiastic encouragement. "Only must take good, long rest and eat. No run around. How lucky! Only two weeks for malaria be gone! You strong girl. Very very much resistant!" he added, taking a pulse which he noted differed drastically from the one just recorded by the nurse. "Worst is done" thought Krishna unconsoled. He didn't know the half of it. Sindhya's letter was a welcome relief.

October 1, 1943

My Dear Akka—

We all know what has happened and we are very worried. No matter how much we plead, Arna forbids us all from coming. He says he does not wish you ill. He says that only in seclusion will you consider why such calamity should come to pass. But you should not be lonely, Akka. Amma and I and even Deepa, Sandhya and Shaku are praying for you every day and thinking of you much. Rahul-dada brings news of you from his friend at the medical college. He learns of your progress from the nurses. I have even an article about you from Jyotsna! We know how the quinine is given you in the arm. They say even your food goes in your arm, but this I do not understand. How then, does it get in the stomach? Yet we pray and so are certain of your full recovery in a short time.

You must be very sad about your ankle. I am sad for it too. Arna says its time to heal is your time to atone. Everything happens just as it should. But Akka, I think it will heal nicely because you are meant to be a dancer just like birds are meant to fly. Last year *M'am* and I sealed a wing back on its bird and only weeks later, away it flew. So why not you also? You once wrote to me that dancing is your duty. Even after a broken ankle, it will still be your duty, isn't it so?

Akka, please take heart. Jyotsna-aunty says she will find some way for the University to keep you. Please do not worry. Have faith. I think of you often and pray for you always.

Your loving, Sindhya

#

While in town, Jyotsa wasted no time in anguish at Krishna's bedside. Her faith was buoyed by her instinctive resourcefulness. She was satisfied when informed by the ever gracious Chancellor that Krishna's medical bills were being covered by an anonymous donor. Jyotsna never doubted divine providence. She relied on it, as a matter of fact. She asked no questions and theorized that one of the many wealthy hosts for whom Krishna had danced over the years was surely to thank. For all she knew, Krishna might even have suitors amongst her class-mates.

The Chancellor was an ambitious, efficient administrator used to getting his way and easily perturbed by hindrances. He had counted on income from Krishna's good work. Without her, he had complications. He disliked confronta-tion and had a penchant for making things work. He hated to issue bad news, which he strategically delivered after the good. When Jyotsna appeared in his offices, he was warm and welcoming despite being troubled by his duties. Know-ing it would be unpleasant, he could have claimed to be busy, but did not. When his secretary let Jyotsna in, the Chancellor practically threw himself across the table to take both her hands in his, eclipsing the formal *namaste* that she had begun to bow. "It is always such a pleasure, Jyotsna-bai…" he enthused, "How many years have you been donating your performances for us now? You do know, we will need to call upon you or one of your students to fill in for our Krishna, I'm sure." Jyotsna didn't miss a beat, although the Chancellor's heartful greetings so charmed her, she strained to remain businesslike. "As a matter of fact, I am here precisely to learn what is to happen to Krishna now that she is injured." The Chancellor hung his head promptly, and spoke sincerely and apol-ogetically, "I fear that Krishna's scholarship must be withdrawn if Krishna is unable perform at fundraisers. You know the terms of the scholarship. I am try-ing my very best, I assure you, but I am not optimistic that the Board will accede to my wishes." The Chancellor liked Jyotsna's feistiness, but did not expect to be victim to it. Jyotsna assessed his words and responded, "With all due respect, may I request that the Board consider an accounting of how much Krishna's events have accumulated for the University, so that they can review the matter from a balanced perspective?" The Chancellor winked at Jyotsna, "You are a clever lady," he complimented, "but that is not the issue. Regrettably, the income from the fundraisers has already been allocated." Jyotsna, irritated, shot back, "So you will do nothing to help? You will simply throw your hands up? The girl has nowhere to turn! She has poured her sweat into fundraising for your university and this is the thanks she gets!" The Chancellor did not like Jyotsna's tone and defended himself. "I am not throwing up my hands. I have put out inquiries as to what can be done. But you are aware this is not my only responsibility. I have a university to run and several priorities requiring attention." He strode back behind his desk, ringing his hands, and sunk into his chair adding, "You are an uncommonly smart woman, you surely understand the economics of the matter?" Jyotsna was not persuaded, and would not be distracted by flattery. She reminded the Chancellor of the sacrifices Krishna had made to earn an education, forsaking long-standing tradition and incurring the wrath of her family. For drama, Jyotsna added that this strictly Brahmin-raised girl lived in daily fear of a formal excommunication by her Swami. Fretting now, and clearly pained at having agitated Jyotsna, the Chancellor leaned forward in his seat to emphasize his concern, "The Board relies on Krishna's continued service, without it, there is no justification for the scholarship. Still, you must believe that I am doing my level best to fund her education. There are only three semesters left! But be clear that it is neither my responsibility nor appropriate for me to put in such effort, as it appears like favoritism amongst the student body." Jyotsna believed the Chancellor and understood his predicament, but she crossed her arms and eyed the Chancellor skeptically, remaining mum like a slighted child. The Chancellor, in his most avuncular tone, urged patience on Jyotsna's part, since anyway, as long as Krishna was hospitalized, she was unable to continue her coursework. "Patience is all you have to offer us?" Jyotsna repeated exasperated. She thrust her chin out at the Chancellor, turned on her heal and stomped out of the office in a huff. The Chancellor couldn't help but be left with a bemused smile.

Despite her faith, Jyotsna knew from experience that the gods operated in divine conceptions of time. She resolved that her faith might be augmented by a little human intervention for the purposes of expediency. She found her way to the university newspaper to mention the matter to its editor. Shuffling through stacks of recent issues tilting precariously near collapse in his disheveled office, the compact, distracted editor assured Jyotsna that the paper had, upon learning of Krishna's fall, immediately printed an article about the accident highlighting the jeopardized career of a dancer in full bloom. "Blow Befalls Bharatanatyam Belle," he read aloud upon identifying the proper issue, pointing at the headline and grinning proudly at the subtle pun in the choice of verb. Jyotsna, in a most conspiratorial tone, intimated the concern over the retracted scholarship, something the paper had entirely overlooked. The editor tugged at his waistcoat as though readying for a performance, and rubbed his hands together in preparation. The scholarship matter added just the kind of controversy he relished in a follow-up piece. The Chancellor, who soon learned of the imminent printing of a disparaging article about how the university was prepared to sacrifice the education of a talented student despite her having earned multifold times her fees in favor of the coffers of the institution, took extraordinary measures to prevent its publication.

Jyotsna withstood courageously the tongue lashing she received from the Chancellor at the front steps of the infirmary a few days later. She had indeed shown little faith in his assurances, he reprimanded. "We have known each other so long, and you undermine me like this? Willing to embarrass me before giving me the opportunity to thoroughly investigate alternatives in good time after I assured you I was doing my best?" Jyotsna hid her smirk behind the veil her sari made when draped over her head. "Good sir," she replied astutely, suppressing inevitable smugness, "I never doubted your own willingness to advocate on Krishna's behalf, only the board's resolve to respond to your pleas without solid incentive to do so—especially considering that the girl is, after all, a girl." "Women!" the Chancellor, retorted irritated, "with you, well enough is never left alone!" The Chancellor continued his tetchy, determined march up the steps whereupon reaching the doors, he couldn't help but revert to his habitual gallantry, and opened them with a flourish and bow to usher Jyotsna in before him in exaggerated English fashion. He beamed as she breezed by and then overtook her right away so as not to be seen to be walking behind. Doctors stopped short their activities to wish the Chancellor good day as he passed; nurses and students scattered, tittering over his unusual appearance at the infirmary accompanied by a woman, and Jyotsna abandoned her customary elegance to keep pace with the Chancellor's scurried stride. He was a good man, she thought to herself, if a tad self-important. She was a well meaning woman, he assessed, if a little wily.

"I will simply not," announced the Chancellor, feigning severity, a twinkle in his eye, "permit any student of this university such indiscrete blubbering at the receipt of what cannot be mistaken for anything but excellent news." The Chancellor had appeared at the infirmary to personally inform the distraught Krishna that her ankle would not be an obstacle to her completing her Bachelor's degree. Her own admirable performance in her mathematics courses had enabled the department to award her a scholarship on the condition that henceforth, her coursework be concentrated in Statistics and Mathematics, and that she maintain the standards expected. "I am ever so grateful," Krishna managed between self-conscious tears, her bedmates cowering under their sheets, astonished to find the Chancellor at the foot of her bed while they lay in disheveled indecency. The Chancellor scanned the room, then commented loudly to the nurses hovering nearby, "Have we so many sick young ladies at the infirmary? Is this something we can attribute to the season or should one take the matter up with the cooks at the ladies' cafeteria?" The appreciative crowd giggled, as did Jyotsna, puffed up with pride on the Chancellor's behalf. "Well then," he concluded, "I wish you all a very speedy recovery and expect no news of the kinds of pranks we must contend with in the boys' ward, yes?" The handful of young ladies sheepishly nodded their consent, donning proper, cheerful faces despite the shame of syphilis, the agonies of dysentery, the dread of nephritis, the doom of a hysterectomy, and the comparatively meaningless disappointment of a dancer's dream spoiled by a twist of fate.

Slowly, Krishna healed, urged by Jyotsna to put *Bharatanatyam* from her mind for the meantime and focus on the good fortune of this second chance. For some time, she mourned and remained miserable. She missed the dancing, the way she had come to feel so easy in it, the appreciative crowds. But forced to concentrate on the load of her new classes, and relieved of the extracurricular burdens of dance, she put greater effort into acquaintance with her classmates. She made good friends with Padma, a plain and kindly girl whose infirmary bed had been next to Krishna's and had spent much of her convalescence sheltered behind the barriers of thick novels, which landed on her forehead with a soft thwack every time she dozed off. With Padma, Krishna shared an interest in strange and faraway places like the ones they glimpsed together at the picture shows. Padma's hysterectomy had rendered her unmarriageable, a disgrace she shared only with Krishna, who felt the stigma of Padma's circumstances in the context of her own.

Krishna's ankle recuperated well enough to dance, but not to Krishna's own standards. She tried, once or twice, in the privacy of her dormitory, to test out the most challenging moves, but writhed in pain and found that she couldn't meet her former speed. There was no point in trying to dance *Bharatanatyam*, if she couldn't execute it perfectly. The gods were meant to be pleased, not insulted. Perhaps, Krishna shared with Padma one night as they sat together lamenting their fates, "the gods hoped to drive the pride from me by keeping me from my passion." Padma understood. She also sensed her lot was some sort of punishment. They wished to find a way to serve their country anyway, as Gandhi would advise. "But how does one serve anybody on earth with statistics?" Krishna wondered aloud. "A teacher? An accountant?" Padma joshed, "A lady cleric wearing a smock in some government office with an inkpad and a blotter, and a small wooden box armed with variously sized rubber stamps?" The girls laughed. No, it wouldn't do. Over the last months in college, no clear future appeared to them, but without having to dance, Krishna managed to devoted more energy to the campus movement for Indian self rule. Over time, she renewed her adoration for the precision of math.

For Krishna, math had its own, neat rewards. She liked its challenges and its tidy solutions; the way everything always worked out at the end. She especially liked the way the problems proposed often began with "Let X be..." She was attracted to the notion of letting things be. Having failed in her duty to her parents, having accepted the punishment of being unable to dance, Krishna took up her new vocation if not with enthusiasm, at least with gracious resignation. Her sorrow over dancing came through in a renewed, more vigorous humility; prayers that asked nothing for herself of the gods, a tendency to work diligently and then discredit herself for the fruit of her labors. Padma admitted to Krishna one day that she dreaded graduation. "Imagine," she said in earnest to her friend, "having to go home like this; as I am, I only add to my father's burdens." Krishna understood, returning home now would hold no comfort for her either. Even if she were taken back, she would always feel shameful in the presence of those she had damaged. She consoled Padma, "At least your deficiencies are not of your own making. I have failed at dancing after choosing to fail my parents, imagine how much more deficient that makes me?" Krishna chose a path that might distance her from those feelings.

September 15, 1945

My Very Dear Arna and Amma:

I would like nothing more than to deliver this letter in person, if only for the honor of beholding you again. I understand that you have no wish to see me, as well you should not. You have returned my prior letters in which I beg your forgiveness. I understand why, under the circumstances, you cannot grant it. I can only hope that the world never visits upon me a daughter such as I have been to you. I know you will garner from your other fine children, and the grandchildren who are so fortunate to have you, all that is lost in me.

This is only to inform you, for if you worry still about me I wish not to burden you in this way, that I have been granted and accepted a further scholarship for completion of the Masters degree that I began last year in Bombay. The scholarship will allow me to finish my Economics degree at the London School of Economics, which is in England. In preparation for independence, The National Government is sponsoring a few students to pursue studies in key fields. The scholarship will supply for me all funds for travel, lodging, meals, and tuition. I have chosen a subject of study that can only be researched abroad, as it is in England that all the meaningful economic records for India have been maintained over the last century. Because my written thesis will address some of the economic impact of the British occupation of India, the government has been generous in granting me this funding. I never forget, however, that it is your generosity that granted me wellbeing for so many years of my life.

I must congratulate you and wish you the happiest returns on the marriage of Sindhya. I have learned of the event from Jyotsna and carry a guilty conscience for the strains my derelictions caused in finding Sindhya a befitting groom. No words can express my sorrow at the distance my actions put between her and you. I know that everybody suffers for it. I can assure you that even I do. You must know that I am no longer dancing. My pride took away everything I love: my dancing, and even you. But it hurts me most that it also took away your own Sindhya, who deserves your love so much more than I. I will never be able to make up for these losses. I only ask you to know that I am as deeply sorry for them as it is possible to be.

I miss you terribly. I will miss you no less when further away. Jyotsna always will know how to reach me. Please do not imagine ever that my staying away is to avoid you. It is only to protect you from the harm I know I have done, and to free you from the burden of an unmarried, over-proud daughter. I am afraid it is my burden too.

I pray for your health, your happiness and the blessings upon you of all the gods. Please give my love and best wishes for health and happiness to all my brothers and sisters who I miss so much. With your blessings, they will surely make you proud in ways I never could.

Your ever loving,

Krishna

Swathed in her fanciest sari and open toed sandals, carrying a single suitcase in one hand and her green, leather-bound passport issued only last week in the other, a nervous Krishna stepped onto the rickety, carpeted gangplank leading to a vast, white ocean liner. Smartly-dressed greeters pinned with labels reading "Peninsular & Oriental Navigation," ushered her in with tight smiles. On the pitch below her, as was Indian custom, families embraced departing members, garlanded them with sweet jasmines and blessed them with colored powders. Mothers blubbered over departing sons, parents blew kisses at joyous honeymooners, sniffling wives stifling emotion waved polite embroidered handkerchiefs at traveling husbands. Nobody but the rickshaw-walla saw Krishna off. She drew a breath at the top landing gazing down at the green water of the bay slapping against the sides of the vessel. She wondered how it was that the boat didn't rock. She gazed wistfully at the sentiment issuing from families, distraught or elated, at the dock. She wished desperately for that sort of love, but knew she didn't deserve it. She gulped hard, steeled herself, remembering the first time she performed on a stage, drew a deep breath and stepped confidently onto the ship. Once again, Krishna left home alone.

In the *Varnam* the solo dancer must tell a story with the movements of her body and the expressiveness of her face and hands. She is expected to portray the lyrical, dramatic and emotional content of a tale. Testing skill, stamina and expressiveness, the chosen story enables the dancer to intermingle a series of demanding dance sequences with a show of emotions. It is meant to exhibit the dancer's capacity for both *nritta* (pure dance) and *abhinaya* (feeling).

#

8

The rooms at Cartwright Gardens, despite their plumbing and electrical curiosities, turned out to be far superior to Krishna's quarters in Bombay. Krishna had braced herself for what the newspapers reported was the "post-War squalor" of inner London. She found nothing of the sort. In her eyes, London was clean and orderly, just the way she remembered the colony at Fort St. George. Compared to the chaos of Bombay, Krishna liked the efficiency of London, its crispness and formality. She liked the way the buses ran on time and the drivers apologized for arriving late. She liked the way the Bobbies, black helmets fixed comically on their heads, stood erect at their stations issuing curt nods in greeting to passers by. She liked the smartly trimmed hedges and the reliable sameness of the grey brick townhouses (black grilles on the windows, and ledges painted in identical white) arranged in the tidy semi-circle that formed what she now called "her" block. Across the street, the crescent-shaped garden under Krishna's dormitory room was neatly rimmed with wrought-iron fencing, each black spoke capped with a brilliant golden spearhead. Ever since she'd spotted the statue of John Cartwright (1740-1824) whose commemorative plaque claimed he was a proponent of universal suffrage and in favor of the independence of the United States of America, Krishna loved the tiny greens of Cartwright Garden best, better even than the more opulent Russell Square nearby.

A number of foreign students, many in the Colonial Studies Programme, were also housed at the Cartwright lodgings, which was comforting to Krishna too. She was surrounded by students as different from each other as from the majority English population at LSE. She noticed that the socialist inclinations of the university came through in its student body and even its staff. Never had she seen so many women in an administration. The refectory even accommodated the eating regimens of the universities' diverse populace, something Krishna would never have imagined. Still, Krishna was especially delighted to have access to a small kitchen at the lodgings, enabling her to maintain her vegetarian diet—though she was expected to dine with her fellow graduate students in the refectory, as her scholarship included meals.

Despite the unexpected cold (she no longer found the notion of it quite as romantic as she'd imagined in the heat of the pre-monsoon season,) Krishna rel-

109

ished the unfamiliarity of London. On recommendation from the friendly President of the Foreign Students Association, she'd ventured to the flea market at Lower Marsh to forage for a warm coat and closed shoes with her very first Negroid friend, Dorothy ("Dot") Hall, a fine featured, coquette Barbadian with a sing-song accent and a playful disposition. Krishna found it absurd that anybody should minimize a name to something as insignificant as a "dot," something that had never impeded Dot herself. Dot's descriptions of Barbados made it seem to Krishna just like Mangalore, with a Christian rather than a Hindu bent. And quickly, Krishna found she had more in common with this *calu* than she would have imagined had she been back home. The girls shared the sorrows of having to imprison their toes and add the weight of itchy wool to their mostly cotton wardrobes. Try as she might, Dot couldn't convince Krishna to give up her silk saris and *salwar kameez* in favor of something more practical during what the girls, in September, were already calling "winter." "You'll ketch your det a' cold!" she'd chant, seeing Krishna fumble out of her dorm-room laden with books, clutching her sari, hugging herself with a woolen shawl over her new winter coat, "all dat chilly air swirlin' 'bout 'tween your bare legs can't do you naw good—'less you waitin' for some boy come warm you up!" Krishna blushed deeply and soon availed herself and Dot of a couple of pairs of irritating wool stockings.

Krishna's course of study for the post-graduate diploma in economics would be challenging, but was well structured as far as she could tell. Dot, who was earning her PhD in mathematics so that she could teach it back home, agreed that the system was well organized. The university aimed to tailor each graduate student's curriculum to the maximum benefit of his research subject. After lengthy interviews with the "Higher Degrees Sub-committee," the subject of each student's research was approved or refined and a senior staff supervisor assigned. The supervisor would guide the curriculum of seminars, lectures, and courses that would complement the students' research throughout the year and would, once a thesis was completed, recommend the students' performance to the Sub-Committee to confer a final degree. The students awaited their supervisor assignments nervously, and gossiped amongst themselves about the faculty—the dreaded and the preferable. To ease the tension of the days prior to assignments, The Graduate Students Association sponsored a party. Dot, who donned unreasonably high heels, shiny lipstick and a form-fitted yellow dress, dragged the reluctant Krishna to the event in the main students' building. Feeling out of place in her ornate silk *salwar kameez*, Krishna was soon impressed to meet, thanks to Dot's insistent introductions, a number of other Indian students amongst the four hundred post-grads, including some dressed in saris. She was happiest to learn that they had not only dress but languages other than English in common, and that in general, the ladies' experiences in London had been good. Some were the daughters of Indian civil servants now permanently in London and being educated as had become expected of them during the war. Others were also there on scholarships, like Krishna, or had been sent by their families to obtain the "broad minded" education that Gandhi endorsed.

Over her years of dancing, Krishna had grown used to feeling like a second-class guest at the formal receptions and cocktail parties. Despite the oak walled, chandeliered and mirrored elegance of the Barley Sugar Room, here, Krishna felt welcomed and included amongst the student body. There wasn't the usual strain between English and colonized, who, she observed, didn't seem to behave like ingratiating boot-lickers the way they might have at home. They presented their hands for shaking as intellectual equals. There appeared a sincere camaraderie amongst the students, if only, she suspected, in public. Everything seemed improbably egalitarian. Meanwhile, Dot indiscreetly pointed out Krishna's admirers in the group, scanning the small clusters of men for searching glances casually executed in the midst of ostensibly stimulating conversations. Krishna ignored the attentions, but admired the boldness of the jovial, cocky Scotsman who threw open the piano and jumped on its bench to pound out a happy tune. She delighted in how an unlikely gaggle of formally dressed, bespectacled boys broke into a heart rending, *a cappella* version of "The White Cliffs of Dover," likely to have been stimulated by the steins of beer they seemed never to put down.

Dot, determining that Krishna was observing rather than participating in the festivities, talked Krishna into her first taste of champagne. "Just try a sip of mine," she urged, brandishing the flute under Krishna's nose, "it's bubbly and it tickles going down." Krishna peered into the glass suspiciously, blinking against the bubbles that burst from the surface of the sparkling yellow brew. She looked around at the other students, invariably adorned with elegant goblets. They seemed to be enjoying themselves. Dot made another plea, "C'mon, it's just a try, it won't kill you!" Krishna took the glass, ejected her pinky finger from the grip as she noticed the other girls had done, threw back her head and emptied the entire contents of the flute down her gullet, her lips never touching the rim. She proudly presented the astonished Dot with the empty flute and then winced, making a sour face and blinking hard against the sting of the bubbles. "You weren't meant to gulp da whole ting just like dat!" Dot cried. "Well it's a good thing I did," Krishna came back, still grimacing at the bitterness, "or I wouldn't ever have had anymore of it. It prickles the throat!" Dot doubled over laughing as a waiter passed by with another tray full of flutes. "May I?" Dot urged the empty flute at the waiter, trading it in for a full one. "Now look, let's try dis again so you can actually taste it. Don't be drinking it all down at once, just take a sip and let it rest in your mout' a moment before swallowin' it, right?" Krishna made a skeptical face, "And what if the glass is dirty?" Dot rolled her eyes, "This isn't Mangalore or Bridgetown, pal! They practically polish da water here before it come outta da tap. You can lick the whole rim o' da glass if you're up to it!" Taking the glass from Dot, Krishna ventured another taste. "That's enough!" Dot warned, just as Krishna tipped back the flute. Krishna let the liquid spread on her tongue. She closed her eyes for a moment and when she swallowed, beamed at Dot, enjoying the sparkles on her tongue and throat and the woozy feeling already taking effect from the last glass.

Krishna's show drew a raised eyebrow or two from the other Indian women at the party. Krishna had transgressed a fundament of her religion without thinking twice. She grew chattier during that evening, finding it strikingly easy to make acquaintances. She stopped a waiter at least four times, remaining careful to hold the glass delicately away from her, pinky aflutter, no matter how giddy she got or how much the room seemed to tilt. When, feeling lightheaded, she spotted a seat, Krishna burst into fits of uncontrollable laughter at being unable to settle onto it squarely behind her. She'd turn to look at the wooden chair, and there it was; she'd turn back to sit on it, and it had somehow shifted right out from under her. Krishna couldn't contain her giggling enough to explain the hilarious predicament to Dot. Wisely, Dot thought it time to lead the tipsy Krishna home.

The next morning, the pigeon-holes in the Students' Common Room were to contain everybody's supervisor assignments. Though she awoke late, thirsty and inexplicably tired, Krishna skipped past the refectory where Dot's note said she could be found, and rushed instead to the Student Center. In her cubby hole rested not only the expected note from the Dean, but her first letter from home. Krishna gleefully tore open the thin blue air-letter splotched with colorful stamps.

October 25, 1945

My Most Dear Akka—

I write to you from my new home in "Cal," as the locals call it. It has so many rooms I am constantly lost. There are even four washrooms with hidgybidgy colored tiles all over the place. It is very distracting. Luckily, the *ayas* and *khansamas* help me to find my way around.

It is cooler here in the North, and everybody is so formal. But I feel most welcome. The Nayels treat me like a real daughter. "Mummy" says she never had daughters and so likes to pamper me. I am grateful and happy because Ranjeet is kind, handsome and quite progressive for a Bhanap. All the Nayels have been very supportive of Quit India movement. "Daddy" even says I can attend the women's college here if I wish. They are highly educated, all of Nayels, and are constantly quoting Tagore. I often feel very stupid in their presence. This college idea may not be a bad one. After all, you did it too, no? But Arna might have a fit!

I miss Amma and Arna greatly and do worry for them now that none of us are at home. I worry even more these days that so much rioting and looting is happening before independence. It seems every day we read of Hindu-Muslim infighting with so many dead. Why so much conflagration? What does that resolve? We pray and fast with Gandhiji but nothing happens. The Nayels say that they used to go to the Club or take walks in the evenings, but now we all stay at home from fear. But do not worry for me. I feel safe. There are so many rose bushes in the gardens of the house that any rascal will get all caught up in the thorns!

Ranjeet leaves early in the mornings and spends all day in hospital. He only can come for lunch a few days of the week. I have lunch with Mummy and we do sewing and gardening or go for the shopping, which she likes to do for herself on her days off. Otherwise Mummy volunteers at the slums. She is well loved there. I have gone with her but I am useless without Bengali. There I have collected a stray puppy we call "Dash" and I am training him into a creditable guard dog now that so many threats come from the outside. I fear he is too friendly, always licking the milkman and rolling around before the postman to be scratched. Even Dash speaks Bengali only. He takes no instructions in English or Konkani from me but when Ranjeet says things he promptly obeys. From next week I will have a daily tutor to learn Bengali properly. Ranjeet has taught me a little but I am hopeless. This language is most properly pronounced only if I tuck a guava in each of my cheeks before making a sentence. All Nayels laugh at my pronunciation, but luckily at home we speak Konkani.

We have a driver and our own bicycle rickshaw. It is very fast compared to Bunty pulling the bullock cart and when we swerve around the corners I often feel sick and dizzy but I do not complain. Traffic in Calcutta is a sight to see! There are so many lorries and rickshaws and bullock carts and often a cow will just sit in the middle of the street and everything will come to a stop because nothing can pass around it. Sometimes I am bored because I am given no chores here. The servants do everything and do not allow my help. I have not cooked a single time after all those lessons from *M'am*. I do miss *M'am* also so much. Even though it is veg, the food here in North is different and not like his. They hardly use any *mirchi* at all and I must always ask for chilis. Also they use barely any coconut. But Mummy has shown the *khansamas* how to make some proper *Konkani* dishes so I have some comforts in the mouth department.

Krishna-akka, I am grateful and lucky in my marriage. Arna worked hard and found me a wonderful match. Ranjeet is honest, good-natured, and very friendly. He comes rushing home from the hospital as early as he can to lavish attentions on me like I have never before had. He brings *mithai* and buys flowers. (Imagine this waste!) He is pleased that I have Dash for company. He calls Dash "my furry coterie." I have not told a soul but you: he was very tolerant with me on our wedding night. Deepa had warned me that grooms can become madly impatient thugs by then, but Ranjeet has been patient and respectful. Never have I had such wonderful treatment in my life, Krishna. He has taken me many times to the cinema and even to the houses of his friends where I meet other Bhanap ladies. He says he likes to "show me off" on Saturdays to his colleagues at the doctors' club and I tell him this is not proper behavior. He even sometimes washes my hair! You will never believe what I learned at the Doctor's club last time…Jyotsna aunty will be coming to Calcutta for a performance. Daddy has already gotten tickets for us. It will be lovely for me to see her dance. Do you miss the dancing, Akka?

Well that is all my news. I am cheerful here even if things have changed so much. Things must be even more different for you. I await your news anxiously. Please tell me about your quarters and your classes and your friends and most important, what is London like? Is it so stuffy like Churchill is?

With much love,

Your Sindhya

Krishna teared up at reading the letter. There was something of home in it which felt good and honest and simple. Sindhya seemed to love her new life though it was far from Mangalore. Most important to Krishna, she seemed as in love with her new husband as he appeared smitten with her. Krishna felt unburdened and was much satisfied by the news. She wondered if the astrologer had predicted so good a match.

By the time she ambled into the refectory, lost in the bulletins from Sindhya, Krishna had nearly forgotten about the Dean's notice. Dot was glad to report that she herself would be supervised by the popular Lady-Professor Travis who had spent three years in the Caribbean for her own research. It was Dot whose impatience reminded Krishna of her Supervisor assignment, and Dot who was aghast to learn that Krishna had been saddled with the prickly Professor Dalton. He was renown in the Economics department for being a task-master and a grumbling curmudgeon. Dot grizzled at the notion that it was in his assessments that Krishna's fate would rest. "He's a dastardly one, dey say. But I'm told he has a weakness for da pretty girls, you know," Dotted winked at Krishna suggestively, "he even recommends da feeble ones just for looking good in a skirt. Den at least you know you can play on your assets." Dot added in a conspiring tone. Krishna intended nothing of the sort. "You well know I don't wear skirts. And if I have to," Krishna informed Dot stridently, "I'll glue my eyelids open so I can't bat my eyelashes even by accident." Krishna's first meeting would be the next morning.

Anxious at the prospect of meeting the venerable Dalton, Krishna braced herself as she sat outside his office door trying to follow the conversation inside. She heard nothing but "bloody" this and "bloody" that punctuating muffled monologue, and no response. She fretted. The departmental secretary sat behind a broad wooden desk across from Krishna's hallway chair. The small plaque on her desk read "Valerie Gupte." Anglo-Indian, Krishna assessed, now more interested in inspecting the woman's appearance. She was petite, older and fairer than Krishna and wore her curly hair short and tightly pomaded against her head, almost like a boy's. She had wide, familiar, Indian eyes, dark eyebrows, and unexpected freckles across her exaggerated upturned nose. She looked across at Krishna, catching her by surprise, and smiled, "Don't worry," she whispered in a broad accent, "just stick ta business an' you'll do fine." The door creaked open, clouds of musty smoke wafted into the hallway. The Scotsman Krishna recognized from the party, not at all his former jolly self, slinked slowly backward through the door nodding intimidated agreement as Dalton barked instructions after him. He was a wisp of a lad, blonde, reedy, and tall, a blade of sea-grass undulating with the waves of Dalton's booming commands. Biting his lip, the boy practically tripped over Krishna as he scurried off down the hall when the roaring came to a close. "Next student!" she heard the Professor bellow. Krishna pressed her hands against the folds of the sari on her lap, flashed a defeated smile at Valerie, took a deep breath, arose and stepped timidly through the door.

The elegant gentleman inside could not possibly, thought Krishna, be the source of all that clamor. He seemed so genteel and cultivated, so formal in his three-piece tweed suit, his grey eyes softened by bushy white brows and long lashes magnified behind studious, round spectacles. He stood surveying the papers on the blotter of his desk and motioned Krishna in without looking up, a pipe swirling smoke poised significantly in his left hand. Leather-bound books lined the shelves in his office from ceiling to floor. Others lay in stacks, unfiled at the base. Through lips now clenched around his pipe the professor growled something about closing the door. Krishna pulled the door closed and remained standing with hands clasped behind, suffocating in the fog of smoke and waiting to be invited to sit. "Mmmmm hmmm," the Professor grunted, flipping through the file before him, then muttered quizzically "dancing?…your Chancellor mentions that you haven't the temperament of an artiste despite having been an accomplished one. Heh heh." then puffing at his pipe again as he flipped through her record, "very good…excellent, yes…" and finally, adjusting the small spectacles on his sharp, Roman nose, turned another page and looked up at the disconcerted Krishna practically pasted against the office door. He considered her for a moment, gnawing at the tip of his pipe. "Madam," he offered gently, looking her up and down, "it is right you should remain standing as this conversation shall be short." Krishna, wide-eyed, nodded quick consent. "Your transcript, if it is true, is exceptional. Your proposed research topic is approved and your proposed methodology seems sound. Your future here requires only that you heed my advice, remain diligent in your studies and synthesize your research into a paper that has social value and practical application. You are best served by observing closely whatever I should propose. Have you any quarrel with this formula?" Krishna, mum, shook her head without blinking. "In that case," he continued calmly, "please see the departmental secretary tomorrow morning by which time I will have proposed a written curriculum for your review. Also have her schedule you for a semi-monthly progress meeting with me. Should you have any objection to the proposed curriculum, I would advise that you return well prepared to challenge it. Questions?" Krishna shook her head quickly no and assuming her appointment had ended reached a hand back to open the door. The professor, boring his gray eyes through the jittery Krishna, stopped her with an inquiry. "Do you ever speak, Madam?" he asked, almost mocking. Krishna, unable to ver-

balize an answer, nodded eagerly. Dalton's severity dissolved into a knowing
smile. He inhaled slowly from his pipe then exhaling, addressed Krishna with
self-satisfied assurance, "Well if you don't speak, we shall get on quite well. I'm
accused of loving the sound of my own voice in any event, and I must admit to
preferring it to the dull voice of a student who presumes to think he knows
what's best for his edification. Or hers, in your case." The professor closed the file
before him. "Very well, then" he added in his crisp Oxford accent, "off you go."
Krishna retreated promptly, making haste toward the secretary. Valerie didn't
give Krishna a chance: "It'll be here for ya by tomorrow at ten" she assured. "And
since you'll likely be scheduled for the one p.m. 'Statistical Analysis and Probabilities' practicums on Thursdays, I'll schedule your regular meetings for twelve-
thirty every second Thursday startin' this week. Awrigh'?" Valerie offered confidently. "Less than a half hour to meet, Miss? Will that be enough?" Krishna
probed politely. "You'll wish for less!" whispered the savvy Valerie rolling her
eyes, "trust me. A pretty girl like you…You'll need to worry 'bout 'is bite, not 'is
bark." Krishna was glad to take the advice. She rushed off stinking of smoke but
satisfied with her first meeting.

The semester rolled on apace. Krishna complied with the curriculum presented by Dalton and found the work before her voluminous, but absorbing.
Inspired by Gandhi as were many in her generation, nowadays she was motivated
by the notion of improving India's lot by gaining skills relevant to its development. She was pleased that she had been given this opportunity to study abroad,
and thought it imperative not to waste it. Krishna's research was easy in London,
as the bureaucracy was meaningfully diminished compared to Bombay, and
refreshingly, there was no need to inveigle attendants to induce them to do their
jobs, whether at the Shaw Library, the book shops on the Strand, or the office of
the Registrar. She spent her paltry spare time with Dot and the few other students she'd befriended. They sometimes went to the cinema, where Krishna
would sink into her seat, prepubescent in her embarrassed over witness so much
passion on screen. They made themselves regulars at the university mixers, which
could always be relied upon for plentiful champagne, and as proper academics,
frequently attended the lectures and teach-ins on several subjects, mainly because
of the free and liberal helpings of wine and cheese. Sometimes, weather permitting, Dot could talk Krishna into accompanying her on a bus to survey the out-
skirts of London. Fashioning cucumber sandwiches at home and swinging a
thermos flask topped up with tea, they'd venture side by side, attracting stares
from the locals, into the misty fields and lanes of the pastoral suburbs. The girls
agreed that the prim English countryside, such a contrast to the bedlam of rural

India or Barbados, was exactly as Jane Austen had described. When unencumbered, Krishna wrote lengthy letters to Jyotsna, Sindhya and Shaku describing everything in great detail.

One morning, after an evening tea social at the dormitory which had recognized a fairly broad definition of "tea," Krishna slept passed her alarm clock. She rushed to make it to class and only half way through her lecture did she realize that she had altogether missed her daily prayers. Weeks later, on receiving a letter from home, she did not become teary eyed or wistful. As she read it, India came through as a quaint and faraway place with little impact on her daily life. Another morning, kneeling before the small shrine in her room, Krishna hurried through her recitations mechanically, making the slightest gesture to indicate a bow rather than performing a proper one at the close. When she sipped her tea, she no longer winced for lacking the taste of goat milk. It happened incrementally but surely: Krishna had stopped craving the comforts of home. She had come to rely on herself entirely. Her comfort, if any, lay only in that.

Krishna felt prudish and left out when Dot took up with Julian, the barman at Dot's favorite local pub. She gazed out her window through the mist of the wintry nights where on the stoop of Cartwright lodgings, the couple indulged in fervent, endless kisses. Though they hid from the faint light of the streetlamps lining the path, Krishna could spy Julian's hands slithering under Dot's coat and could divine Dot's ecstasy from her rapt expression. Krishna liked Julian's company well enough, and was enthralled by the stories he told of growing up in Southern Rhodesia with an English judge for a father and a native for a mum. His family had moved back to England when he was only ten. He had never quite fit in either in London or back home. Perhaps this is what made Julian so courteous and attentive to Dot and Krishna, who he perceived as equally displaced. He didn't drink, he didn't carouse, he had served in the war and lost his brother in combat. There was something resigned and melancholy in his disposition which Dot's presence entirely eclipsed. Though not nearly as bright as she, he was enough enamored with Dot to disregard their intellectual differences. Julian took satisfaction in possessing the simple, steadying, sensibilities that could counter Dot's flighty enthusiasms—a role Krishna suddenly recognized that she herself had grown used to playing. He was inquisitive about Krishna's upbringing in India, something she began preferring not to discuss. "I come from a back-water village without distinction," she'd offer in dismissal, "nothing's ever changed there, and nothing ever will."

Over the Christmas intersession, when everybody else went home, most of the foreign students remained on campus and fashioned house-parties of their own.

Christmas held no meaning for Krishna, but she liked the way it lit up the city just like *Diwali*—except for the fog and the cold. Bundled up so only her nose poked out from under her bulky garb, Krishna wandered the lively shopping streets dotted with Christmas trees, their branches neatly tied with red velvet ribbons. She meandered endlessly through the festive shops, sampling puddings and chocolates and sips of sherry offered for tasting, and gazing at the window displays aglitter. On Christmas eve she found herself gazing up the Thames from a pillar at the Tower Bridge, a fine mist of rain settling upon the velvet cuffs of her coat and damping the shawl she'd draped 'round her head. Dot was gone to Julian's to meet his family for Christmas dinner. Krishna didn't mind the time to herself. London was quiet tonight: nary a car on the street, and few pedestrians to contend with as in the hectic days before. "You always choose ze same desk at ze Shaw librareee" announced a deep voice from behind her in a French accent so exaggerated it was nearly a lampoon. Krishna turned to face its owner. "Pierre-Andre Sarlat," he extended a hand, "enchanté." Krishna, curious at how this gent would know her habits, poked frozen fingers out from under her shawl. He bowed to graze her hand with his lips, a gesture Krishna had only ever seen at the picture shows. "May I intrude upon your solitude, Mademoiselle?" the dapper stranger inquired as he rose. Suspicious, but charmed, Krishna ceded some space on the narrow stone walk of the overlook where both now perched gazing out over the water at the twinkling lights of the city beyond. "I'm afraid I cannot admit to recognizing you, sir." Krishna offered in all honesty. "Unlike yours," smiled the Frenchman in mock self-effacement, "my face is rather forgettable. I am a fellow in the Philosophy department and live at the Osborne lodging. I must admit your mere passing at the Cobden room or the refectory diverts me much from my work." Flattered, Krishna blushed and took note of the Mediterranean features of this welcome admirer: sallow skin wanton for sun, moss-green eyes darkened by long, bountiful lashes. His polished, august profile was marred only by an unfashionable cascade of dark, curly hair. "Philosophy?" Krishna proposed, skeptically "as in Socrates and Kant?" "Or as in *Samkara* and *Gangesa*," replied the Frenchman, with a wink. Krishna was intrigued. They ended up strolling together through the misty streets of London, sharing stories of adjusting and recounting their academic woes. Their conversation lasted long into that exquisite Christmas night. The next day, a dozen red long stemmed roses were delivered to Krishna's door.

"A genuine beau." Announced Dot mischievously settling herself on a stool beside Krishna at the pub. "Just a friend!" protested Krishna unconvincingly in Julian's direction. "Well, a special one den!" insisted Dot, who relished the idea that the priggish Krishna lately found excuses to visit Shaw at precisely the times Pierre would happen to be there. "It's only that I find him interesting and so unlike the other fellows here. Did you know that when I told him I was from Mangalore he asked whether by chance I spoke *Kannada* or *Konkani*? Have you any idea how few the people are who even know my language exists?" Krishna gushed, defending her distraction. "He knows the names of Indian logicians and can tell of the Brahmins, and the migration of the Aryans from North Western Eurasia down through the Indian subcontinent!" Krishna was proud and excited in recounting Pierre's scholarly achievements. "Well la-tee-dah," Dot replied bemused, "impressin' you wit all dat cleverness, is he? An' you don't tink the roses have anytin' to do wit' it? Did I mention,' Julian, about the roses yet?" Julian laughed affably. "There's no denying it, Miss, where there's roses," he assured, "there's fire." Krishna rolled her eyes and sat back in her stool defeated. "Roses," she commented, "are about as common in India as bricks are here. You're just silly romantics the two of you." But Krishna was pleased. And there was no denying it to herself. Krishna knew from the way her breath went shallow and her heart beat faster when she came across Pierre that she felt something uncommon. His mere glance would fluster her entirely, spoiling her normally level-headed conversation and transforming her into the sort of tittering flirt she never knew she could conjure.

Krishna especially liked to watch Pierre smoke. Nestled into a deep, leather club chair at Shaw, a book invariably balanced on his lap, Pierre would ceremoniously unwrap his stash of tobacco from a worn leather pouch. He'd sift a pinch of it into a carefully laid square of paper, and tap it ever so gently between two fingers to settle the tobacco into a fold. He tended to it almost lovingly, rolling a thin tube and tapering the ends with exaggerated strokes that stretched far beyond the tips he fashioned with his fingers. Before lighting it, he would hold it up to eye level, observing his creation with intense satisfaction; and then would strike a match and squeezing his eyes shut, draw a concentrated breath from one end until the other flickered. Then he'd exhale, as though relieved, lips loosened into a lazy "w", eyes squinted against the smoke. It was an automatic set of motions that never varied, but were performed with a sensuality, an elegance, that rendered the ritual, to Krishna, at once comfortingly familiar and singularly captivating. Mesmerized, Krishna would fix her eyes on his every move from across the quiet room where she was meant to be studying, and quickly avert her glance if Pierre looked up to meet her gaze. Suddenly self-conscious, Krishna would hastily flip a page in the book open on the table before her, and perhaps readjust her shawl, her fingers lingering at its edges and combing through its fringes in nervous titillation. And so it was that Krishna began to learn yet another language. One in which Pierre was appreciably more fluent.

It began far more innocently than Pierre would have preferred. They had been at the pub together one night when on parting, instead of the usual graze of the hand, Pierre leaned in and kissed the flustered Krishna square on the lips. She neither resisted nor consented but was more embarrassed about the public airing of what she considered a private act than interested in the meaning of the impulse itself. Pierre found this refreshing and compelling. Krishna would have to get used to private acts performed in public. Her lodgings permitted no guests of the opposite sex and Pierre's quarters, being far from the main campus, weren't welcoming in winter. Stolen kisses between lectures or at the cinema were the most that Krishna would hazard, using considerable skill to oust Pierre's stealthy hands should they venture into perilous territory. He was persistent and insistent. He had heard much, he suggested, about the *Kama Sutra*—and wasn't it Krishna's duty to please her partner? "Her husband," Krishna would insist, "and I'm not that kind of a girl." "That," Pierre conceded twirling fingers around a lock of her hair, "is precisely what makes you so desirable, *ma cherie*..." But such amusement was rare, and more than anything, Krishna preferred to explore the terrain of Pierre's fertile mind. She could spend hours parked before a fireplace in one of the common rooms listening to Pierre discuss anything from German literature to the optimal grind for peppercorns. She even liked watching his lips move, liked the way he sometimes forgot the English word for something and would just use the French one to get by. He rarely asked her opinion having quickly gathered that she seemed indisposed to offer a contradiction or challenge to his. He had once asked her thoughts on a film they had seen and she'd answered "I'd so much rather know what you have to think; you seem much more an authority on these subjects than I. I have such little experience by comparison." Pierre proffered, "Is it that you've made no judgment or that you fear your opinion might be incorrect?" Krishna was surprised by the query. She considered for a moment. "I suppose I just don't think my opinion matters." Pierre took Krishna by the hand and whispered in her ear "Self doubt clips the wings of hope."

Dot and Julian's company took the edge off the couples' inclinations toward heady intellectual discussion. At the pub, the motley international cluster sometimes raised eyebrows, easily dispelled by a single, haughty eyeshot from Pierre. The four enjoyed making fun of each others' accents. Pierre was hopeless at pronouncing his "h's" and Dot didn't believe in the letter "g." Krishna's v's and w's seemed randomly interchangeable, leaving Julian, the least schooled of the lot, in the unlikely position of locution instructor. "Hhhhheart!" he would insist at Pierre, mocking and exaggerating the "h," "art is another matter altogether!"

Krishna often felt like Pierre was on a mission to free her from her modesty, but only once were the two caught *in flagrante delicto* when Pierre snatched Krishna into an empty classroom as she hurried down the hallway on her way to her next lecture. "There's no point kidnapping me," she warned, muffled between fierce, wet kisses, "nobody would trouble to pay the ransom!" Pressed against the wall beside the door so as not to be detected through its port-hole, the two were tussling, Pierre ever bothered by the layers of shawl, coat, and slippery silk *salwar,* and Krishna playfully dodging his insistence, when the door swung open and in blew the beleaguered Professor Dalton, having abandoned his lecture notes at the lectern after class. He was as astonished to discover Krishna cowering behind the frisky Frenchman as she was embarrassed to have been so exposed. "Perhaps I should let it be known to the Sub-committee that the university has not provided adequate venues for the graduates to acquaint themselves with the student body?" the Professor suggested sarcastically, eyeing the two with scorn. The couple made a brisk escape.

Over the past months of meetings Krishna had come to understand that Dalton was not so much a grouch as, much like herself, a perfectionist. She had never found him genial, but as long as he perceived his charge as attentive to his guidance (something at which Krishna never failed,) and he remained unopposed, he seemed appeased. Krishna followed his instructions to the letter, not seeing why she shouldn't, and efficiently offered up her lecture notes upon demand, as well as drafts of her research for Dalton's review. He seemed to respect her methodic, steady approach, and assessed her progress as "more than adequate"—high praise according to Valerie. They had come to a peaceable equilibrium wherein, over the course of six months, Krishna was no longer intimidated by Dalton's naturally surly demeanor. Still, after the lecture-room incident, she was mortified over her next supervisor meeting and braced for some sort of scolding. To her surprise, Dalton didn't flinch. He was nonchalant, and if anything, gentler than usual, making not even a sidelong comment on Krishna's conduct. Then, just as she started to go he proposed, "You're but an exploit, madam, though he may try to convince you, indeed even believe, otherwise." "Excuse me?" Krishna blurted, somewhat overwhelmed by the proposition. "The boy is toying with you, my girl." suggested Dalton smugly, "Sees himself as the tamer; you as the feral creature wanting civilization. You are a dalliance until somebody suitable; you know, of his own kind, comes along. He will never marry you. But I presume you know this already, so clever a girl you are. Not at all as guileless as you appear. Perhaps you have something to gain from him, then do you?" "No sir," Krishna stammered, and unthinking, "thank you, sir." as though Dalton had just done her some sort of favor. Humbled, Krishna gathered her things, and parting in a great hurry, carelessly slammed the door behind her.

Krishna couldn't concentrate in lectures that afternoon. Running over in her mind professor Dalton's warning, she stumbled down the stairs from class, careening into a hapless undergraduate chap who, startled, broke her fall. She neglected to thank him for his ministrations in collecting her belongings and ensuring that she was alright. Walking home after classes, the notion still plagued her. Was it possible that Pierre was just dallying with her? Was she merely a temporary intrigue on the way to something more "suitable," as Dalton suggested? Now that the milder spring weather made the long walk more plausible, she thought of making for Pierre's quarters and questioning him on the subject. But then she reconsidered. It was only two weeks before examinations and her thesis was soon due. She must put it out of her mind and focus on her studies. She had nothing if not that sort of discipline. Plus, she rationalized, Dalton knew nothing of Pierre, nor how much the two shared. He had never witnessed Pierre's extravagant attentions to her or his sweeping, romantic flair in her presence. He knew nothing of the comfort Pierre provided just by his company. He was unaware of Pierre's fondness for all things Indian; knew nothing of his keen interest in her culture and her art; and nothing of his passion for the details of her traditions. Pierre had inspired Krishna in her studies and openly admired her self-reliance. When Krishna was applying to the PhD program in Demography at Princeton University in America, Pierre had supported that effort entirely: encouraged her, even helped her organize her documentation—for which only her final transcripts and recommendations remained outstanding. Marriage had never been a consideration when they spent time together. But why not? It suddenly occurred to Krishna. Why, indeed shouldn't it have been? Had Krishna been behaving improperly? Certainly by Hindu standards, but here, where life had now led her? Everybody seemed to have a girl or a boyfriend—and many remained as such, "un-affianced," as Dot liked to say, for ages! Krishna flushed the pointless doubts from her burdened mind and focused on the work before her. She assured herself that Pierre had no reason to dishonor her. He was a solid, earnest man in whose company Krishna felt comforted and elated. It escaped Krishna's attention entirely, in considering all these practical matters, that she had fallen blindly in love.

Instead of finding it tiresome and depressing, as Dot did, Krishna thought the near incessant drizzle and mists of spring made for lush greenery in the city, and at the lawns of Russell Square. The girls studied there when it was dry enough, weighing down the fluttering pages of open books with pebbles from the tidy gardens. Pierre too was studying for examinations, making the fewer meetings with Krishna more precious to her as a result. Nowadays, in Pierre's company, Krishna had to struggle to suppress the yearnings that swelled and heaved inside her. She found it harder to resist the roaming of his hungry hands. In the tender silences, when she and Pierre gazed at each other endlessly searching something telling in each others' eyes, Krishna felt freer to eschew her usual modesty. She began to relish Pierre's sensual ventures; the feeling of fullness they imparted, the way they lured her into wanting to surrender. Even in public, their kisses grew deeper, less playful, more rigorous and prolonged. The way he fixed his eyes on her, or tenderly brushed aside a strand of hair from her eyes undid Krishna entirely. She was engrossed and discomfited all at once. She distrusted men instinctively but somehow could not keep herself from collapsing into Pierre's fulsome attentions. He was admirable and cultured and paid a type of attention that Krishna had never known before.

Perhaps it was the contrast between the punishing days of written and oral examinations and pressures of completing her thesis, and the relative ease of being in Pierre's company. Perhaps it was the champagne he'd popped to celebrate the end of the term, making her muddled, giddy and pliable. Whatever it was, Krishna felt no regrets at awakening cosseted in Pierre's arms at his dorm one early summer morning, her thick, black hair stark and hot against his moist, pallid skin. He had been tender with her, insistent on stirring her pleasure despite the sting for which she hadn't braced. Pierre's sureness and obvious experience had stilled Krishna's distress. His rapture had numbed her pain. "Relax," he assured her, "There is nothing more natural in all the world." She couldn't seem to help herself. Eventually, Krishna's own voluptuous satisfactions gave her ample motivation to find herself frequenting his quarters during that indulgent summer. When alone, her thoughts strayed to Pierre. When in company, she longed for Pierre's embrace. In her sleep, she dreamed of Pierre and wished always for more of him, as much of him as she could draw. She relished the way he encompassed her, the way he filled her up entirely, eclipsing all self-consciousness and shame. There was unexpected freedom in this intimacy. So much so that she confessed to him one of those nights that she would be willing to forgo her doctorate in favor of his proposal. "Is that so?" is all he commented in his cool French manner, insinuating nothing. Nobody ever said "I love you" and Krishna never wrote about him in her letters home.

In the meantime, Dalton resisted issuing the recommendations still due for Krishna's doctorate application to Princeton. He said he was aware, having had other students attend, that Princeton had the only specialization in Demography offered internationally, and that Princeton awaited the completion of her application. But he refused to recommend her until after Krishna's examination results were posted. Luckily, there was still some time, as she would be unable to attend Princeton or travel to America without the Fulbright scholarship she also awaited. But the delays did not put Krishna out. She had set out to specialize in demography, population and family planning so that she could return to India equipped with the skills necessary to improve her country's lot. Her current government scholarship supported her plans as, with a population crisis looming, the independent India would require trained professionals to guide a rational policy. Only at Princeton was there a program available at a doctorate level, and she had determined to pursue it. But now that she had given over to him, the contemplation of alternate future with Pierre softened her drive. She could, if she had to, repay her civil service debt to India right here in London, she rationalized. What a relief it would be not to have to sustain herself alone any longer. Krishna half hoped that neither the acceptance nor the scholarship would materialize.

The note in her pigeon hole read simply "5:00 p.m. tomorrow. Office of Professor Dalton." It was written in Valerie's familiar hand with no further instruction. Krishna came when bidden. Valerie typed feverishly at her desk as Krishna waited anxiously: it would be her results, for sure. Valerie smiled at her across the hallway, knowing and tense, uttering not a word. Again the familiar ruckus behind Dalton's office door pulsed into the hallway. These days, Krishna paid no mind. It was not for her. When a disgruntled undergrad stomped out of the office, Krishna drew a breath and plunged in. Dalton surveyed her smugly. "You have passed your examinations with honors." He announced. "Your research on the economic effects of the British occupation of India, with the slightest luck, will be published before the beginning of the next term. Your work here, Madam, is done. The recommendation I owed you was posted to Princeton two weeks ago, for which you can thank your compatriot, Valerie. Your results have even been sent to your benefactors at the Indian Embassy. Your Master of Science in Economics degree will be issued in the post within the month." Krishna resisted her temptation to beam before him. He moved around to the front of his desk and leaned back upon it, his arms crossed in front of him. Incapable of withstanding the possibility of such unabashed glee, Dalton augmented…"Highly inadvisable indiscretions aside, you have represented ably the potential of your heritage. Would that all my students were as dedicated to their labors as you have been. But in the academic world, dear lady, you will want to see that your personal standards are maintained. Nothing will cast doubt upon your academic credentials quite so much as personal imprudence." Krishna's eyes dropped, embarrassed by the implication. Dalton, noticing, narrowed his eyes and suggested softly, "I can assure you this from personal experience." Then, trying to bolster the confidence he recognized he'd just shattered, he added, "Your parents will be exceedingly proud of your performance." These words stung. Krishna did not expect the tears that bulged in her eyes. Her parents, she knew, would not be pleased. No matter what she managed in her lifetime, they would remain ever disappointed. The delight of just seconds before devolved visibly into hopeless, helpless sorrow. In what Krishna thought was a fatherly gesture, Dalton reached out to her, quite unexpectedly, stroking her hair and embracing her in consolation. He pulled her in closer as she sobbed. Krishna was as grateful for the comfort as she was ashamed to need it. Dalton began pressing kisses into the nape of her neck. Krishna, incredulous, flailed free, and surprising herself, slapped him hard across the face. A memory of the Lieutenant glinted in her mind. Anger flashed across Dalton's brow. Hatred brandished across Krishna's. She wanted to spit at him but she didn't. She grabbed for the door and fled, distraught.

Valerie, familiar with this sequence of events, followed with her eyes Krishna's embarrassed evacuation. Calmly, she slid the spectacles off her nose and folded them into their case, which she snapped shut, congratulating herself. Just this once, she had persuaded Dalton to issue the recommendation before examination results had surfaced. She had even drafted the document herself, modeling it on those for other students. She had cleverly inserted the letter into a pile of papers he was to sign one early morning when he was too rushed to attend to the details. Later that day she had casually asked him whether he intended the Nayam recommendation to be sent via express or parcel post. He had behaved unsurprised at learning that it was already signed, responding that it made no difference. He would have nothing, they both knew, with which to induce this comely student to his will. Valerie had never been so bold before, but she could stand it no longer. Nary a fetching student had crossed this lofty professor's office without suffering his nefarious misuse. Proper, sweet, untainted girls, eager to stimulate their fecund minds left hardened and embittered; educated, to be sure, but always degraded, their intellectual victories ever contaminated by his depravity. The farthest from refuge, the most innocent, the loneliest, invariably the foreign, were reliably victimized. If he couldn't seduce them by "mentoring," playing the surrogate father, he would vengefully stoop to extortion, withholding his approvals until they conceded to his lust. Even if the faculty were aware (there was rumor, but never any confirmation), no reprimands came. No fuss was ever made. If Dalton could maintain his position, Valerie would undermine his ploys. It gave her immense professional satisfaction to clear the way for these girls. Nobody had been around to do so for her.

Krishna returned to her quarters shaken and confused. Memories of the wicked Lieutenant flashed through her mind and she shuddered. Just like with him, she had done nothing to tempt Dalton, nothing to deserve such mistreatment. Had Dalton drawn conclusions about her since finding her with Pierre? Had she done something to make him believe she welcomed his advance? He had only just finished telling her how impressive was her academic record, and then to accost her under the guise of comforting her! Was she meant to be flattered? Even worse, had his academic endorsements been founded on his attraction rather than her skills? Krishna found Dot and recounted the episode, leaking tears of shame. Dot, listening empathically, showed neither surprise nor outrage. She sighed heavily, struck by how green was this little Indian lass. "What" she inquired in earnest, "did you ever expect from dat ol' skirt-chaser? You should be glad he didn't go in for it sooner! He could've had you over a barrel what wit' your recommendations 'n' your results still waitin'! Underneath all that lah-ti-dah, he's just a randy bloke like the rest a' dem. You can't have been expectin' any different, could you?" Krishna felt dim-witted. Of course. She should have anticipated it all along. Any worldly woman would. At least, Dot consoled her, no real harm was done. Krishna hadn't had to sully herself for Dalton's favor and, Dot exclaimed joyfully, she'd even managed a good right hook! She should consider herself lucky. Krishna wondered at how many students had been compromised by Dalton. She wondered what he would do now that she'd rebuffed him. What he could do, if anything. She wondered if it would always be like this. Not, she assured herself, if she were married. She would tell about it to Pierre as soon as his exams were finished. She imagined he was likely to defend her honor. Dot encouraged the idea, "Anyhow, he sure has been making himself awfully scarce lately, dat frog of yours."

There was nothing but to wait now that her work was done: wait for replies from America, for her degree, for Pierre's proposal most of all. She had promised not to disturb Pierre this week, his research deadline still unmet. A celebration at the pub would come soon enough, as Dot and Julian had become engaged. An unexpected note from Valerie came one morning at her pigeonhole. "Supervisor meetings suspended henceforth. (Nothing to worry about.)" Krishna was glad of it, anyhow, they were no longer necessary. She ambled frequently through Hyde Park that week, where summer had begun to flourish. She waited obediently outside the gates of Buckingham palace to see for herself the infamous changing of the guard. She accompanied Dot to shop for a wedding dress, becoming accustomed to being eyed suspiciously by the guarded shopkeepers who did little to attend them. She wrote home about her accomplishments as well as about her plans.

At last the envelopes came. Both arrived on the same morning. The Fulbright Grant offered one year of financial support, including the cost of room, meals, tuition and even a cash stipend of Two Hundred and Seventy US Dollars for the academic year, pending admission to Princeton University's program in Demography at the Office of Population Research.

Princeton University

The Graduate School

August 1, 1947

Princeton, New Jersey

Mr. Krishna Nayam
c/o The London School of Economics
Houghton Street, Aldwych, London, WC2 England

Dear Applicant:

I am very pleased to inform you that you have been appointed as a Visiting Graduate Fellow at Princeton University's Office of Population Research for the academic year 1947-1948. The status of Visiting Fellow entitles you to use the library, instructional and supervisory facilities of the University in pursuit of your Doctorate degree, but it does not include any stipend. Arrangements will be made for your housing, room and board.

The OPR notes that although your academic record, recommendations and credentials are in order, you are required to register for and complete two undergraduate courses (Mathematical Statistics and Calculus) concurrent with undertaking your PhD research in order to qualify for the degree.

The University will open on Monday, September 15th, 1947. Please register in the Department of your specialty when you arrive at Princeton. The OPR can make arrangements for your transportation to the University campus if you will submit detailed travel plans.

Very sincerely yours,

J. Thorn, Assistant Dean

Krishna couldn't contain herself. She would not wait to see Pierre tomorrow as planned. His research should have been submitted today and he was sure to be at his quarters if not already at the pub. She would present Pierre with the letters proudly and announce her intention to leave for America. He would be foolish not to ask for her hand in marriage.

That evening, Krishna attended more to her appearance than ever she had. She found her favorite, fine, silk sari that shimmered slightly pink to pique her femininity. She drew kohl around her eyes, although more subtly than when she danced, and borrowed a smudge of lipstick from the ever-willing Dot. She touched her wrists with the perfume that Pierre had given her from France and per Dot's sound advice, instead of raising it into a tight bun, bound her long hair low at the nape of her neck with a most delicate pink ribbon. Confidently, she strode to the distant Osborn lodging, her letters of acceptance folded carefully into her satchel, and tapped playfully at Pierre's door. She heard movement, but got no response. She insisted. The tall and slender girl who opened the door, barely covered, a slippery silk robe draped hastily around her, only stood there looking bothered, waiting for Krishna to speak. "Oh, forgive me," Krishna offered, embarrassed at the girls' indecency, "I was looking for Pierre Sarlat—I was so rushed, I must have mistaken the doorway. Do excuse me…" she repeated as she began her retreat. *"Cette ici,"* replied the gamine, nonchalant, then directing her voice indoors, *"Pierre, une nana pour toi mon cher."* The door opened wider. Pierre, nothing but a towel wrapped around his waist appeared cheerily, slipping a hand around her waist as he sidled up to the woman's side. On beholding Krishna, his face dropped. Nothing at all came to Krishna's mind. She stared at him momentarily, then back and forth between them, trying hard to conceive any innocent explanation. A pang of anguish shuddered through her. Pierre didn't go after her as she scuttled down the stairs, stumbling in her rush to escape. All she wanted was to run. Krishna trotted urgently through the streets, her ankle stinging with familiar strain. She could not muster anger. All she felt was shame. Back at the Cartwright lodgings, Dot was nowhere to be found. Krishna gazed at her reflection in the small mirror in her room. She thought herself painted like a trollop. She thought herself stupid. She thought herself the most undignified creature ever to suffer the earth. She felt humiliated. She felt despicable. A familiar loneliness set in. She hadn't cried herself to sleep since her early days in Bombay. She collapsed upon her bed, and despairing, did just that.

It was not her own will by which Krishna woke the next morning but the clamor in the hallway. Dot was banging down her door—"open up Krishna," she pleaded, "it's all over the papers! India's won its independence! Come read the good news!" Krishna rolled out of bed and stumbled, groggy and bleary-eyed, to open her door. Dot came rushing at her announcing Nehru's words from the paper open before her: "Long years ago," Dot announced cheerily, deepening her voice as though to imitate the Prime Minster, "we made a tryst with destiny, and now the time comes when we shall redeem our pledge...At the stroke of the midnight hour, when the world sleeps, India will awake to life and freedom. A moment comes, which comes but rarely in history, when we step out from the old to the new, when an age ends, and when the soul of a nation, long suppressed, finds utterance." She paused dramatically for the full impact, then noticed Krishna looking disheveled and overwrought. Krishna tried to absorb Nehru's words through her sorrow. "My god," whispered Dot, as Krishna began sniffling, "What's happened?" "He was with another woman, Dot." She whimpered almost to herself. Then breaking down, whispered "I am...nothing to him." Dot rushed to embrace Krishna. Krishna thought her shame unbearable. She sobbed generously in kind.

August 1, 1947

My Dear Akka—

I write to you with a heavy heart knowing how much this will afflict you. Yet, there is nothing but to tell you: Jyotsna-aunty has perished. She was returning by train to Bombay, where she was to marry your own University's Chancellor, who had offered himself last month. The rail car that she boarded was put alight by rioters. It is difficult to learn accurately the particulars, so much is the commotion. There are eighty fatalities from trampling and asphyxiation; many charred so that they cannot be recognized. It is Rahul's uncle in the railway service who learned first of the news, and Shaku who therefore relayed this to me. The newspapers have printed no particulars. An effort, we are told, to encourage calm.

Do not despair, Akka. Our beloved Jyotsna made her good marks. She has danced so much for the gods, she is assured liberation for her deeds in this merciless world. She lives in all our hearts, does she not? Even Arna has shed tears (Amma has told me so.) Imagine this! A soul that could move Arna to tears has surely had some good effect! And then of course, she helped to mold you. So we are most assured that she is blessed in the afterlife.

We are all well in the family. Thank god, Amma and Arna are healthy and fine, though troubled. It has not been so bad in the South. Anirudda is growing like a weed. Though I am expected to be expecting, I am not yet, and we worry and pray. But I start college here in Cal in September—with the blessings of my parents-in-law. I hope I will someday do even half as well as you.

It is comforting to learn of your rise and of your progress in these mean and terrible times. One would think that independence should be a good thing. It has not been, as a practical matter. You know from the newspapers that it has been bloody and difficult. It is comforting to me that there is a light that shines outside this country if there can be none within. You shine for us, Akka, do not persuade yourself otherwise. Please write of your adventures in America and on the way. May your travels be always safe. The Queen Elizabeth should bow down to have one so bright as you aboard!

There is nothing but to accept our fate, Akka. Jyotsna-aunty would not have wanted you to grieve.

With much affection and condolence from your ever loving, Sindhya.

9

No matter how much Sindhya-Aunty assures Suhasini and me that it's a routine and fairly straightforward procedure, I remain stubbornly unconvinced. "A Mayo Clinic study on thyroidectomies," she suggests, morphing the diminutive, maternal *bon vivante* we're used to into an industrious, authoritative doctor (pediatrics) steeped in experience, "showed over fifty years that less than three point five percent of operations resulted in either damage to the laryngeal nerve or permanent hypoparathyroidism. The prognosis is excellent." Ranjeet-Uncle (endocrinology) cheerfully chimes in, "Better to be safe than sorry, no? At this age, no point waiting for the growth to turn cancerous or metastasize. Though with the thyroid, little risk of spreading. Fairly isolated gland it is. Nowhere for the cancer to go." I protest as politely as possible, "I thought the thyroid regulates the metabolism? Seems pretty pervasive to me...Isn't it sort of an important thing to have?" "Not so much," Ranjeet-Uncle responds, "An essential gland, but also one of the few we can compensate for synthetically without effect." Suhasini shifts in her seat, uncomfortable with my persistent inquiries that seem to challenge their wisdom. Sindhya-Aunty, reverting to her consolatory role almost completes his sentence, "Once we land on the right dosage of Synthroid to replace what the thyroid was emitting, mummy should be back to normal. It's a highly effective replacement for the natural thyroid hormone." "I just don't like the idea of an operation with general anesthesia." I continue, trying to ignore Suhasini's beseeching glare. I know she thinks my inquiries are disrespectful, but I'm skeptical of the medical world and even if they are my aunt and uncle, right now I'm more concerned over their medical expertise than their genealogy. "It's only because it's stressful to the patient to remain immobilized for so long under regional anesthesia. Particularly uncomfortable to have to hold her head back for an operation at the throat. It's more for her own comfort than anything, Sushi." Sindhya-Aunty assures seriously, possibly slightly miffed at the challenges. I drop the argument. It's too late anyway. Somewhere down the hall mom's changing into a gown and getting pre-examined before they put her under.

It all happened very fast. I was at a lunch meeting in Zurich when I got the call. It was so unusual to hear from Sindhya-Aunty, and on my cellphone no less. Recalling the day mom phoned to tell me of dad's heart attack, I braced promptly

for the worst. "What's happened?" I panicked, barely letting Sindhya-Aunty finish her greeting. (It occurred to me at that moment that I've never called her
"Aunty Sindhya," but Sindhya-Aunty, maybe a direct translation from the Konkani.) As it turned out, in my absence a couple weeks ago, her doctor had
detected a strange growth on my mom's thyroid. A biopsy had showed nothing
but "papillary tissue," and the family consensus, including my mom's, was that
the gland was best removed. A surgical cancellation made it possible for mom to
be operated upon day-after tomorrow at the Virginia Hospital (not far from my
sisters' place in DC) where Ranjeet-Uncle practices. They had scheduled the surgery and wanted "just to inform me of it and assure me it wasn't a big deal."
Sindhya-Aunty stressed that it was a normal procedure, nothing to worry about.
"Is papillary tissue another way of saying cancer?" I squealed through the phone,
forgetting that the very proper Swiss clients with whom I was at the time lunch-
ing might consider the conversation somewhat inappropriate at the table. I raised
my finger apologetically, pointed at the phone and excused myself, making for a
more private corner of the restaurant. "No dear," Sindhya-Aunty sighed, "it's just
neoplasic cells amassed on the thyroid, best to remove in case of progression into
carcinoma." Do all doctors assume everybody knows what the heck they're talking about? Now I felt like an idiot having to ask questions she imagined she'd just
answered. "So it's not cancer? But it's best to take it out?" I confirmed. "Yes, but
don't worry: we'll get it out quickly. It's only a two-three hour, outpatient procedure." Sindhya-Aunty assured. I got as much out of her as I could, then returned
to the table and excused myself from the meal, indeed from the entire city of Zurich, by awkwardly announcing "I'm so sorry. My mom might have cancer. I need
to go home." The clients were concerned and gracious, but my boss leered at me
through a politely strained smile as if to ask why on earth this couldn't wait till
after our client lunch. Even if it could have, having recently lost one parent, I
wasn't about to take my chances with another. I shook hands around the table,
apologizing profusely in the best Switzer-Deutsch I could muster. I recognized
the "can't-handle-the-big-leagues" implications of my departure, exacerbated by
being a younger, brown woman defecting from the company of five older, white
men, and left.

Back at the hotel I called Suhasini at work to get the real scoop. Sunny gathered that the growth was benign as it stood, but could turn cancerous. That was
the concern. Mom, she said, seemed fine about it, or at least resigned to the idea
of having it removed. If she was worried, she wasn't showing it. She claimed to
like the notion of getting it over with in a couple of days rather than sitting
around stressing that it might turn into cancer. Sunny had accompanied mom to

the original gyn appointment where they found it, and had also been there for the biopsy. Why, I wanted to know, had I not been informed earlier? There was nothing to tell, she defended, and mom didn't want to bother me in Zurich when it could turn out to be nothing at all! "You know how mom is," Sunny explained, "she'd rather do stuff on her own than bother anyone about it. She's always worrying that she'll worry us!" Good point.

After organizing a re-ticketing to get to DC the next day, I braced to call mom. She wasn't home. No way was she at work two days prior to her operation! Indeed, there she was. "Mom!" I yipped into the receiver, "what on earth are you doing at the clinic?" (Okay, that was definitely the wrong opening, but it's what came out.) "What do you mean?" she retorted incredulous, "Just because I volunteer doesn't mean they don't count on me to be here." Between consulting jobs, mom volunteers at a Latino community clinic in DC nowadays. Retirement didn't, in fact, suit her. She likes having somewhere to go, something to think about outside of her deteriorating self. Meanwhile, she's probably in better physical shape at her age than either my sister or I ever have been. "Mom?" I bleated out, "I spoke to Sindhya-Aunty and Sunny. Are you doing okay? I can't believe you're at work..." "I'm fine," she came back, "it's just a pesky bump in my throat. Sindhya-Aunty called you? What a big fuss for nothing...I'm not looking forward to the operation. But better to be safe than sorry." "I'm coming back for it, mom. I just arranged to get a flight straight there. Sunny's getting me at BWI tomorrow. She's already got my flights. So I'll see you then." I informed, trying to cover up my anxiety with administrative detail. "Don't be ridiculous!" commanded mom, "You'll lose your job! I'm not dying for heaven's sake! It's just a standard procedure. How can you just drop everything and come just like that all the way from Switzerland? You have responsibilities there! Don't be absurd." "Mom," I sighed, "I won't lose my stupid job and an operation is plenty good reason to take a couple days off. I've never taken a single personal day my entire time here! Anyhow, this isn't open for discussion. I'm coming." "Fine," she responded, defeated. "You always do whatever you want anyway. I'm not going to convince you differently, I suppose. But really, it's not necessary." I rolled my eyes. Mom would never acknowledge herself as important enough to be bothered over. She was about to undergo surgery and didn't think I should show up. "I hope you're at least taking tomorrow off, mom?" I suggested, changing the subject. "Absolutely not!" She protested, "You think Latina teens stop getting pregnant just because I get a growth? What am I going to do at home anyway but sit around and worry?" "Okay mom," I conceded, "...Well, I'm thinking about you...I hope you're not losing sleep. I'm sure it'll be just fine just like Sindhya-

Aunty says. I'll see you tomorrow night, okay?" "Thanks for calling, Sushi," she confided. "It isn't necessary. But I'll see you tomorrow if you insist." Nobody said "I love you." In Indian families, we love by worrying aloud.

Before the surgery, my cousin Jag ("Jagadeep,"—hem/onc), Ranjeet and Sindhya's son, swoops into the waiting room unexpected. "Hi there!" he announces, buoyant in his lab-coat and stethoscope, "what's a nice family like you doing in a place like this?" He's dropped by to check on the patient, but is on call at his hospital nearby so has to get back. We're always pleased to see each other, Jag and I. He's closest to me in age of any of my cousins, and the only one I know well on my mother's side. He's going through a divorce, something that won't be raised in this venue, though I try to load it into my inquiry, "So...how are you doing?" Jag beams falsely as though nothing's the matter, digs his hands deep into his pockets, "okay, you know, considering...lots of work...keeping busy. What really matters is how's Krishna-Aunty?" We would not, of course, discuss what's really happening, certainly not within earshot of our folks. It's an unstated rule amongst all first-generation Indians that no feelings shall be raised in the company of the older generation. It's to protect them from our reality. We all get it. We all comply.

The last time I talked to Jag in any detail was on the phone a few weeks ago, to solicit his opinion on a D&C. It felt right to contact somebody in the family before I did it, and I figured Jag was understanding and objective enough to see me through it long-distance. In fact, he was informative medically, reassuring emotionally, and supportive enough to offer to come up to New York for the procedure (which I would never have allowed). He called the doctor's office before and after it though, just to let her know she was being monitored by a pro, and checked on me often, even sending roses to cheer me up at home. Other than Jag, it was an entirely private event. I didn't even tell the perp about it. We'd dated only about two months, trying our best to "make it work," before recognizing that anything that forced wouldn't. I'd learned I was knocked up immediately after we split...(Figures.) Anyway, it's done and over. I got through it. No point getting all pointlessly emotional. Bygones.

A nurse pages Ranjeet-Uncle (must be calling us into the pre-op) so Jag and I agree to catch up later. We're led in procession down the pastel-colored hall into the bustling prep room where mom's laying on a stretcher covered with a papery white sheet, her hair mashed into a flimsy shower cap, a pink plastic tag around her wrist. She turns cheerily to face us as we file through the door. "Oh hi!" she chirps, uncommonly content to see familiar faces. "Even you!" she beams, addressing Jag. I wonder if she's just putting up a chipper front. "They wanted to take my wedding ring, Sindhya!" She complains uncharacteristically. It occurs to me that she looks weird; a little woozy and perplexed. "But then the surgeon said 'twas 'kay." She adds, flinging her hand lazily in the air to present the wedding band, then dropping it back on the stretcher with a thud. "He was so ver nice. They're all so ver nice. Nice hospital, Ranjeet. Really...all ver nice." Ranjeet-Uncle explains for our benefit, smirking "They must have given you some sedative already, eh?" "Yes. A setitive." Mom confirms, still smiling agreeably, vast eyelids dropping slowly, then gaining momentum to slam down like a rampant garage door. She forces them open again, as my sister bursts into giggles. Nobody's ever seen mom quite so out of it. We find it hilarious. "Mom," Sunny offers, squelching her laughter now, turning encouraging and concerned, "We'll see you in a few hours, ya? Sandeep and the kids are just outside with us waiting when you come out." Sunny wobbles her head through the sentence in agreeable Indian fashion. I notice that her accent gets thicker, more lilting Indian when we're amongst family. I wonder whether mine does too. Mom, looking gratified, struggles to keep her eyes open and settles into a dopey grin. It was funny a moment ago but something about seeing mom so helpless and outside herself, so vague and vulnerable splayed out on a glorified shopping cart now makes me shudder. I desperately want not to lose her. I reach for mom's hand, clasping it tightly, suddenly petrified and not knowing what to say. She manages a wan little squeeze back. Like a big idiot, I start to cry. I can't help it. Tears just stream down my cheeks. "Don't cry, Sushi" mom comforts me through her grogginess, "It'll be alrigh..." What a moron. Here I'm supposed to be all confident and reassuring and I'm blubbering like a toddler. Good going, Sushi. Just what mom needs as she goes into surgery. Ugh. Sindhya-Aunty urges a tissue at me as she distracts mom with the drill. "So when you wake up, we'll all be here waiting. You won't be able to swallow. It's likely to hurt once the painkiller wears off, but they'll administer more as you need it. Don't worry dear, we'll all see you very soon." Jag adds jovially, "Hey, and when you get out, you get all the ice cream you could ever want!" Mom nods agreeably, her glazed eyes shutting against her will and her smile widening as the words sink in. A waiting nurse gestures that they're ready to wheel her in. Sindhya-Aunty bends to kiss mom on the forehead. I lean down and do the same. Mom smiles gently at me as I rise, flaps another sloppy blink, then confesses in a whisper, "...So glad you came for me." Like a god-damned spigot, I erupt into more tears.

The main redeeming feature of the waiting room, I've determined, is the unbridled access to trashy magazines I'd never buy for myself. Problem is, I can't concentrate on a single word, much less an entire article devoted to how some b-list celebrity shed fifty pounds in six minutes and maintained her weight-loss with an easy regimen of seventy-five minutes of cardio eighteen times a week and ten minutes of weightlifting every half hour. Sandeep's taken Ranjeet-Uncle, Sunny and the kids to lunch in the real world while Sindhya-Aunty and I elected to sit here and fret, availing ourselves of the cafeteria. I've coached her on programming it, so Sindhya—Aunty's taking the time to feed all the right people into her cell-phone. I'm also speculating on who the others in the room might be waiting on and why. A balding man in his fifties taps anxiously on the shared, fading upholstered arm of his modular plastic seat. I don't get why chairs in hospitals and airports have to be connected together. Why can't everybody just get his own damned seat? He's risen at least five times for coffee from the machine. Two young black women, sisters no doubt, probably in their twenties, communicate little but take turns with the remote, flipping relentlessly through the only six channels on the wall-mounted TV. They settle on a soap opera. No wonder, it occurs to me, TV dramas tend to center around hospitals. So much potential for tragedy and relief. I notice the herds of Desi doctors swishing by (always in wire rim glasses, stethoscopes swinging.) We're so reliably unimaginative when it comes to careers: medicine, i.t., banking, hard science research and academia…Understandable, of course, ever seeking security and urged by the pressure to please our parents.

"Hmm." Sindhya-Aunty humphs, smiling at some memory, "Did you know, that the first time your mummy was in the hospital, nobody in the family was allowed to visit her?" It had never occurred to me that mom might have been hospitalized before Sunny was born. "Really?" I inquire, intrigued by the notion, "why was that?" "As a matter of fact," Sindhya-Aunty adds, "She was alone through a really rough time." For the next four hours Sindhya-Aunty distracts me from the surgery with stories about mom I could never have imagined.

The whole family's back by the time the surgeon shuffles into the waiting room looking for us. He thumps Ranjeet-Uncle on the back and embraces Sindhya-Aunty with familiarity. "Fine, fine altogether…" he tells us, "the operation took a little longer than planned because the strap muscles were tight across the throat. We surely distressed the laryngeal nerve, so she'll have some hoarseness of course, but it should restore itself over time. We've sent the specimen to the lab for testing. You can go in as soon as she wakes up. The nurses will tell you what room she's in. We're keeping her overnight just for monitoring, yes? Nothing to worry about—only that we spent longer in there than we expected, and we'd like to keep her under observation. You never know…Better to be safe then sorry, no?" Effusive in their gratefulness, Ranjeet-Uncle and Sindhya-Aunty congratulate the surgeon. A tad understated, I evaluate. The operation took a full two hours longer than predicted, leaving those of us without medical training utterly freaked out. Meanwhile the operating room sent not an iota of information down. In over-considerate Indian fashion, the family agreed not to disturb the surgeons in progress, even though Ranjeet-Uncle could easily have made some inquiries. No, we decided. They're obviously working on it. If there've been complications, why add to their pressures? Why, I had to wonder, is it okay for them to add to ours? Doesn't matter now, I suppose, but still.

When they finally let us in the recovery room another hour later, the mom I encounter on the cot isn't the one I'd seen get wheeled away. It's not the bandages across her throat or the tubes burrowed into her forearms. Other than drier lips, and a novel air of exhaustion on my generally perky mom, her appearance is no different. For me, she's become "a woman with a past." She's been rounded out with inconceivable history and improbable adventure. She's an animated, Technicolor version of what used to be to me a comic strip sketched in black-and-white. I can't fathom why she'd not have let us in on it, nor why Sindhya-Aunty decided now to spill some of the beans (and there's more to come! She's promised to find for me the stacks of letters she kept from mom's travels.) My mom's been infused with a strange and fascinating veil of glamour. I'm relieved she's alive and well, but it's like she went in for a thyroidectomy and came out with an extreme makeover.

When she blinks her eyes open, they fall first on Aarti and Mulund, who squeals "Hi Amma! How was it?" excited, as though mom was just back from a birthday party at Chuckie Cheez. "I don't know." She tries to respond, her voice reedy and straining. "Is it done already?" She seems in a sunny mood, perhaps relieved to be out. "Look at all this attention!" she fawns in a taut whisper, winking at Aarti. "And well deserved!" Sindhya-Aunty propitiates. Ranjeet-Uncle informs mom of why the operation took longer, tells her that she'll have to stay overnight and that one of us will stay in the room with her. He cautions her to rest her voice considering the stress on the vocal chords. Mom, who I expect to be feisty, ever wanting no fuss made over her, is uncommonly placid and amenable. She clears her throat, wincing from the soreness. Meanwhile, the family negotiates. Everybody volunteers to stay overnight. We out-nice each other, give each other heaps of reasons why the others shouldn't be put out. Very Indian, this gleeful volunteering for inconvenience. Just another way to express our love without having to confess it. Finally, I convince them that I have the least to manage outside the hospital and that I'm jet-lagged anyway. I should be the one to stay. "Good," mom croaks mischievously, "maybe you'll meet a nice Indian doctor."

The gang chuckles at the well timed joke. Mildly embarrassed, I smile at the good-natured candor of her aspirations for me. Another expectation I wish I could fulfill.

Within the *Varnam* is often a "*Padam*" sequence where the dancer's capacity to express *abhinaya* (pure feeling) is put to the test. Phrases may be repeated several times at the singers' choice, each one to be interpreted differently by the dancer, enabling the audience to experience the *rasa* (mood or flavor) that each line conveys. To evoke the *rasa*, a dancer must have an imaginative faculty—which is most difficult to teach. The *Padam* requires nuance and personality and is the only part of the repertoire that permits improvisation.

#

10

The grandeur of her conveyance was lost on Krishna over her seven days on the Q.E. Nothing would cheer her, though she felt better on deck alone than in the company of the garrulous strangers on show in the extravagant pavilions. She leaned on the cold railings gazing out over the grey Atlantic and brooded for hours, her sari fluttering with the capricious winds. Sullen, she surveyed the satisfied passengers, invariably coupled, playful and insouciant, swinging gaily like their strings of perfect pearls. A mere whiff of cigarette smoke, reminding her of Pierre, would make her dizzy, nauseous, and launch her into another bout of lament. At first, she only mourned her losses and wept her grief. But it was during this passage that surges of anger started pulsing palpably inside her. Breaking from her usual politeness, offered anything at all, she'd snap a fierce "no," at the obsequious staff members moved to relieve her obvious distress. Even the chipper Captain couldn't seem to break through her new-found bitterness. His attempt at extending himself was met with a curt and dismissive "It's all lovely. Thank you very much." Resenting having constantly to turn down their kindnesses, one afternoon she barked back at her well-meaning cabin steward who passing her on deck had merely offered a cup of tea. "No, do you hear me? No!" Krishna cried, "I do not want tea or anything else from anybody! I do not want to be helped. I do not want company or drinks or to be escorted to dinner! I do not want to have to be polite to strangers. I do not want to be admired. I do not want a darned thing, from you. I will help myself!" The flustered boy regarded Krishna with awe, wondering what might make so gentle seeming a woman erupt with such venom. The staff began to give Krishna a wide berth.

One evening on returning to her cabin in her usual state of desolation, she spotted on her cot a small, dog eared book she didn't recognize as her own. She read the title embossed in gold on the dark blue cover, "Leaves of Grass. Walt Whitman." Krishna's impulse was to return it to the cabin crew, imagining it had been left behind by a housekeeper. She flipped the cover open and read a little note inside, "Dear Lady. May this bring you some relief. It often does the trick for me." The note was not signed and tears came to Krishna's eyes in recognizing that it was for her. She could not fathom from whom the book had come, as she had made no friends on board and had gone far out of her way to avoid anybody who might make an attempt. She sat down on the bed and began to read.

The little volume came to sustain Krishna for the rest of her journey though it did little to diminish her grumpiness. With every swell a memory flooded through her of each time she had been denied, each time she had been curtailed, each time she had been wronged or suffered loss or been marginalized. She could not muster rage, but instead turned cantankerous. She appeared on deck almost always with arms crossed, resenting the cheerful crowd. So petty she felt for having slapped Professor Dalton, no matter how he had misused her. So helpless she felt that a generous life such as Jyotsna's could be extinguished through no fault of her own. So humiliated she felt for having given herself so easily to the philandering Pierre. She hated Pierre. But the fury that grew inside her had no permissible outlet. It was safer to retreat into the familiar loneliness of self-reproach than suffer the starker isolation of abhorrence and outrage expressed. It was how she was raised, what she was taught, the way women were meant to be. The most Krishna could manage was to remain in a bitter snit. She came to detest her conduct and made up her mind to reform it before reaching land. She spent long hours staring out at the rolling sea and up at the scudding clouds, aggrieved at her predicament and deploring the gods. Why was it necessary to exact so much revenge? She pored over the small volume she now kept with her at all times. She was grateful for the hope it promised. Even then, she resolved never to let herself fall in love again, and just as Amma would have done to purify, Krishna began to fast. Like the liner piercing through the vast, relentless ocean, she focused hard on just forgetting and moving on.

She arrived at the port of New York thin, depleted, disoriented and still bereft. Worse, though the Office of Population Research had written that somebody would fetch her, the terminal had almost emptied, and Krishna still sat waiting atop her battered leather trunk hopefully searching the eyes of every seeker passing by. Accustomed to detailed questioning, she had not minded the haughty demeanor of the sparkling-buttoned immigration officer who surveyed her paperwork skeptically, concocting at least five ways to inquire whether it was her intention to return to India after her education was complete. She was irritated, however, by the irresponsibility of the O.P.R. and just on the brink of making her own way to Princeton when a dark and skeletal, distressed, Indian chap marched up to her looking purposeful and concerned. "May I inquire, Miss, have you been just coming off the Q.E.?" he queried politely in a heavy Indian accent. "I have, yes, but not just. We disembarked at least three hours ago." She explained. "I might be imagining that you are Indian as well, yes?" the man probed, his generous suit hanging off his bony limbs. "Indeed, from Mangalore." Said she. "Oh Mangalore! How wonderful, I myself am being from Madras! So unusual to find a lady in a sari Stateside...I am hoping you don't mind my asking. By chance while you were aboard might you have made the acquaintance of another Indian lad, a Mister Krishna Nayam? I am coming here to collect him and he doesn't seem to be anywhere. I have been asking almost every Indian disembarking to no avail. He was meaning to be waiting for me right here at the terminus, you see, but I am being unable to locate him." Krishna was pleased that she would relieve the agitated fellow. "I did not meet Krishna Nayam aboard, sir," she beamed, recognizing the common mistake, "I am Krishna Nayam!" "Dear me!" came the flustered reply, the man reaching for his chest. "No, no, this cannot be!" he insisted, growing visibly nervous now, wringing his thin hands before her. "But I am!" confirmed Krishna, searching his demeanor for what so worried the man, "You must be here to collect me from the university! I am so very pleased to finally find you. I feared I had been forgotten and would have to make my way to the campus on my own." "Oh dear." the flabbergasted fellow uttered now pacing in front of her and patting his forehead nervously with the handkerchief he produced from his breast-pocket. He removed his spectacles, swabbing them mercilessly with the same hanky till they almost snapped between his fingers. "But...but," he stammered as politely as he could muster, "the arrangements, you see, the accommodation, the meals, the, well, everything. They are making them for a mister, you understand? The graduate college has been planning on a mister." The man continued pacing, stopping only when he himself spoke. "I see, yes well..." Krishna agreed, though not quite understanding why the arrangements should cause such a commotion. "Well, there's nothing to be doing but bringing you in, is there?" The man now determined, resolute. "We can't very well just be leaving you here at the terminal, can we? Surely not your own fault...Well, then, come along." he became suddenly officious and determined, hailing over an attendant to cart the luggage, "I've parked the car across the way." Krishna scuttled after the agitated stranger oblivious to the attention that her exotic dress drew from passers by. "An apology," he announced formally, whilst unlocking the boot, extending a hand to Krishna in greeting rather than a *namaste*, "I have not introduced myself. I go by Naga. I am a fellow at the O.P.R." "Then we shall be colleagues!" Krishna responded with delight, "and thank you for fetching me. It is so comforting to be welcomed by a countryman. You will have to tell me all about your experiences here." On her way to Princeton, on the wrong side of the road in so large an automobile she felt it might have been a barge, Krishna made a very agitated friend.

The problem was not, explained Dean Thorn at the office, that she was a lady per se, the problem was that she was expected to be a gentleman. Her housing had been arranged at the Graduate College, which would also serve as her eating club. Princeton's Graduate College served a strictly male student body. While the university admitted women students at a doctoral level for coursework and research, it had no facilities to house them nor could they matriculate. Krishna was astonished. If she could not matriculate, she could not obtain a doctorate from Princeton. Even if it was the only program available for a degree in demography, it simply could not be done. Dean Thorn regretted that there was nothing but to admit the mistake, deny her application and send her home. Temporary arrangements were made to house Krishna at the parsonage of the Miller Chapel. The minister and his wife had kindly agreed to accommodate Krishna until she could be returned to India. It was preposterous, lamented the efficient Dean Thorn, that neither Fulbright nor the Department of State had caught the error. It was common knowledge that Princeton was a male institution and something of which at least her advisors at LSE should have been well aware. Dean Thorn was sincerely sorry, had organized to ensure Krishna's safe (though temporary) stay and would contact Fulbright and the State Department to explain the situation on Monday morning. In the meantime, the fretting Naga helpfully carted Krishna and her belongings to the home of Reverend Carter and his wife. Krishna, too surprised to be distraught, meekly accepted all that was explained. There appeared nothing to do but accede.

The couple was informal and welcoming under the unexpected circumstances. They were awful sorry to learn about the mix-up and were happy to oblige in any way they could. They said it was the Christian thing to do. The elongated reverend was dressed in a red checkered shirt and loose grey slacks, appearing not so much a clergyman as perhaps a gardener to Krishna, who had grown used to the formal black capes of the Anglican clergy in Mangalore and London. Mrs. Carter, plump and bright-eyed, wore pearls and a black and white polka-dotted dress that clung tightly to her generous bosom, every stitch doing more than its job. "So far from home," bewailed the doting Mrs. Carter, "and so disappointed, you must be…But my oh my, expecting that a lady could so easily end up at Princeton University, well, that was fanciful, wasn't it? But what a special costume you have! Isn't it elegant? Must it be quite uncomfortable?" Ushered to a banana yellow themed bedroom with three windows neatly framed in white trim and optimistic, daisy-printed curtains that matched the bedspread, Krishna mournfully unpacked from her trunk as little as she could. She marveled at the size of the carpeted room, larger than any she'd ever occupied—including the cabin in the

Q.E. She grizzled at the immense painting of Jesus that hung over the wide bed. She had seen the figure in this pathetic pose before: kneeling, hands clasped and beseeching the parted clouds, as though praying for rain. He always seemed, compared to the riot of Hindu gods, so pitiable and woeful, so altogether color-less—how could somebody so insipid inspire anyone at all? She was glad the painting hung over her, so she'd be unable to see it while laying down. After cleaning up, (remarkable how there was a single faucet for cold and hot water, making it convenient to combine the two for a comfortable temperature) she was called down to supper and thought it appropriate, despite the circumstances, to put on her brightest face.

She did not want to insult her hosts, so when Krishna's plate was presented with nothing but a heap of potatoes and the odorous white flesh of a fish whose rusty skin sizzled and made her wince, she sat mum and aghast and wondered if she should mention. She was entreated to bow her head and clasp her hands for a short prayer. "Good friends, good meat, good Lord, let's eat!" the reverend joked, winking at Krishna on closing, and picking up his fork. "William Trevor Hunt Carter!" Dolly Carter scolded, "that's no way to give proper grace!" Still, she smiled at him, conceding, and picked up her fork. Krishna nibbled at her pota-toes, careful to avoid the meat. She made polite small-talk about the beautiful houses in Princeton, the weather over the Atlantic and yes, how they must con-stantly have to pay attention to readjusting the clocks on the Q.E. "But you haven't touched your cod!" exclaimed the reverend who had tucked mightily into his. "I'm afraid, sir, I don't eat meat. I'm so very sorry, but I'm vegetarian." Krishna admitted, feeling awkward to make the confession. "Vegetarian?" exclaimed the bewildered Mrs. Carter, "Such newfangled ideas…Now why would anybody want to put all that good meat to waste when there are people starving in India…Oh my, India, that's where you're from, isn't it? Silly me! Is that why they're starving, maybe? Because nobody's eating their meat?" "Excuse me, madam," Krishna intervened, surprising even herself, "It is not that we waste any meat in India. If we are Hindu, we don't slaughter the beasts in the first place. We think it is not right." "I see," replied the baffled Mrs. Carter consider-ing the proposition momentarily, then dismissing the notion and turning to the problem at hand, "but you've barely had anything to eat! How about a peanut butter and jelly? Now that would be vegetarian, wouldn't it?" She hurried off into the kitchen without awaiting reply. "So you would be Hindu?" the reverend inquired, interested. "Yes sir. I am." "Reincarnation and all that, eh?" he pro-ceeded, pleased with himself for knowing the implications. "Do you know what I'm going to do for you little lady?" The jolly man slapped his knee, smiling proudly, "I'm going to make sure you don't leave this great land of ours without a bible of your very own! I'm sure you'll find it a most fascinating bit of reading!" he added, pleased at the prospect. "How thoughtful of you." Krishna replied, suddenly overcome with exhaustion. "And tomorrow, perhaps you'd like to accompany Dolly to the Y? It's a Saturday after all, and there'll be a social in the evening. The ladies there'd be tickled pink to meet you. Don't think they've had many Indians there before—especially ladies. What do you think of that?" inquired the parson, leaving Krishna little choice. "I'm sure that would be lovely," Krishna acquiesced, then struggled to remain ladylike against the challenge of her first of many a peanut butter and jelly sandwich.

The Daily Princetonian
September 17, 1947.

Ooops!

Imagine his surprise when expecting a Mr. Krishna Nayam
as a new Visiting Graduate Fellow at the Population Section,
a Miss Krishna Nayam came to register instead! The Daily
Princetonian has learned that due to a series of administrative errors, the Office of Population Research accidentally
admitted a lady student from the London School of Economics into its visiting fellows program as a candidate for a doctorate in demography. Unwilling to comment on the details of
the flub, Dean Thorn of the O.P.R. has informed the Princetonian that, it being University policy, it would be impossible
to matriculate a female. The O.P.R. is working diligently to
quickly return the student to India, her country of origin,
and taking steps to refund the Fulbright organization for the
scholarship she received for study at Princeton. Having no
other recourse on campus, the would-be student is temporarily housed by the Reverend and Mrs. Carter. We at the
Daily Princetonian believe it should be mandatory for admin-
istrators at the O.P.R. to register for basic coursework in the
Biology department.

The Daily Princetonian
September 19, 1947

AAUW Takes Up Cause of Accidental Admission

In an unexpected turn of events, the Dean of the Office of
Population Research is being challenged by the American
Association of University Women to make an exception in the
University policy regarding the matriculation of female students. On September 17th the Daily Princetonian reported of
a female, Indian student whose application was accidentally
accepted by the O.P.R. as a Visiting Fellow in pursuit of a
doctoral degree. Miss Krishna Nayam, of Mangalore India,
applied for admission, having completed her M.S. in Economics from the University of Bombay with honors. Her coursework included a stint at the reputable London School of
Economics which supported her application to Princeton for
completion of her doctorate in the field of demography. Miss
Nayam's application was accepted, and a Fulbright scholarship provided for travel, tuition, room, board and incidentals.
She arrived on campus last week with great expectation, only
to be turned away in what the O.P.R. described as an unfor-
tunate case of mistaken identity.

Miss Marjory Fisher, a member of the A.A.U.W. and wife of
Professor Randall Fisher of the Physics Department learned
of the student's peculiar plight at a recent Y.W.C.A. social.
"The lady was admitted on her academic merits," commented
Mrs. Fisher to the Daily Princetonian, "she told me herself
that whilst applying to Princeton she had no reason to believe
that so advanced a university would be closed to women.
After all, even the London School of Economics is open to
female students at all levels. I contacted the A.A.U.W. in
Washington to inform them of the matter. The Association is
enthusiastic to support Miss Nayam in remaining at Princeton to complete the degree for which she came."

The fetching Miss Nayam, resplendent in her traditional
Indian costume, said in accented English "I very much appreciate the interest the A.A.U.W. has taken in my situation. I do
not wish to cause trouble to the University. I hope only to
return to India with skills needed to improve my country's
conditions. This is why I came. I applied to Princeton because
it is the only program in the world for the study of demogra-

phy. It never occurred to me or my advisors at LSE that the University was closed to girls. Had I known, why would I have applied?"

The recently established Fulbright organization, sponsored by the United States Government, granted Miss Nayam's scholarship. Fulbright made no formal statement to the Princetonian. Representatives explained that the organization reviews applications for scholarships on the basis of academic merit. It's mission is to increase mutual understanding between the peoples of the United States and other countries through the granting of scholarships for international study. They added that the organization had no reason to question the veracity or appropriateness of the O.P.R.'s acceptance letter, issued to Miss Nayam last August. The Fulbright organization provided the grant in good faith of the University's due diligence in reviewing the student's eligibility for her course of study.

Dean Thorn of the O.P.R., recently elevated from his position as Assistant Dean, said, "It is preposterous that an educated lady would be unaware that Princeton University is an all-male facility. It is impossible to revise that principle for the sake of a single student without having to open the institution to all women. I have contacted the office of the President of the University to review the matter but doubt that the decision to return Miss Nayam to India shall be reconsidered."

###

The hearing took place in the imposing Board Room at Nassau Hall—a building, Mrs. Carter informed Krishna, which had housed the Continental Congress and had been visited by George Washington in revolutionary times. Krishna, appropriately intimidated, was ushered into the room by the Reverend and Mrs. Carter, who primped and smiled widely at the few Members of the Board of Trustees already seated at the long conference table. The hastily scheduled meeting was closed to the university community, but Krishna was pleased to see Naga in a knitted blue sweater seated in one of the several seats against the far wall. He waved eagerly. She bit her lips into a smile and perked her eyebrows up in response. Krishna had not yet met the A.A.U.W. representative, a Mrs. Wallace, who sat beside Mrs. Fisher at the far end of the table and jumped instantly to greet her. She welcomed Krishna in a whisper and invited her to take a seat between the two ladies, advising her not to be nervous and assuring her that she had reviewed the papers closely and would do everything possible to enable her stay.

Krishna had never met a lady like Mrs. Wallace. She was built square, like a bullock-cart. She wore a dense, dark blue, tweed suit cut like a man's and not a hint of color to brighten her freckled face. (Even Krishna had taken to wearing lipstick under Dot's influence.) Mrs. Wallace's red hair was cropped to military minuteness, her deep-set blue eyes could have pierced through blocks of cement. She shook Krishna's hand so hard between the massive sponges of her palms, that it verily throbbed from the rigor of her greeting. Something about her reminded Krishna of Jyotsna, she couldn't quite determine what. Krishna's crisp, powder blue sari rustled as she took her seat at the table and the Carters found their way to the seats in the second row, Mrs. Carter smiling politely and making sure to leave an empty chair between herself and the unnaturally cheerful Naga.

At ten minutes to ten, several seats around the table remained empty, and the Trustees (all men) who occupied the few remaining had not looked up to acknowledge Krishna's presence. They shuffled the papers before them in silence, perusing them intently, cleared their throats and issued curt nods in greeting to the other men who trickled in, surveying the wood-paneled room or shaking hands before taking a seat. Finally she recognized Dean Thorn, who entered and shook hands with all the men seated but ignored Krishna and the ladies entirely. Mrs. Wallace leapt up to introduce herself, her deep voice resounding through the room. "Good of you to come," Thorn responded in a hushed tone meant to dampen Mrs. Wallace's fervor. When President Dobb entered at ten o'clock on the dot promptly commanding the single seat at the head of the table, everybody stood until he had settled into his chair. He welcomed the crowd and expressed appreciation for their appearing on so short a notice. He stressed, in a booming voice more suited to a stadium, that the Board had determined to consider the matter at hand because of the importance and credibility of the government's Fulbright grant. "The funds from Fulbright, having already been accepted into the universities' accounts," he continued, "impinge upon us as the Board of Trustees to address the mistake in a responsible fashion. And I intend to keep this hearing short. I expect we all understand that we are working from the premise that this admission was made in error." He then presented Mrs. Fisher, Mrs. Wallace, Dean Thorn and the Carters to the Trustees. "The lovely lass seated between Misses Wallace and Fisher must be the subject at issue?" he inquired at Dean Thorn. "Yes sir, Miss Krishna Nayam, who we had expected was not of the fairer sex" replied the Dean, eliciting chuckles from the men, and an exaggerated, silvery twitter from Mrs. Carter.

First to be called upon was Dean Thorn, who described in detail the process by which Krishna's application had been received, reviewed and accepted by the Office of Population Research. He referred frequently to the mimeographed papers stacked before each Trustee. In an effort to absolve himself of responsibility for the mistake, he stressed that the recommendation letters from London and Bombay repeatedly identified Miss Nayam as "the applicant," "the student," or "the candidate," and only once referred to her as a "she." When sternly questioned by a Trustee, he readily admitted that the review panel knew the name "Krishna" to be typically held by Indian men and assumed that the extraordinary credentials and transcript could not but belong to one. "In fact," he added, much to Mrs. Wallace's satisfaction, "there was nothing in Miss Nayam's record to indicate that the applicant should not be eligible for a doctorate." Had the fact that there was record of her having been a classical Indian dancer ever been considered? "Not at all," replied the incredulous Thorn, "would you question the gender of Mr. Fred Astaire or Mr. Gene Kelly?"

The Trustees glanced nervously at each other as Dean Thorn finished speaking. His information did not bode well for the university's position. President Dobb leaned an elbow heavily on the table, pinching the bridge of his nose between thumb and forefinger, then summoning Mrs. Wallace to comment. She stood confidently, and thanked the Board for considering the A.A.U.W.'s position, one, she stated "which would be irresponsible to dismiss in this advanced day and age." Authoritative in her manner, she as good as commanded the Trustees to review their documentation "with a fine tooth comb" to locate where on the Application for Admission to Princeton University's post-graduate programs there was any spot for indication, perhaps a check-box, for specification of gender. The Trustees busily flipped pages, scanning to no avail. "It has already been stated by the Dean that there is nothing in the record to indicate that Miss Nayam should be denied the posting for which she applied and was accepted." she announced emphatically. Krishna was at impressed at Mrs. Wallace's direct, impassioned style. Unlike Dean Thorn, she stood when she spoke, and looked the Trustees boldly in the eyes as though challenging each of them personally. She spoke loudly in declarative sentence without doubt or hesitation. "Moreover," she continued, "Miss Nayam has done nothing for which her education should be made to suffer. She not only meets, but exceeds the university's stringent academic requirements. Her documentation was submitted completely and on time. Her references are outstanding, and her transcripts are extraordinary. Her tuition, room and board fees have already been paid. Should she be faulted merely for her gender when even the university's own paperwork does not demand to know it? And how was she to imagine, in the rural boondocks of India, embroiled in its own political and social turmoil, that a university as reputable as Princeton would be closed to her when even the London School of Economics had embraced her with open arms?" Krishna stared up at Mrs. Wallace, who she appreciated for defending her cause with all her might and wit. She recognized what this woman shared with Jyotsna. Mrs. Wallace was unapologetic. Unlike Krishna, she was bold and unashamed.

"It is," President Dobb interrupted in just as commanding a tone, "a matter of practicality, Mrs. Wallace, as much as anything else. The university has no accommodation for women in the dormitories or eating clubs. Even the few ladies who do take up coursework on a graduate level cannot be accommodate and arrange for their own meals and lodging." "So you would offer that if Miss Nayam were to find her own lodging, the university would matriculate her?" Mrs. Wallace cleverly interceded. "Nothing of the sort!" shot back a Trustee, outraged. "We cannot simply throw the doors open to all sorts of women because of a bumbling administrative error! The matter must be considered from a rational perspective. After all, the university has operated as it does for more than a century." "Yet," Mrs. Wallace replied in calm response, her hands now leaning on the table, "the O.P.R. admits that Miss Nayam's qualifications make her no different from the gentlemen who are so readily admitted." "Mrs. Wallace, with all due respect to your cause," grimaced another Trustee in frustration, "imagine if every institution were to open its doors to women? Our military, for example? Or the ministry? Outrageous!" "Yet," Mrs. Wallace glowered back angrily, "you are willing to cheat a qualified candidate of her education as a result of a mistake that the university admits it made? Is there nothing so outrageous about that?" A tense silence engulfed the room.

In a mild effort to relieve the unease, President Dobb addressed the reverend Carter. "Reverend, have you anything to contribute with respect to the character of the candidate at issue?" the reverend stood to answer. "Why yes sir," he responded amiably, "she's a proper lady, I must say. The little Missus had her doubts about putting up an idolater…who knew what to expect? But we can't complain, can we Dolly? Keeps to herself for the most part. Neat, quiet, stays outta the way. Helps around the house wherever she can. Even cooked us a fancy Indian-like feast one night without meat, isn't that so Dolly?" Mrs. Carter, lips pursed, nodded in agreement. "Mr. Dobb!" cried Mrs. Wallace who had had just about enough. "I do not believe Miss Nayam's character, diet or religion are at issue here! Her academic achievements and her right to earn the education for which the Fulbright organization has sponsored her are the only matters relevant to this discussion." "It always helps, Mrs. Wallace," Dobb suggested patronizingly, "to be assured that a student, particularly one so out of place, would contribute positively to the Princeton community, wouldn't you agree?" He surveyed the room to gather consensus from his peers. Mrs. Wallace, disgusted, did not respond. More papers were shuffled, more throats were cleared. The Trustees glanced nervously at their watches. It was already past noon.

Suddenly, Dean Thorn piped up. "But she does not, after all, meet the academic criteria for candidacy! Why it says so right here in her acceptance letter! She has not fulfilled the credits for Mathematical Statistics or Calculus. As a matter of fact, those courses remain outstanding…Surely sufficient ground to deny the application." Mrs. Fisher, proper in her cream colored suit and matching pillbox hat was not meant to speak, but interrupted to protest. "Mister Thorn! Why this is ridiculous! You know full well that the university frequently asks graduate students to make up for undergraduate credits that haven't been properly fulfilled! It's a common procedure—not one that would ever have resulted in denial of the application—in fact, it didn't in the first place!" The Trustees shot looks at each other bolstered by the discovery, Mrs. Fisher's outburst being of little consequence.

"Excuse me," Naga chirped from the back row raising his hand meekly. "Excuse me, sirs!" Dobb, hadn't noticed the lad who blended neatly into the dark corner, but acknowledged him to speak. "I am also being an Indian Fellow at the O.P.R." he knew he might raise Thorn's ire by speaking, but felt compelled to contribute. After all, Thorn had invited him to attend. "I was sent to collect Mr. Nayam, well the now Miss Nayam, from the port in New York as I am having a vehicle and well, I was available and always am being happy to encounter a coun-tryman, well even a country lady, and of course, delighted to welcome them and share stories and news from back home as well as introduce them to the..." Dobb raised his hand to halt the nervous yammering. "Sir, have you something relevant to add?" he inquired. "Oh, right, yes, do excuse me," stammered Naga, "yes, only that I too was lacking those very same courses and was accepted into the doctor-ate program. It is only that mathematical statistics is not generally being taught as a regular economics curriculum and the calculus portion is not its own course, but part of an advanced maths class, for the most part, in other universities. So you see, I was accepted and I had to take those courses, as a matter of fact, many of my colleagues..." Again, Dobb raised his hand to silence the fellow and thanked him for his comments.

"Miss Nayam," President Dobb addressed Krishna for the first time. "Have you yourself anything to add?" As the meeting went on, Krishna had grown hopeless. She was sure she'd be sent home. Mrs. Wallace nudged her to stand, which she did, looking disconsolate. She had prepared a small speech, but forgot it entirely. She clasped her hands behind her back. Her dark eyes grew pensive as she addressed herself solely, intimately, to President Dobb as though no-one else were in the room. ""If you will permit, sir, I am reminded of a poem. When I was very young and learning English in school, my teachers used to have us memorize English verses from Shakespeare and Longfellow. I must confess that I didn't understand what most of them meant at the time, but one always stuck in my head. It was from the Bengali Nobel Laureate, Rabindranath Tagore, who wrote a book of prose called Gitanjali. If you'll indulge me, I hope I can remember it properly to recite it for you. It says: 'Where the mind is without fear and the head is held high; Where knowledge is free; Where the world has not been broken up into fragments by narrow domestic walls; Where words come out from the depth of truth; Where tireless striving stretches its arms towards perfection; Where the clear stream of reason has not lost its way into the dreary desert sand of dead habit; Where the mind is led forward by thee into ever-widening thought and action—Into that heaven of freedom, my Father, let my country awake.'" She paused to let the poem sink in, then continued. "That is all I wish for, sir: to help my country awake into that type of freedom. I come here not to take anything from you that you would not wish to give. Your institution is in the business of education. I am here to be educated. I have arrived here only by my wits and by my work and with very little to call my own. But I did arrive with hope. I hoped that earning an education would help me improve the lot of my country. I thought these things because I grew up under the influence of Mahatma Gandhi, a man, who you must know, has been a great leader." She paused for a moment, considering what to say next and remembering that it's best to say something kind. "But still," she stammered, "it is a wonderful aspect of your America that even a foreigner such as I would be granted a hearing here. And that the A.A.U.W. would choose to support the cause of a complete stranger. I have made friends here. The Carters have been so welcoming, and Mrs. Fisher and Mrs. Wallace and Mr. Naga. I am ever so grateful for all that the O.P.R. has done to accommodate me during my stay. I can assure you that I will go home with a most positive report of my experience here. I believe that it is my responsibility to do what I can for my country, and I also believe it is your responsibility to make sure that Princeton keeps its word. But of course, I will accept any decision you make." Krishna, on that note of defeat, settled quietly back into her seat. For the first time, it hit Krishna that she might end up back in Bombay. Mrs. Wallace, impressed at Krishna's strong start, now sighed at her easy attitude of acceptance toward the end. She wondered if it was the Gandhian influence: to resist by not resisting. After having come so far, Mrs. Wallace was amazed that the girl was readying to settle for the shortest possible straw. President Dobb asked everybody but the Trustees to take their leave.

The Daily Princetonian
September 24, 1947

An Exceptional Studentess?

The Board of Trustees today issued a recommendation to the Office of Population Research that it honor its admission of a female doctoral candidate: Miss Krishna Nayam of Mangalore, India. Deliberations after an unusual emergency meeting of The Board of Trustees resulted in a letter, addressed to Dean Thorn of the O.P.R. stating that because there is no other doctoral program available in the field of demography, because the student was admitted on her academic merits, and because the Fulbright organization's scholarship funding for the student has already been accepted, there is no responsible choice but to allow Miss Nayam to pursue the coursework and research for which she applied and was accidentally accepted. The Board of Trustees emphasized that the student will not be permitted to matriculate and that the decision is exceptional, implying no policy change with respect to the admission of women to the University.

The Board of Trustees reached a compromise with representatives of the American Association of University Women, which put forth Miss Nayam's case. Miss Nayam had applied to the O.P.R. unaware that the University does not matriculate women. Her gender had escaped notice as her first name, (Krishna) is typically a name given to Indian men. It was determined by the Board of Trustees that while Miss Nayam's coursework and research can be undertaken at Princeton, another university must accept the credits and matriculate the student as well as issue her doctoral degree. Similarly, Miss Nayam will be permitted to enroll in two undergraduate courses in the mathematics department, credits for which will also have to be recognized by another qualified university. This will be the first time a lady sits for any undergraduate courses at Princeton University.

Representatives of the American Association of University Women said this was a "red letter day for the furtherance of women's education." They were highly satisfied that the administration had chosen the proper course of action under the circumstances. The A.A.U.W. will assist Miss Nayam in finding a qualified University to matriculate her, transfer her credits and issue her doctorate.

Dean Thorn of the O.P.R. explained that it has been a challenge to find accommodation for the studentess, who is temporarily housed by the Reverend and Mrs. Carter at the Miller Chapel parsonage. Without access to an eating club, arrangements have been made for Miss Nayam to have use of the faculty dining facility for meals. Miss Nayam is working with the YWCA and representatives of A.A.U.W. to locate appropriate housing near the campus.

Miss Nayam, an elegant Indian national in colorful traditional garb has already been spotted on campus, and can't help but be conspicuous in class. "We will treat her just like any other student," commented Professor Rodney Philips of the mathematics department, "we will expect her to perform at the same level as her classmates and place before her the same challenges as must always be met to maintain academic excellence." The Board of Trustees, the O.P.R. and the Mathematics Department were careful to stress that this decision was made by exception and that university policy remains firm on the matter of admitting females on campus. It is expected that documentation related to application to the several university programs will soon be revised to state the university's policies more explicitly.

###

"We recognize how weighty a decision it would be for you." explained the Reverend Carter. "It's simply that Dolly doesn't think it proper for us to put up a pagan like this, understand?" Krishna had never taken a shine to Mrs. Carter. Only yesterday, she'd noticed how Mrs. Carter could discredit anybody she pleased by preceding the criticism with an invocation. "Marge Shaw," Mrs. Carter would beam, "God bless her soul…" (this is where Krishna learned to brace for the insult) "couldn't bake a pie if the Lord himself came down to roll the dough!" She imagined Mrs. Carter's complaints at the possibility of Krishna's staying on at the parsonage. "That pretty Krishner" (she pronounced her name with an e-r at the end,) "God forgive the little savage, I couldn't bear to think she's in that bedroom bowing down to all those barbaric little idols she's installed." Krishna considered her options. The Y had no more rooms, the A.A.U.W. had come up empty handed, and it seemed that private homes on campus area were unwilling to take in a paying Indian boarder for heavens knew what ridiculous reasons. Naga had mentioned something about getting used to being thought of as a negro, but the repercussions hadn't fully dawned on Krishna as yet. Mostly she was concerned that she had already missed a week of classes. Krishna couldn't afford to fall behind on her school work when she was under such scrutiny at the university. She would be wasting time looking for housing and was already comfortable here at the parsonage as long as she could steer clear of Mrs. Carter. After all it was, she figured, just another god to her. "Yes," she stretched her hand out to the Reverend Carter, who accepted it joyfully, "I'll take the classes to convert." "Means you'll have to go to Sunday school with the children for just a little while…" laughed the Reverend Carter, "but we'll make a good Christian outta you yet!" With the housing matter settled, Krishna could finally get to work.

Mrs. Wallace found it peculiar that a certain Professor Dalton at the London School of Economics, who had even issued a glowing recommendation for the student, denied the request to transfer her credits and matriculate Krishna at LSE. He hadn't even the courtesy to explain the refusal. Perhaps, she concluded, it was a simple matter of policy. She did not have the heart to tell Krishna the news, as the girl had suffered more than sufficient hurdles, and the battle wasn't over. It was remarkable that Princeton had allowed her to commence her classes and research at all. Mrs. Wallace wrote off to Cornell University in view of its strong program in Economics and its receptivity to women. She had the presence of mind to include the Bombay University in her list of addressees as well.

October 18, 1947

Miss Krishna Nayampalli
c/o The Reverend and Mrs. Carter
The Miller Chapel Parsonage
Princeton, NJ 08544

My Very Dear Akka:

We are delighted to hear of your safe arrival in America and of the excellent news at Princeton. Ranjeet has renamed you "the Accidental Pioneer." What a grand debacle! It is shocking to imagine that so important a university in America would deny admission to qualified girls when even in Bombay and Cal they are readily accepted. Ganesh must have been labouring intensively on your behalf to garner you so much favour!

You have said little about your journey. Was the Queen Elizabeth as splendid as they say? How fortunate also that you have so quickly met a nice fellow. Are you keeping secrets to yourself about Mr. Naga? Do share with us all the details. Is he at least Brahmin? It would bring us so much joy to learn that even at this age you have made a good match. Or must you now seek out a Christian?

As you asked, we have, of course, uttered not a word about this matter of conversion. We cannot imagine the difficult circumstances that put you in this predicament. And how horrid that landlady must be! How droll to think that so many years we all spent walking far out of our ways to avoid the English missionaries in Mangalore, only to find oneself entrapped for the sake of a roof over one's head! But isn't it even so with the converts here at home? Christians of convenience they are, gaining favor with the occupiers or escaping the rigours of low-birth. In any event, we do not think Brahma would mind. After all, even Ranjeet believes that our *sangha* has not stood properly by you. Do Presbyterians celebrate Christmas then, and must you also learn Latin? What is this Sunday schooling all about? Isn't that meant to be the day of rest?

We are still only speculating about it, but I am bursting to tell you. Ranjeet and I may come to America! He has corresponded with a hospital in Nebraska, a rural place that has trouble finding doctors with particular specialisations. With so much paperwork and rules to follow (you will notice that the Indian bureaucracy runs circles around the English,) the prospect of going may be as much as two years away (perhaps you will be already back by the time we come!) But I am hopeful that it can be sooner. Ranjeet expects that the earnings there would be much better than they are here at home. After only a few years we could come home and retire. He wonders if, being there, you think also that this is so?

The University is going well for me. I am very busy with my studies. I enjoy the challenges and am quite happy with the distraction. I am pursuing biology because Ranjeet thinks it will help me in all the work with the animals. (We now have four sweet new pups to feed!) And talking of pups, she will report to you herself, but Shaku is expecting again! We hope that Aniruddha will have a small brother, but that is still six months off. I remain, regrettably, without child. Arna and Amma worry about this, but otherwise they are fine. Ranjeet hopes to transport them here to visit me in December. He will even bring our M'am, he says (because I miss them all so!) Though I bring him no children, he is yet so very sweet to me. He says we mustn't worry, that they will happen in their own time.

You remain always in my happiest thoughts. Do keep writing as you can. It is such a joy to hear your news.

Your ever loving,

Sindhya

Krishna went headlong into her studies. She paid no mind to the undergraduate boys who before the professor arrived directed hooting and cackling sounds at her under their breaths, imitating the monkeys they were implying she descended from. She did not think their behavior insulting, only branded them as undignified. She learned to arrive just in time for class so as not to have to suffer their abuse. Much to her relief, she felt neither leniency nor demand from the professors, who appeared unfazed about her presence in class. They droned on with their lectures glibly oblivious to their audiences. Naga helpfully showed her all the ropes at the O.P.R., taking pains to accompany her to the library and make elaborate explanations about the resources essential to complete her research. He was engaged back home to a girl easily half his age, and not being a Brahmin, it was understood between them that their relations would be strictly collegial—though it was a question whether she herself was still one, particularly now that she had "converted." By November, the A.A.U.W. informed Krishna that the Chancellor at the University of Bombay had confirmed matriculation and said he would transfer her credits with pleasure. She was assigned a supervisor for her research at the O.P.R. and was inordinately happy to learn that he was legally blind.

Krishna attended church on Sundays, and followed the children to Sunday School immediately before the sermon. She was consistently surprised each week by the remarkably miniaturized furnishings of the colorful room, and didn't mind the innocent questions about the length of her "sorry," or the dot on her forehead. She elected not to participate in the children's Christmas pageant already being planned in November, but volunteered to assist in fashioning the elaborate costumes for the event which she sewed in the company of other members of the Y. Her plentiful schedule ensured deep and restful sleep. She never disposed of her little shrine of Hindu figures as she was meant to do, only transferred the small retinue neatly into a shoe-box which she lowered carefully into her trunk. If this Christ had any credibility, she decided, he should not feel threatened.

11

Beyond its title, there was nothing so special about the faculty dining club. It was inconveniently remote from the Office of Population Research and while she expected the mature faculty might make more of an effort to extend themselves to her, Krishna often found them more clannish than the students. The wintry walk to the building wasn't in the least justified by the uninspired menu offerings and despite her "conversion," Krishna couldn't help but remain a vegetarian. The paltry provisions available to a vegetarian in 1947 were limited to chopped lettuce (which constituted the "salad course") an overcooked, buttered vegetable (generally "succotash," green beans or boiled beats), white bread, boiled potatoes or plain, insipid rice. Had Krishna not discovered Tabasco sauce that year, she might not have eaten at all.

One early evening after classes Krishna appeared at the faculty club smarting from the blustering winds that pierced her as she skittered across the wide walkways between buildings. The silk sari, woolen stockings, sweater and coat suited to London in winter proved insufficient for Princeton even in the autumn. While she found the brilliance of the fall leaves riveting, Krishna detested the daily battle against the wind that insisted on sealing shut the entrance door to the club. She heaved at the brass handle of the dense, wooden, door, brittle leaves fluttering against her, the door remaining stubborn against her will. She learned to wait patiently for the fleeting instants when the winds died down to yank hard, and would end up catapulting herself into the club, an ever harrowing form of entrance. She would remain in the darkened vestibule for a few seconds, shivering, rubbing her cheeks with her frigid hands, or smoothing her hair, and recovering her dignity. Krishna was hungry that particular day, cold, and reluctant to relinquish her garb to the cheeky coat-check boy, an underclassman who she suspected of pilfering loose change from the pockets. Since it was improper to enter the dining hall fully covered, she handed over her heavy grey, British coat with its perky velvet collar, making sure to empty the pockets first. The dining hall was desolate save for two professors who chatted at a corner table, too involved to acknowledge her entrance. At least the serving-men behind the counters, negroes with sympathetic smiles and doting welcomes, could be counted on for pleasantries. "Cold enough for you?" one of them winked. "A bit too cold," she answered, recognizing that she had shed much of her former modesty, "might you be able to arrange to have the wind turned down?" The waiter chuckled at her, "For you, Miss, we'd do our very best I'm shor."

Miss Krishna stood apart for the waiters. She surely wasn't white, but she wasn't colored either. She didn't shy away, afraid the way so many white folks were, but neither did she order them around without pleases or thank yous or would you be so kinds...She'd introduced herself to each of the staff the first time she'd arrived, shaking hands as simply as at church on Sundays. Few professors ever did such a thing. They had learned that she was a misplaced student and were always pleased to see the young lady come, so exotic she was in what they called her flowing gown. Today, she read the menu with predictable disappointment and ordered the special "hold the chicken" as she'd often heard repeated. "Why do you always go taking the special part right out of the daily special, Ma'am?" her waiter commented. "Not even a rabbit could live on yo rations!" "Because where I grew up," she replied in earnest, "we try not to eat anybody who isn't trying to eat us." They had a good laugh and her server tutted while heaping her plate with extra servings of succotash.

Krishna had not taken notice of the bedraggled, elderly fellow, presumably a professor, who'd shuffled in after her, comfortable in a thick wool sweater. His hands, clutching a pipe, were clasped humbly behind his back. He had observed their interactions and now saluted the staff with nods and gave a wave to the professors at the far end of the room, both of whom stood nervously and came back with strange, formal bows. Krishna did not stir. She only smiled at the unkempt man, noticing the way his frazzle of hair almost defied gravity, and continued to gaze out the brass-grid windows at the shimmering leaves and the howling, biting wind. The scene reminded her of something from her past, she could not recall what. Soon the gentleman approached her, inquiring in accented English "Vud I prevent you from enjoying your solitude if I ver to join your tebl?" Krishna, her mouth full, could not speak but nodded, and motioned to the chair beside her. "Zo, you must be ze young ledy meking all ze commotion, eh?" Krishna didn't know what to say. Again, she nodded, quashing the smile that wanted to burst forth in response to his outfit and his accent, both disheveled. "An ingenious leadership in your country. You have much to be proud of." He continued. "Many changes and difficulties lately," is all Krishna replied between bites. "I have not, unfortunately, been home to witness them." The waiter came to take the professor's order. The man considered the offerings, then looked over Krishna's plate intrigued. "Exactly what she's having!" he commanded "zo ve von't offend ze fegeterian ledy." "Please sir," Krishna jumped in, "select as you wish. I am quite used to it." "Perhaps it vud suit us better in ze Vest to learn a little something of your veys," he replied, adding, "Look, ve can do even better together…I see you haf entirely missed ze scalloped eggplants!" "Oh no," Krishna explained, "I fear I don't touch eggs." The man chuckled to himself, then offered gently, trying hard not to sound patronizing, "Eggplant, dear ledy, might be known better to you as aubergine." Krishna was happily surprised "aubergine? Have I all this time been turning down the aubergine?" The man repeated his order, adding a plate of scalloped eggplants that would be shared, then extended his hand saying, "vud you be zo kind as to remind me of your name? I do not belif ve ver properly introduced." "Oh do excuse me, I am Krishna Nayam," Krishna reported, extending her hand. "And I am Albert Einstein," the man responded sweetly, taking it. Krishna nearly fainted in her chair.

In 1947, Krishna celebrated her first Thanksgiving at the Einstein's home on 112 Mercer Street. Professor Einstein was uncomplicated, jolly and kind. He played the violin and chatted with his few guests in German. He had made sure that there was plenty for Krishna to eat aside from the obligatory turkey. The Einsteins welcomed Krishna with warmth, and expressed a constant interest in her culture. Krishna, intimidated by it, was also flattered to be included in the company, but didn't feel she could much contribute to the lofty conversation. She tried to make polite conversation with the guests but found she was happiest when "put to use," and most satisfied when Professor Einstein consented to letting her do the dishes.

The only reason Krishna agreed to perform in the Y's winter fundraiser was that it was Mrs. Fisher who'd asked. After all her support, how could Krishna turn her down? The theme, it had been decided, would be "Dance Around the World." Already, said Mrs. Fisher, they had found amongst the membership a remarkable treasure of dance talent. Mrs. Armstrong, as it turned out (nee Solino), had grown up in Spain dancing Flamenco. Professor Hochburger's two daughters had been studying it in New York and would be dancing a Russian ballet. Mrs. Vanderveer from the English department was a clog dancer in the Dutch tradition. And how exotic it would be for Krishna to perform a traditional Indian dance! Krishna hadn't tested her ankle in ages, but limited to a single, ten-minute piece, she imagined it would hold up just fine. Her biggest challenge would be to get ahold of the music, for which as it turned out, Naga thought he might have a source. An Indian graduate student in the engineering department had a remarkable collection of reel-to-reels with *ragas* and *ghazals* from back home. Surely, something in there would do. Soon, Naga reported that Jacob Rao had happily agreed to lend his collection to the cause, if the infamous Krishna

Nayam (was this the girl he'd read about in the papers?) would concoct a *pukka* Indian meal in return. If he offered the kitchen and the ingredients, said Krishna, she would happily take on the task.

Feeling laughable in her new woolen cap (she had never worn but a scarf before) and armed with the spices Sindhya had sent, Krishna sought out the house that Jacob Rao, who Naga said was a Christian from Darjeeling, rented on Prospect Avenue. Krishna was meant to show up early to start the cooking. Naga would join them later. On December 1st 1947, Krishna first set eyes on the man she would marry two years later to the day. Jacob Rao bounced merrily down his stairs and flung open the front door with the enthusiasm of a kindergartner on Christmas morning. It was this joie-de-vivre which would ultimately win Krishna's heart, though at first meeting she thought Jacob quite the buffoon. He was tall and athletic, with shiny, mischievous eyes, and a brazen smile as wide as its boulevard of glimmering teeth. He wore a tightly knitted sweater of brilliant, kaleidoscopic colors ("Peruvian!" he later announced, proudly, pinching it away from his chest) and his laugh, which was frequent, was equally unrestrained. There was nothing dark about him. He had nothing to hide. "Why you're beautiful!" were Jacob's first words to Krishna upon beholding her. "I'd been expecting a miserable old spinster and look what you've turned out to be!" Krishna didn't know how to respond. She extended her frigid hand formally and with caution, "Pleased to meet you as well, I suppose."

There was none of the Indian formality in Jacob's jaunty company. He herded Krishna through the house and promptly corralled her in the kitchen, pointing out where the "*dekchis*" could be found and unsystematically yanking open every drawer and cabinet so she could "survey her territory." He'd set out the ingredients he'd bought on the white kitchen table. Directly over it hung a framed calligraphic print of Tagore's poem, incredibly, the very one Krishna had quoted to the Board of Directors not so long ago. A recent gift from his sister, Jacob explained, who had done the calligraphy herself at art school.

The meal would be considerably vegetarian for Naga's sake, though he himself, Jacob confessed, was raised a carnivore. He'd also taken the liberty of making some music selections he thought Krishna could listen to while cooking. He'd just keep playing different pieces he said, and Krishna could yay or nay them. Each happily set to his task, Jacob noisily unboxing the rickety reels and threading, dedicated, the slippery tape through the convoluted pins and levers that poked from the sound-system he'd erected behind the brown checkered living room couch. They made small-talk in elevated voices across the swinging kitchen door. "All let to me" Jacob chirped in response to Krishna's inquiry about the house, revealing the traces of an English education, "by a jolly good professor gone off on sabbatical."

In the brightness of the kitchen, Krishna unbundled the *masalas* that smudged with vivid colors the waxy brown paper in which Sindhya had wrapped them. They were *M'am's* customary blends and when the smell of his curry struck her nostrils, a lump came to Krishna's throat and tears bulged, pending behind her eyes. She turned quickly to the sink, spun the faucets and put herself to flushing the vegetables of their grit. "Fine, thank you," she answered in a wavering voice, when Jacob asked if all was suitable in the kitchen, just as the haunting warble of a *vina* leaked into the room. At that, Krishna gave in. The sound and scent combined to tease the depths of her loneliness. She leaned over the sink, and riding the melancholy music, gave in to her tears.

In my imagination, this is when my father bursts in, not giving mom time to compose herself. He intuits correctly the source of her anguish. He wraps merciful arms sweetly around her, needs no reassurance himself, demands no explanation. He simply takes away the pain. But I know it must have happened differently for there was nothing to suggest, growing up, that anything tempered my mother's loneliness. Once it had taken root so long ago, it simply swelled. Most experiences went to substantiating it. It enveloped her, invaded her, ensuring Krishna would always remain apart. It saw itself in every mirror, slipped into every interaction, flooded her bloodstream, infused her DNA, even passed itself on eventually, like the smallness of her fingers or her need for reading glasses, into me.

Jacob, who as it turned out had come over to Princeton with the intention of completing his studies in divinity and joining the clergy, found it uproarious that Krishna had taken Christianity on so lightly. Jacob had left Princeton's seminary disappointed at the church as an institution, still buoyant in his Christian faith, but distrustful of the system and the functionaries that fostered it. His facile mind had adapted easily to the study of soil engineering (though he hankered for the spiritual, he had always been adept at the more mechanical and the practical,) which both interested him and he came to believe, under Gandhi's influence, would be more useful to India. Like Krishna and Naga, Jacob was in America only to learn, and would return home to serve. Unlike Krishna and Naga, Jacob's family was wealthy, having earned its fortunes in the verdant tea estates of Darjeeling where for generations the family held sizeable plantations—augmenting Jacob's interest in studying the earth. The Raos had been Anglicans for eight generations, ever since missionaries riding the coat-tails of the British trading companies had converted (though Jacob freely admitted they had actually co-opted) so many Northerners. Krishna was impressed at the breezy telling of Jacob's history. He told it matter-of-factly, without stressing the hardships, although she knew that such matters as his parents' early deaths (he was just seventeen,) or his decision to leave the clergy could not have been easy. Naga was pleased by their acquaintance. He was certain they would become fast friends.

The performance at the Y would be atrocious by Krishna's standards, but nobody in this audience would have known the difference. Without access to a proper costume or the jewelry to go with it, Krishna donned a nine-yard sari, which she tied between her legs in the sensible Maharashtrian style. She pinned a borrowed rhinestone bracelet around the bun on her head and used crimson nail paint (which she didn't realize would be so difficult to remove) to feign a *mehndi*, covering the tips of her fingers and toes. Between classes she had practiced diligently in the basement at the Y, having convinced Jacob to teach her how to use the reel-to-reel so that he wouldn't have to attend her rehearsals. She had found amongst his collection an adequate *pada* full of *bhakti*. Its tempo was slow to start and increased markedly in the middle, making it possible to show both *nritta* and *abhinaya*. The song told of a devotee of Lord Krishna, who knowing that those who brave the Lord's anger can attain salvation, questions and challenges the deity about playing so recklessly with human hearts and minds. It had been so long since Krishna had danced, she did not expect the steps to come back to her with ease. But the sentiments of the narration felt true, so the steps to mime them came naturally. Krishna felt no pain in her ankle when she danced, only occasional twinges of sadness that she forced herself to ignore.

Naga occupied a seat in the very first row that Thursday evening, having arrived early to secure it. The Carters, dressed in their Sunday best, also featured prominently up front. Krishna recognized nobody else in the audience though she thought she detected the frizz of Dr. Einstein's head at the back of the stuffy room. Her dance was third in the line-up. All the dances were introduced by the charming Mrs. Fisher who for Krishna's dance read out a translation of the words of the *pada*, explaining its devotional nature and stressing that the gestures of the dancer were meant to interpret the words of the song. Jacob, who'd been roped into managing the sound system for all the performances, watched Krishna, mesmerized, from the wings. He had assessed her as good-natured, unfrivolous, determined and adroit, but he noticed that when she danced a kind of splendor showed through. She became a passionate version of her usual, pragmatic self: the kind of girl a boy could come to love. The audience appreciated the footwork, but found the twelve-note scale unsettling. When her piece was over, they applauded politely, as a scholarly, Christian gathering would, though not enthusiastically as they had for the clog-dancers—except for Naga, for whom the piece lent a wistfulness that brought him to unexpected tears.

Final examinations and the Christmas holidays kept Krishna from her friends. Jacob had gone to Pennsylvania where he had a brother, and Naga to New York, where an old class-mate had wound up. Krishna, in the meantime, reveled in her first sightings of American snow. It fell just as gently and wonderfully as it had in all her dreams. She wandered down the streets of Princeton in boots borrowed from Mrs. Carter, delighting at the sight of children sculpting crooked snowmen, and playfully dodging the snowballs that she imagined strayed in her direction—or had they been purposely lobbed? After a quiet New Year's eve, which she spent at home in the company of the Carters and their friends, Krishna signed up for her first outing to New York City with a contingent from the Y. They would travel in a group by train and see a Broadway show. Thirsty at the Princeton Rail Road station, Krishna located signs over two drinking fountains that read "whites" and "coloreds." She knew the latter meant negroes and rating herself as fair, headed gingerly for the one for whites, glancing around to ensure no offense. A dour-faced matron, prim in pink velvet gloves and a matching hat clopped up behind her on noisy heals. On noticing Krishna in a sari sipping from the spout she tutted loudly, thrust out her chin, and stomped off in a snit. Krishna was summarily reclassified. Like flakes of snow, such disappointments settled softly upon Krishna's shoulders and melted into her, no one of them sufficiently weighty to cause the structure to cave in.

Krishna was thrilled by the tea-time at the Horn and Hardart in the thrumming of Times Square. Only in America would she ever be issued a cup of steaming coffee from a nickel-eating steel contraption that clanked and lit up like a fire engine. Later she would tell the waiters at the faculty eating club that they shouldn't worry for their jobs as unlike them, it was stingy on the cream and hadn't a single comment to make about her vegetarian food selection. She was amused at her reflection distorted on the glass of the vending vault entrapping an enticing, hilly triangle of apple pie. She fancied herself its liberator upon depositing the twenty cents required as ransom. She marveled at the way the red light above the coin slot flashed to signal that it had counted the right change, and was startled when the encasement door popped so eagerly open. She huddled up to the vending units with them every time, thrilled, as her companions rescued everything from bubbling bowls of baked navy beans to congealed macaronis with cheese. They gathered together to eat at one of the neat rows of tables and discussed at length the wonders of the automat. On the way back to Princeton on the train, they debated the relevance of Arthur Miller's "All My Sons," which

Krishna had not so much enjoyed. Professor Fisher said he thought it was about morality: whether the protagonist was more responsible to his family or to his work. For Krishna there had never been a question. His family should have clearly come first.

Jacob returned from Pennsylvania just a week before the Spring semester started. As Naga had taken the train up, the two had access to his Plymouth and hatched a plan to teach Krishna how to drive—a skill, Jacob thought, without which no American education would be complete. Jacob collected Krishna from the parsonage in the titanic, gleaming, sea-green sedan. He introduced himself, respectfully, to Krishna's hosts explaining that he would have her back by sundown. "Not to worry, boy," Carter declared, "I'm sure any good Christian can be trusted." The two drove off merrily in search of an unpopulated parking lot as Jacob drilled Krishna on the names and purposes of all parts of the dashboard. When it was her turn to get in the drivers' seat, Jacob laughed aloud at how diminutive she appeared behind the wheel, her eyes barely clearing it. No wonder, he realized, so many women didn't drive. They struggled from either side of the car to readjust the front seat and managed, together, to heave it into its forward-most position. Krishna climbed back in. Jacob chuckled. It wasn't enough. He folded his coat into a lump behind Krishna's back so that she could reach the pedals. He pretended not to mind the cold.

Maneuvering took more strength than Krishna had expected, and she frequently confused the clutch for the break, causing the car to throb and jerk and sputter out in pathetic gasps. Jacob remained encouraging, focusing on what Krishna did right. Krishna, meanwhile, berated herself for being so clumsy a learner. She feared she would ruin Naga's car, she worried she wouldn't be strong enough to turn the wheel in time to make it around the curve, she even fretted over crushing Jacob's winter coat. Jacob reassured her about the car (he had helped Jacob to buy it used and did all the repair work on it himself.) He leaned over to help her turn the wheel, and promised that this was his everyday coat, nothing special, really. He laughed heartily when Krishna slammed on the gas instead of the break, jolting the car and stalling it out yet again. When finally, hours later, her hands almost numb against the steering wheel (he could not persuade her to wear his gloves, which were enormous, while hers made the steering wheel slip from her grip,) Jacob convinced Krishna to try the open road. An empty street, he promised, one with few houses or other cars to challenge her. Feigning courage, Krishna agreed.

She was doing fairly well she thought, keeping to her own lane. Jacob joked "No point staying in your lane if yu're only willing to go ten miles per hour." So

Krishna sped up at his urging, and was proud to overcome the struggle of engaging the next gear. At the end of the first long street, it was easier to turn right than to turn around, and so she did. Then, without warning, she swung another right too quickly, sending Jacob rattling against the car door and prompting him to question her as to when Indian women had become so bold. She responded ably, slowing her speed and down-shifting when a dog skipped across the street in front of them as Jacob concealed bracing himself (just in case.) She was still nervous about making left turns and stalled the car out a couple of times before managing one successfully. Satisfied with today's lesson (parking and driving in heavier traffic was planned for their next adventure,) Jacob directed Krishna down the wooded, scenic route back to the parking lot, "You'll like this road. It has the most magnificent estates!" Fearing distraction, she dared not turn to admire the vast homes that Jacob kept pointing out along the way, ribbing her that if she didn't look around once in a while she would never know where she was. Jacob would later tell Naga that it was because Krishna couldn't take his eyes off him that it happened, but it was actually a darting squirrel that unnerved Krishna causing her to swerve the car clear into the stem of a free standing roadside mailbox which promptly snapped, launching the painted white coffer against the browned and frozen ground, and shattering it into jagged wooden bits. Krishna thumped hard on the break while swerving, so that the car screeched and jerked. Jacob braced himself against the dashboard and gasped. Closing her eyes in disbelief, Krishna collapsed over the steering wheel shaking her head, as embarrassed as she was rattled. The long and winding street was empty save the squirrels which scampered, flustered somewhere in the trees.

"Dear me!" Jacob understated his own alarm, "this certainly wasn't in the plans, was it?" He leaned over Krishna to turn off the engine and thought he'd better inspect the damages before backing up the car. He patted Krishna on the shoulder, "are you alright?" he queried with sincere concern. She nodded, yes, obviously embarrassed. "Be right back," he announced, and sprang the door open purposefully, letting in a chilly gust of winter wind. He moved around swiftly to the hood, frozen hands jammed deep into his pant pockets. Krishna, worried, poked her head over the steering wheel searching Jacob's expression as he bent over the fenders. Jacob, rising, smiled cheerily at her across the hood, signaled a thumbs up, then set out toward the bits of mailbox scattered on the lawn. From where they were, they could hardly see through the woods to the mansion that belonged to the mailbox. Jacob collected some of the larger fragments of wood and rounded up a couple of fluttering envelopes as Krishna hopped out, shivering, to confirm the damages for herself. "The good news," reported Jacob as he climbed back into the car, offering her the shards he'd collected, "is that if I can get ahold of the wood at this hour, I can probably build another one by tomorrow." "And the bad news?" Krishna had to ask. Jacob handed her one of the letters he'd found. The address read "Dr. R.M. Dobb, President, Princeton University…"

Though she was terrified at the prospect of coming up against Dobb, the two immediately agreed it was best to fess up. After collecting the remaining strewn bits of mailbox into the boot, readjusting the seat to his preference, and parking the car properly, Jacob was somewhat disgraced to have to bundle himself into his now rumpled coat to accompany Krishna for his first visit to the university President. He put on a confident face and on the awkward walk up the driveway prayed to himself that nobody would answer. Regrettably, President Dobb answered the doorbell for himself, in checkered slippers and black and orange striped sweater which bore no relationship to his slacks. "Ah if it's not the controversial, Miss Nayam!" he recalled, "Now you are aware, isn't it, that if this is an academic matter, I have office hours. And you can imagine that I much prefer not to be disturbed at home. Yes?" He warned, quite ready to dismiss the couple. "I fear it's not, sir." Krishna responded timidly, beginning to blush. "It seems…well…I'm so very sorry to…" she had not prepared her speech. Jacob interrupted, stretching his hand out to shake the President's. "Jacob Rao," he announced, confidently, "we have not been introduced, sir. I am a graduate student in engineering and a friend of Miss Nayam's. We are so very sorry to disturb your afternoon, sir, but we thought it best to inform you so that you wouldn't be alarmed that perhaps it was some sort of eating club prank." President Dobb assessed Jacob. "You see sir," he continued, "I was showing Miss Nayam the sights in town, the lovely residences on this block amongst them, and a squirrel ran across our path just as we were driving by. We had to swerve to avoid hitting it and, well, sir it seems we've quite exterminated your mailbox. I am so very sorry, sir. But I assure you that I shall have it restored by morning—even better than it was sir. And I am sincerely, so very sorry." "Is that what all the racket was about?" Dobb responded, putting his wonder to rest. "Raccoons in the trash cans, as usual, I'd guessed." He added, fashioning a smile. And then, with unexpected kindness, to ease the nerves of the shaken couple standing before him, "Well, the damned thing's always stuffed with bad news in any case, isn't it? I might not welcome getting it back quite as quickly as tomorrow!" A smile beamed across Jacob's face. Krishna, still embarrassed, but also touched by Jacob's gesture, stared down, like a schoolgirl, at her feet. Jacob had chosen his words carefully, making sure Krishna didn't seem to blame. "I assure you, sir, it will be fixed by tomorrow morning, and it shall be better than before. Perhaps I can mount it on a metal post, rather than wood so it can withstand any future run-ins? Though I do fear this might take a bit longer." Jacob added, stimulated by the prospect of designing a new mailbox. "Not to worry, young man," Dobb offered, "as long as it works and isn't much of an eyesore, I'm sure it'll do just fine. Now everybody's alright I expect, yes?" "The squirrel emerged unscathed, sir!" Jacob reported brightening even more, "as did the car. Which reminds me..." he reached into his pocket and produced the two envelopes he had retrieved, handing them to President Dobb who accepted them with a quick bow of thanks. "Well, Miss Nayam," Dobb remarked "I trust all else is in order, then?" "Yes sir," she whispered, still bowed in chagrin, "all is exceedingly well thank you." And in that moment, she felt it was indeed.

Krishna, though charmed by his gallantry in taking the fall for her blunder, was satisfied that Jacob made no other romantic gestures toward her. She had grown stalwart about not falling in love. They built a friendship instead, provided easy companionship for one another, and slowly gathered more about each others' habits, histories, and aspirations. Krishna learned more of what it meant to be Christian from Jacob than ever she did at Sunday school, at sermons or in the company of the Carters. She found that he preferred not to indulge in gossip; remained impressively optimistic even in dire circumstances; and forgave quickly, without lingering on reproach. He was unselectively generous, supportive and helpful. Judgment, even self-judgment, he happily left to the almighty. He had, soon after the accident, gently prodded Krishna to "get back on the horse." "You are a fine driver, and you were doing mighty well before I started pointing out all those distractions." He encouraged. She wouldn't take the bait, "I am jittery and hopeless in a car. You must be some sort of saint or at least a glutton for punishment." Krishna rejoined. Jacob valued Krishna's modesty and self consciousness. "Nope," Jacob retorted, "But speaking of saints, even Christ would have given you a second chance, don't you think? So I feel obliged to do the same." "So you fancy yourself omnipotent do you?" Krishna suggested, smirking. Jacob recognized the presumptuousness and smiled at himself, urging the car keys at Krishna, "Just a regular sinner trying to do the best he can. So will you take the wheel? I'm sure you'll do better this time. I believe in miracles." Krishna most appreciated Jacob's confidence, which was as quiet and automatic as was her self-doubt. He looked not a bit concerned about her taking the wheel again, not even venturing a single caution as she would have expected. She proceeded as vigilantly as she could muster. "I'm certain you can keep control even if you go a little faster..." he suggested, mildly. Krishna sped up the slightest bit, casting nervous glances in Jacob's direction to see if she could detect any apprehension. "You can do better than that!" he urged, "C'mon now." Krishna sensed the fearlessness in Jacob. Biting her lip and bracing herself, Krishna gunned it. Jacob didn't bat an eye. "That's the spirit!" he exclaimed.

Naga began to treat them as a couple, and even Reverend Carter at some point started referring to Jacob as "your young man." But still, Jacob made no romantic advances as he sensed Krishna wished none made. Her sense of undeserving kept Krishna at bay. She thought of Jacob as tender, wide-eyed, and unsullied, meriting the like. She was satisfied to have Jacob as her friend; got used to the notion of dedicating herself to the worthy cause of her country; planned on remaining unmarried, a lesser indignity than enslaving herself to a virtuous husband who might use the stain of her lost virginity against her. She resigned herself to the comfort of her familiar loneliness, collected it around her like a blanket, and cozy within it, let warmth neither escape nor penetrate the woolly layers of insulation.

That winter, Gandhi was assassinated. The threesome gathered at Jacob's house in the void of a February night. They listened to his Indian music, and told stories of growing up inspired by Gandhi's promise and by his courage. They gathered around for the hourly radio reports, wondering what on earth was Ground Hog's Day, and wept together, worrying for the future of their country. Dr. Einstein, not finding Krishna at the Carter's home, thoughtfully traced her to Jacob's house to offer his condolences. Jacob opened the door and turned white, as though he'd seen a ghost. "Wait till I tell the folks back home," he mused to Naga and Krishna after the peculiar professor had left, "that these days Albert Einstein drops by for tea!" For thirteen days thereafter, Jacob grumbling over not ever even having been a Hindu, they agreed to fast in solidarity and mourning. After twenty four hours, they revisited their program to encompass coffee, tea, soup, and fruits. Jacob started attending church services again just to spend time with Krishna on Sunday mornings. He suppressed childish giggles, snorting to control his laughter, when the sweet but ancient Mrs. Samson, tottering in the row behind them, sang the hymn vibrato. Jacob shook so much from laughter, the hymn book trembling in his hands, Krishna could not help but chortle, earning glares of disapproval from Mrs. Carter in the choir box. Jacob taught Krishna to whistle. She felt foolish even trying it. On the way to the cinema, Naga driving, Jacob having insisted she occupy the space between them rather than the back seat, he pinched her mouth into unlikely shapes while she hooted. Krishna taught Jacob and Naga how to cook a Keralan curry. They stood around the pan watching the seeds of fennel dance in the hot oil and cracking jokes about how

Naga, once he got back to India, would impress his new bride by replacing her *khansama.*

They drove into the countryside one brilliant afternoon for a picnic, unraveling a worn blanket onto the slope of a hill, new with tender grass in springtime. They had *pao-bhajji* which Krishna concocted with Wonder bread and cabbage curry, sweet pistachio *meethai* that Naga's mother had sent from home, and drank sour wine which made Krishna wince and pucker. Naga drank Mrs. Carter's lemonade poured from a metal canteen, for which she had kindly supplied small paper cups with perky pink tulips decorating the rim. He sneezed incessantly from the wispy dandelions that floated on the breeze. Krishna wished they had a tiffin carrier so she could have made warm food. Naga wished he hadn't developed these pesky allergies. Jacob wished he had asked Naga if he would stay behind. It would have been a perfect way to propose.

On the way home they had a flat. Jacob and Naga struggled with the replacement tire while Krishna loitered beside them on the country lane, the train of her sari wrapped around her head, the skirt billowing widely with each car passing by. One car slowed down, to help, they thought. They looked to it hopefully as it approached. The passenger-side window rolled down, "Niggers go home!" screamed the boy in his baseball cap, attempting a spit which thwacked against his own back-side door as the car sped off, laughter trailing behind it. Until the tire was mounted, they all avoided meeting each others' eyes.

On Easter Sunday morning Jacob helped Krishna situate the sloppily painted children's eggs in strategically obvious spots around the school-rooms for the ritual hunt. Krishna had graduated to teaching Sunday school to the youngest of the children, a strategy the Reverend thought an ingenious manner of steeping her in the good book. Jacob attended today's lesson, folding himself onto one of the abbreviated wooden chairs beside the children and raising his hand high and waving it for even more attention when Krishna asked the children, "Can anybody tell me what resurrection means?" He sang the loudest, leading the group in the pre-snack rendition of "Jesus loves me." And he helped put out the milk and chocolate bunnies that day, instead of the usual sugar cookies. The children taught Krishna & Jacob the recommended method of consuming an Easter rabbit: ears first, one by one, must be followed by the tail, then the paws if they "stick out." For the body, one was left to ones' own devices. Jacob wondered aloud if by eating a rabbit in effigy, Krishna was violating her vegetarianism. At first bite, hollow bunny carcasses cracked into fragments and tumbled, smudging natty Easter outfits and littering the polished parquet floors.

When the children had been collected and Krishna and Jacob turned to cleaning up, Jacob located a stray, abandoned chocolate bunny. "Look," he raised it, so its silvery-blue foil face was turned toward Krishna, "I've been left behind," he squealed in his best bunny voice, crouching as if he couldn't be seen behind the small confection, "Please eat me! I shouldn't be left out." He cried. Krishna smiled at Jacob's foolishness, rolling her eyes and taking the bunny gently from his hand. She heard it rattle inside and shook it to her ear, shrugging her shoulders, then peeled the wrapping, and offered it to Jacob. From her hand, he bit off the left ear, announcing "exactly as instructed." Krishna bit off the right. "No you," Jacob commanded, redirecting her hand to her mouth when she presented him with the tail. "It's the best part." The tail bent off without resistance between her teeth, something shiny fell to the floor, bouncing. "Heavens!" cried Krishna, a mouthful of chocolate tail "what was that?" Jacob had not expected the ring to fall out. He had taken such care to slice off the tail, press the ring into a corner of the interior, melt the chocolate with a lighter and splice the tail back on, smoothing the foil carefully over the fracture. Both ended up on hands and knees, searching. "Look!" Krishna cried, holding it up, delighted to find it, "think of that! It's a ring!" "Yes," Jacob nodded, turning to behold her. "It's for you." Krishna gazed down at the small sparkling diamond sunk into its typically Indian, 22 karat, oval setting. Jacob edged closer to her, both on all fours.

"I was hoping," Jacob admitted, seeking out her eyes, clutching her empty hand, "that you would honor me someday soon with your hand…in marriage." Krishna blushed, could not look him in the eyes. Her heart swelled and thumped. A tear verged at the corner of her eye. Jacob reached up to wipe it raising her chin with his hand, and though nervous, drew himself closer, intending to kiss her. Krishna turned abruptly away, leaving Jacob devastated. "You do not fancy me." He realized, his heart sinking. He paused, awaiting her response. When nothing came he added, dejected, "I understand. You surely deserve better. I'm only one of many chumps gone mad for you, aren't I?" "No," Krishna interjected, sobbing now. She paused a long while, then whispered. "I do not deserve better, Jacob. It's you who does. Please believe me. I cannot…You should not…" Krishna, was folded onto her knees. Jacob collected her into a tight embrace. She whimpered now, trembling. "It's alright," he whispered, stroking her hair, sinking into the softness of her shoulders. "It's alright…really. I didn't mean to make you cry. I know that I am not enough for you. I knew it all along. I only fell in love is all. I won't bother you anymore. I promise." He reassured. "No," Krishna shook her head into Jacob's shoulder. "No, don't say this thing, please." She urged, her voice muffled against his Sunday suit, "It is I who am insufficient, Jacob. You cannot know…Believe me. You would not want me if you knew me." "But I do know you," Jacob urged, "and it's you I know I want." "No, no, Jacob" she insisted, "you only think you know…" He held her tighter. She loosened her embrace sinking back onto her haunches, wiping hot tears from her face. "Is it children then?" he questioned, seeking explanation, "You can't bear children, is that it?" She shook her head no. "Don't do this, Jacob, there's no point. Really. Just believe me, you will not want me." Determined to save him from her, she looked him in the eyes and repeated gravely, "You will not want me, Jacob. You will want a woman who is…pure." Now Krishna blushed again, her eyes beseeching his understanding. Jacob did not comprehend. "You mean a Christian born woman? Is that what you mean? Don't be daft. You're pure! You're a pure-bread Brahmin for heaven's sake. What foolishness! Of course I want you." He went to embrace her again, but she raised her hand against him and turned away. "No Jacob, please don't…Please, just believe me." She pleaded. Jacob, his eyes squeezing shut against the tears that threatened him, fumbled to a stance. He brushed the knees of his pants, collecting himself. Krishna followed his dejected movements with sad eyes. He edged closer to the classroom door. "Here," she sniffled, reaching her hand out toward him from her kneeling pose, "you've left the ring." Jacob turned back, went to take it from her and held onto her hand for just a moment, searching once again her eyes. She blinked up at him, knowing he deserved an explanation. "I am not a virgin, Jacob." She whispered, twisting her eyes closed and recoiling to avoid facing his response. Jacob let go her hand which dropped with a thud to her knee. He rubbed the ring between his fingers momentarily, considering the admission. He knelt on both knees beside Krishna and kissed her tenderly on the cheek, gently taking her hand between his, slipping the ring on the first finger he could find. "Neither, I have long suspected," he whispered in her ear, "was the Mother Mary."

With Jacob, Krishna didn't get butterflies the way she remembered feeling with Pierre or the way they said in the movies. She loved Jacob intensely, and trusted and admired him, but something about her insisted that she remain somewhat detached. What she gave to Jacob, and what she got, was acceptance, companionship, like-mindedness, solidarity. He augmented this with protection and passion, a passion that she could feel from him but could not return, having learned to fear the consequences of her own. She knew that she could stand by Jacob and expected that his playful, open, heart would compensate for whatever deficits in hers. Marriage would restore some sort of social position. Even a love marriage was better than none. It was not as calculated as all that when it was happening to Krishna. It was natural, pragmatic, delightful, obvious, perhaps even a heaven-sent second chance. She didn't know which god to thank. She took no chances and thanked them all.

They did not specify a date, but quietly announced their engagement, first to Naga, then the Carters, and little by little, by letter and telegram to family and friends farther away. Jubilant response returned from Sindhya, warmest wishes from Sandhya, delight from Shaku and even somber congratulations from Deepa. Kishore, too close to Arna and Amma, would not be informed. They all regretted being unable to attend. Krishna knew it was not a question of inability. It was not worth risking the wrath of Arna, on whose good graces her siblings had still to rely. Jacob was outraged. "Aren't they happy for you, wouldn't they want to celebrate your joy? I have even offered to pay for their passage, how is it that they would spurn their own sister like this? Are they kowtowing to your father to preserve an inheritance or something?" Krishna didn't let the disappointment penetrate her. She calmed Jacob, "It is simply a matter of tradition, Jacob. My brother and sisters are conferring the respect my father deserves and I do not blame them. I perhaps should have done the same thing. Don't you see, it is in them to obey Arna's dictums, without question, without challenge, and without doubt." Krishna admitted no sting from being shunned, she proffered unconvincingly, "You see, I had expected it, so I am not disillusioned." Jacob intuited a need. From that moment he took on for a lifetime the faint strain of placating a partner ever braced for disappointment.

Krishna worked straight through the summer session. In June she was baptized, a puzzled, but ever-cheerful Naga amongst the congregation. With the help of his brother in Pennsylvania, Jacob set about preparing for the wedding, which was scheduled for October. But it was in mid-September that the telegram arrived at the Carter's house. Telephone connections were difficult from India and Sindhya-Aunty said it was the most verbiage that, at the time, they could afford. It only read: "REGRETS. ARNA DECEASED."

Following the emotional *Padam*, the *Tillana* alternates sculptural poses with variegated patterns of movement, to remind the audience of the technical skills of the dancer. All the tempos are used in a *Tillana* (2,3,and 4 beats) with dance cadences which give the impression of a mobile sculpture. It gradually livens the mood of the onlookers, preparing them for a satisfying conclusion.

#

12

I e-mailed mom yesterday about whether Shaku-Pacchi & Rahul-Mama would be offended if I were to buy them an air conditioner. They wouldn't be offended, she replied without embellishment, but they would never use it. They'd give it away to a village hospital or to some elderly person for whom the heat might be truly intolerable. So I'm laying, depleted, in the muggy swelter of Aniruddha's former bedroom, tormented by an ardent mosquito and the clatter of a dodgy overhead fan that threatens to whirr clean off its brackets and impale me. It's 3 a.m. I'm jet-lagged. I'm at desperation's edge. If I duck under the covers to shield against the beast, I suffocate. If I kick them off, it's open season. If I flip off the fan switch, abating the racket, I might get some sleep, but the marauding heat of Bombay at once encloses me, a dense and stifling veil. Meditate, I tell myself, focus on something else. And so I do, fixing in on what it means to live only within one's needs, as my aunt and uncle do, isolating their whims and hankerings, eschewing the frills. I wonder if their ascetic choice is burdensome or liberating. Does wanting less make one want less? Does choosing less make one choose better? Does that constant sense of relinquishing for the greater good make one feel less lonely? Is anybody on this planet really that much better off right now just because this heavy air hangs about me, unconditioned? My quandary lasts only an instant, the whining mosquito returns to remind me of my lot. I bat at it in vain, my fury stirring. I want rest goddamit! I want comfort! I want, I want, I want. I shift to examine the little pile of books on the bedside table. I find "Leaves of Grass." Haven't read that in a while. It distracts me entirely from the bug.

Mom is nervous about my being here, and about my having quit the bank. I had no sound explanation. Just couldn't do it anymore. "I feel trapped here, mom," I explained after I'd done all the planning so it would be too late for her to veto the idea, "I don't know why India, but it feels right that I should go." I didn't let her know that Sindhya-Aunty's stories were a big draw. "But you'll hate it! Everybody there is so rigid! You hardly know them at all. And you weren't raised to conform to their traditions. You'll feel even more trapped." Mom implored in response. Perhaps mom worries that I will embarrass her, ask uninformed questions, stick my rootless foot in somebody else's traditional mouth.

Perhaps she worries that I am, myself, an embarrassment—un-legitimated by marriage, unemployed, unsure of anything these days. "And what about getting a new job? When are you going to attend to that?" She added, ever vigilant of my recklessness. She worries that I'm drifting, heedless of the future. She's right, I'm more intrigued at present by the imprints of the past. I'm trying, for a change, to forge my own path despite the burden of her anxieties.

I have come to South India to meet my extended family—mom's—many, for the first time. It's amazing how easily everything fell in place. I quit, and a bit worried about spending savings on coming to India, was going to put it off. Remarkably, I got a giant tax refund I hadn't expected. And, contrary to mom's concerns, the family has been wholly welcoming from my very first contact. In the planning they enthusiastically concocted meticulous itineraries for me. E-mails flew, cc'd all around, eagerly detailing the plans: who would pick me up and when and where and what they would be wearing to be recognizable; with whom I'd stay and for how long and what they'd take me to do and see. "If you're a real American," one e-mail from a cousin read, "then you'll want to shop. So Manu will take leave from work on Thursday to accompany you to the safer shopping districts. He is a champ at haggling!" Since my arrival, they have been without exception welcoming and ebullient, not at all as rigid or formal as I'd invented in my mind. They enthusiastically answer my endless questions about their upbringing and about my mom—things I didn't even know that I wanted to know. I find them open and unpretentious, genuine and inclusive. They expect little of me as it turns out, so there's no pretense on my part either. I'd come up with twenty excuses, but nobody asks twice when I tell them I'm just taking some time away from nine-to-fiving. They're used to sabbaticals and unemployment here. It feels easy to just be myself.

The tea, thick and milky, spiced and redolent, whirls slowly on after it's stirred as Shaku-pacchi offers it to me smiling softly, careful not to burn herself or me. "Deranged marriage, you said last night. Do you really think it is deranged?" she asks, sincere in her interest. It's only five in the morning. She heard me bumping around in the bedroom and wanted, she said, to give me company. Had I been her, I'd have covered my head with the pillow and rolled over. But there's some-thing natural about the way she says it, as if it's so obvious that I shouldn't be up and alone. She's already washed, and her hair swings down her back in a neat, wet braid. She wears a light cotton sari, pressed, the faintest tinge of blue. Her colos-sal brown eyes search mine for meaning. Though older than my mom, there's an innocence about her that brings forth her youth. Even unadorned, she is radiant. I make light of the glib comment. "I was only joking, Shaku-pacchi. It was a stupid play on words. I just wanted to know if Aniruddha's marriage was arranged. I did not mean disrespect." It's true, I didn't. But the comment was surely charged. "It made me wonder," she explains. "We think it is better this way, you see, because it is so long in our tradition. And the Saraswats are fading out. We have become only fifty thousand now in India. If we do not arrange our marriages, who of us will be left? This is why Arna was so worried; why he was so distressed about Krishna-bai. He had a responsibility to grow the community and also take care of his daughter's future. He must have felt he had failed in his duty to both." I feel remorse now for my kidding. I must seem to her like some sort of plodding, insensitive, American oaf. Here she is all quietly dignified and elegant bearing the weight of her culture. And me, challenging eons of tradition, in an oversized Yankees tee-shirt, my hair mussed and my teeth un-brushed, whilst slurping unreasonable volumes of tea which her slender hands generously and repeatedly decant for me, not a single drop asputter, into a dainty cup. "I am honest, Shaku-Pacchi. I was only wondering if the match had been to your liking. I wasn't criticizing the practice. I don't really understand how it could be satisfying, but I accept it as the way things are done here."

It is barely 5:30 and there's a gentle knock at the door. Shaku-pacchi pops up to get it. It's the milkman, delivering two old-fashioned bottles of goat's milk. I'm enchanted. He's scrawny and dark, dressed in white overalls covered by a dark-blue smock and wears a white cotton cap, the visored version of a beret. I've never seen a live milkman. This one presents precisely like the Bollywood version of what might have been the American classic. He smiles a sheepish grin at me through the half-opened door, surely wondering who I am as he hands Shaku-pacchi the bottles and retrieves the empties that were left outside the doorway. No words are said, no money is exchanged. A placid, polite transaction in nothing but smiles and gestures. "He's new," Shaku-pacchi explains, promptly pouring both bottles into a pan and setting them to boil. "Just replaced the last one who we had for twenty years. Nice man. But Tamil. Doesn't speak a word of English, or Marathi or even Hindi. Anyhow, it's so early in the morning, nobody wants to speak!" Just as she says this we hear the sing-song call of a street vendor peddling his wares. I lean over to the window. A man in a colorful *dhoti* balances a small basket on his head. It contains what looks suspiciously like an iron? "He's selling irons at this hour?" I exclaim. Shakku-pacchi giggles, joining me over the window. "No you silly girl, he does the pressing!" Remarkable. Labor's still so cheap in India, that most of it will come to you. I watch windows thrown open across the way, addresses yelled to the peddler who points at each caller, yelling back "ek," "donn," "teen…" "He's telling them where he'll go first, second, third," explains Shaku-pacchi. "He's quite good, but I like the Tuesday-Thursday lady better. She takes more care with the saris. Rahul doesn't like me to hire them, but I do it because they need the money. Even that is why I have the sweeper come. We are so lucky, you know? We have everything we could ever want. These poor people live only from hand to mouth." This modest apartment in the Bombay suburbs has a single telephone to serve six rooms, gets frequently victimized by rolling blackouts, and doesn't stock even an extra pillow for comfort. Yet my Aunty has everything she could ever want. I had almost said something about the air conditioning. I feel like an overindulged brat.

Getting back to the subject, in her measured, dispassionate manner Shaku-pacchi launches a sensible defense of arranged marriage. She clarifies that Aniruddha's was an "arranged introduction," where if the couple didn't find each other suitable after a few dates, either could back out without shame. She stresses that arranged marriages have a meaningfully lower divorce rate than love marriages. She says that when a couple is supported by its community, and the raising of children is shared amongst extended family the way it's still possible to do in India, there's a lot more cohesion, more "family values," less truancy on the part of the kids, even less adultery she ventures to guess. She wonders, sincerely, what all the fuss is over love marriage—why Western books and movies romanticize it the way they do. Even Bollywood, she says, has hopped on that bandwagon. Don't they see how lonely and alienating that search for such idealized love can be? She knows, she says. She watched Aniruddha from a distance. She could see his heartache every time. I fear she can divine the fallout in me. Passion fades, she admits, in any relationship—but this is what gets all the billing. Deeper love grows from familiarity and commitment, and as couples come to rely on each other, particularly when they have joined based on common values, shared beliefs and with a similar upbringing. And from a practical perspective she adds, "Just think of the amount of time and effort you invest trying to find a match. Imagine how much more you can contribute in the world if that is taken care of when you are young and ready. All this energy expended on something that is, after all, quite predictable. It's not something to jeer at, you know! I said this same thing to Aniruddha. Finally, after so much trying for a love match, he agreed and we posted an advert in the Saraswat magazine. And a good thing, it was. They are married six years now. They have the children they always wanted. And by now, it is obvious, they are quite in love!" Shaku-pacchi is plain-spoken, considered in her delivery, entirely unconflicted. She also makes a decent point. I find myself seriously entertaining the notion.

I am warmed here by the way the extended family gathers so casually and frequently. I have never had so much contact with extended family, growing up moving from country to country, as we did. Here, there's a lot of dropping by for tea and "checking in," particularly on the elder members. On our way to the open market, it occurs to Aniruddha (who had just dropped by to check in on me and his parents), that we should stop at Kishore-Mama's to see if he needs anything. It's only 7 a.m. and we reach there to find that two other cousins (with their kids!) have arrived before us with the same agenda. Pots of milky tea ensue. Maya-pacchi starts clattering in the kitchen. The last cricket game, the Bush family war-mongering, and how to find the asthmatic Sandhya-pacchi a more reliable sweeper are all discussed with equal vigor. My ten and twelve-year old niece and nephew, my cousins' kids, are not off playing together somewhere but have stayed with us adults, absorbed in the conversation. Soon, steaming *idlis* appear on the coffee table accompanied by spicy *sambar*, coriander chutney and a fragrant pan full of *poha*. There's no big to do, no formal serving dishes or fanfare. Everybody chips casually in to help, distributing bowls and refilling tea-cups based on whomever's closest, fetching napkins and extra spoons (for those of us too Westernized to use our fingers.) When the eating's done, the kids, unbidden, leap to clear the table, neatly stacking bowls and cradling them with both hands on the way to the kitchen. Everybody's right at home, part of the action, including me. As it turns out, Maya-pacchi could use some gramm-flour, so we take the order and a bunch of us travel to the market, two hours later, en masse. Back at Shaku-pacchi's, nobody's put out by our delay. Things happen here. They're used to it. If something had gone wrong, they would have come to know.

Later today the whole family, all of whom live within an hour of each other in the Bombay metropolitan area, will meet at a *dharshan* at the temple. The swami of the Saraswat community makes yearly visits to the now dispersed congregations. Rahul-mama's enthusiastic that my sojourn coincides with the Swami's Bombay-area tour. "If you want to learn more about the way your mummy grew up," Rahul-mama offers smiling and widening his eyes, "I think you will pick up a lot." After naps, over even more tea in the early evening, Deepa-pacchi casually questions whether it's proper for me, a non-Saraswat, to attend the *dharshan*. Rahul-mama inquires authoritatively, "But how will the *sangha* expand if it keeps people even from learning about it?" Deepa-pacchi responds softly, deferring to her brother-in-laws' wisdom by posing her challenge as a question. "I raise this only to respect the tradition, you know. Technically, Sushi isn't a follower. Only one parent is Saraswat, no?" I interject that I have no desire to offend anybody, and that if my presence would cause any controversy, I would be just as happy to stay home. A general discussion ensues. The cousins in my generation think it's perfectly acceptable to bring me along. The older generation ponders, Shaku-pacchi voicing the main concern, "We do not want to be disrespectful, isn't it?" But inclining toward their good-natured wish to include me, the group satisfies itself that as I am half Saraswat by birth, if not by upbringing, it should be alright. "If you come with a spirit of curiosity instead of judgment," Kishore-Mama settles the matter as the oldest brother, addressing me just as much as the rest of the family, "then there should be no harm, isn't it?"

Soon everybody turns to worrying that I've only Western clothing to wear. The women put themselves to finding me a sari and blouse that'll fit. The blouses are all too small to get around my chest and my cousins joke good-naturedly about my American proportions. I feel enormous. "Too much McDonald fries!" Deepa-pachi giggles, shaking her head. I feel ashamed but realize the comment is in good fun. Earlier at tea with everybody, Deepa-pachi was making fun of the size of her own feet. I suppose in a land with such diminutive men, petiteness in women gets highly valued. Despite their protests that a woman my age should really appear in a sari, I insist on borrowing a more comfortable *salwar kameez* instead. The only ones that might fit are from when Santosh, Aniruddha's wife, was last pregnant! So over my complaints that we not go through all this fuss, I walk Santosh back to their place to fetch it in the grubby heat of a Bombay afternoon. The *kameez* is a vertiginous shade of Sweet-n-Low pink with a white floral embroidery around the cuffs and collar. If I have a style at all, it's clean-lined, urban, and practical and as is mandatory for a New Yorker, relies heavily on black. In this I look like a swirl of cotton candy and I wince at my own reflection, but everybody cheers when I return with it on. Shaku-pacchi wraps an arm around me as I survey myself in the mirror. She pastes a small red *bindi* on my forehead, making sure it's aligned between my eyebrows. When I look back in the mirror, I feel changed. Something falls into place. I look like everyone else here. I fit in. Shaku-pacchi raises her hand to hip height and beams, "When you smile," she says, "you look just like Krishna-bai when she was so big. Isn't it, Deepa-bai?" Deepa-pachi surveys me momentarily, remembering. "And you are precisely as self-conscious and also as self willed." She adds, leading me into the washroom, "Come, you must wash this make-up off your face. It isn't modest." I take pains to point out to her all the ways I'm nothing like my mother, all the while gently prodding if it's okay to keep just a bit of eyeliner on. "Nothing doing," says Sandhya-pacchi, "See, you are even as determined." She smoothes my hair back into a tight pony tail. She recalls nostalgically how Amma used to do this for all the girls when they were young. "When we asked Amma why the hairs had to be so high and tight on our heads she would say, 'so you don't fall asleep in your classes!' It's true, our buns were so tightly pulled back we could hardly blink for all of elementary school!" Sandhya-pacchi cracks me up.

The perimeter of the small white temple hall is hung with bright garlands of marigolds and daisies. At the front, a gold-painted dais in the form of an "*om*" awaits the swami, two sagging pillows stacked under it. The men, uniformly in white cotton *dhotis*, are cross-legged on the floor on the right side of the hall, separated by an aisle from the women in colorful saris on the left. Straw mats are rolled out for the women to sit on as we arrive. There must be three hundred people in attendance, and everybody chats and laughs, issuing waves and cheerful greetings to new arrivals. The atmosphere's chummy and informal, not the least bit reverential as I'd expected. We are late by half an hour and have lost nothing for the delay. I notice eyebrows raised at my presence, smiles flashed at me when I look over at twosomes leaned into each other, pondering my provenance. I am grossed out at having to remove my shoes and walk in bare feet across the marble floors, where thousands of other bare feet have crossed. Shaku-pacchi, noticing my worry, reassures me, "They are not saying anything bad, don't worry. They're only curious because you're new." I spot Rahul-mama across the aisle explaining something to those gathered around him. "*Dhuve America rabta*. Kishore Nayampalli's niece!" a voice bellows from the crowd unexpectedly. It was a man shouting the news to his elderly, deaf companion. The crowd titters. He had not meant to be overheard. The ladies gathered around me smile politely at Shaku-pacchi's introducing me. "Oh I see," one says sweetly, taking my hand and reminiscing, "What a firecracker your mother was! I do remember her so well! Are you so talented like she was too?" They speak of her as though she's dead. Later at the reception, chatting with the elderly women who come to tell me how much I remind them of Krishna, I learn that these, her peers, had over all this time come to assess her as glamorous and courageous, not scandalous, the way Sindhya-Aunty had imagined.

A procession of orange-robed priests moves up the aisle. One of the younger ones, strikingly handsome, accommodates himself at the dais as the crowd quiets down. He chants in a clear and moving voice what I imagine is an invocation. Half-way through his song, the congregation joins in, swinging gently side to side with the rhythm. I can only make out the names of some of the deities in their song, the rest is completely lost on me. The monk begins to speak to the gathering, humble yet self-confident. I may not understand the language, but it's clear the speaker has conviction. He goes on longer than I expect for an introduction. I gently elbow Shaku-pacchi next to me and whisper "when does the swami come on?" She looks at me puzzled, "this is our swami!" I'm incredulous. "But he's a total hunk!" I blurt, unable to help myself. My cousins, surrounding us, overhear me, break into wide smiles and cover their mouths with their hands, suppressing laughter. "What's a chunk?" Shaku-pacchi whispers back, curious. Beside me, also barely containing a giggle, Santosh-akka leans over to explain, "Not a chunk! A hunk!" then defines it in Konkani. Shaku-pacchi, scandalized, her eyes widening at me, covers her mouth with one hand and grabs onto my hand with the other. She doubles over to hide her laughter, shaking her head. Around us, women are clearing their throats, shifting on their haunches and struggling to contain giggles.

Another twenty minutes into the lecture and I think I've fallen in love. The swami has a generous demeanor, and tender, sparkling, eyes. His sermon is chatty and matter-of-fact. When he speaks, his eyes shift calmly from one in the congregation to another. He does not smile often, but it's clear that he's cheerful. A largesse, and benevolence comes through. If he'd been raised in the US instead of a monastery in the South of India, he'd have probably ended up as a news anchor, or maybe a Benetton model. Except for the distraction of three ashen stripes across his forehead, he really is that much of a stud. He must be saying something that's worth translating. Again, I elbow Santosh-akka, who has by now calmed down beside me. "What's he talking about?" I inquire. She takes a moment to boil down the subject, then whispers, "He says that above all, we must not betray ourselves because our human birth is precious. That means also we have a duty to forgive ourselves. We must develop compassion for our ignorance, which is very human, and for bad choices in the past. If we don't forgive ourselves then we cannot really forgive others, and this can make a very lonely life. The laws of *karma* will make sure we are troubled for our misdeeds. We do not have to go on punishing ourselves." This doesn't strike me as particularly deep at the time, nothing Oprah hasn't already filled me in on, but I realize I'm considering it while indulging in the sarcastic judgment I'd promised to enter this temple without. I'm listening to the hypnotic voice of the swami and something softly sinks in. Unforgiven, comes the message, and naturally, alone. Looking around me at the comfortable crowd of which I feel a part, I settle into another recognition. Here, I'm not constantly caught up in meeting some sort of personal goal. Nobody is. Everyone's just keeping on, together, and it feels good.

Later, on our drive home, six women squeezed inelegantly into a car made for five, I apologize to Shaku-pacchi for what I said earlier about the swami. "I am sorry if I was irreverent, Shaku-pacchi, I thought he'd be some shriveled up old bit like the Pope, not so young and handsome." Shaku-pacchi pats my knee and wobbles her head in acquiescence, "Not to worry." She says, "No harm." Santosh-akka, who's driving, turns to me and winks "We all think the same thing, only nobody has the nerve to say it." The car-load bursts into chuckles, Deepa-pacchi, most modest, turns almost purple from trying not to laugh. "Don't be naughty, Santosh," she scolds, trying to restore dignity to the subject, "We should not sexualize the swami like this. He's remained celibate since he was ten so he could learn and become a *saddhu* for our benefit." "Presumably," I kid, "he was celibate before he was ten!" Sandhya-pacchi roars with laughter now, and even Deepa-pacchi can't help herself. "Oh my," says Sandhya-pacchi between chortles, squeezing my knee with one hand, "always so fresh and candid." I have never heard myself described as either of these things. In fact, I feel like I've spent a lifetime remaining stifled, and here, I somehow feel free to bridge the gap between my private and my public self.

From: sushilarao@yoohoo.com
To: knadghar@calberk.edu
Subject: The dedication
Date: Feb 17 2001 10:10:06—1000 (CST)

Dear Dr. Nadghar:

It has been a long time since your kind response to my inquiry about the dedication in your father's book. I trust you received the small response I wrote in sympathy for your loss. I also lost my father not so long ago, spurring my interest in learning more about my mom while I'm still lucky enough to have her around. As a matter of fact, I've been traveling in South India (see travel-log attached), visiting family and gathering some family history.

As you had expressed an interest, I hope that you are not alarmed to learn that the dedication was probably directed from your father to my mother. I have learned that my mother, who was a Bharatanatyam dancer at the time, had been arranged to marry your father but chose instead to pursue an education, and therefore did not.

It seems, however, that both fared well despite that turn of events, and that your father ultimately appreciated her decision. After all, I suppose you would not have resulted (nor I!) had they stuck to original plans.

I hope this note finds you well.

Sincerely,

Sushila Rao

From:	knadghar@calberk.edu
To:	sushilarao@yoohoo.com
Subject:	The dedication—a question
Date:	Feb 18 2001 11:51:06—2300 (CST)

Dear Ms. Rao:

Thank you for the surprising information about the dedication. I was shocked to learn that my father had been engaged before meeting my mother. Indeed, isn't it difficult to imagine that ones parents had any sort of lives at all before we came along? I must also confess that I am selfishly pleased that it didn't work out!

It might explain my father's interest in Bharatanatyam. I do recall him talking about once seeing a performance that he said "transported" him. He would drag us out on the rare occasions any dancers came to Kenya. We never understood what was going on on stage, but we sat through it. I remember how happy it made him to watch. He was a big fan.

I must also admit to some surprise. Since you made the initial inquiry, I imagined your mother had also passed, as otherwise, presumably, you could ask her directly about the dedication. Unless of course she is somehow incapacitated. If so, forgive the stupid assumption.

Your travels in South India must be very interesting. I have never made the trip myself and confess I am intrigued by the place, as it is also in my heritage. I would welcome hearing any more of what you learn there. I have not yet read the attachment but will get around to it soon.

Thank you, again, for the information. I'm sure my sister and brother will be fascinated to learn of this—although I think it best if we keep the news from our mom.

With warm regards,

Kamath Nadghar

13

She does not recall how it was, that first time on an airplane. She does not recall how they postponed starting the semester, nor any of the details of getting back to Bombay. She only remembers that she floated through those days, entirely reliant on Jacob, suffering nothing but the constant torment of knowing that she'd lost her father without the chance to make amends. So used was she to taking care of herself, that had Jacob not had this opportunity to be so solicitous in his care, cocooning whatever might be left of her spirit, Krishna may never have come to appreciate the best of him. He ran marathons for her, made every last arrangement, paid for the tickets, got her packed, got them excused from classes, got them to Idlewild, through London and on to Bombay, managing every last detail, even exchanging currency and remembering to stop the rickshaw on the way to Kishore's to pick up some mourning garlands from a roadside flower vendor.

The moon was high in the sky by the time they arrived in Mangalore. They were not expected. Krishna, reeling from heart-ache and jetlag and drawn by the dreamy jasmine air, kept asking to slow the rickshaw so she could make out the trails of her past. She had forgotten the address of Kishore's house, perhaps never had cause to have known it. But she remembered the way. The bamboo hedges out front were taller now, obscuring the bright green doorway, but she recognized it, and on seeing the stoop recalled a moment when she was young, when Amma was home and pregnant with Sindhya. At this very spot, Arna had lifted her out of the cab of a rickshaw much like this one and entrusted her with the paper sack of *jalabee* that M'am knew Kishore so relished growing up. In her excitement to present Kishore and Maya with the treat, she'd flipped the sack from one hand into the other, grabbing it by the wrong end. When she thrust her hand out to offer the bag, beaming, to Maya, who'd kneeled to receive it, the sticky *jalabees* came tumbling out, clinging briefly to Maya's now gummed up sari and breaking against the marble floor. Horrified, Krishna had squatted on the spot, making herself small, hiding her head beneath arms crossed above it in shame, and had started to cry. The others had knelt to console her, Arna coaxing her out of her misery and prodding gently "what's so much fuss about? No harm done, it's only a little accident!" "No!" She had cried "No Arna! M'am made them because Kishore-dada loves them, and I was clumsy and I wasted. And now nobody will love me!" Arna was at pains to unravel this twine of childish logic. He paused, collected Krishna lovingly into his lap and asked her, "Did you want to throw the *jalabees* on the floor then?" Krishna shook her head no. "Then we have nothing to worry about I should think. If you did not hurt Kishore or M'am on purpose, then wasting was not your intent. Why would M'am or Kishore love you any less?" Krishna remembered that she stopped sobbing to please her father, but somehow, she was not convinced. She had spent days berating herself for wasting the *jalabees*.

When Maya-bai opened the door, sleepy-eyed, she gasped and clasped both hands over her mouth before widening them to embrace Krishna who she held tightly to her, muffling tears. Krishna had not known what sort of greeting to expect. Assuming he was her driver, Maya-bai commanded Jacob to drop the bags in the corner and ran off to fetch him a tip. Jacob was puzzled by the offer of a crumpled note and smiled politely as he folded his hand over Maya's out-stretched palm to enclose it. "You must be Krishna's sister-in-law," he whispered in English, "I am Jacob Rao. I am at university with Krishna. She was not in a state to come alone, so I have accompanied her home." Krishna had removed her ring. They would keep the engagement from Kishore and Amma until the mourning was over. Maya-bai was embarrassed. "Forgive me, please." She explained, "it is such a shock to see our Krishna after so long. You must be so tired from traveling. Please, come, rest, sit, let me get you some tea and I will wake the others." She turned back to Krishna, "Come, will you want to wake Amma for yourself? Kishore will be so..." It occurred to Maya that she had no sense of how her husband would respond to his sister's return. He had, since her departure, as any first-born son would, given his full support to Arna's determi-nations over Krishna. But now that Arna was gone, would it be up to Kishore to maintain the distance? Krishna lay a mourning garland, fragrant with dark yellow marigolds over Maya-bai's head. Tears welled up in Maya's eyes. She grabbed Krishna by the hand and led her down the hallway.

Krishna stopped in the washroom on the way to the small bedroom now allot-ted to Amma. She rinsed her face and scrubbed her hands ritually, as she would have before any *dharshan*. In the hallway, Krishna spied the opening to a closet she remembered used to hold the linens. Its door had been removed, replaced with a flimsy sari draped across a curtain-rod to fashion a covering for what was now the household shrine. She could smell the coconut oil that flickered in the small *diya* lamps, aflame before a silver-framed picture, garlanded, of Arna. A radiant silver bowl offered a coconut, some bananas, and sprigs of jasmine to the exacting pantheon. She drew the makeshift curtain, and examined the photograph more closely. Arna wore a neatly pleated white dhoti and the stiff white, boat-shaped cap so popularized by Gandhi. He was walking away from a building alone, and smiled mildly, kindly, at the camera, his hand indicating the intention to wave, the afterthought of being caught off guard. He seemed calm in the photograph, at ease, though perhaps unprepared for the shot. There was not a trace of bitterness in him, no shadow of disappointment. He looked almost jaunty, though the folds in his face had grown deeper. Drawn by the familiarity of the little shrine, Krishna dropped instinctively to her knees, bowed deeply and began to chant a mantra in a whisper. As the words slipped from her lips, tears dribbled from her eyes. Krishna wondered if she had continued to cause her father suffering. She hoped deeply that she had simply been forgotten. She heard the shuffling of feet and felt supple, bony, hands settle from behind upon her shoulders. By now the kitchen was aclatter, lights had been flipped on, and she could hear the bass in Jacob's voice and the familiar sing-song of Kishore's, though she could not make out their words. She tilted her head back into Amma's lap for just a moment before twisting to lay her hands at Amma's feet. She meant to get up for a proper *vandana*, but could not. She remained coiled on the floor instead, her forehead pressed against Amma's ankles, her arms wrapped tight 'round her haunches. Clutching each other, wordless, the two rocked together and cried.

Krishna was relieved to learn that Arna's passing had been quick, if not painless. Amma, irritated that Arna hadn't turned up to dinner at his regular time, had sent M'am to check on him in the office. M'am had knocked, then opened the door, peered into the darkened, empty office and assumed Arna had stepped out. He reported back to Amma that he was nowhere to be found. Neither of them recalled seeing him leave, though both had been quite occupied that day. They waited, imagining he had trotted off to meet with one of his farmers and absentmindedly forgotten to inform them—he was, they consoled themselves, forgetting so much more these days. But neither had heard the sound of the bullock-cart, and in fact, they went and found Bunty grazing in his corner of the barn undisturbed. Still they waited patiently, delaying dinner another two hours, and finally, when Amma thought it was excessive, she sent M'am home, resolving to serve dinner herself. On his way out the back, however, something tugged at M'am and he went to check the granary. There he found Arna curled on the floor, clutching his heart, his cold body no longer pulsing with life, his face frozen into a soundless shriek. As the eldest son, he knew it was Kishore who would now head the family, so M'am did not return to the house to fetch Amma. Instead, he ran the two miles to Kishore's house on foot, and returned with him by motor-car. Kishore now mourned to Krishna, his voice cracking, "Imagine, my first job as head of the family was to break my own mother's heart." He sighed and hung his head at saying this and Amma reached out and stroked his forehead lovingly, adding in Konkani, "Otherwise, it would have been such an ordinary day…" M'am, they reported, blamed himself for not checking the granary along with the office. He thought if he had checked both he might have found Arna in time to save him. In shame, he resigned from his 30-year post the next day. He did not even show himself at the funeral, hiding behind palm trees by the river, where the pyre was, so as not to cause grief to the family but still be able to pay his respects. The men had all tried to persuade him to return to his post or at least join the funeral procession in dignity, but M'am felt responsible. "I would not," he said resigned, "offend the family in that way."

Jacob, who had been given one of the boys' rooms, and Krishna the other, spent the rest of that week watching and waiting, smiling and nodding and staying carefully out of the way. He understood no Konkani and wished not to interrupt Krishna's rapprochement to solicit translations for his own benefit. He had to be careful not to give the impression of being over-familiar. The family included him appreciatively, but once they determined he was a Christian, fairly cautiously as well. Still, they insisted that he stay at Kishore's, so inhospitable it would be to put him up elsewhere after he'd accompanied Krishna all the way. They hoped he did not suffer from the vegetarian diet. To stay out of the way, he took long walks through the streets of Mangalore, visited the libraries, the bookstores, the churches and the night fairs. He understood that back in these circumstances Krishna would observe her Hindu rites and he watched her, protectively, play the part of the prodigal daughter. He noticed that Kishore had spared her any harshness in the least and that Amma had welcomed her with more than open arms. As Shaku and Sandhya eventually visited, they too embraced Krishna wholeheartedly, as though nothing had transpired. It was Krishna who carried the cross of her unworthiness, not anybody who imposed it now upon her. Deepa's impression was slightly more nuanced. In her world, Krishna's exile was something everybody had to tolerate until Arna had passed. Beyond that, all seemed to be forgotten and forgiven. But Jacob, who came to be known by everybody as "Jacob-ji," neither judged nor commented on what he witnessed. He remained silently respectful and considered whether when he asked for her hand it would be best to approach Amma or Kishore. Though it was past the two-week mourning period, Jacob thought it becoming that all the women in the family continued to wear white. Clustered in white saris in the kitchen or sipping tea in the back yard, they looked like a band of angels contriving their next salvation.

That week, the men of the family, (except for Kishore, all brothers-in-law) decided that the business, which had been ailing, would have to be wound down. The farmers, most of whom had attended Arna's funeral, mourned for their own futures in addition to Arna's demise. They pleaded with Kishore to follow in his father's footsteps as they needed a trustworthy broker for their produce. But Kishore, an accountant, said he had neither the training nor the talent to carry that load. The property would be sold, as everybody but he had moved to Bombay or the bigger cities, and because it would enable him to keep Amma more comfortably. A portion of the sale, of course, would be tithed to the temple at Shirali. The entire family, minus Sindhya, who could not come from Calcutta, and Amma, who was spared the agony of going back, congregated at the homestead to clear it of remains. Jacob went along to pitch in. Krishna trod softly through the rooms, perhaps to keep from disturbing the bittersweet memories that seeped from the walls. Jacob would periodically run into a couple of the sisters weeping together, consoling each other over some memory or having come upon some trivial item no suddenly rendered precious. In time, they managed to pack the few belongings and distributed the minimal valuables (carpets, paltry silver) amicably amongst themselves, arguing not over what each wanted, but what each wanted the others to have. Whatever they chose not to keep would be sold with the property or given to the temple. Jacob noticed how a sparse, Saraswat Hindu household was so easy to disassemble. There was simply so little to parse out. Krishna kept only one item, and that was but of sentimental value—the ink pen from Arna's office, the one he'd use for "special papers," with its little accompanying pot of watery India ink. She was careful to make sure everybody else had chosen first, and specifically asked Kishore whether she could have it. She prefaced her request by stating that she knew she was not worthy of making any claims at all.

It was an afternoon when the women, all but Amma, who was still fragile and not inclined to socialize, had made yet another unsuccessful pilgrimage to persuade *M'am* to return. They had estimated that Krishna's reappearance might inspire *M'am*'s reappearance. The sun cast long shadows in the back yard and Amma, with little else to do, offered tea once again to Jacob and Kishore, who had just come back from finally sorting out the knocking sound in the hood of Kishore's car. They were proud of having done the trick, and Kishore was grateful for Jacob's "technical consulting." Though Jacob felt grubby and unpresentable, having just spent two hours tinkering with an engine, he thought it a good opportunity, and seized the moment.

"May I take a spot of your time?" he asked, peering into Amma's eyes as she poured the tea before them. "Certainly!" Kishore replied eagerly on her behalf, "we have quite been monopolizing most of yours." Amma, concerned, only took her seat across from the men at the small garden table and cautiously raised her teacup. Jacob continued, unexpectedly addressing himself to Amma rather than Kishore as he had planned. "I have the intention, rather, I have the wish and have already expressed my desire to Krishna, to marry her. But I would like to do so with your blessings." He stated it plainly and quickly and the words hung in the humid air for a few seconds before anybody spoke. Kishore broke in, somewhat displeased. "I see…" He pondered, "then you will be seeking a dowry?" Amma stared into her tea-cup, concerned. "No fears!" Jacob replied, "Not at all. I wish no such thing." "What then…what would you want?" Kishore questioned, suspicious. "Well, only your agreement. It is important to me that Krishna's family be satisfied with her spouse." Amma was serious and mum. She kept staring down into her tea. Kishore remained puzzled. "But what is your incentive then?" he inquired, a tinge of anxiety in his voice. "Incentive?" Jacob repeated the word as though it had been launched as an insult. "My incentive is that I love her. That I wish for her to be my wife." Amma's face grew perturbed. "That you love her?" Kishore continued, still incredulous, "And you will want nothing from us to take her then?" "Nothing but your consent, no. Only your blessings." Jacob confirmed. Kishore persisted. "Then you expect to be able to return her, yes? I mean, should the match not turn out to your satisfaction. Is that it? If we give you nothing, then you will want the right to return her I imagine?" Jacob was stumped. "No, by golly, I love her. Don't you understand? I have no intention ever to return her. I wish to be her husband. I intend to keep her, forever, as my wife." Kishore, about to challenge the proposition yet again, felt his mother's hand upon his knee. "Love marriage, then?" Amma questioned Jacob, whispering as though it were to be kept a secret. "Spot on!" Jacob cheered, a bit puzzled himself at what the others might have had in mind. "Yes. A love marriage." He beamed back at them as though they should be pleased. Amma, disbelieving, clarified for her own sake, "If love marriage, then why do you ask us? What can we do?" Jacob remained puzzled but answered honestly. "You can say yes. You can agree that it is something you would wish for Krishna…to be married. Well, to be married quite specifically to me." Kishore still did not comprehend. "But you see, if it is a love marriage, then there is nothing for us to agree to. We would only have terms to agree upon if the marriage were arranged." Now Jacob was at wits end. "Then you would like to arrange Krishna's marriage?" Amma tutted, Kishore threw up his hands exclaiming, "Heavens no! Impossible at her age! All we could ever do was hope for a love marriage." Jacob, frustrated by this incomprehensible conversation now implored, "But then why aren't you consenting to my offer?" Kishore drew a breath, put down his tea cup significantly. Amma broke in again. "If love marriage," Amma explained, "then we cannot say yes, you see? Who agrees to love marriage? Only you two. For family, big disaster!" "Disaster?" Jacob repeated, uncomprehending, "I am promising to take care of and honor and love your daughter for her lifetime! I should think you would delight in this! What disaster is there? Unless of course you have a more suitable candidate in mind?" Jacob's spirits flagged. A curt exchange occurred in Konkani between mother and son. Amma, turning again to Jacob, tried gently to explain. She cleared her throat. "Everybody in all of family very extremely happy please if Jacob-ji marry to our Krishna. We love Jacob-ji very much. We are very much grateful." She wobbled her head with delight, then added, "But we cannot say yes." She sat back on her seat, pleased at herself for the clear explanation. Jacob slapped his hand to his forehead. The words Amma pronounced made sentences but they did not make any sense. "Then you would not like me to marry your daughter?" he persisted. Kishore clarified, smiling wide. "We would like her very much to be married to you. Yes, we would be pleased if you would take her. But it is improper for us to support this union, you understand? It is outside of the tradition. So we will not consent. But we encourage you to do this thing. And we will work very diligently not to be pleased. Not at all pleased." Jacob finally understood. He thumped Kishore on the back, beaming, took up Amma's left hand, and much to her alarm, pecked his lips upon it. She drew it away quickly, shaking off the impact. They all smiled upon each other, Jacob and Amma competing for who might be most gratified.

Later, when Jacob told Krishna what had transpired, Krishna erupted. "What on earth made you approach Amma without discussing the proposition with me?" It was the first time Jacob had heard Krishna raise her voice. "I only wanted Amma to know how much I care for you and how I intend to take care of you. And of course, to get her blessing." He explained in earnest. "But I am no longer theirs to give! Once my father sent me away, I am not somebody over whom they should be concerned. And she does not need to be troubled with me now—specially while she's still in mourning!" Jacob, though still confused about these Hindu manners, was contrite. "I did not mean to disturb anything. I just thought it was the right thing to do. I should think your family would be happy that you are to be married. It would be good news, I would imagine. A relief. Particularly as you'll be married to me!" Jacob joked to lighten the mood. Krishna couldn't help but smile and confess. "Amma told me that all these years she's prayed that

Ganesh continually remove obstacles from my path. She wanted for me to be happy in a love marriage. She is doing *pooja* now for Ganesh because you have come along. They are happy for me. But it is not the way we do things here. We could have married and informed them of it without obtaining their consent, you see? Then they would not be in the position of offending the community." Jacob understood better. He smiled to hear the news and squeezed Krishna appreciatively. He was gratified that her other siblings had been welcoming and solicitous with him. He reluctantly agreed to postpone the wedding. It did not feel right to Krishna to be married in the same year that her father had died. Plus, in another year, they could both complete their studies and be free for whatever came next. Krishna, feeling fortunate for a change, joined Amma in her *pooja*. Amma hugged her tightly with relief.

After Mangalore, the couple headed North to visit Jacob's family. By contrast to the memory of her first airplane ride, Krishna never forgot the rickety train that strained its way up the slopes to the town of Darjeeling in the Himalayan foothills, ever threatening to tumble off its tracks. It was thundering and lightning the way it often can in that mountain region, as the train made its painstaking, winding way up the hillsides. Even the goats had trouble keeping their footing, skidding on the diagonal as they trotted up the slopes until a rock or branch broke their slide. Though they were caught in the mists of a cloud, obscuring the Himalayan backdrop, the flourishing greens of the tea estates, the endless rows of neatly laid hedges that seemed to march down the mountains on spindly vine legs, distinguished themselves to Krishna, remaining as clear and unforgettable as her first sighting of the Grand Canyon. Arriving at the mansion in the torrents was an even greater to do. As usual, they had not been expected, but unlike at Mangalore, here, legions of *ayas* and bearers and brothers and sisters and nieces and nephews swooped down on the rickshaw, hollering their delight, pinching cheeks, thumping backs and whisking belongings swiftly out of sight. Just as she had been at Jacob's house on Prospect Street, Krishna was hurtled through the mansion and shown to what would be her room; one that looked upon no less than an acre of rose gardens, boasting wrought iron benches and fountains, British in their tending and formality.

A bright-eyed young *aya* soon appeared bearing Krishna's suitcase in one hand and in the other, a box wrapped in silvery paper and tied with looping ribbons of blue satin. She bowed a quick *namaste*, "From your soon sister-in-laws!" she announced, "as velcome for you visit. Please put!" Krishna was touched and also taken aback to find a magenta *kanchi* silk sari, its intricate border patterned in threads of gold. Her *aya* tutted at seeing Krishna hold up the blouse it came with.

"So big!" she shook her head, then took it from Krishna's hands, "I fix. You small." And scuttled away. Minutes later she returned proudly bearing a box full of safety pins. "We put now!" she pointed at Krishna and then at the blouse, "more later, I sew." Krishna didn't remember the last time she'd had such attention. She was uncomfortable with it, having grown used to managing things for herself. "What is your name?" she asked the young *aya*, politely. "I Sona." Came the response. "I'm Krishna," replied Krishna bowing in *namaste*. Sona was startled. "You Hindu?" Krishna nodded yes, then remembered, "No, well Christian now…And Hindu also." Sona was puzzled but let the matter drop as she held up the sari to shield Krishna from her view so Krishna could slip into the blouse with privacy.

No less than five of Jacob's brothers and sisters still lived at the mansion, each with some responsibility over the tea production, accompanied by their husbands, wives, children and caretakers. Krishna soon learned there were three cooks, two bearers, six *ayas*, a rotating team of tutors, a couple of gardeners, a driver and a flurry of pets. By tea time, within an hour of their arrival on a Wednesday afternoon, every one of the family had been summoned to meet "Tail's fiancé." Jacob, the youngest of ten siblings (there had been eleven, but one had died at birth), was nicknamed for having come in last. Not a single of the others bore a proper name. The room was filled with "Kooklus" and "Chicoos" and "Povis" and "Bunnies." The family spoke English at home, not Bengali, and Krishna sipped tea (not spiced, sweet and milky, but delicately scented and poured from bone china tea pots, with warmed milk and sugar added in British style) in the formal sitting room with the chatty relations, properly perched on a Louis VIX fauteuil, lavish Persian carpeting under her feet. Out came warmed scones and improbably, clotted cream. Everybody, including the bearer, bowed his head for a prayer said in thanks for Jacob's safe return and to bless the couple's future. The family launched promptly into founts of conversation. Everybody spoke loudly and all at once so that Krishna didn't know where to direct her attention. "Do tell how you two met?" they pleaded, and extended earnest condolences for the passing of Krishna's father and assured her that he must be looking down upon her from heaven. "Is it true that in America hardly anybody had an *aya* but almost everybody has an ice box?" Between inquiries and pleasantries, Krishna admired the portraits of dignified ancestors, the vases littering the rooms stuffed with colorful and fragrant roses and the wrought silver candelabras flickering and sparking even in daylight. She scanned the mantelpieces, chock-a-block with florid Murano glassware, prismatic Waterford miniatures, and the most fragile of porcelain collections she ever could imagine. She was reminded of the

Governor's mansion at Fort St. George as rife with gleaming silver tea settings and sparkling crystal chandeliers. Except that place had been smaller.

She heard the stories, told in crisp English accents, of Tail's antics growing up, and flipped through picture-albums filled with Jacob and his brothers of varying age and size—gangly Indian lads in British school-boy uniforms grazing the grounds of the venerable St. Paul's. She sensed a strange nostalgia for the British raj, a feeling of grandeur manquee. A coterie of delighted children escorted Krishna through the sprawling mansion screaming "Aunty, Aunty, this one is my room!" and "Look here see, when this clock comes to the next hour, a small bird comes out and sings coockoo! You will hear it in the morning!" Krishna was content to have met the family when finally bedded for the night, but also quite certain that she had more in common with the staff.

Sindhya and Ranjeet came to visit from Calcutta. Despite the bitterness of her father's passing, these were welcome, happy days for Krishna. Reunited, the sisters made up for years of missed company, reveled in each others' familiarity, giggled madly and conspiratorially over nothing in particular, and on occasion burst, embarrassed, into floods of sentimental tears. Jacob impressed the group at the luxurious Planter's Club where the waitstaff treated the foursome like recently crowned royalty. He also whisked them off to see the mountainous vistas of old Darj. From Tiger Hill they gloried in the peaks of Kanchenjunga and could just about make out Everest nearby. They picnicked at Senchal Lake, tiffin carriers laden for them with all vegetarian fare, by the meticulous cooks. They wandered through the town bundled in furs borrowed from soon to be sisters-in-law. They met Tibetan monks at the Ghoom Monastery, and at the bazaar they found *sherpas* and *ghurkas* and *Bhutias* and Nepalis, many of them friends of Jacob and Paulites themselves. Jacob and Ranjeet worried aloud, joking that the sisters, inseparable, might plot to run away without them. Krishna confided in Sindhya: "I'm not so sure anymore, to tell you the truth. Look at the way he grew up, the way he has lived…Such abundance, such excess, so much taken for granted!" Sindhya, upset by the implications, was quick to answer. "You're being ridiculous! You should consider yourself blessed. This man loves you. It's obvious. He is handsome and charming and educated and caring. What does it matter how he grew up? The gods are giving you a golden chance! At this age, who are you to throw it away?" Krishna considered Sindhya's plea. "Of course, you're right. He is all those things. He has been a gem to me. I may not deserve such a blessing, but it would be folly to throw it away." Sindhya recognized that the habit of self-punishment dies hard.

Back at Princeton, everything seemed less of a struggle. Having spent a month away, both Krishna and Jacob had much to catch up on, but responsible and diligent, they set to work without complaint and felt fulfilled by their recent memories. Krishna was charmed to learn that the staff at the Faculty Club and even Dr. Einstein had noticed her absence. The children at Sunday school said they'd missed the way she told the stories—not just reading them straight from the bible, but explaining the big words and asking their opinions on what they might have done in such situations. Even Mrs. Carter mentioned something about the house seeming so empty without her. For the months before the graduation, which she was not permitted to attend, Krishna came to feel like Princeton had become home. She celebrated in the audience at Jacob's graduation, and Naga lent her his mortarboard and let her toss it up in the air at the send-off celebration they threw for him at Jacob's, as many as eight other Indian students now in attendance. By the time Krishna and Jacob got married the next December, Naga had already written from Madras that his wife was three months pregnant.

Of the family, only Jacob's brother in Pennsylvania and his American wife could attend. Dot, who Krishna asked from England to be her matron of honor was pregnant with her second and couldn't come. Padma was now running a charity back home and couldn't be spared for the trip. The wedding was held at the Miller chapel, the Reverend Carter presiding. Friends from the Y, class-mates, church-members, and even professors came. Professor Einstein, who was traveling, again sent regrets. Scandalized by the notion that she walk down the aisle alone, as Krishna had proposed, Dolly Carter arranged for two of the Sunday school boys (one on either side) to give the bride away. The selection was made based on which of the boys in class could recite the names of all the books of the bible (old testament and new) the fastest and without errors. One of the girls, unaware the contest was open only to the boys, raised her hand, was called upon to speak and reeled them off first and fastest. After the boys had taken their turns, and two of them been selected, Krishna felt at pains to include the true winner in her wedding. The wedding party quickly incorporated a flower girl. The men all wore dark suits, thin ties, and white carnations on their lapels. Krishna, who were this a Hindu wedding would have worn a red sari embroidered in gold thread, wanted somehow to honor her roots. She wore a gold-trimmed, white sari instead, which Sindhya sent as a gift and a substitute for her own attendance. Dolly Carter finagled the post of Krishna's witness and matron of honor. For the humble reception, held in the wood-paneled church basement and common room, Mrs. Fisher baked a most magnificent white wedding cake in multiple layers, which she thoughtfully topped with her miniature frosted vanilla-wafer rendition of the Taj Mahal. The couple were delighted by the surprise. They were both too polite to mention that the Taj was a Muslim monument built for a wife who'd died in child birth. Aside from the cake, they had vegetarian *samosas* all made by Krishna and served disappointingly tepid, sweet champagne, and Mrs. Carter's infamous punch. For days the guests related how they'd "attended an Indian wedding."

The honeymoon, a gift from Jacob's brother, consisted of three days at a hotel edging the thunderous Niagara Falls. The couple left for their train directly after the reception and arrived late at the hotel where the eager, freckle-faced lad who checked them in, making small-talk, inquired into their provenance. "Indian," Jacob replied, proudly registering them into the honeymoon suite as "Mr. and Mrs. Jacob Rao." "Indian?" repeated the boy delighted, "Really? From what tribe?" It was Jacob who was deflowered on his wedding night, having waited patiently like the gentleman he was, despite Krishna's admission. He was never one to take advantage of anybody's weakness. Eager but inexperienced, Jacob didn't muster in Krishna the kind of passion that Pierre had. For this, Krishna was grateful. She still believed she didn't deserve satisfaction. Having suffered from Pierre the consequences of indulging the baser pleasures, she learned to prefer that her own bliss be curtailed.

The couple moved back to India to make a difference. "It is what we had envisioned before Ghandiji died, and what we must follow through on to honor his life." they explained to Indian friends who couldn't understand why they would want to return. "Don't you see? India needs us even more now. We have been trained and we are skilled in ways that the government can exploit. By serving in government, we can improve the conditions of more people. How is it that you can sit back and watch your motherland fail while you prosper here so far away?" they charged back at their peers, inducing guilt and sighs of hopelessness in their now American colleagues. They moved to Delhi, where the engines of centralization had started chugging and where both imagined the greatest opportunities to contribute. Because the government now required it, they learned Hindi together, finally establishing an Indian language in common. They had to speak it at work. At home, they still spoke English. Through Jacob's family connections, they got well placed in government posts and volunteered for church work on the side as much of India in the 1950s still subsisted on charity. They visited often with relatives both North and South, everybody nudging about when they'd be expecting. Back in Mangalore Krishna would revert automatically to her Hindu traditions. In Darjeeling, at church with the family on Sundays, she'd just as easily recite the Lord's Prayer or chant the Apostles Creed. Maybe she was hedging her religious bets. It didn't work. God, or the gods, disciplined her with two miscarriages. Had she known the statistics on how common they were, she might not have felt so inadequate. Neither time did she burden Amma with news of the hardships. Only Sindhya, who had by now become a doctor, came to Delhi to care for Krishna through the discouragement and isolation. Jacob was somehow too naturally optimistic to be of meaningful comfort. He was always certain that the next one "would stick." For Krishna there was the searing pain of the event itself magnified by the torment of unmet expectations. Sindhya sympathized and tried to comfort her, "It happens to all of us, Krishna. Even I have suffered like this so many times as you know. It's only that nobody talks about it when it happens, so we think we are alone. How many times I see patients, even younger girls, have miscarriages. It is not your fault. How can you blame yourself?" Krishna didn't agree. "It's not the same for you and me Sindhya. Your calamities have only been accidental. For me, this is karma coming back to roost. I can feel it." Krishna didn't even give herself the luxury of depression. She took her three days of mandatory rest, bore her disappointments and moved on.

Amma died in her sleep during the monsoon season. On hearing the news, Krishna's knees buckled under her and she began to tremble so violently that even Jacob's embrace could not contain the rumbling. She remained doubled over on the cold marble floor, sobbing, with Jacob wrapped around her for no less than two hours. He resolved not to budge until she was calmed.

Nothing presaged Amma's demise. Only in her late sixties, though delicate, she was healthy and well kept. She had remained active with her temple volunteering, involved with the grandchildren nearby, and integrated in the family and the community. She had missed Arna, yes, but was satisfied that he was soundly reincarnated. She complained of nothing, not even diminishing eyesight, and had good genes to boot. There was no reason to believe that, like her relatives and ancestors, she wouldn't live well into her nineties. But one dark dawn, Maya-bai, noticing that Amma had not come out for her morning prayers, knocked mildly on her door and on hearing no reply found her peacefully, eternally asleep. Kishore called on the whole family. He felt always encumbered by the strain of bearing bad news. Despite the rains, they all arrived within a day. Despite the rains, the funeral pyre burned brightly on the riverside, and Amma's ashes were scattered into the river as had Arna's before her. Despite the rains, the mourning women all wore white. They wailed together, the sisters, reminding themselves of the benevolence and quiet tolerance of their simple, servile mother. They clung onto each other in a batch, like seaweed adrift, recognizing they would never again be graced by such unconditional love.

The last time Krishna had seen her mother, they had sat together on the floor of Kishore's living room before a spongy pile of brilliant white mums and fragrant jasmine blossoms, threading garlands for a temple *dharshan* which it was understood Krishna would not attend. Amma had admonished Krishna for having forgotten her garlanding, letting the threads peak through between the buds, unlike the tight knots Amma had accomplished. Then she had corrected herself good-naturedly, patting Krishna on the knee and exclaiming "Silly me! Perfection is only an aspiration—even for the gods. We humans...sometimes we come undone, sometimes our threads stick out!" It was Amma's way of reminding Krishna that her foibles had long been forgiven. Krishna didn't get it. She unwound her garland and started over, tightening the strings so much they dug red grooves into her fingers. Amma watched her little perfectionist now all grown up, gratified with pride. Krishna had thought Amma was scanning for mistakes.

It was a combination of Amma's passing and Ranjeet and Sindhya's decision to move to Nebraska that got Jacob and Krishna thinking. After several years in the bureaucracy into which India's government had stagnated, their passion to improve its lot had waned. Nehru's cries for "*roti, kapada aur makaan*" for the people got lost in the need to quell the constant Hindu-Muslim riots in the North, the border wars with Pakistan over Kashmir, the restructuring of Southern state boundaries along linguistic lines, and the folding in of formerly Princely States and their maharajahs into the Indian union. While the central government was strong on ideology and theoretical foundation and staffed with honorable civil servants with the best of Gandhian intentions, there was still far to go with respect to practicalities, and the functionaries had no experience at spinning the wheels of a country so vast. Those few who had come back waving higher degrees from abroad and anxious to contribute to Indian self-rule found themselves stymied by a populace skeptical of centrist efforts and raised on the habit of resistance and non-cooperation. Waves of famine kept devastating any advances. Things in India weren't changing fast enough. Jacob determined that the couples' personal disappointments were being exacerbated by the erosion of their ideals. They optimistically applied for jobs at the United Nations, a new and international organization brimming with prospects and twinkling with hope. Their first postings took them to Peru.

They were happy together outside of India. They felt like they were making a difference with the U.N. and Krishna, perhaps feeling less pressure to reproduce as she had in the family context, seemed to Jacob slightly softer on herself. She had indeed grown more in love with him as her trust evolved, appreciative that Jacob had stood by her despite her perceived deficiencies. It was years before

Krishna became pregnant with Suhasini, who was born in Lima. Her first language was Spanish, which she learned from the Peruvian nanny who raised her while her parents were at work. Krishna was shocked on coming home one evening to find her toddling little daughter in animated conversation with the maid. Suhasini hadn't said a single word in English yet and Krishna didn't understand the Spanish exchange. Jacob hired an English tutor for Suhasini as well as for the nanny. Five years later, when the thrill of the first-born had long faded, I came along. We grew up speaking English at home, my parents having had no other languages in common when they met. I must admit that mom was always pleased that her girls were so independent from early on.

14

"What rot!" cries mom, scoffing at even the suggestion, "when are you going to stop all this nonsense and put yourself to finding a job? Enough of this now, Sushi, you're really beginning to worry me." We've been on the phone about an hour now. I've been trying to get her buy-in on the novel but, stubborn and dismissive, she won't budge. I returned from India all pumped up about it, notebooks crammed with what I now term "research," and mom is my first phone call. While she's glad to have me home safe and sound, delighted of the reports on her family back home, and pleased that I had such a good time, my big plans just aren't flying. She determines that I'm tired, probably jet-lagged, and should do my laundry and get some rest. We'll chat tomorrow, she says "when you're thinking straight."

Sindhya-Aunty, on the other hand, thinks it's a splendid idea. Of course she'll cooperate with me, she says, she's happy to help with as much detail as she can remember. But, she cautions, she wouldn't want to upset my mother. She really wouldn't want to act against her wishes. Have I thought, she asks in earnest, about why I really want to do this, even if mom isn't on board? Sindhya-Aunty gives me pause. I suppose it had never occurred to me that mom wouldn't want to cooperate. After all, it would be a celebration of her life. Sindhya-Aunty questions in all fairness, "It's not as though she's ever been so interested in sharing her past with you before. Why would she start now?" I suppose the question for me is really why she wouldn't. I explain this to Sindhya-Aunty. "Well maybe, Sushi," she suggests in her most effective bed-side mannerial voice, "maybe you should examine why this is so important for you to do and just tell her. The reasons it's important to you may be the only thing that gets her on your side." Ugh. She's right. Introspection…and a dreaded heart-to-heart.

So it's later. I've unpacked, downloaded the digicam pics and e-mailed them around, done the laundry, returned messages and sorted the mail into neat piles for "act now," "consider," and "recycle." It's still early, and I'm jet-lagged so the chances of sleep are low. I set myself to updating my resume, something I haven't thought about, and certainly not acted on, in at least a couple of months. Mom's right. I should get on it. But the whole damn thing's demoralizing, and I've been procrastinating. Now I'm staring at the chunks of time I've spent marinating at one finance job or another. I suppose when you look at it all neatly formatted and appropriately euphemized like this it has the veneer of a career, but I can vouch that it yielded none of the requisite satisfaction. The most I can say was that it was lucrative—designed to support a lifestyle, not to sustain a life. I'm realizing that I just can't do that to myself again. There's no soul in it. It quashes hope. I simply can't go back.

"Mom, it's me again."

"Oh! Hi. I thought I wouldn't hear again till tomorrow. It's so late! Are you okay? Jet-lagged?"

"I'm fine. Yeah, jet-lagged, I suppose."

(Long pause while she waits for the other shoe to drop.)

"Mom, I really…It's really very important to me to write this book. About you."

"This again?" she blurts. I can just about hear her rolling her eyes, so I break in before she can speak.

"The thing is, mom. I know you don't see it that way, but a lot of what you went through, a lot of what you did, you know, it's amazing. It's heroic. It's, well, it was pioneering…And I, well…I want to celebrate you mom, you know? And I feel like I'm just getting to know you lately. And I don't really understand yet why you didn't share your experience with us growing up, but now I know it's an admirable story…It's just, well, impressive. And I want to write it. I want to write and tell people about how amazing my mom is! Plus, you know that in my heart I've always wanted to write…And here the universe hands me this brilliant story, and I'm probably the only person who can tell it—well, other than you—and you won't help me. I just don't understand. But it's important to me, mom. I mean, you're important to me." It occurs to me that adding some sort of social value might inspire my mom. "And you know mom, you're a role-model. You have exactly the kind of story that girls from traditional backgrounds need to hear more of. You're an inspiration." It never occurs to me to tell her that I love her.

There's silence on the other end. I think I detect a sniffle. "Look, Sushi," mom announces, her voice cracking (is it the operation or is it tears?) "This is important too. And I don't want to repeat it. So just listen once and for all, alright?" She swallows, then pauses again before launching in, her voice quavering slightly. "Look, what you see as pioneering and, what did you call it, heroic? It's not like that. From my point of view, it's just not like that. Everything I did growing up, whatever you know of it, it was all very selfish, you understand? I was just a girl who thought she knew what she wanted, having her flights of fancy without the least concern for how it affected anybody else. I know for you, for your generation, here in America, it all seems so progressive and liberated, no? It wasn't. It isn't. It was all very damaging. It was defiant and improper. It damaged me and my parents and it insulted a whole tradition. It's nothing I'm proud of. You understand? It's shameful. It's nothing to be touted. Once I had made certain mistakes then I had no choice but to just get on with it. So I just went on. I wasn't making the liberated, courageous choices you think I was. I was following my adolescent, egotistical whims and then I had no choice but to keep doing whatever was necessary to get on with life. I'm not proud of any of it. I don't want you writing about all that as if it's something to be proud of."

What she's saying brings a lump to my throat. I know it took nerve to admit all that, and I'm reeling at the words. I want to weep but I swallow the tears. I can tell that mom feels badly now, and I feel like a jerk for pushing her.

"Oh." Is all I can muster. "I didn't know that's how it was for you, mom. I really never thought of it that way…I'm sorry. I'm really, very sorry." The lump feels bigger now. I hear my mom sniffle, swallow her own tears. "It's okay, Sushi" she whispers, "just forget about all this, okay? It's over. Now go to bed. You've got a lot ahead of you these days, eh? I'll e-mail you tomorrow or something. Alright?"

"Okay mom. Sorry mom. I didn't mean to upset you, okay? Goodnight."

"Okay Sushi. Goodnight."

"Mom?"

"Yes?"

"Mom, I…nothing mom. Sleep tight mom."

"Goodnight."

When I hang up I climb into bed and try to get to sleep. That horrible, familiar, loneliness flushes through me once again. I shudder and squeeze shut my eyes, fearful of giving into it. I pull the covers closer to protect against it. But it doesn't work. I spring a leak. A single tear escapes my eye and trickles down my cheek, seeping a splotch into the pillowcase. A vast sorrow inundates me. My body convulses as I resist the pangs that wrench and threaten to flood through my gut. It dawns on me that rather than resisting, I should just let the tears flow for a change. So I give in. The dam bursts. I sob freely and melodramatically. I ride the waves of shame that sluice through me; I shiver as the loneliness surges and cascades across me and I wail. I writhe there, awash in the floods of emotion for what feels like hours though I know that only a few minutes have gone by. Soon enough, I transition into sniffles, and then to an unfamiliar calm. I lay there in the darkened silence, blinking. Something feels different. The torrent that ran through me seems somehow remote and impersonal now, not mine. Like the brittle banks of a river that can't help but burst when the waters rage by in spring-time, I am merely the vessel for the water's violent flow: its conduit maybe, but not its source. The shame and guilt gush through me, but I recognize that maybe none of it was ever mine.

When I next talk to Sindhya-Aunty I tell her about my conversation with mom. Even she is shaken to learn that all these years her sister remains so dis-tressed over what happened so long ago. "I suppose it affected every one of her choices ever since," she surmises aloud. "In many ways," says Sindhya-Aunty, "you, Sunny, Jag, all of you…you're so lucky that you don't have the burden of responsibility to a tradition the way we had growing up. You're deprived of that culture, but you're also very free." She takes a deep breath, "Maybe, Sushi, you're even free to pursue whatever you think you need to do without Krishna-akka's support." I've been pondering the question. I wonder if being free from the stric-tures of tradition actually brings a greater burden in demands and expectations of oneself.

The thing is though, in the last couple of weeks, while purportedly looking for a job, I've actually been writing. It all just started pouring out one day, coming together into a story. The dance imagery thrums in my head. I can feel the ten-sions, the themes of the pull of tradition versus the passion of youth and will. I am getting a handle on the loneliness that seemed always to engulf my mom. I understand now that the dance of my mother's life was to live in the shadow of a tradition she could never really escape. Maybe she was never liberated from the burdens of her culture, but just by understanding that culture, I've come to appreciate her better, and learned to distinguish some of her burdens from my own. There's no point slamming my head against the wall of my mother's rigid-ity. In the end I realize that I'm going to see this novel through with or without her approval. If she won't cooperate, I'll just have to imagine the blanks. And just resolving that I have to write this thing makes me feel hopeful and strangely com-plete.

From:	knadghar@calberk.edu
To:	sushilarao@yoohoo.com
Subject:	Coming to New York!
Date:	March 18 2001 11:51:06—2300 (CST)

Dear Sushila:

Thanks so much for including me on your list for the travel log from India. It was so amusing, I hope you don't mind that I forwarded it to a couple of friends. (I also forwarded the jokes.) You are a vivid and entertaining writer. You really should see if you can get this stuff published! (Maybe the Kanara Saraswat magazine?)

I am writing because I just learned I must be in New York for a conference next week. It is also possible that I will be teaching at Columbia starting in the fall. If you are available, it might be interesting to meet. After all, we might have been siblings!

Please send my best regards to your mother. Your stories of her family in Mangalore remind me very much of the few folks I've met from my own. (By the way, I get that same stuff about being 38 and single...so don't worry, the harassment is equal opportunity.) Looking forward to your response.

Best wishes,

Kami

The classical *Bharatanatyam* program ends with a *Mangalam* or benediction. Here, the artist will again salute god, guru and audience and complete the traditional order by dancing to a simple devotional verse. The final number is meant to be gratifying to the audience, a reminder that the dance series is devotional and is also where the promise of the *Alarippu* is fulfilled.

#

15

It's spring in D.C. and the cherry blossoms, splendid in their bloom, release flurries of petals that flutter and drift on the breeze. I'm looking forward to my nephew's first little league game tomorrow and my niece's dance recital tonight. (She saw a performance at an international dance festival four years ago and decided she wanted to try Indian dance. Sunny, in perpetual search for anything that'll distract the kids from the television, signed her right up for classes. She took to it like a housecat to napping. She's been dancing every weekend ever since.) When they come to fetch me at Union Station, Mulund assesses me with wonder, "Aunty Sushi!" he cries, returning my vigorous hug with the uncertain embrace of an eight-year old boy, "you got so dark!" He means it as a compliment. "Sushi!" exclaims mom, wrapping me in a full-on embrace, "didn't you take any sunblock to India?" I did. It was pretty pointless in the South. "Fair and beautiful" comes to mind. "No time to drop your stuff off," Sunny explains while leaning out of the drivers' side window to kiss me. "The performance is at six! We're headed straight for the auditorium. Sandeep already took Aarti, and Sindhya-Aunty's meeting us. Get in!"

At the elementary school auditorium, before Aarti's recital starts, we're mingling with the crowd. I'm surprised to see so many non-Indians in attendance, many of them in *Salwaar Kameez* or swathed in colorful Indian shawls. Friends I figure, guests of the dancers. Sindhya-Aunty arrives on time but flustered anyway. Like most Indians, she's used to making excuses for running late. She surveys the crowd to find us. I wave at her from our seats. Her 4'10"s are just about eclipsed by the giant bouquet of flowers she's thoughtfully carrying for Aarti. She makes her way to our row, embraces mom and Mulund both at once, then Sandeep and Sunny who've saved a seat for her beside them. I climb over bags and shawls to greet her. "So tan!" she remarks, "is that still from India?" Then, whispering in my ear as she hugs me, "Hey, there's a boy for you to meet while you're here. Doctor. Works with Jag. Divorced. Come for dinner tomorrow? I know you don't like Indians but he grew up here, and he's only half. Will that do?" I giggle at the generosity of these random attempts to matchmake me. We may have nothing at all in common, but the guy's the right age, available and half Indian, so he'll probably fly. "Believe it or not," I whisper back into her ear, "I may have met somebody. A doctor! Really good guy. Half Saraswat. Will that do?" She beams, pinching my cheek. "*Amichi Gele?* Met in India?" she suggests. "Long story." I explain in a whisper, having decided in advance that I'm not bringing Kami up at all until things are more gelled between us.

The crowd settles when Aarti's petite, softspoken dance teacher takes the stage. In a refined, unAmericanized accent, she reads an abbreviated history of *Kuchipudi*, emphasizing that this form of dance-drama was initially performed by men and only taken up by women in this century. "Like *Bharatanatyam*," she says, "it is a devotional dance form, but *Kuchipudi* has more of a folk idiom and greater flexibility in form and subject matter, enabling the dancers to express more humor and drama and more of their own personalities, often even singing for themselves." After the invocation with all the girls, she tells us, the first dance will be the popular story of the competition between Kartikeya and his brother, the elephant-headed god, Ganesh. "Kartikeya was proud of his mount, a peacock, and confident of his own speed on a flying beast. He challenged his brother to race around the world seven times. Kartikeya managed to tour the world only three times before giving up. But Ganesh, having only his wits and a mouse as his vehicle, merely circumambulated his parents, the Lord Shiva and the Goddess Parvati, seven times and then bowed down to them with reverence. With that, he claimed victory. When Kartikeya questioned Ganesh on how he could claim the prize with such little effort, he replied 'My parents are the universe. All of creation is a manifestation of the Shiva-male and Shakti-female form. It is an act of delusion to attempt to go round this phenomenal world. To encircle my beloved parents, from whom I am sourced, is the true circumnavigation of the cosmos.' The story can be interpreted on several levels, but is often told merely to impress on children the importance of attention to their parents."

Aarti, who I can't believe is already thirteen, appears in the first number. She plays the Goddess Parvati, whose role seems mainly to praise and prostrate herself and revel obsequiously around the proud and angry Shiva. I am surprised at how convincing she is in her fawning, subservient, demeanor and I wonder as I watch her graceful obeisance, what she thinks about her part. Aarti is growing up to be so independent, somewhat defiant by nature and I now realize, quite unlike Sunny, her easy-going mom. Last week we were i.m.-ing and I asked her if she was nervous about this performance. "Nope." She replied, promptly. "It's fun to pretend to be other people. I get to be silly sometimes, or mean or stupid. Stuff I'm usually not." At her age, it seems a healthy way to indulge a whole range of sentiments that might otherwise remain constrained. By the time her number ends I'm so proud of my niece, so charmed by her courage and dedication that

I'm hooting and whistling the loudest, much to my family's embarrassment. Since the rest of the performance doesn't feature much of Aarti, I find myself daydreaming, thoughts of Kami softly seeping in.

We'd had a pretty remarkable week while he was in town. We met at the Strand at seven one evening, poked around a bit and went for drinks, then dinner. I was loitering at a book-bin, flipping through something when I looked up and saw him making his way through the chaotic maze of bookshelves and rolling carts that epitomizes the bookstore. He looked exactly like the kind of guy I've avoided my whole life: preppy, scrupulously combed, shorter than I'd expected and of course, unmistakably Indian. His youthful, angular face spread into a bright smile when he spotted me and from across the room instead of waving, he raised his hand into a little pistol, winking and shooting a blank at me as he made his way over. There was an instant familiarity about him, and when he arrived he poked at the book I was paging through to read the title, commenting, "Hmm. A travel guide eh? Leaving already and we've only just met!" He didn't extend a hand, but wrapped me in a warm embrace, "I'm Kamath. I sure hope you're Sushila." "I am" I giggled, "But everyone calls me Sushi." "Yup," he came back, "everyone calls me Kami." Without a trace of an accent nor the formal mannerisms I would have expected from an Indian, I got easily thrown off the scent. We fell promptly into easy conversation, none of the awkwardness of a first date, though it hadn't meant to be a date at all. When we decided to move along for drinks he managed to disarm my regular guard with self-deprecating, sidelong comments ("cheap as a Desi doctor") and a relaxed manner that evinced a quiet self-confidence. He didn't need to select the ideal bar like your average metrosexual, "You're the New Yorker, what could I possibly have to add to the subject?" And he didn't try to impress me with his knowledge of wines. "If it's red, doesn't require a mortgage and doesn't taste like something you pour into your car, I'm sure it'll be fine" he chirped at the bartender, inspiring me to add, "I'll have the same." We covered zillions of topics, laughed ourselves silly and gazed into each others' eyes dreamily, quickly picking a new subject when one of us noticed our own absorption. We moved on to dinner where I braced for the usual litany of food restrictions Indians tend to endorse. You know, vegetarian, no cheese (cholesterol, not lactose intolerance), no salt (blood pressure.) Again, he took it easy, "May I ask if there's something you're known for?" he inquired politely of the waiter, taking his suggestion without modification. He was effortless company. We chatted for hours. The next time I looked at my watch it was 2:30 a.m. It was thoroughly unlike me to let a guy pay. But I did, and without the usual fuss. We saw each other every night of his conference before he headed back to the West coast. I never expected to date an Indian (not even half of one), and even less to like him. But he's surprisingly progressive, intelligent, warm; a feminist even, a good kisser and even better, a great cook. He gets me. I get him. We've agreed to play it by ear and see what happens. He expects to end up in New York in the fall.

Later that night on my way to the pull-out in the basement of my sister's house, where I'll be sleeping, I pass by my mom's bedroom. I notice her through the half-open door in the striations of a streetlight filtered through vertical blinds. Even though she has her own place, mom spends enough nights at Sunny's babysitting or just hanging out, that she's merited her own room here. She's a tapering hump under the duvet now, clinging fast, in fetal position to the right side of the queen-sized mattress. I realize that for years I've done the same thing. Although I could sprawl out across the entire bed, I sleep on just "my" half of it, perhaps leaving room for completion.

Mom blinks, smiles at me sleepily through the doorway and murmurs "good-night, Sushi." For some reason I'm drawn to push the door open further and let myself in. She pats the empty space behind her and I crawl on the covers so we're spooning, tucking one hand under my head and embracing her with the other from behind. "Long day for you," she comments, "but I'm really glad you came." "Me too," I concede. In adjusting my arm across mom's tiny frame, my fingers find their way to her supple, velveteen earlobe, and absentmindedly I stroke it between thumb and forefinger. "Hmmm." She humphs, with pleased recognition, "you used to do that when you were really young, when I used to put you to bed. You'd hang on to my ear with two fingers." Funny. "Did I?" I don't remember this. I must have been very little. We cuddle together for the first time in as long as I can remember, mom facing away. "Sushi," she proffers timidly, "you told Sindhya-Aunty today that you've met someone special." She pauses for a moment. My arm rises and falls with her inhale and her exhale, then she whispers "…but you didn't tell me…"

My heart stings. It's not like my mom to let out something like this. Mom moves on quickly. She bears her slights stoically, without complaint. I start to jump to my own defense: "It's nothing serious, mom. Just a couple dates. Nothing worth mentioning really." "Oh." She allows, unsatisfied. Tears want to form in my eyes. I realize I should elaborate. "Mom, I just didn't want you to be upset if things don't work out, you know? I didn't want to get anyone excited. But more than that, I just didn't want to disappoint you." "Disappoint me?" she blurts almost before I've finished my sentence, then she swallows whatever she was going to say, considering for a moment. The bed heaves as she flips turning to face me, settling into the same curled position, but on her right side. I tuck both my hands under my head on the pillow. She reaches across with one of hers and strokes the hair away from my face as she looks at me benevolent, intent. "Sushi," she whispers, "what about your disappointment?"

I'm alarmed. My eyes close shut and I can't help the tears that start to scud down my cheek. "What good am I?" she continues, "if I can't share the burden of some of that?" I blink, looking back at her, the tears flooding faster now. "You know," she intimates, "maybe keeping disappointments to yourself is like twice the burden: there's the thing itself, and then the strain of having to hide it. If you share the disappointments, then maybe each of us only gets half?" She pitches it, doubtful over whether it'll actually work that way. I understand her meaning though. I nod childishly in agreement, tears still flowing, and it occurs to me to whisper between sniffles. "But Ma…you have to do it too, you know? It can't just be one way…" That way, I figure, maybe we'll both feel less alone. She strokes my hair gently, and wobbles her head agreeably in patronizing ascent. She has no intention of sharing her disappointments, but tonight I'll get to fall asleep in the boundless comfort of my mom's embrace. "I love you, mom" I croak. My mom hugs me tighter. I hear her sniffling into my hair.

I've brought a suitcase full of gifts from everybody in Bombay to everybody here, and after breakfast the next morning, the kids don't conceal their keenness to break into it. "I can't believe you lugged all of this back!" My brother-in-law remarks on being assigned the task of hauling it from the car into the living room. "Me neither!" I lament. "But you know how it is…" Sandeep knows. Every time they go to India, they take two empty duffels: one for the shopping and one for the gifts. We tuck into it at once. All the packages are tightly wrapped and neatly labeled. Third-world wrapping (or is India second world these days?) delights Aarti to bits. She loves the way they'll swaddle even a pre-scription for you at the pharmacy, the brown paper sealed tidily with a stretched, yellowing snippet of gummy "celotape." I parcel out the contents, setting aside the bundles for Sindhya-Aunty, Ranjeet-Uncle and Jag. Mulund, playing Santa, distributes each package as I decipher its intended recipient and try to remember from whom it came.

For the children there are light blue tee-shirts emblazoned with the flag and logo of India's cricket team, costume jewelry for Aarti's *Kuchipudi* and a dwarfed, extravagantly embroidered Jodhpuri *kurta*-pajama for Mulund who models it for us, revealing his inner maharajah. For the women there are saris of course, each one more ornate in its gold threading than the next, and glass bangles of varied colors, sparkling with geometric gold designs. We shudder in fear that they'll snap as we squeeze oiled, pinched hands through the hoops and then admire our wrists as the bangles, in unison, jingle and bounce. Sandeep is surprised to get a case of elegantly boxed clove cigarettes (he doesn't smoke) and passes around the colorful folder full of handmade writing papers with matching envelopes he gets, the hefty kind that warrant calligraphy.

Mom opens a laden cardboard box, the red and gold dotted *Bandhani* tie-dye print on it as dazzling as the contents: two silver *diya* oil lamps small enough for a home shrine; a plastic bottle of rose water and another one of *Gangali* water taken from the Ganges; a litter of smaller boxes, printed exactly like their container and filled with cloves, raw turmeric, *jaggery, aggarbati* incense sticks, betel nuts, red *Moli* holy threads, cotton wicks and camphor oil for burning; and finally, a bulbous and modern statuette of Ganesh looking sleek in polished silver for the 21st Century. These are all the ingredients for the making of a *pooja*. Inside the box Kishore-Mama has tucked an envelope. His note is written in Konkani, and it comes with some sort of receipt. Mom translates aloud, pausing to remember her words. "My Dear Krishna-bai: what a joy that you sent us your Sushila to know. Just like you, a determined and curious girl." Mom glances at me and winks. "She has had us all dredging up such memories and even mining our old boxes. I did not realize I had held onto Arna's account books. The tax authorities advised us to keep them for ten years after his passing and I must have overdone it. You may be as surprised as I was to see what I've found! I did not know that Arna had carried this expenditure after you left home. I thought you might like to learn of it. Many sincere thanks for all of the gifts you sent with Sushila. You are most clever to send only useful things or else Maya offloads them immediately to the temple. Affectionately, Kishore."

I smile at the formality of the closing, remembering how Kishore-Mama somehow imparts a stiff, almost reluctant warmth. Mom inspects the enclosed receipt more closely. She squints to read what's written on it. She draws a breath and drops the hand holding the paper on her lap, the other she raises to pinch the bridge of her nose under her glasses. She squeezes her eyes against the tears. "What is it?" Mulund asks, concerned to see his stalwart grandmother weaken. Mom sniffles, wipes her eyes hastily with her fingers to compose herself. "It's just an old checkbook stub. From my father's records." she responds, her voice cracking. "Can I see?" I ask, reaching for the thin blue receipt. She releases it. I inspect. It's hard to make out the date on it, but it's in English and the "To" line says something about a University Hospital in Bombay. The payment was made in rupees, the tight, rounded numbers almost indecipherable, 330 Rupees? 380? 980? The "For" line reads quite clearly: "Krishna hospitalization—ankle, malaria." Aarti takes the slip from me, deciphers the same. "Why does it make you sad?" she asks her grandmother with concern. "It doesn't," mom responds, still wistful, "it makes me happier than I ever thought possible."

Glossary

Abhinaya—feeling. The suggestive imitation of emotions or psychological states in a drama or dance drama.

Aggarbati—incense.

Akka—(Konkani). A suffix. Honorific for elder sister.

Alarippu—in a typical Arangetram, *Alarippu* is the first dance number. It is an invocation, offering obeisance to the gods and the audience.

Amichi gele—(Konkani). Literally "one of us." Used to specify the caste and clan, and generally used by Saraswat Brahmins.

Amma—(Konkani). Mother.

Ammu—(Konkani). Term of endearment. Literally "little mother."

Aniruddha—cooperative; the manifestation of Lord Krishna as the One Who Cannot be Obstructed.

Arangetram—(Tamil). The first public performance of an artiste. A debut and initiation ritual wherein the audience judges both the guru's expertise and the disciple's talent. The guru or nattuvaram determines when a disciple is ready for public appearance. If successful, this appearance marks the launching of a solo, public career. When the Bharatanatyam dance form was a form of devotion in Hindu temples the Arangetram initiated the dancer as a "Devadasi" (servant of the lords.) The Arangetram can last up to three hours, requiring great stamina and concentration. The order of the dance repertoire in the Arangetram is prescribed: Alarippu, Jattiswaram, Shabdam, Varnam (and Padam), Tillana, Mangalam.

Arjuna—peacock; also a mythological archer and the protagonist and hero of the Indian mythological epic, the Bhagavad Gita.

Arna (or Anna)—(Konkani). Father.

Atcha—(Hindi). Yes or agreed.

Avidya—(Sanskrit). A Vedic philosophical concept implying ignorance. The natural tendency of the human mind to misperceive reality. (This differs from Maya, which is a state of pure ignorance.)

Aya—maid/servant/nanny.

Ayurveda/Ayurvedic—an ancient Indian system of medicine employing herbs, oils, minerals and massage.

Baba—Literally, father. Sometimes used as an expression equivalent to "gee" or "gosh."

Bai—(Konkani). Kannada and several Indian languages, an honorific suffix for any lady (usually addressed to elders.)

Bala—meaning young girl or ear-ring. Can also be a name for the mother goddess.

Bandhani—a tie-dyeing style from Jamnagar (a suburb of Bombay) that features intricate patterns for saris and other fabrics. The style incorporates colored dots, circles, squares, waves and stripes against a background of another color.

Batcha—(Hindi). A term of endearment implying "young one" or child.

Bhagavad Gita—perhaps the most popular and most loved religious text in Hinduism dated to between 200 BCE and 200 CE. It a small section of a much larger epic, the Mahabarata. The Gita is a dialogue between the famous warrior Arjuna and his charioteer, who is actually the god Krishna in disguise. The primary theme is the idea that faith and devotion to god are the primary means to attain liberation from the cycle of rebirth.

Bhakti—devotion.

Bhanap—nickname for Chitrapur Saraswat Brahmin.

Bhangi—a derogatory term for an untouchable. Likely derived from the association of smoking "bhang" (marijuana.)

Bharatanatyam—literally "Indian drama". The oldest classical dance form of India. Originated in South India, where its chief exponents were the Devadasis (temple dancers) who performed as a form of devotion to the gods. The dancer was a worshipper on behalf of the public, and was offered to the gods as an embodiment of the beauty, charm and grace known to please them. The style of dance traces its origins to the Natya Shastra a recounting of several of the Hindu creation myths and stories of its pantheon. The Natya Shastra was purportedly written by the sage Bharata in the 4th Century B.C. The strenuous, complicated, yet sensuous dance form was handed down as a living tradition by generations of temple dancers, who eventually received the royal patronage which kept the art form alive over centuries. The (well educated) dancers also did the illiterate community a service by dancing the mythological stories which otherwise would not have been conveyed.

Bhutia—(Hindi). A native of Bhutan.

Bindi—also known as kumkum, mangalya, tilak, sindhoo—The holy dot on the forehead, is an auspicious makeup worn by young Hindu girls and women. The term is derived from bindu, the Sanskrit word for a dot or a point. It is usually a red dot painted onto the forehead and made with vermilion (finely powdered bright red mercuric sulfide). Considered a blessed symbol of Uma or Parvati, a bindi signifies female energy (shakti) and is believed to protect women and their husbands. Traditionally a symbol of marriage (widows generally wore a black bindi,) it has now become a decorative item and is worn today by unmarried girls and non-Hindu women as well. No longer restricted in color or shape, bindis today appear in many colors and designs and are manufactured with self-adhesives and felt.

Brahmin—In Hinduism, the brahmana varna is the highest of the four traditional castes. It is identified with the priests in society. There is no relationship, traditionally, between wealth and caste. Brahmins are often ascetics, and therefore can often be amongst the poorest.

Bullock Cart—normally a wooden carriage on wheels drawn by water buffalo and used to haul farming loads or to carry people.

Calu—(Hindi). Slang. "Darkie."

Chitrapur Saraswat Brahmin—an Indian ethnic community of Brahmins roughly associated with the South-Western area of the country. Speakers of a

Sanksrit-based language known as Konkani. A coastal social, political, spiritual and economic clan known to have played an important role in the evolution of Indian society since 2000 B.C. The CSB's give their allegiance to a lineage of spiritual leaders (Swamis) who provide for religious guidance and aim to preserve the caste purity through dictums and measures for social control. CSBs are credited with pioneering the creation of cooperative credit and building societies (worldwide.) Historically, it is believed the CSBs originated in the North West of the Eurasian continent (currently Afghanistan) and traveled down the (now defunct) Saraswat River to end up in a colony at its mouth—in the Konkan region of India.

Dal—a lentil curry or soup.

Dada—(suffix) Honorific for elder brother.

Deepa—lamp or lantern.

Dekchi—cast iron pan or pot.

Desi—A slang term for Indian or "from the Indian sub-continent."

Devadasi—literally "servant of the gods." Historically, a devotional temple dancer (woman.)

Dharshan—literally a school of thought. Used colloquially to mean a "teach in" or spiritual gathering and celebration.

Dhoti—an Indian drape generally worn by men. A cotton cloth that is pleated and wrapped around the waist to mimic a form of pant.

Dhuve America rabta—(Konkani). "Daughter from America."

Didi—(Hindi). An honorific for elder sister.

Diwali—the Indian "festival of lights." Possibly the most important holiday in India. Sometimes considered the Indian New Year and celebrated annually in honor of the Goddess Lakshmi.

Diya—small oil lamp used for ceremonial purposes; often made of silver or brass.

Dupatta—the long, trailing sash or scarf sometimes worn as a veil, that accompanies the salwar kameez.

Durga—the fiercest of the female deities in the Hindu pantheon, remarkable for her beauty and her fidelity.

Ganesh (Ganesha or Ganpatti)—In the Hindu pantheon, the portly, elephant headed son of Shiva. He is the God of the Beginning (so much so that "to Ganesh" is the verb "to begin" in many Indian languages), the God of elimination of troubles, of removal of obstacles, and; a deity known to be easily pleased with offerings of good food.

Ganpatti (or Ganapatti)—festival and feast in celebration of the elephant god, Ganesh. Also used as a name for Ganesh.

Gayatri—a Hindu goddess known for purifying, and eliminating sins. She is also thought of as the mother of the Vedas.

Ghazal—A poetic form of Indian and Pakistani music. Strictly speaking, it is not a musical form at all but originally, a poetic recitation. In this form of music, primacy is given to the lyrics.

Ghee—clarified butter used in Indian cuisine. Butter that has been boiled down so that milk solids and water evaporate. Ayurvedic medicine posits that ghee is the best shortening for cooking, because it stimulates the digestion and can increase immunities.

Ghurka—(originally, "Ghorka")—a military group, originally from Nepal, who were recruited under Queen Victoria to fight on behalf of the British Empire. Considered a highly organized, efficient and effective elite fighting corps.

Goa—The smallest State of India, located in the middle of the Western Coast on the Arabian sea. A former colony of Portugal.

Gori and Gomti—(Konkani). Literally "fair and beautiful." The implication of the popular phrase is that to be light-skinned is also aesthetically preferable.

Gotra—a clan or a family whose ancestry is traced to any one of the eight rishis (seers) known to have composed a portion of the Vedas.

Hare—(Hindi). Hail or praise. An expression of devotion, as in: "Hare Krishna."

Harijan—literally "the children of god." A euphemism used by Gandhi to refer to the untouchable caste (those below or outside of the four "legitimate" castes described in the Vedas.)

Idli—a steamed rice-flour dumpling.

Isfahan—an elaborate carpet from Persia (named after the city in Iran where the design originated.)

Jalabee—a fried, sweet, confection (something like a funnel cake) made of lentil paste and dipped in syrup or honey.

Jamnasthi—the Indian festival and feast in celebration of the Hindu god Krishna.

Jattiswaram—The second act in a typical Arangetram. This pure dance number is performed to the beat of mnemonic syllables, but introduces the element of melody. The movements do not necessarily convey meaning, but the steps are more complex and can require astonishingly sculptural poses. The purpose of this dance is to show the technical skill and accuracy of the dancer in meeting a demanding rhythm as well as holding still for challenging decorative postures.

Jyotsna—moonlight or moonbeam.

Kajal/Kohl Kajal—black eyeliner, originally made from charcoal.

Kama—literally "sexual satisfaction." Usually interpreted to mean desire. Also the equivalent of Cupid in the Hindu pantheon. He is represented as a beautiful youth, with a bow of sugar cane or flowers.

Kanchi—a highly gold-brocaded variety of sari and weave said to have originated in the South Indian town of Kanchipuram. The sari is distinguished by the brilliant colors of its silk and the detail and width of the gold borders.

Kannada—also Kannara or Kanarese. The language of the Dravidians, spoken in southwestern India; it is the official language of the State of Karnataka (formerly Mysore.) There are a number of regional dialects of Kannada and at least three distinct social dialects. A dichotomy, called diglossia, also exists between the formal, literary language and the informal, spoken version.

Kartikeya—In the Hindu pantheon, a warrior god and the second son of Shiva and Parvati. The brother of Ganesh.

Kathak or Kathakali—traditional dance drama form from the Indian State of Kerala. Generally employs colorfully painted masks.

Khansama—in the North, a generic term for cook or chef.

Kshatrya—the warrior and ruling caste; the second in the Hindu caste system.

Kishore—a name meaning teenager or youngster.

Konkani—(from the Sanskrit). A language of South Western India predominantly spoken by the Saraswat Brahmins of the Goan region. Etymologically, "Kum" represents mother earth and "Kana", dust or an atom. Historically, worshippers of "mother earth" were recognized as Konkanis, and were associated with farming.

Krishna—or Krsna—A Hindu god and the main character in the mythological Indian epic, the Bhagavad Gita. An avatar or incarnation of Vishnu. Krishna is the playful blue-colored god of myth and legend.

Kuchipudi—a dance form originating in the state of Andhra Pradesh. It aims to convey scenes from Indian mythology to a relatively unsophisticated audience and was traditionally performed by groups of men. It differs from other forms of Indian dance in that the dancer usually also sings for himself during the performance.

Kurta-Kameez or Kurta Pajama—a tunic and baggy pant-suit worn by Indian men. The tunic is often heavily embroidered, features a "Nehru" collar and is used as formalwear.

Lassi—a drink made of yogurt. Mangos and sugar can be added for richness. Also sometimes made to be savory.

M'am—see also, Khansama; a term of endearment for cook or chef, a variation on "Mama," the suffix for "uncle."

Madhurai—A major city in the Southern Indian state of Tamil Nadu. The site of one of the most elaborate and largest Hindu temples (Meenakshi.)

Mahaballipuram—A city on the Eastern Coast of Southern India(State of Tamil Nadu) known for its archeological and architectural features. Specifically known for its religious (Hindu) monuments and detailed devotional sculptures.

Maharashtria—A state in India where the City of Mumbai (Bombay) is located.

Marathi—The language of Maharashtria.

Mama (Konkani suffix)—an elder, or maternal uncle.

Mangalam—The classical Bharatanatyam program ends with a Mangalam or benedictory verse. Here, the artist salutes god, guru and audience and completes the traditional order by dancing to a simple devotional verse.

Masala—a blend of spices used for cooking or marinades.

Maya—(Sanskrit). Illusion or the ignorance based on form. It is considered a limitation of physical/material manifestation.

Meenakshi—the fish-eyed Goddess also associated with the moon. An infamous Hindu temple in the city of Madhurai in the State of Tamil Nadu.

Meethai—sweets; confections made with sugar, clarified butter and a variety of pastes (almond, pistachio, lentils, milk solids).

Mehndi—the decorative art of henna body painting used in India to adorn women for festivities, weddings and other celebrations.

Mem Sahib—a respectful title for a woman or lady; generally the word used to address the wives of gentlemen of European descent.

Mirchi—in Hindi; hot, as in spicy or piquant. Another term for chilis.

Mithuna—sexual union; describes the amorous couples in classical Hindu and Buddhist figurative art and architecture.

Moksha—in Hinduism, enlightenment. The Hindu equivalent of "nirvana." The blissful state of freedom from rebirth aspired to by Hindus and Jains.

Mudra—highly stylized, complicated hand gestures used in Vedic ritual, and featured in Hindu, Buddhist and Jain art and dance. Each gesture symbolizes the teachings and life stages of the spiritual seeker.

Namakarana—the Hindu naming ceremony. Due to a high infant mortality rate in India, Hindu babies were often not named until they survived three to six months outside the womb.

Namaste—a respectful greeting between Hindus performed by clasping the hands together as though in a prayer pose, and bowing.

Nataraja—the manifestation of the Hindu deity, Vishnu, as the Lord of the Dance.

Nattuvanar—Bharatanatyam dance teacher and guru. As the repositories of centuries of accumulated knowledge and experience, the nattuvanars were greatly sought after during the renascent phase of Bharatanatyam in the 20th century. They became indispensable guides to the women of the so-called "good families," who took up this art for the first time, without any background or exposure to it. There was no other access to the art except from this singular stronghold of an oral tradition, which could be imparted only in practice. Their cultural matrix and racial memory made them intuitive in their teaching methods.

Nightsoil—a euphemism for human waste. Nightsoil collectors in India are generally "untouchables" engaged in the cleaning of latrines and outhouses.

Nritta—pure, non-expressive, rhythmic dance movement (as differentiated from expressive dance movement.)

Odissi—A classical form of Indian dance which originated in the (current) State of Orissa. Highly sensual, it traces its origins to the ritual dances performed in the temples of ancient northern India. Like other classical arts of India, this ancient dance style had suffered a decline as temples and artists lost the patronage of feudal rulers and princely states, and by the 1930s and 40s, left few surviving practitioners of the art form.

Om—(Sanskrit). A word of solemn affirmation and respectful ascent, sometimes translated as 'yes, verily, so be it' (and in this sense compared with "Amen"). It is placed at the commencement of most Hindu works, and as a sacred exclamation may be uttered at the beginning and end of a reading of the Vedas or prior to prayer. It is also regarded as a particle of auspicious salutation [Hail!] Om appears first in the Upanishads as a mystic monosyllable and is there set forth as the object of profound religious meditation. The highest spiritual efficacy is attributed not only to the whole word but also to the three sounds A, U, M, of which it consists, and are considered the resonating sound of the universe.

Pacchi—(Konkani). Aunt.

Pada/Padam—literally a song. Often a devotional piece of music that appeals to god for protection and betterment.

Pakora—a battered, fried vegetable hors d'oeuvre.

Paratha—a layered Indian flat-bread made of wheat flour.

Parvati—also Shakti, Durga, Kali, and several other manifestations of feminine energy. Parvati is the consort of the god Shiva. She is constantly beside Shiva, watching him as he dances, admiring him in his deeds of annihilation, joining him in games of dice or playing with their two sons, the elephant headed Ganesha and the warrior Kartikeya. Shiva and Parvati, whose love is deep and abiding, represent the paradigmatic divine family. Shiva and Parvati are often united in a single form (half man-half woman) to represent the concept that the divine is both feminine and masculine.

Phuranpoli—a sweet, South Indian flat-bread made with gram flour and layered with a sweet paste made of clarified butter, sugar, coconut powder and sometimes, dried fruits.

Poha—a South Indian dish made of beaten or flattened rice flakes, onions, grated coconut, chilies, curry leaves and ground peanuts. Often a breakfast food.

Pooja (or Puja)—in general, worship of Hindu deities in the form of prayer, offerings and sacrifices. Pooja rituals can entail offerings made to the fire (Agni devta), which is viewed as the mouth of the Divine—(or feeding of the God.) During a Pooja, sixteen prescribed steps occur (symbolic of the sixteen ceremonies to be completed in the life span of a Hindu) including the welcoming of the deity, giving the deity a place to sit, the washing of the feet, decorating the deity, and the offering of food items, clothing or money to seek blessings. Fresh, sweet-scented flowers along with specific herbs and plants are used, as well as a combination of milk, ghee, honey and spices. The planting of flags with significant colours associated with the deities is sometimes used to symbolize the offerings.

Prakash—light or airy.

Prasad—food blessed in temple sanctuaries and shared or distributed among devotees.

Pukka—authentic.

Radha—In the Hindu pantheon, the lover of Krishna; also means prosperity. Radha was the mythological mistress of Krishna. They were known to have been close friends since childhood: they played, they danced, they fought, they grew up together and wanted to be together forever, but as the myth goes, the world pulled them apart. Krishna departed to safeguard the virtues of truth and came to be worshipped as a lord of the universe. He was compelled to marry Rukmini and Satyabhama out of duty, but so great was his love for Radha that even today her name is often uttered when Krishna is invoked, and Krishna worship is thought to be incomplete without the deification of Radha.

Raga—a musical tune. Ragas are derived from Thaats or parent modes. North Indian music recognizes ten such modes. A Thaat is a group of abstract tonal forms, but a Raga is a combination of notes with the power to generate emotion.

Rahul—historically, the son of Gautama Buddha (the Buddha.)

Raja, Rajah, Raj—king or royal.

Rangoli—an intricate geometrical pattern of colored rice powders laid at the entrances to homes and temples on special occasions. The art of pouring rangoli is highly specialized.

Rani—queen.

Ranjeet—victor in wars.

Rasa—a primary emotion. The nine moods expressed by a dancer through movement. They are: joy/mirth, anger, fear, disgust, wonder, valor/heroism, compassion, peace/tranquility and love.

Ratna—gem.

Roti, Kapada aur Makaan—(Hindi). Literally "food, clothing and shelter."

Saddhu—sage, ascetic or holy man. A seeker of spiritual knowledge. Often a monk.

Salwar Kameez—a long tunic-like top with baggy, ankle-hugging trousers generally worn by Muslim women, but popularized all over India for its practicality.

Sambar—a spicy soup generally served with idli.

Samosa—a kind of dry dumpling; a stuffed savory made with a flakey crust and filled with potato or meat curry.

Sandhya—evening or twilight.

Sangeeta—musical.

Sangha—a spiritual community.

Sari—the typical dress of an Indian woman; a 6-yard length of cloth (usually highly ornate silk or cotton) which is wound around the waist, tucked into a petticoat and draped over one shoulder. It is worn with a short, torso-exposing matching blouse.

Saraswati—the Hindu goddess of music, purification, fertility, knowledge and learning. Also known as the most beautiful of the goddesses. She is the wife of Brahma.

Shakuntala/Shaku—Mother of Bharat (India, or the Universal Monarch.)

Shabdam (or Sabdam)—the third act in a typical Arangetram. A composition generally in praise of a particular deity or king describing his qualities, deeds or accomplishments. The dancer adds "abhinaya" or feeling to her repertory during the Shabdam, requiring employment of gestures to express a story (albeit a simple one.)

Sherpa—a Himalayan porter who climbs mountains laden with luggage and necessities; also a mountain guide.

Shiva—Along with Brahama and Vishnu, Shiva is one of the three principle gods in the Hindu pantheon. Shiva is regarded as the "destroyer" god. Whereas Brahma creates and Vishnu maintains the world, Shiva is responsible for destroying the world and, thus, regenerating the cycle of birth and death. Although at times Shiva is portrayed with a necklace of skulls to emphasize death, Shiva is not reviled in Hindu mythology. It is acknowledged that death and destruction are necessary parts of life. Shiva is identified with the phallic symbol and male energy in general. It is thought that without destruction there can be no regeneration, therefore he represents an integral part of life.

Shudra—the servant caste, also the lowest of the four castes in the Hindu caste system. (The "untouchables" are considered to be outside of the caste system.)

Sindhya—ocean.

Suhasini—ever smiling.

Sushila—well behaved one; one with good conduct.

Swami/Swamiji—the title for a holy man, priest or spiritual community leader. The suffix "ji" is added to connote respectful familiarity.

Swaraj—literally "self-rule." The synonym for Indian independence coined by Mohandas (Mahatma) Gandhi.

Tabla—a "two headed" drum carved of wood. Each conical head is covered by a composite membrane.

Tiffin—a light meal or snack. Tiffin-carriers are usually stackable, tightly sealed metal containers that can keep food warm. Equivalent to a pic-nic basket.

Tillana—The pen-ultimate pure dance number in a Bharatanatyam performance. Its presentation breaks what may have been the slower tempo of the Padam. It is vivacious in nature, with a number of sculptural poses and variegated patterns of movement.

Vaishya—the third, or merchant and trading caste in the Hindu caste system.

Vandana—a respectful salute; a bow in praise of the recipient.

Varnam—The most challenging part of a Bharatanatyam performance. Here, the solo dancer must tell a story with nothing but the movements of her body and the expressiveness of her face and hands. She is required to portray the lyrical, dramatic and emotional content of the tale. It is an elaborate synthesis that brings out the best of both nritta (pure dance) and abhinaya (feeling).

Vedas/Vedic—the sacred original writings that are the fundaments of Hinduism. Estimated to have been written between 500 and 1000 BC, these are the sacred scriptural philosophies that underlie Hindu rituals and beliefs. The Vedas are the oldest scriptures of Hinduism, composed in Sanskrit and gathered into four collections: the Rig-Veda, the Sama-Veda, the Yajur-Veda and the Atharva-Veda. The Vedas are not a revelation like the scriptures of Western religions. They are instead considered elaborations on the nature of life and existence derived from a communion with the general, impersonal spiritual forces of the cosmos.

Vina—(or Beena) a flutelike musical instrument.

Vishnu—the Hindu god considered the preserver, restorer and protector. As one of the most important gods in the Hindu pantheon, Vishnu is surrounded by a number of extremely popular and well-known stories and is the focus of a number of sects devoted entirely to his worship. Vishnu contains a number of personalities, often represented as ten major descents (avatars) in which the god has taken on physical forms in order to save earthly creatures from destruction.

Walla—A suffix implying occupation. A peddler or one who occupies himself with the preceding noun. A "chai walla" is a tea peddler.

978-0-595-34556-4
0-595-34556-5

Printed in the United States
33772LVS00003B/148